Sojourner

AN EXETER NOVEL

KEN ARTHUR

Round Table Group Publishing
2018

Copyright © 2018 by Ken Arthur

ISBN: 9780980180824

Round Table Group Publishing
8817 Compton Street
Denton, TX 76207

2119

All rights reserved. No part of this book may be reproduced without written permission from the publisher, nor may any part of this book be reproduced, stored in a retrieval system or transmitted in any form or other without written permission from the publisher.

Manufactured in the United States of America.

Cover picture by Kevin T. Arthur

This is a work of fiction. Names, characters, places, and incidents are either the product of the author's imagination or are used fictitiously, and any resemblance to actual persons, living or dead, business establishments, events, or locales is entirely coincidental.

Dedication

To Mary – for making my life a joy;
To Kristi – for being a lady I'm always proud of;
To Kevin – for being the kind of man I wish I were;
To Celia – for being a daughter-in-law from Heaven;
To Rob – for being a great son-in-law… you did it right;
To Ember Fae (Emmy) – For bringing a new light into our lives;
To Aiden Thomas – For brightening our lives even more;

To Mom, Terry, Thurman, Granny, Dad & Mom Campbell,
Jimmie Lee, Gerald, & Sonny…
Requiescat in Pace.

Special thanks to

Major General Maury Forsyth, USAF (Retired)
for his invaluable suggestions and insight into test flying

Mario Alfonsi
for his expertise with the weapons and police tactics.

Tom Lemke, M.D.
Emergency Room Physician and Professor of Emergency Medicine
Brown University School of Medicine
for helping keep the medical parts accurate.

Steve Johnson
for knowing everything there is to know about
editing, publishing and marketing…
Genius is not too strong a word.

Acknowledgements

Thanks to everyone who read *Exeter* and encouraged me to write a sequel. Encouragement like that keeps you writing when you really want to go play Pickleball. (Look up that game if you're not familiar.)

A special thanks to everyone mentioned above for all for their expertise in keeping the technical material accurate. In addition, thanks to Captain Kevin Arthur for allowing me to use his photo for the cover. Also, thanks to Captain Kel Trott for his help with the T-38 information.

Finally, everyone who has ever written a book knows how important a good editor is. The writer knows exactly what he or she wanted to say and that's what they'll read every time. It takes a gifted individual to read those same words with discernment and a critical eye to find grammar and syntax mistakes the writer would never see. I was blessed with three incredible editors. My deepest thanks to Patti Lafferty, Steve Johnson, and Dr. Mary Arthur. Their work was amazing!

It is in the shelter of each other that the people live.
Irish Proverb

Chapter One

May 21, 2022
An Air Force installation somewhere in Nevada

Major Monty Desplain was trying to shade his eyes from the glaring afternoon sun. He was riding in an Air Force van that badly needed shocks and every slight bump went directly to its occupants.

"Son," Desplain said to the airman who was driving, "when you get back I want this damn rattletrap sent to the motor pool. These shocks feel like they were made by the French." The young driver had no idea what the major meant by that comment, but he wasn't about to admit his ignorance.

Their route from the squadron building to the flight line took fifteen minutes. Along the way, the van was stopped at three checkpoints where both men had to show their government and flight line identification badges to military police. Security was expected to be tight when the flight line was in the middle of one of the most classified military installations in the world.

Monty Desplain was a graduate of the prestigious Air Force Test Pilot School and was on temporary assignment as pilot liaison to the program defense contractor. He didn't mind the security hassles. He didn't even really mind the administrative crap of being the de facto Executive Officer of the small Air Force test detachment. Flying the newest top-secret jet in development was the best assignment he had ever had. After completing these development flights, his promotion to Lieutenant Colonel and getting an assignment as commander of a frontline fighter squadron was a certainty.

After the pressure of flight testing, Desplain's wife and two children were all looking forward to the more normal life of being attached to a real fighter squadron on an actual Air Force base with its spouses' club and activities. The hours would still be long for Monty, but at least he would be able to talk about his work, or most of it anyway. Now, all he ever said about work was, "I had a good day today."

Two hundred yards beyond the final security checkpoint, the van stopped at the entrance to a closed hangar. Inside the building was the

Air Force's newest and most classified stealth-fighter, the oddly shaped FX-121.

Desplain stepped out of the panel truck prepared to show his line badge to the security guard. He was surprised to see one of his favorite enlisted men patrolling the hangar entrance perimeter.

"Tank, what the hell are you doing carrying a rifle?" Desplain asked while returning the guard's crisp salute.

"Just getting a little exercise, sir," was the reply. "The colonel thinks I'm getting flabby."

"Yeah, right." Desplain knew he was being kidded. There wasn't an ounce of evident fat on the guard. "Well, I guess everything's okay out here?"

"Yes, sir. We got a call an hour or so ago that someone had wandered out into the restricted area. The command post sent a helicopter out there, but they didn't find anything. My guess is that those damn remote sensors are going weird again. They're supposed to register anything the size of a man that moves in the area, but I'll bet some jackrabbit set them off."

"Well, if the helicopter crew didn't see anything, that's good enough for me. The command post didn't call the squadron, so they must be sure the area's clear. Will you still be on duty when I get back?"

"How long is the flight, sir?"

"Tank, you surprise me. You know that type of information is classified. If I told you, I'd be guilty of revealing secret information, which of course I won't do. Having said that, if you just happen to still be here in about an hour and fifteen minutes, I'll see you get to ride back to the squadron in the air-conditioned aircrew van with bad shocks."

"Thanks, sir. I'm supposed to be relieved before that. But, what the hell have I got to do but wait for you to land? I'll hang around."

"See you later, Tank," Desplain said as he entered the hangar.

Senior Master Sergeant Daniel Tank Harris had already been on duty for four hours. The strap from the M-4 he carried cut painfully into his shoulder, and no matter how he shifted it there was no relief. Harris ignored the ache. He understood, and had an almost stoic philosophy, that discomfort was sometimes part of the job.

Harris was an imposing man with ebony skin, close cropped hair and arms that were the size of most men's thighs. His uniform was so heavily starched that it was still crisp after all his time on duty. *Tank*, as his friends called him, looked exactly like what he was, a professional noncommissioned officer.

Normally, someone with far fewer years in the Air Force would be walking this security detail. Harris had heard the young airman assigned to the location was about to become a father. The airman and his bride were both only nineteen, and Harris figured the kid should be with his wife instead of carrying a loaded weapon on the flight line. He had sent the young man home and was covering the post. *The Colonel will probably be pissed when he hears about me doing this, instead of doing my normal duties, but that's his problem*, Tank thought to himself.

Senior Master Sergeant Harris was a second-generation military man whose father had retired after twenty-three years in the army. Tank's enlistment in the Air Force, one month after graduating from high school, surprised no one. From the beginning, he was the perfect recruit — intelligent, motivated, and mentally tough. He had easily adapted to his chosen career, and was recognized by the officers he served with as an exceptional man. Tank had moved up rapidly in both responsibility and rank. Within the next couple of months, he would be sewing on the stripes of a Chief Master Sergeant, the highest enlisted grade. His promotion would come good six months earlier than any of his contemporaries would receive it.

Tank Harris liked and respected Desplain. The major was a graduate of the Citadel, a decorated fighter pilot in several conflicts around the world, and was now an instructor at the elite Air Force Test Pilot School. In Harris' opinion, the best indicator of Desplain's character was that he was a popular officer with the security and maintenance enlisted personnel on the flight line. Those officers who acted aloof and felt superior to the enlisted corps were shunned and often ridiculed by the men. This was not the case with the major.

Harris had also met Desplain's wife and two children during a chance encounter at a restaurant 30 miles from the base. Meeting was not that remote a possibility. Despite its distance from the base, the restaurant was the closest off-base eating joint. Sometimes working in such a secret location was a pain in the ass. Few creature comforts were available for personnel. Harris and his wife were having one of their few evenings away from their children and had walked into the restaurant two minutes after the Desplains had entered.

Monty Desplain had invited Tank and his wife to join them for dinner. Desplain and, just as significantly, his wife Annette made Sergeant and Mrs. Harris feel completely welcome and comfortable. Both men knew when to act like civilians.

Annette Desplain was a lithe woman with strawberry blond hair, green eyes, and even some light freckles across her nose. She looked like she was in her mid-twenties instead of her actual 37. Annette had been raised in a close-knit family on a cattle ranch in the Western Oklahoma plains. She had graduated from the University of Arkansas along with her twin brother, Justin.

Immediately after graduation, Justin received his officer's commission from the University of Arkansas ROTC program. He broke with tradition and decided not to enter the Army but instead chose the Air Force and pilot training. Justin's pilot training was at Vance Air Force Base in Enid, Oklahoma. Fortunately, Vance was only two hours from the family ranch. Justin allowed himself one weekend a month to visit the family, or for them to come see him. The other weekends were spent studying.

Early in training, Justin brought one of his pilot training classmates home for a weekend, Second Lieutenant Monty Desplain. Monty and Annette were instantly attracted to each other. After a whirlwind romance, they got married the day after Monty's graduation from pilot training.

In the intervening 14 years, they had lived the nomadic life of an Air Force family, but had been so deeply in love, the moves and frequent separations were only distractions from their happiness.

Tank had been charmed by the Major's children as well. His daughter, Elise, was nine and a miniature of her mother. She was very polite and proper in her dinner manners. The Major's son was seven and all boy. His given name was Clive, a generations old family name, but for some unexplainable reason everyone called him Tex. From the first moment they met, Tex had stared at Tank's massive arms in unconfined amazement. Tank looked at the boy and asked quietly, "You wanna arm-wrestle?"

Wide-eyed, but smiling broadly, Tex shook his head quickly up and down. "Sure!" he responded at the same time.

Senior Master Sergeant Harris enclosed the boy's small hand in his enormous one and then put up a feigned attempt to win the arm-wrestling match. When Tex easily pinned the man's hand to the table, Daniel Tank Harris had a young friend for life.

While the Desplain and Harris families had not become close, that evening had been a pleasant memory for both.

Major Desplain knew his maintenance crew assigned to the FX-121 was comprised of handpicked specialists from the entire Air Force and were quite simply the best team anywhere in the world. He was also certain the ground crew had meticulously gone over every inch of the aircraft. However, he was the one who was going to strap his butt into the cockpit and fly the jet, so he was personally going to inspect the aircraft for hydraulic leaks, fuel leaks, loose panels, or any of a myriad of other problems.

As Desplain walked around the aircraft he reflected for a moment on the dull gray color of the jet. The finish of the jet was the result of its metal alloy skin which cost just shy of ten thousand dollars per square foot. In wartime, many fighters had been lost when the sun had reflected off their wings and seen by a distant enemy pilot. The skin of this jet would prevent that. This covering was responsible for almost a fourth of this prototype jet's four-hundred-million-dollar price tag. Once in full development, each fighter would cost just shy of three-hundred fifty million dollars eclipsing the cost for any previous front-line aircraft.

As he reached the rear area of the plane, Desplain considered, as he always did, the almost magical tail section of the jet. There was nothing that even remotely resembled any air-to-air fighter or fighter bomber ever designed. Every civilian who had attended an air show recognized the nozzles at the end of jet engines where the thrust shot out. That radiant blue shock of flame exploding from behind a plane was what air shows were made of.

The FX-121, however, had no nozzles. Instead, the thrust of the engines was vented through ports that hid the vast majority of its heat signature. The exorbitantly expensive metal that covered the jet included the exhaust ports. Since the outer skin of these vents remained cool regardless of the temperature or velocity of the air going through them, it virtually defeated infrared detection of the FX-121 from any direction.

That same metal alloy had a secondary benefit that eliminated a long-standing problem for supersonic fighters. A surprising fact about those jets in the past was that friction generated by going through the air resulted in high temperatures on the skin of the aircraft. For many fighters of the 1970's and 80's, skin temperature was the limiting factor in how fast they could go and for how long. Fighters of the past were easy to track and target for IR missiles because their high skin temperatures were impossible to hide, but the FX-121's metal alloy skin prevented friction from generating an IR signature. The aircraft was designed and built to have almost zero temperature rise from friction. Military planners recognized the exorbitant cost of the alloy skin would be well worth it because the FX-121 would be virtually invisible to all IR tracking.

While the metallurgical discovery of the new alloys almost eliminated the IR signature of the jet, a discovery in the food preservation industry did even more to hide the engine's heat from detection. As often happens in research, scientists working in one area discover something that profoundly affects an entirely different field. The FX-121 was the recipient of such a discovery. Scientists working on a way to flash freeze food had developed a process that produced a near instantaneous drop to subzero temperatures. Best of all, the effect did not require heavy compressors and caustic gases. Instead, two chemical compounds were sent through a small centrifuge. The chemicals were together only a moment before being separated by the action of the spinning. This sealed system was cheap, easy to maintain, and required chemicals that could be safely handled by almost anyone.

Super cooled air would soon be available to refrigerate homes, schools, businesses, and even large commercial buildings with refrigeration units much smaller than the current size and at a tiny fraction of the cost. Unfortunately, since these units were so effective, economical, and had virtually zero environmental impact, they would never be seen by the public. Several key congressmen and senators, from states with multi-national chemical corporations as contributors, were preventing the technology from ever getting out of their fact-finding committees. Those corporations, who had been so generous with their campaign contributions, would lose proprietary control of cooling gases and the billions of dollars that resulted annually. So, naturally, the EPA and other governmental agencies, who relied on Congress for their operating budgets, found the new technology to be impractical. In short, virtually free cooling, that could be available to even the most remote part of the world, would never be made available because of politicians who so righteously campaigned as Champions for the Poor.

While rapid temperature technologies were lost to the public, they could be used in top secret military applications. A tiny cooling unit producing subzero temperatures aimed into the tail sections of the FX-121 would further reduce the heat of the exhaust to almost the exact same as ambient air. As a result, even in full afterburner, the FX-121 produced a tremendous thrust with a near zero temperature deviation.

The test pilots and design engineers had been astonished when the venturi function of the ported engines provided far more thrust than had been expected. The aircraft could easily fly at almost three times the speed of sound, Mach 3.

Conventional radar was also not a concern at all. The same metal alloy skin that was so effective in eliminating the heat signature, could also absorb or deflect every known or anticipated detection radar system used by both allied and adversarial countries.

Once infrared detection was minimized, if not totally eliminated, and radar was defeated, there was still one final problem for the FX-121 engineers to address—airflow. Sophisticated computer systems could now probe the skies in ways that would see the disrupted airflow that any jet, no matter how aerodynamic, produced in flight. Airflow anomalies were impossible to completely hide. However, the FX-121 had an aerodynamic design so complex and construction so precise that it penetrated the air with a minimum of disruption.

The only aerodynamic factor that could not be hidden was the supersonic bow wave that happened when a jet became supersonic and created the well-known sonic boom. There was no actual or planned detection suppression system on the table to address this problem for low level supersonic ingress to a target.

Supersonic flight at low altitude with the most advanced stealth technologies still made the FX-121 virtually impossible to be defeated by ground or airborne enemies.

Today, Desplain would fly supersonic low-level test runs to assess the FX-121's operational capabilities. Specifically, aspects of the fighter's control-by-wire flight system was being tested and evaluated.

The advanced control-by-wire system did far more than just direct the basic maneuvering of the aircraft. The aircraft systems still did that, of course. Control-by-wire gave the pilot more instantaneous feedback during air-to-air combat engagements to command one hundred percent of his jet's maneuverability in any given flight condition.

In the hangar, Monty Desplain quickly completed the exterior inspection of his jet. Satisfied that everything was in order, the Major climbed the ladder, settled into the ejection seat, and waited for the crew chief. Because of the cramped cockpit, the young crew chief was the only one who could connect his pilot's parachute harness. Desplain then reached into the bag he carried and removed his helmet. The customized interior of the helmet made it extremely comfortable, and the tight molded ear cups reduced the flight line sounds to just above a whisper. The crew chief then connected Desplain's radio communication cords, oxygen system, and anti-g suit hose.

To prepare his jet for the flight, Desplain only had to move the battery switch from "Standby" to "On". With that move, power was established and without any further pilot input, dozens of internal systems checks were automatically accomplished. In Desplain's previous fighter, there had been seventy-one different switches that had to be set properly. There were also ninety-three warning lights that had to be out before the plane was ready. Despite hundreds of hours of practicing preflight checklist procedures, a proficient pilot still took several minutes to methodically set and check the cockpit switches. With the FX-121, those same procedures that once took minutes were internally self-tested in less than three seconds.

    The first action Desplain accomplished after establishing power was to create a private and secure link with his jet. Right after the three second self-test was accomplished, a small red light appeared on the heads-up display in front of Desplain. The major looked at the light without blinking for two seconds. The light turned green. Next, he removed a hard-plastic sleeve from his flight suit pocket and broke it apart. Inside he found a card containing a ten-character code. An hour earlier, the squadron intelligence officer had used an encrypted secure data link to insert that same code directly into the jet's memory system. The pilot spoke clearly and read the code, "Mike, Alpha, Romeo, Yankee, Six, Six, Lima, Oscar, India, Sierra." The green light flashed several times.

    When the pilot spoke the code correctly, the jet verified a two-factor recognition process. Using the red light as a focal point, a micro-camera feeding data to the fighter's facial recognition software had first identified the man in the cockpit as an authorized pilot. The resulting green light showed this was accomplished. When Desplain spoke the correct verbal code, a second verification was completed and the jet was then paired to his voice, and only his voice, for all oral commands. That was verified when the green light flashed and then went out. Everything from engine starts and pre-takeoff checks would now be accomplished simply by the pilot verbally ordering them.

    Desplain took the throttles out of their cutoff position and spoke a single command into the microphone inside his oxygen mask. "Sierra Hotel 01, engine start…now." Immediately, the whine of spinning turbines echoed through the aircraft hangar as an internal activation motor began the start process on the powerful jet engines. The decibels increased radically when a high-pressure spray of synthetic jet fuel was introduced inside the combustion section of the engine and ignition was added at just the perfect moment in the start sequence. Soon a smooth vibration enveloped the airframe and reverberated through the cockpit. To the pilot, it was a welcome and gentle massage.

Unlike most small civilian airplanes and even many commercial jets, there was not a single instrument on any surface in the cockpit. Instead, three large and two small glass panels displayed all the engine gauges, systems instrumentation, navigation information, and warning messages. Desplain quickly scrutinized the myriad of displays before him. His practiced eye perused every screen quickly and satisfied him that all the instruments displayed were well inside their acceptable parameters. Desplain verified the remaining checklist items had been accomplished internally. He was soon ready to taxi to the runway.

In a way understood only by those who have been there, the pilot and his unique aircraft were now one.

Even with all the high-tech and sophisticated magic built within the FX-121, it had been designed with a single and long-established role as an air-to-air fighter—a predator to enemy aircraft. That mission had changed radically in the past couple of decades. Dogfights between enemy jets, known in every major air battle from WWI through Vietnam, were mostly a thing of the past. Now, with modern weapons and long-range sensors, most pilots never actually saw their adversary. Instead, fighter pilots often discovered, identified, and engaged enemy aircraft in what was called BVR or Beyond Visual Range situations.

In high-threat environments, every wartime task could be executed by voice command. If the FX-121's warning systems recognized a hostile jet well beyond visual range, the pilot would be able to lock his weapons on the threat, arm the specific missile he deemed best for the situation, and then fire the rocket all by voice commands alone. Once released, that missile was completely autonomous. It could rarely be fooled by chaff or flares from the enemy aircraft. It could out-maneuver the most advanced fighter any prospective enemy possessed. The joke among the pilots was that once the missile had been released, they could go home and have a beer. The enemy was dead from the second the fire command was given.

Despite the capability to engage the enemy BVR, no tactical planner could ever totally discount the possibility of conventional air-to-air dogfights where pilots aggressively maneuvered their jets to use aircraft guns or missiles to destroy an enemy. If an FX-121 pilot found himself in an air-to-air dogfight, he had the advantage for two reasons. First, the jet's control-by-wire automatically provided 100% of the aircraft's aerodynamic turning ability at all times. The pilot could neither over-stress the wings by pulling too many G's in a turn nor stall the aircraft by allowing its speed to decrease too low. Both ends of the performance envelope were constantly monitored and compensated for by flight control computers. Second, the ability to speak commands allowed the pilot to always keep visual contact on his adversary. A maxim of fighter pilots has always been "Lose sight, lose fight". Once an adversary was seen, if visual contact was subsequently lost, the advantage immediately went to the bad guy. For that reason, in a dogfight, pilots never wanted to look away from an enemy jet even to arm a weapon. The FX-121 fighter pilot's ability to engage his weapons without looking inside the cockpit eliminated that danger.

Verbal commands, however, were not limited to wartime. In day-to-day flights, even emergency situations were handled by verbal commands. The days of a pilot having to fly a stricken aircraft while simultaneously reading and accomplishing a long emergency checklist were gone. Now, regardless of the problem, all the pilot had to do was call for the proper checklist verbally and the jet would then automatically accomplish the procedure. The pilot was no longer in danger of being distracted reading a checklist while still flying a malfunctioning aircraft.

Major Monty Desplain moved his left hand slightly forward to advance the throttle. Powerful engines hidden deep inside the fuselage instantly responded and the jet slowly inched forward. Desplain's crew chief, standing to the left of the nose, bent over to take one more look at the jet—he called it his jet—to make sure there were no hydraulic or fuel leaks of any kind that had developed since the engines were running. There were none. He stood up and gave a sharp thumbs up sign then a salute to Major Desplain who returned it.

Twenty yards away, Senior Master Sergeant Tank Harris watched the jet begin to taxi. He saw, as the plane moved away, that Major Desplain was looking his direction. Suddenly, the pilot raised his dark visor and crisply saluted the guard. Harris immediately came to attention and returned the salute. *That was damn nice*, he thought.

Five minutes later, across the expanse of desert, there came an increased pitch from the whining engines. Even though the plane was out of sight, everyone at the hangar could tell the test pilot was now on the runway and doing his last engine checks. Finally, there came a loud boom as the pilot pushed the throttle past an indentation and into the afterburner range. Raw fuel was being sprayed into the post-combustion area of the engines to augment their thrust for takeoff.

Harris watched as the fighter flew by a hundred feet above the ground and climbing steeply. The pilot was just retracting the landing gear and retarding the throttle out of afterburner as he streaked by. Harris thought how great it must be to fly something that powerful. He looked forward to the return ride to the squadron with Major Desplain. It sure beat riding in the open jeep security would have sent for him. On top of that, the Major was a good guy. *Yeah, it'll be neat riding in with him*, Harris thought.

The trip with Major Monty Desplain never happened.

Twenty minutes after his takeoff, Desplain was dead. His top-secret advanced fighter was so totally destroyed that the largest piece of recovered fuselage was less than six inches square. Ground tracking cameras recorded his last seconds of flight. During the scheduled supersonic low-level pass, his jet simply appeared to go uncontrollable. It pitched up, then down several times within one and one-half seconds. Each undulation was more severe. The resulting aerodynamic stresses were horrific, far exceeding any design specifications. The aircraft simply disintegrated in flight.

The death of a fighter pilot or test pilot rarely makes the news, and the crash of a top-secret military jet during testing never gets coverage. Those two factors alone meant that no civilian would ever know how or why Major Monty Desplain died.

The post-accident Air Force review board was hampered by the fact Major Desplain's radio transmissions for several seconds before the crash were garbled and unreadable. His thoughts during those last few moments of life were a mystery.

Inexplicably, prior to the actual aircraft breakup, along with the radio transmissions, there was also a total disruption of the telemetry signals from the sophisticated on-board test equipment. In short, the accident review team had no clue why a highly-trained pilot had allowed the most expensive experimental fighter ever created to be torn apart over the Nevada desert.

The answer was simple. He had been murdered.

Chapter Two

May 22, 2022
Corpus Christi, Texas

Nicholas Schumer was in his office after a tough night of little sleep. Thirty minutes before, Schumer had landed in his company jet after an early morning flight from Las Vegas. A week-long annual convention of electronics manufacturers had been held in there, and Schumer had been the keynote speaker for the closing meeting. Being chosen for that particular address reflected the status he held in the industry. Schumer was the founder, president, and CEO of Winter Triangle Physics (WTP).

At thirty-six, the man's jet-black hair was just beginning to show gray streaks at his temples. Dark piercing eyes sat deep under thick brows. There was just the hint of a dimple in his chin. His five-foot eleven-inch body was still thin and rock solid. Most women would have considered Schumer handsome. Most men found him intimidating.

Schumer had a personal net worth of over one hundred fifty million dollars, but that figure would soon grow exponentially. Unlike most self-made men of his age, Schumer's wealth had not come from the Internet or software design. Instead, thirteen years ago, as a graduate student in physics, he had discovered and patented a process for protecting sensitive communication and computer systems. The technology had made Schumer wealthy. It had also been the start of his reputation as a ruthless man who would allow nothing to stand in his way.

Soon after Schumer's original patent had been filed, his major physics professor contested the patent in court. The professor claimed that he was the one who had actually discovered the process. Schumer, as a graduate assistant, had merely done support work. Almost everyone agreed with the professor. Very few graduate students were given the opportunity to do independent research and the professor claimed to have physical evidence to prove his case.

The legal proceedings were ended when a mysterious fire in the physics lab destroyed all of the professor's research papers. Two days later, his body was discovered on the sidewalk behind his apartment building. Investigators decided the man had been despondent over the loss of his lab, and apparently committed suicide by leaping from the roof.

The suicide ruling was questionable. No suicide note was found, and the professor, a devout Roman Catholic, had a life-long opposition to ending life before—as he put it—God's time.

With the professor dead and all the contradictory research papers destroyed, there was no way to contest Schumer's patent.

Winter Triangle Physics occupied a sprawling complex of research and production facilities on the outskirts of Corpus Christi. Forty physicists and a research staff of over a hundred made up the core of Schumer's employees. Most of the physicists held doctorates from prestigious universities. The fact that their employer had never finished his graduate degree made no difference to these researchers. His high salaries, superior facilities, and virtually unlimited research budgets made Winter Triangle Physics a desirable employer. WTP even had the world's most advanced and powerful WIFI system. Encrypted emails could be sent anywhere in the complex with absolutely no chance of interception nor decoding.

Nicholas Schumer's assistant was a woman, a beautiful woman. Catherine Austin's flawless face and taut six-foot tall body invariably caused heads to turn when she entered a room. She had striking Irish features—shoulder length iridescent red hair, pale blue eyes, and an hourglass figure with an emphasis in the top half of the hourglass. Catherine Austin knew the power of her appearance. She wore clothes that accentuated and drew attention to the firmness and fullness of her breasts. For Austin, her physical attributes were merely a powerful tool to be used as needed.

Catherine Austin exuded a sexuality that most men could not ignore, but behind her beauty was a calculating business mind. She had had more than a few lovers in her twenty-eight years. Men, for her, were creatures to be played with and discarded.

In Nicholas Schumer, Catherine had met her match. He seemed

impervious to her hedonistic charms, but recognized and encouraged her ruthless drive for power. She was the perfect assistant for a man with no conscience.

"Nicholas, I trust your trip to Las Vegas was worthwhile," Catherine Austin said as she sat on the corner of his walnut desk.

"Our little project was highly successful." Schumer smiled, but his eyes were still cold. "Time is getting short for the final test, however."

"There's time. The launch is in ten days and we have all our equipment at the facility. According to your guy there, the test schedule has been adapted to carry out the work."

"Are you telling me everything will be ready?"

Catherine Austin looked down at her boss. "Have I ever not been ready?"

"Don't be a shrew with me, Catherine. I won't tolerate it." Schumer said sharply. "Will everything be complete?"

Catherine Austin stared into Schumer's eyes for a moment. She fought successfully to control her temper. "Yes. We will be ready," she answered slowly.

"Good! It's one thing to destroy a jet. I need to know I can carry out a much greater area but with the same accuracy. After we demonstrate our prototype, we'll hold every business in the world hostage."

"Nicholas, I told you. We'll be ready," Austin repeated.

Catherine Austin walked around the corner and reached the private entrance to her office. Once inside, she punched the button on the intercom. "Red, I'm in the office."

Red, whose given name was Anastasia O'Callaghan, got her lifelong nickname from the fiery color of her hair. She looked across the outer office to the man waiting there. "Miss Austin, there's a gentleman here to see you for your 9:30 appointment."

Austin glanced at her appointment calendar and confirmed that she had indeed forgotten a scheduled meeting. "Shit!" she muttered to herself.

After a moment, Austin walked to her office door and showed the radiant smile that always disarmed any man she met. "Sorry to keep you waiting. I'm Catherine Austin." She moved gracefully to the visitor and offered her hand.

"Cam Forsyth, Miss Austin. It's a pleasure to meet you." Forsyth was chief research correspondent for *The Journal of International Tech Research and Development,* the most prestigious scientific publication in the U.S. He was the holder of a Pulitzer Prize for his work, and was considered by many to be the best technical writer in the world.

"Come in, Mr. Forsyth." Austin turned and strode to her office. She knew there was no way he could be ignoring the tight fit of her dress as she walked away from him. He wasn't.

The woman sat across from Cam Forsyth. She made her assessment quickly. He was probably about forty, trim, had muscular arms, and walked with an easy grace. She expertly moved to show the maximum thigh to her visitor. Again, the sight was not lost on him.

"Miss Austin, my magazine is doing a series of major articles on women in technology."

Austin smiled warmly. "Mr. Forsyth, my degrees are in business administration, not physics or engineering. I serve Winter Triangle Physics as assistant to the president, Mr. Nicholas Schumer."

Forsyth was not fazed. "Not to worry, Miss Austin. My focus will be on those who have become successful in fields other than research."

"I don't believe I am interested in being the subject of any such article, Mr. Forsyth." The sarcasm in her voice could not be mistaken. "My work here is both important and confidential. My personal life is just that ... personal. The last thing I want is a national magazine invading what little privacy I have."

Cam Forsyth was momentarily taken back by the direct and acerbic response. He was not accustomed to that kind of reaction to his magazine's offers. "Miss Austin, first of all, IJTRD is not exactly a nationally known magazine. Our subscription demographics are somewhat narrow in scope. Second, you assist one of the most powerful men in the industry. Nicholas Schumer is known as a man who does not tolerate anything less than perfection." Forsyth smiled. "As a totally impartial and unbiased outside observer, that describes you precisely." He paused for a moment, carefully chose his words, and allowed his eyes to take in the beauty before him. "I recognize perfection when I see it."

Catherine Austin was not at all affected by the man's overt flirtation. She had been hit upon more times than she could count and in virtually every contact with men, she was the one who controlled the situation. However, for the moment at least, Cam Forsyth had her on the defensive. She decided that maybe he had qualities she might enjoy exploring. Austin softened her tone noticeably. "Mr. Forsyth, perhaps I overstated my opposition to an interview." She licked her lips seductively, pretending to be thinking about her next words. She knew Forsyth was now totally engrossed. His eyes kept glancing at the front of her dress. "What I meant is that our work here is highly sensitive. I couldn't talk about that, and I have very little personal life outside of work so that wouldn't be too interesting for your readers either."

"If you have no personal life, then you're too busy, Miss Austin."

Damn, he's charming, Catherine Austin thought. *What the hell, he might be fun.* "Cam, may I call you Cam?" He nodded before she continued. "Cam, I'm not that busy all the time," she said with a hint of playfulness in her voice. "I've actually been known to take an entire day off once or twice a year. In fact, I was thinking of leaving early this very afternoon."

Forsyth nodded thoughtfully. "What an amazing coincidence. I happen to be free this very afternoon, too." Forsyth leaned forward in his chair to get closer to Austin. "Now that you're calling me Cam, do you prefer Catherine or Cathy?"

A glacier cold stare was the initial answer. Austin then smoothly responded, "No one who knows me would ever dare call me Cathy. It brings out the instantaneous bitch that lives just under the surface, I'm afraid."

"Then I guess I'll call you Catherine. Catherine," he said carefully, "I haven't been to the beach since a wild spring break trip when I was in college. Since you were considering leaving work early this afternoon anyway, is there a chance you could show me Padre Island? I'll even throw in dinner."

Forsyth's smile easily pierced through the tough shell of Catherine Austin's cynicism and independence.

For a full thirty seconds Austin stared at the man across her desk. Normally she would have smiled at such an offer and quickly turned it down. For some reason, instead, Austin thought, Why not. The offer and her response were a surprise to Catherine Austin herself.

"I'd be happy to, Cam." She quickly wrote an address on the back of her business card then paused a moment looking at it and reconsidering her spontaneity. After a second, inwardly smiling at herself, she slid it across her desk to Forsyth. "This is my home address. Pick me up there at two o'clock this afternoon." Austin glanced at her watch and immediately offered her hand to Forsyth. "It has been an unusual pleasure meeting you, Cam. I'll be ready at two."

Recognizing that he had been summarily dismissed, Forsyth got up and turned to leave. As he reached the door to her office, the man turned to look again at Austin. She was already examining some papers on her desk. "We're going to have a great afternoon, Cathy."

Catherine Austin looked up to see the back of Cam Forsyth as he closed the door. She shook her head in disbelief, but was still smiling as she told Red to cancel her afternoon appointments.

Chapter Three

May 22, 2022
Kennedy Space Center, Florida

In 2010, a nearsighted American government decided the space program would not buy as many votes as would entitlement programs. The original Space Shuttle Program had lived a mere thirty years and produced 135 flights. Even though those decades of research in space had produced countless products in everyday use around the world, the program was deemed too expensive. When STS-135 landed in the pre-dawn hours of July 21, 2011, most people believed only the International Space Station would include manned space flight, at least for many years.

Fortunately, within nine years, the stupidity of the cancellation was obvious to enough politicians that funding was pushed through Congress to start rebuilding the nation's space program.

Along with the new push for basic funding, there had also been a fundamental change in attitude regarding how to pay for the expensive programs. On the original shuttle flights, almost all the experiments and studies were funded by either the military or different government agencies. On the new-generation shuttles, however, many of the experiments and products on each mission were funded by private corporations. To further cut costs, most of the numerous support facilities and activities that had once been completely funded by the government had been privatized. The result of these funding changes had been huge savings to the taxpayers and a much more efficient and economical accomplishment of the tasks.

The first new-generation space shuttle had been completed in 2018 and was now operational. She had been named Explorer. The second one built was named Sojourner. She would be launched on her maiden flight in ten days. Both shuttles were larger than the first-generation shuttles had been, could accommodate larger crews, and stay in orbit for longer missions. Sojourner's first operation in space would last fifteen days…fifteen very full days.

Five men and three women were sitting in a study room. On the heavy oak table before each of them lay reams of study materials and checklists carefully bound in white notebooks with NASA emblazoned on the cover. Each person was wearing a light blue flight suit upon which had been sewn a name tag and the circular patch designed for the space shuttle mission they would be flying in ten days. Almost the entire crew, with one exception, had been working together for a year and had developed an incredible trust level.

The leader of the group was an imposing man. "One more time," he commanded. The team collectively shook their heads with fatigue. "I'll make you a deal," he said with a smile. "Get the procedure right and we'll take a break."

One of the ladies, Dr. Janelle McLain, responded, "You said that an hour ago." McLain, a medical doctor with a lithe body and a bubbly personality, was about to make her first flight into space. She would be conducting experiments on the effects of microgravity on bone and muscle cells. "Keep this up, Bubba, and you'll lose all credibility with your audience."

Everyone laughed, but they knew there would not be a break until the man said so. The speaker was Navy Captain Thurman Ledwell, a tough-minded man who carried his one hundred ninety pounds of dense muscle easily on a five-foot, ten-inch frame. His dark brown eyes peered at the group from a totally bald head.

Ledwell was a no-nonsense Navy officer assigned to NASA. Credibility was not a problem for him. A little more than three years before, Ledwell had been mission commander on the maiden flight of Explorer. That shuttle flight was the United States' giant step into becoming once again a credible nation of space explorers. Eighteen months after the Explorer mission, Captain Ledwell completed four months in the International Space Station (ISS) as commander. He returned to Earth from the ISS and was unexpectedly given his third major command. Much to the dismay of some other astronauts who believed they should have received the assignment, Ledwell was to take Sojourner on her maiden flight.

Titles for astronauts on the flight deck was misleading to most civilians. The *mission commander* was responsible for the entire flight and everyone on board. This astronaut actually flew the orbiter. The title *shuttle pilot* was given to the astronaut in the shuttle's right seat. Surprisingly, this person did not actually fly the shuttle, but instead assisted the commander by monitoring the flight instruments and systems.

Usually there was a much longer period between missions, but Ledwell had earned his new role. On the first mission of Explorer, the launch and orbital insertion had been flawless. Once on orbit, cameras installed on the newly-designed robot arm were used to ensure the shuttle had sustained no damage on ascent. Robot arms carried on first-generation shuttles had not been long enough nor articulated enough to make this inspection, and that meant every shuttle had to fly by the ISS for a visual check. The new arm's design eliminated that time-consuming requirement.

While the entire flight had gone well, once the shuttle's orbital maneuvering system (OMS) engines were fired to slow the craft and initiate re-entry, Ledwell had demonstrated extraordinary coolness and skill when three of Explorer's five primary flight control computer systems failed at an altitude of sixty miles above the ground which was during one of the most critical phases of reentry. NASA's press release had later downplayed the situation by saying a backup system had immediately functioned to control the shuttle.

In fact, the backup system had not worked either. Thurman Ledwell, sitting in Explorer's left seat as mission commander had recognized the problem with the secondary system and immediately reacted by flying the shuttle himself. This had been considered an impossible feat by most engineers who believed only a computer could provide the precision flying required to stay on the paper-thin arrival corridor.

Later, in the flight simulator, it was determined the shuttle had been within two seconds of tumbling out of control and disintegrating when Ledwell bypassed the computer systems to fly the shuttle himself. His skill had prevented a disaster that would have halted future shuttle flights indefinitely, perhaps permanently. NASA's administrator often said privately that Captain Thurman Ledwell had single-handedly saved the entire shuttle program.

Everyone at NASA considered Ledwell the current dean of

shuttle astronauts. He was held in near awe by everyone, but surprisingly, despite his reputation and experience, only military members and strangers called him *Captain*, and only his wife called him *Thurman*. All the rest of his family, friends and everyone on his crew called him by the nickname he had had since childhood, *Bubba*.

The upcoming mission would be Ledwell's last, and the team sitting before him knew he wanted it to go perfectly. He had pushed and cajoled each and every one of them to practice their duties and responsibilities time and again until every contingency had been rehearsed. They were tired, but for the most part, were ready.

At the far end of the study room table, Lt. Colonel William (Bill) Weaver, the team's shuttle pilot, raised his hand. "Bubba, next time you schedule one of these study sessions, let me know earlier. I didn't have one of those famous low residue meals, and I'm on my third cup of coffee. When I have an accident in my shorts, the flight surgeons will ground me for physiological and psychological problems. They won't believe it when I say you wouldn't let me go potty."

Again, everyone laughed.

"Okay, okay," Captain Ledwell raised his hands in mock surrender. "Take ten minutes to handle your physiological and psychological needs. Then we'll go over this procedure one more time."

As the group moved towards the bathrooms, three of the team members, two men and one woman, hung back to see Ledwell. "Bubba, how are you feeling about all this?" one man asked.

Ledwell looked squarely into the eyes of Dr. Jim "Tunes" Dalton, a brilliant biomedical payload specialist with one previous shuttle mission to his credit.

Dalton had been given his nickname, Tunes, by the crew after he and one of the training supervisors Muriuki Sales, had discovered a mutual love for classic rock music and had started a garage band as a way to relax during the stressful training for the mission. They called their group *Exit Orbit*. Dalton played keyboard and Sales played guitar and did vocals. The rest of the band was made up of other astronauts and mission specialists from different crews.

"I'll be ready, Tunes," Captain Ledwell said with a light laugh.

"That's not what Tunes means and you know it, Bubba. You were born ready," the woman, Dr. Terry Lee, responded.

The other man, Lt. Colonel Tom Fredrick, glanced around to be sure they were alone. This would also be Fredrick's second shuttle mission. He was a shuttle flight engineer raised in the heart of Nebraska. He had more than fifteen hours of experience performing space walks on his first mission. "Bubba, the new guy's not ready. He won't be ready. You can't get him ready. Hell, I can't get him ready!"

The "new guy" was a payload specialist named Dr. L. Scott Elder who had been added only four months prior. He had worked hard to fit in and catch up, but still was far behind the other crew members that had been together over a year preparing for the mission. Fredrick had been working the closest with Elder since the experiment would require a four hour extra vehicular activity (EVA).

Dalton, Fredrick and Lee were reflecting the entire crew's frustration. A frustration that had been growing. "You've never told us who the hell approved the change?"

"Which change? Do you mean the experiment or the addition of Elder?"

Dalton immediately responded. "Both! We didn't like bringing in a new specialist to a crew that had gotten used to each other. We already had the crew cycles planned out. I had to shuffle everyone's schedule for the entire shuttle flight. He brought new experiments, more equipment, and one extra EVA to the agenda. Bubba, this mission had a pretty full plate before the boy wizard showed up to screw with my system."

Fredrick chimed in, "Bubba, I'm doing a long EVA to set up Elder's antenna array and I don't even completely understand what it will do when it's completed. How am I expected to handle problems if they happen—and we all know they will happen— if I haven't been trained on the entire experiment? Most of all, I'm really tired of being told there isn't enough time to train me to a deeper level. I'm only supposed to set it up and Elder will run it. This is crap, Bubba."

Captain Thurman Ledwell looked at the ceiling for a moment in an attempt to formulate his response. He knew several weeks of irritation were behind the comments. "Look guys, there isn't a hell of a lot we can do about this. Orders to put the 'boy wizard', as you've so eloquently labeled him, on the crew came from Maclemore himself."

"I still don't like it," Lee sighed. "I'm sure Dr. Maclemore had a good reason." She glanced over to Dalton, who shrugged his shoulders in defeat. "It's probably not a good enough reason, but who are we to question the burning bush?"

The addition of L. Scott Elder to Sojourner's crew had started almost seven months earlier. Dr. John Francis Maclemore, NASA's Director of Flight Operations, was the one person at the Johnson Space Center who had the authority to bypass the normal acceptance protocol for experiments or personnel. He had only done so twice in his twelve years at the position. Both times he had been strong-armed by the Chairman of the Senate Appropriations Committee.

Senator Maxwell Bellow was a politician from the old school. His state received far more than its share of government contracts and programs because of Bellow's arm twisting. Even though he pretended not to know about it, the Senator took great pride in his nickname of *Quid Pro Quo Bellow*. His tactics didn't make him popular with other Senators, but in his home state of California, Bellow's reelection was always a forgone conclusion.

Senator Bellow had called Maclemore to testify before his committee. NASA's Space Shuttle budget was being reconsidered, and major cuts were a distinct possibility. Maclemore was being grilled about every aspect of the program.

All eight Senators on the committee were doing their best to appear sincerely interested in protecting the nation's taxpayers. To that end, they questioned NASA's Director of Flight Operations for two solid days.

At the close of his testimony, Maclemore knew with a virtual certainty that his program would soon again be decimated. It was just like the 2010 decisions all over again. That sickening realization lasted until the Director returned to his hotel suite and found Senator Bellow sitting in the room. The Senator had his feet up, his jacket off, and was nursing a bourbon from the mini bar. Maclemore didn't even ask how Bellow had gotten into the room.

"You did a fine job of defending your programs, Johnny," Bellow said to Maclemore. The younger man deeply resented being called Johnny even by a United States Senator. "Too bad it won't be good enough. My distinguished colleagues want to shrink the space program. There are still more reelection votes in social legislation than there are in space exploration."

"Senator, if you're here to bring me bad news, I'd appreciate first pouring myself one of those drinks you're having."

"Bad news? Johnny, I think I may have found a way to actually increase NASA's budget for the next fiscal year." The old politician smiled flashing his perfectly capped teeth. "Of course, I do have to show some sort of compromise on your part."

Maclemore did not look up from the drink he was pouring. He knew he was about to be forced into a situation he didn't want. "Okay, Senator. I'll bite. What exactly do you want from NASA in exchange for protecting our budget?"

Bellow stiffened slightly. He didn't like being forced to reveal his hand too soon. "Nothing NASA wouldn't have wanted anyway, I assure you. Let's just say I have a friend whose company has some technology that needs to be tested in space. He doesn't have time to wait for the normal formality of selection committees."

Maclemore knew that friend translated to contributor, probably a big contributor. He also knew his budget was dead without the chairman's intervention. "Okay Senator, give me some details."

The two men drank for a couple of hours. In the end, Maclemore agreed to add the experiment and its developer to the next shuttle mission.

Three days later the Senate Appropriations Committee, after due deliberation, found nothing in NASA's budget that required major reductions.

At the same time as the Sojourner's crew members were resuming their study session, President Larry Robertson was sitting alone in the Oval Office.

Robertson was breaking a personal rule. It was late in the afternoon and there was nothing on his schedule for the next twenty minutes. The President was taking a break. His feet were on the desk and a small glass of his favorite Maker's Mark bourbon was in his left hand. Normally, the only place the President had a drink was in his private study or in the family quarters upstairs. *The hell with it,* he thought, *I'm in charge here. I'll have a drink if I want one.*

President Robertson had not started out to be a politician. He had been a successful and popular physician, a dermatologist, after spending six years as a flight surgeon in the Air Force.

Reacting to what he considered the lack of leadership in Washington, Doctor Robertson had run for the House of Representatives. Surprising most professional pollsters, he had won. After three terms in the House, he had been elected to the Senate where his charisma, common sense, and no-nonsense approach to government had made him a national figure.

Many felt it would be impossible for a fiscal and social conservative to win the White House, but Larry Robertson had decided early in his second Senate term to run.

The Republican party had been in shambles for several elections because of their seeming inability to present a true conservative candidate. In Robertson, they had a chance to correct that mistake.

After an arduous nomination process and campaign, he had won the Presidency with a fifty-five percent majority popular vote and an overwhelming Electoral College selection.

During that first term, Robertson's administration had gone a long way towards reestablishing the honor and decorum of the Executive Branch.

One of President Robertson's first actions had been to eliminate numerous redundant regulatory groups that his predecessors had allowed to grow. By ordering the consolidation of agencies from different departments, many often-conflicting government regulations had been ended. At the end of his first term, the size of the Federal Government had been reduced by eighteen percent, but he strongly felt there was more to do.

Robertson's second Presidential campaign had been even tougher. Many had tried to paint him as "unfeeling" and "against the poor" because he had successfully pushed through legislation obligating any state receiving Federal HEW funds to require drug testing for welfare recipients. Anyone found to be using drugs would be required to enter and complete drug treatment in order to continue receiving assistance. The welfare rolls had dropped by almost thirty percent as a result. Many liberal politicians had tried to claim this was racially motivated, but their claims had fallen on deaf ears as the country was seeing the fraud, waste, and abuse of the welfare system being reduced.

With a promise to continue reducing the intrusion of the federal government, Robertson's administration had sharply curtailed the power of the Environmental Protection Agency. The economy had reacted to this action by reaching new and unprecedented growth levels. The doomsayers had predicted that the environment would be destroyed since the EPA could no longer unilaterally subject any business venture to unnecessary and expensive regulations.

The sanctity of the Oval Office was absolute and there were only a few people in the world who were allowed to just walk in. One of them was Donna Morr, the President's personal secretary. Early in his private practice, Dr. Robertson had hired Morr, first as a receptionist and later as his office manager. When he had been elected to Congress, she moved to Washington to head the freshman congressman's office staff. She had been his key administrative assistant for his entire elected career. He completely depended on her, as did his wife, Amy. Amy Robertson saw Donna Morr as her husband's watch dog. The two women had been close friends for more than twenty years and trusted each other completely. Amy knew she would get a call from her husband's secretary at the first indication that he was pushing himself too hard. A secretary could not tell the President of the United States to take a break, but his wife could.

Donna Moor walked into the Oval Office unannounced and handed the President his daily military abstract. Every afternoon, someone in the Pentagon prepared a synopsis the country's troop and arsenal strength for the White House. The summary often included single paragraph reports of pertinent military events. Even though the cover said For President's Review, it was rare that the President ever saw it. His Chief of Staff and National Security Advisor both reviewed it and decided if there was anything that the President should really see.

Today the President's Chief of Staff, Di Dennington, had highlighted one paragraph and left it on the President's desk. It detailed the initial information on the crash of the developmental FX-121 fighter.

All Air Force flight surgeons are required to spend time flying with the pilots they treat. This requirement was established so flight surgeons would be familiar with the stresses and problems faced by pilots. Dr. Larry Robertson had spent his entire military career working with fighter pilots. Therefore, it wasn't surprising that as President, Robertson had been keenly interested in developmental programs for new fighters. He was one of the few who believed that a cold war would likely take place again. This time, he was convinced, both Russia and China would be the driving forces behind a new arms race. The FX-121 would be a major addition to the front-line military. Any disruption in the programmed research and development (R&D) would be unfortunate, and ultimately, even more costly.

The President took a pen from its holder and scribbled a note beside the report. "Di, keep me informed on this. I'd like to know what happened. Was this a problem with the jet or simply a mistake by the pilot? How long will it delay testing?" Robertson took his role as Commander-in-Chief of the nation's military very seriously. He added to the memo, "Get with the Pentagon. I want to know where to write the pilot's widow. I want her to know I was personally interested in what her husband was doing. Also, tell the Sec Def I want to know what the Air Force is planning regarding an appropriate medal and see if a posthumous promotion to his next rank is feasible."

Robertson closed the report and finished off his drink before pushing the button on his intercom. "Donna, call upstairs and see if Amy is in the mood for pizza tonight. Why don't you join us?" The First Lady was almost always ready for pizza.

"Yes, Mr. President. I'll call her right now, but I'll pass on dinner. I've got a date."

President Larry Robertson smiled. He and Amy had been trying to introduce Donna to eligible bachelors for years with no success. "Need me to get a background check on this man?" he joked.

"No sir, you already have. He checks out okay. Thanks for doing that!" came the chuckled reply.

Chapter Four

May 22, 2022
Padre Island, Texas

"This is my favorite time of the year here in Corpus," Catherine Austin said. "The offshore breezes are still cool. By July, the heat and humidity keep me in the air conditioning." She laughed and took in a lung full of ocean air. "Besides," she said haughtily, "there are fewer tourists to deal with." The beach was deserted as far as they could see.

"Well, I can't argue with your logic, Catherine. This is a great way to spend the afternoon. Living in Corpus, I imagine you're out here all the time."

"Actually, I don't really remember the last time I came to Padre Island. I think it's like those people who have lived all their lives in New York City and have never been to the Statue of Liberty."

Austin was wearing a light blue jogging outfit. Underneath was a matching color spandex swimsuit she kept at her office for swimming in the company pool during her lunch hour three days a week. She was warm despite the wind, and had the jersey top unzipped. The swimsuit barely covered her breasts.

"Too bad the water isn't a little warmer," Austin commented naughtily. "I'd love to go skinny dipping in the bay."

Cam Forsyth instantly pictured the cold water swirling around Catherine. The effect was immediate. A quiet throaty giggle came from her as she glanced at his swimsuit. "Looks like you might need a little cold water, too."

"Miss Austin, you're a tease."

"Nope, I'm many things. A tease is not one of them." With that Catherine Austin quickly removed her jogging outfit and ran into the surf. "Damn!" she yelled, "It's cold out here!" Moments later, the spandex suit was thrown on the beach.

Forsyth stood on the shore admiring the view. "You know, Cathy, this isn't exactly what the readers of my magazine are expecting to read about. They're expecting a hard-hearted, business-before-pleasure, workaholic feminist. You're dispelling all those notions."

"I told you not to call me Cathy. Get your butt in this water, you wimp. It's really not too bad once you're numb."

"Sorry, there are parts of me I don't like numb."

Catherine Austin stood up in the waist deep water. "I'm disappointed. A big-time writer afraid of a little cold water."

"Well, I'm not really afraid of cold water but, I do have one question. How exactly do you plan on drying off after your little romp with nature? We didn't bring towels."

"Oops. I guess occasionally even a hard-hearted, business-before-pleasure, workaholic feminist doesn't plan ahead. Sorry to disappoint you, Mr. Forsyth."

"Right now, Miss Austin, there is no way you could disappoint me."

Catherine Austin walked out of the surf and bent down to pick up her wet bathing suit. She was shivering slightly. Forsyth handed her the cotton jogging suit. She pulled the pants on. The top came next, but she left it unzipped.

"My place is perfect for warming up. And, if you're still interested in interviewing me, that would be as good a place as any."

"Usually, my meetings are held in office buildings. Your place sounds better."

Four hours later, Cam Forsyth was propped up in a king-sized bed with a legal-sized pad of yellow paper sitting on his knees. Catherine Austin was lying beside him, a crisp sheet covering her. After making love twice, her makeup and hair were mussed. Forsyth thought she still looked amazingly beautiful.

"Cathy, perhaps I could get a handle on your spontaneous personality a little better if I understood what Winter Triangle Physics does."

"Cam, even though, based on the past few hours you and I could probably write our own version of the Kama Sutra, you may not call me *Cathy*. Do you understand? Cathy makes me angry. Cathy makes me want to grab someone by the throat. I prefer Catherine. I expect Catherine. If you worked for me, I would fire your ass for calling me Cathy." Austin waited for a response that was not forthcoming. After a moment, she continued. "Now that we have that little item settled, Winter Triangle Physics is a research facility primarily dealing with electromagnetic radiation spectrums. How familiar are you with that area?"

"I did an article on electromagnetic pulse in the late 90's. I've forgotten almost everything except that it has to do with the effects of a nuclear detonation. Doesn't the blast create some kind of supercharged particles?"

"Not too far off. Remember I'm not a physicist, so this may not be the most technically precise explanation, but it should be close enough for your use." Catherine paused to gather her thoughts. "A nuclear detonation produces gamma rays. Photons from those gamma rays hit electrons in the surrounding air. Those electrons gain energy and shoot off in different directions." Catherine stopped for a moment. "Is this too much detail?"

"It's too specific for the article. But remember the project is to write about you, not really your company's research. I just want a generalized grasp of the material so I can flavor the story with some details. When you totally lose me, I'll let you know."

"All right," Austin said while tucking the sheet around herself. "Where were we? Oh yeah, these electrons of various speeds and weights and charges create an electrical field. This electrical field only lasts a fraction of a second, but it's powerful enough to destroy electronic components. Communications and computer systems are particularly vulnerable, but automobiles that rely on computer chips for their electronic ignition systems would probably also be fried. Even modern aircraft that have fly-by-wire or control-by-wire flight controls would become uncontrollable by EMP."

Forsyth searched the recesses of his memory. "I do remember someone saying that the effect was like a bucket of water turned upside down. It sort of splashes out in all directions."

"A pretty good analogy. It's not one hundred percent accurate but, for purposes of your research, it's close enough."

"And Nicholas Schumer devised a method to protect systems against EMP. Right?"

"That was his original work. Your magazine did an article on him ten or eleven years ago didn't it?"

"Yeah. Before coming down to Corpus I looked over that old material. He was pretty tight-lipped back then. Now, I understand, he's like Fort Knox."

"That's true. It's the nature of the business. Our current research and development projects are highly classified. Winter Triangle Physics has diversified into so many areas that I can't discuss. It's better if we just drop any further discussion about it."

"Okay, but if we can't talk about your work, I need to concentrate my attentions elsewhere." With that, Forsyth lifted the sheet to admire again the physical attributes of Catherine Austin. "You are a writer's dream; a fascinating subject to write about and a wonderful distraction from writing."

"That's a compliment…I think."

"It was intended as one." Forsyth pulled Austin close to him. "I wish I could stay here in Corpus longer."

"Do you have to leave right away?"

"I leave tomorrow night. Headed to my home for a few days then to Florida. I'm covering the next space shuttle launch. My sister is Dr. Terry Lee. She's a mission specialist on the flight. I've got permission to follow the crew through the last few days of preparation. In fact, I'll be the first journalist ever allowed to ride in the crew van and be on the gantry as the crew enters the shuttle and are strapped into their seats before flight. Then I'll be in the closest pad bunker for the actual launch."

Catherine Austin felt the color run from her face. "God, no," she whispered. "Your sister will be on the shuttle?"

"Sure. She has a doctorate in electrical engineering. She's doing several research studies on energy generation in space. It's been her life-long dream to be on a shuttle mission." Forsyth could tell that Austin was troubled. "What's the matter, Catherine?"

"Nothing. I guess I was just hoping we could have more time together," she lied. "I haven't been with a man for a long time."

Forsyth was a reporter. He made his living interpreting other people's words. He wasn't convinced for a moment, but he was confused by her sudden change of character. "I've got a great idea. Why don't you come with me? My editor wouldn't bat an eyelash at the extra expense, especially considering the exclusive article I'm writing about the Sojourner crew." Warming to the thought, he continued, "Take a few days off, Cathy. Come with me."

"I can't, Cam. We have a very big project that's being tested in less than two weeks. I have to be here for it." Catherine's pale blue eyes were still locked on Forsyth.

She didn't even notice I called her Cathy, Forsyth thought. *There's something going on here that she's not going to tell me about. Whatever it is, I'd better let it drop.* "Listen. I've got to go. I'll pick you up in the morning for breakfast. We can go over my notes for your article." He smiled thinly. "You can have first editorial review of my manuscript. How's that?"

"Breakfast sounds good. I don't have to read your writing. I know it'll be great." Austin hugged Cam Forsyth. It feels good holding him, she realized. She made a difficult but absolute decision at that moment. Once her mind was made up, Catherine Austin felt herself relax and calm down. She could tell her muscles were less tense, too. "Do you have to leave at this moment? Won't those notes wait another hour or so?"

"Maybe we can watch TV," Cam answered jokingly.

"Look around. Do you see a TV? I don't even own a TV."

"Well," Forsyth answered. "My laptop and I have an agreement. It will process words as fast as I can type them. Fortunately, I'm a very fast typist, so another hour or so will not be a problem."

The two lovers kissed gently. The past few minutes of conversation were forgotten as passion, for the third time that night, took its place.

Chapter Five

It was nearly midnight as Catherine Austin kissed Cam Forsyth goodbye. He had turned down her offer to stay the night by reminding her that his first draft of the article had to be written sometime. "Let me type this tonight, grab a few hours of sleep, and then pick you up for breakfast at seven-thirty."

Reluctantly Austin agreed. There were a few things she had to do tonight, too. As she watched him drive off, Catherine reached for her phone. She dialed a number from memory. She had no doubt the phone would be answered immediately.

"Yes," was the only greeting as the phone call was answered. Nicholas Schumer's private office number was known by very few. He felt no need to be cordial or sociable to anyone who called him on it.

"Nicholas, I must see you tonight."

"I see." He waited for more explanation. There was none. "I was just finishing up here. Perhaps we can meet first thing in the morning."

"No! It has to be tonight," Austin responded quickly. Then she caught herself and got control of her voice. "Nicholas," she said slowly, "this will not wait until morning."

"Alright. I'll stay until you get here." The line went dead.

Twenty-five minutes later Catherine Austin logged into the computer at the security desk of Winter Triangle Physics. The guard was not especially surprised at seeing her even though it was nearly midnight. The senior researchers and staff often worked weird hours.

Austin walked tall and tried to project far more confidence than she was feeling. She stopped outside the heavy mahogany door to Nicholas Schumer's office. There she took a deep breath and pushed it open.

Schumer was not there. She stopped for a moment and looked around. Suddenly a side door opened and Schumer walked out. He was wearing a white towel around his waist. "Sorry, I didn't hear you come in, Catherine. I was in the sauna. Give me a moment to shower off, and I'll be right back in."

Austin knew her boss was making her wait in order to gain a psychological advantage. The urgency of her demand to see him was thwarted by his apparent indifference to the call.

Several minutes later Schumer returned. He was wearing a black pinstriped Italian suit, and was combing his hair into place. He sat down and looked across the massive desk at his administrative assistant. "Okay, what's so important that would not keep until morning?"

"Nicholas, I've been thinking. There's really no way we can be ready to test the project on the next shuttle mission. There's another one in three months. By then all the bugs will be worked out, and we can have a full-up test of the weapon."

"Remember it's not a weapon, Catherine. It's a bargaining chip." Schumer spoke slowly and patiently as if to a toddler who has been told the same thing several times and still didn't understand. "Think of the years when countries were stockpiling nuclear weapons. Those fools in power called it MAD, Mutually Assured Destruction." Austin knew all of this, of course, but she let her boss rant. "Their idea was that no one would use nukes in a first strike because the other side would be able to respond in a totally devastating counterattack. There is no longer a necessity to destroy cities and kill millions. All you have to do is cripple them. Our system will be inexpensive, mobile, and virtually foolproof. Focused EMP is finally a reality, but we have to test it against an actual target from space."

"Couldn't you simply demonstrate against a power station somewhere? Wouldn't that accomplish the same thing?"

"Catherine, this is not like you. No. We both know that the government would sit on that kind of information. We'll use the shuttle to demonstrate our power. We've known since the beginning that the shuttle will probably not survive our test. That's unfortunate, but necessary. The fact that no one will know exactly how the catastrophe happened does not matter. We have to know for certain that our worldwide system works."

Schumer stopped to examine his fingernails. "Didn't you tell me yesterday in this very office that we would be ready? You were gone all afternoon. How could you have changed you mind so radically in just a few hours?"

"Nicholas, we can't kill all those people!" The words tumbled out before Austin even realized what she was saying.

"Really? Your conscience didn't bother you when the FX-121 pilot was sacrificed for the project."

"I didn't really think about it. You were causing the crash of a jet. I thought about it as an inanimate object."

"Well, hell, Catherine, how did you think the jet got airborne?"

Anger flowed from Catherine Austin. "Damn it! I said I didn't think about it. Now I *am* thinking about it. We have to find another way to test the equipment."

"You feel that strongly about it?"

"Yes," was the simple reply.

"All right. I'll give you four days. If you can come up with another viable way to test the system, I'll gladly change my plans. Agreed?"

"Thank you, Nicholas. I'll meet with the senior research staff in the morning. We'll come up with another plan, I'm sure." A sense of relief flooded Catherine Austin's whole body. "Thank you again, Nicholas."

"Make it a good plan, Catherine. I have a lot riding on this."

Two minutes after Catherine Austin signed out at the security desk, Nicholas Schumer walked out also. He never signed in or out, but the guard on duty logged the time and inserted a personal note in the computer record anyway.

Forty-five minutes later, Catherine Austin was standing in her shower enjoying the hot steamy water as it stung her flesh. She had returned from Winter Triangle Physics too wound up for sleep.

Catherine had fleetingly considered going to the bay front hotel where Cam Forsyth was staying. She discarded that idea because he would still be typing his article and didn't need any distractions. Instead she decided to relax with a long, hot shower. The water cascaded over her skin and seemed to wash her tension down the drain.

Catherine had her eyes closed enjoying the sensation. Suddenly a hand reached through the shower curtain and grabbed her by the hair. Another hand clamped over her mouth.

In terror, Catherine Austin opened her eyes wide. The attacker jerked her backwards and with a powerful movement smashed her head into the tile edge of the seat ledge in her shower.

The last sight Catherine Austin saw before dying was the face of Nicholas Schumer.

Chapter Six

May 23, 2022
Corpus Christi, Texas

When Forsyth left the hotel the next morning, a young man was handling the hotel parking valet stand. His pure white shirt, shorts, and shoes accentuated the man's cocoa brown complexion. A plastic oval name tag with "Paco" engraved on it adorned his uniform.

Paco jumped off the tall stool when the hotel customer approached with his parking slip in hand. "If you'll just give me the keys I'll get the car myself," the man said.

The young man was disappointed when Forsyth made that comment. "Sir, the car is up on the top level. I'll be happy to retrieve it for you," he answered cheerfully. "Besides, the car will probably be really hot. By time I have it here the a/c will have a chance to cool it off a bit."

"Thanks, but I need the exercise," was the response.

Paco was certain he had lost out on the chance for a tip. "I'll get your keys, sir." He checked Forsyth's red parking slip and found the corresponding car keys in the lock box. The young man felt better when a five-dollar bill was exchanged for the car keys.

It took Cam Forsyth only a few seconds to realize he had made a terrible mistake as he reached the top level of the garage. Even at seven o'clock in the morning, the humidity and heat were stifling. To make things worse, there was not even a hint of breeze. When he opened the door to his car, a wave of hot air hit Forsyth in the face. It took an effort to slide into the driver's seat to start the car. Once the engine was running, he set the air conditioning on high cold. Forsyth's highly starched shirt was already spotted with sweat.

That kid was right. I should have let him go through this heat. The car would have been a little bit cooler by the time he drove it down to the bottom level.

Forsyth's impatience was understandable. He wanted to get to Catherine's apartment as soon as possible. He had tried to call her before leaving the hotel room, but there had been no answer. *She's probably in the bathroom*, he thought.

Driving out of the hotel garage, Forsyth made a right turn on North Shoreline Boulevard towards Catherine's condominium. As he drove, Cam glanced left to see the beautiful Bay of Corpus Christi. Behind him were the harbor bridge and the USS Lexington aircraft carrier. The carrier was permanently moored and turned into a museum. *This is a city I will want to explore more*, he thought.

It took twenty minutes to reach the gate that opened to the two-story luxury condominiums within. Beside the gate was an ornate box with silver buttons. Forsyth punched in the code Catherine had given him and the gate immediately opened. He drove straight ahead into one of the two parking spaces reserved for her condo.

A lush garden of tropical plants and flowers lined the walkway and were in full spring bloom. They were shaded from the hot Texas sun by tall palm trees. It was, Forsyth figured, at least twenty degrees cooler here than in the uncovered parking area.

The reporter reached the front door and rang the bell. Thoughts of Catherine and the experiences of the day before filled his mind. *It's amazing what can happen in just twenty-four hours*, he thought. Forsyth pushed the bell again then looked at his watch. It was seven twenty-five. *Okay, I'm five minutes early*, he thought. *I can't believe Catherine would not be ready to come to the door.*

Suddenly Cam Forsyth began to feel uncomfortable. Something is not right. Something ... but what? Years of training had honed Forsyth's intuition. He trusted his instincts. Carefully, Cam slowly turned the brass doorknob. He was more than a little surprised when it turned. He was even more surprised when he realized the dead bolt was also unlocked.

Slowly Forsyth pushed the door open. "Catherine," he called. "Catherine, it's Cam."

No answer.

Cam Forsyth entered the condominium. He could feel his heart pounding in his chest. He slowly walked through the living room and into Catherine's bedroom. Her king-size bed was exactly as he had left it late last night. The pillows were in the same places the two lovers had thrown them and the sheets were still messed up.

Catherine did not sleep there, he realized. With a foreboding dread, Forsyth looked at the closed door to the bathroom, then turned the knob.

The sound of the running shower momentarily relaxed him. *She's in the shower. That's why she didn't hear the bell or me call her.*

"Catherine," he called. When there was no response, Cam Forsyth pulled back the thickly opaque shower curtain. There before him was the body of Catherine Austin. Shock at the sight momentarily stunned Forsyth. Then he quickly felt her wrist and neck for a pulse. From the color of her face and lips, Cam could tell she had been dead for several hours.

Two officers from the Corpus Christi police department were at the condominium within three minutes of Cam Forsyth's 911 call. A detective and the medical examiner were there shortly afterwards.

Forsyth was sitting in the living room with a glass of water. After a quick look in the bathroom, the detective sat down to question Cam.

"Mr. Forsyth, I'm Detective Sam Cessnas." He showed his badge and identification to Forsyth. "I'm sorry about the death of your friend. I'm here as a formality. Right now, it looks like she slipped in the shower and probably hit her head. We'll know more when the medical examiner finishes his exam."

"This was a homicide, Detective Cessnas."

"Really? And you know this how, Mr. Forsyth?"

"Catherine is at least six feet tall. That shower is less than five feet across which includes a twelve-to-fourteen-inch seat at the end. To slip and hit with enough force to kill her, Catherine's legs would have to be out in front of her. Instead, they're folded back at the knees. Someone had to push her back and down in order for her to die in that position."

Cessnas' interest was piqued by this revelation. Keeping his eyes firmly on Forsyth he yelled out, "Doc, don't move the body yet. I need to look at something." He then spoke to the man sitting beside him. "Don't leave, Mr. Forsyth. I'll be right back."

A curt nod was the only response.

The detective was gone for only two or three minutes. When he returned, one of the uniformed officers was with him. "Mr. Forsyth, would you be kind enough to go with this officer. We would like you to give a statement at headquarters."

"Am I being arrested?"

"No sir. You're the one who found the body. We just need to know what you saw. If you have an attorney you want to accompany you, then that's your privilege."

"I do need to make a phone call. May I use my cell phone?"

"Of course, Mr. Forsyth. As I said, you're not under arrest. We just need to get some details from you."

Cam Forsyth was no fool. He knew he was the prime suspect in what Detective Cessnas now believed was a homicide. Forsyth took a cellular phone from the inside pocket of his sport coat, and dialed a number from memory. When the call was answered on the first ring, he pushed four more buttons quickly.

The phone sounded a second ring, then a third. Forsyth was considering hanging up when his sister, Melissa, answered it. She knew at once who was calling.

Melissa was a perpetually cheerful twenty-year old. She possessed a vivacious personality that was evident even over a phone call. "Good morning, Cam. Mom and Dad are still asleep. Want me to wake them?"

Forsyth ignored the friendly greeting. "Melissa, I'm in Corpus Christi, Texas. The police here are taking me in for questioning regarding something I found. I would appreciate it if you would find someone local who can give me some help."

"Do you want me to get Dad?" she repeated.

"There isn't time for that. They are waiting for me right now."

"Okay Cam, I'll find out who we have in the area there. Are you in danger?"

"No. An assistant or someone like me would be nice, though."

"I understand. I'll get right on it."

"Don't worry, Melissa. I'll be okay. This is just a misunderstanding."

"You'll be at the police station then?"

"Yes. If anything changes, I'll let you know."

"Take care of yourself, Cam." The line went dead.

Forsyth's call had not been answered in what anyone would consider a normal home, but it was just about to create a stir in the most advanced civilization on the face of the Earth: a place called Exeter.

Exeter, known by many names, had been a source of legend for centuries. Before the written word, all great ancient civilizations had oral traditions passed along around campfires from the elders to the children. This was the way history and legends were shared from one generation to the next. One oral tradition, common in many civilizations, concerned a tribe of warriors who could not be defeated. Supposedly, this nomadic tribe had warriors called Protectors who were without equal.

While most ancient oral traditions were a combination of truth and exaggeration, the stories of the unknown warriors describing Exeter were remarkably accurate. Throughout the centuries, even though the people of Exeter tried to avoid conflict with any other civilization, inevitably others would discover and attempt to conquer her. Their intentions were always devastating for them. Never once were Exeter's Protectors, defeated even by the most formidable army.

Eventually, in an attempt to finally live secluded from any adversaries, the tribe of Exeter migrated to an area so distant that no one discovered them for almost 100 years. During this time, they were at peace, but the Protectors were still always prepared.

In 1544, conquistadors from Spain came exploring what they called the New World. As a result of those Spanish explorations, the tribe of Exeter was once again discovered and their desire for peace put at risk. The King of Exeter, in an attempt to avoid a confrontation, presented himself to the leader of the Spanish invaders to negotiate safe passage through his domain. The King was unarmed and seemingly alone. Unfortunately, one of the conquistadors, acting on his own, shot the King, mortally wounding him.

From hidden locations surrounding the conquistadors, Protectors exacted instantaneous revenge. Within seconds, all of the Spaniards, except their leader, were decimated. As the King lay dying, his final command to his son was to continue searching for a place to live in peace. His last utterance was to "Always keep the Protectors learning." The new King was determined to fulfill his father's last command. The tribe found, in a most unusual location, such a place of peace and serenity. Exeter, a tribe of over 50,000 people, has since lived in that hidden location for centuries in complete secrecy.

Anyone who has ever visited the Carlsbad Caverns of New Mexico has been told by Park Rangers that the caves open to the public make up only a very small part of the system. Some experts believe the Carlsbad Caverns actually has hundreds of miles of undiscovered and unexplored massive underground rooms and passages.

They are right.

In 1544, Exeter discovered, explored, and settled in remote areas of those caves. Their civilization flourished in the seclusion and protection provided by living in the massive rooms and passages of the cave system. They turned the rough stone and impossible rubble into smooth and finished areas where families could live in comfort.

Regardless of the temperature on the Earth's surface, the deep caves remain at a constant 64 degrees. Through the centuries, the scientists of Exeter produced many crucial modifications to the caves. Exeter's internal environmental system and infrastructures alone were engineering marvels. Decades before electrical power was in common use outside Exeter, family homes in the caverns had lighting, cooking, and communications systems. Inhabitants traveled throughout the civilization using high speed trams that moved seamlessly and were programmed to maximize speed and avoid conflicts. There had not been a single collision between trams in more than 80 years.

The far superior technology of Exeter had allowed many other crucial enhancements to their home. Since human beings have an intrinsic need for a circadian rhythm, normal day and night cycles had to be established. In all the common areas, tiny wires were woven into an almost invisible matrix that covered every wall and ceiling. These wires produced a perfect mimic of sunlight whenever an electrical current was passed through them. The amount of current directly resulted in different levels of light. So, at 'sunrise' a tiny charge was used which was increased during the day until reaching its highest level around noon. As the hours passed, the electrical current was slowly decreased and 'night' was created. This process provided the false day and night cycle humans required.

Exeter's main chambers contained shopping, schools, hospitals, and all the infrastructure anyone would recognize above. The only difference was they were housed six hundred feet below the surface.

Exeter had never been reluctant to share its scientific and engineering knowledge with those above. Many of the Protectors who were living under pseudo-identities in countries around the world had been pivotal figures in history. Some of the greatest medical and scientific discoveries through the ages had been made by Protectors while living their assumed identities outside Exeter. The names of those Protectors were known to every school child above. Biographies of these men and women were in libraries around the world. Even the list of Nobel Prize winners who were actually from Exeter was long and distinguished. No one would have ever imagined that these giants of science, medicine, literature, and technology were in fact citizens of another civilization called Exeter.

Even during the centuries of total isolation, Exeter's Protectors continued to be trained as warriors. Instruction for these select individuals began at age five and continued until age twenty-one. They became experts in every kind of martial art and were trained in tactics and weapons deployment. Land and water survival skills were honed. In short, by the time a student was initiated into the Protectors, he or she was capable of defending themselves or others regardless of where help was needed, using whatever was available.

Part of the Protector's life included studying other cultures and civilizations. For centuries, Protectors had left Exeter to live among other countries, but not as a visitor or stranger. Before infiltrating a society, the Protector would know the language, customs, and dress of the indigenous people.

Generations ago, it was easier to manage the task of moving a Protector into a new place. Word of mouth was the primary means of communication. People moved from place to place easily, and Protectors could assume any identity they desired. Today, the job is more difficult because of computer databases. To be effective, these men and women had to have identities completely established.

Technological sections of Exeter constantly developed new methods of incorporating Protectors into societies around the world with cross-referenced histories in computers. Birth certificates, school records, Social Security files, credit references, university attendance and degree awards, military service files, and a thousand other seemingly authentic identifications were placed into secure federal, state and even local government databases. In some cases, even employment records were established into corporate computer records.

Even though Protectors and other members of Exeter had lived in almost half of the countries of the world, never had one pseudo-identity been compromised. This was a remarkable accomplishment particularly considering the sensitive areas where many of these men and women worked. They were involved all over the world with governmental, military and civilian intelligence agencies, sensitive research and development departments, and even within NASA. Knowing the Protector's assumed persona would receive the most complete background investigations, the establishment of those identities had to be perfect. None had ever failed to be authentic in every detail. It was a source of great pride among those who were responsible for fabricating these fictitious lives. Evidence of this elite attitude was humorously demonstrated by a hand painted sign in the work chambers that said:

Only God Can Create the Body, But We Can Create the Person.

As soon as she hung up from Cam's call, Melissa went to her parents' room. The phone call had stirred them.

"Who was that?" her father asked.

"Cam. He's being taken to the police station in Corpus Christi, Texas."

Moses and Tame Forsyth were now fully awake. "Tell me exactly what he said," her father demanded.

Melissa gathered her thoughts before answering, then carefully recounted everything her brother had said. "He is being taken to be questioned about something he found. He said he wanted an assistant or 'someone like him' to come there. I guess that he meant another Protector. He did say he was in no danger."

"Good. Thanks, Melissa." A few moments later he was on the phone. "This is Moses Forsyth. I need to know if we have any assistants in the Corpus Christi area." He did not like the response he received. "Yes!" he said sharply into his phone. "I have both the need to know and the right to know."

Almost instantly a new voice was on the phone, "Sir, I'm the control supervisor. I'll have that information for you in just a moment."

Moses Forsyth was an Elder in Exeter. These men and women were elected from the different colonies of the tribe. They were primarily advisors to King Annu, but exercised great control over the day-to-day operation of the dominion. He had been given the name Charles Moses at birth to honor his maternal great grandfather, Charles Moses Hammond. The grandfather's name was known to every school child in Exeter.

In the late 1880's, Hammond had been the first to develop a method for farming large areas of Exeter's subterranean caverns using a hydroponics technology that no one who lived outside Exeter would know about for almost fifty years. His work and discoveries had ensured the people of Exeter would never face famine regardless of what happened outside the caverns they lived in.

Charles Moses Hammond had a son, Millard, who took his father's technology to the next level. At a time when cities above still lit their streets with gas lamps and only homes of the every affluent had electrical power, Millard refined his father's hydroponic process using electricity. He modified the matrix of minute electrical circuits used on the chamber walls and integrated them into the growing cycle of the hydroponics sections. This allowed for far greater production of light sensitive plants. Prior to this discovery, the people of Exeter grew most of their vegetables in carefully camouflaged gardens placed in surrounding mountain plots. This had become more difficult as the area above was being developed and populated. Millard Hammond's discovery removed the need for outside gardening and thus the danger of someone discovering Exeter.

Despite the history associated with his name, at age 5, Charles Moses Forsyth decided he would only go by the name Moses. He told his family in no uncertain terms he would no longer answer to anything else. They all laughed but soon discovered the strength of his pronouncement, whenever someone slipped up and inadvertently called him "Charles", he simply would pretend he hadn't heard them until he was addressed as "Moses". Now, as an adult, no one ever called him anything other than Moses. He was an Elder in Exeter, a Protector, and one of King Annu's closest friends.

The supervisor Moses Forsyth was talking with did indeed know who was on the other end of the conversation. Moments later he had an answer for the Elder. "Sir, we don't have any Protectors in Corpus Christi. The closest one is Prince Isha. He and his wife, Deidre, are visiting Temple, Texas. That's where she was born," he added parenthetically. "We don't have any assistants in Corpus. King Annu may have some business associates in South Texas, but I wouldn't know about those."

"Thank you," Forsyth said and disconnected the call. He glanced at Tame, and realized her deep brown eyes showed the look of concern a mother feels when one of her children, even a grown one, is in trouble. "Don't worry, Tame. Cam is ok."

"I know," she replied. "He's a Protector, but he's alone. I want to get someone there with him." She had that tone Moses recognized meant *right now*. Tame Forsyth was married to an important man, but she was a force to be dealt with, too.

Moses Forsyth smiled back. "He's okay," he said again. "He's a man, not your little boy. Plus, he's been a Protector for many years, and I don't think he needs his mommy to rush to his aid."

"Moses, I'm not kidding," she responded seriously. "I've got one child about to blast off into space and another one in some kind of trouble with the law. I don't want to hear any more of this Protector business." She gave her husband what he called the look then she spoke her next words one-by-one very slowly,

"Make. Something. Happen."

Tame Forsyth was in many ways the antithesis of her husband. Where he was quiet with a dry sense of humor, she was gregarious. His calm and professional leadership style was effective because people just recognized his skill and did what he wanted done. They also recognized that he never asked a subordinate to do anything he couldn't do or wouldn't do himself. That trait alone gave Moses a well-earned reputation as a man of integrity and honor.

Tame had a more participation style of leadership. She was known for the committees she led and organizations she patronized. Tame had the gift of giving 100 percent of her attention to whoever she was speaking with. That attribute plus her warm and engaging personality made her a popular leader. However, she could also be as forceful as necessary to accomplish her will. Moses knew not to make light of her make something happen comment.

"Tame, Corpus Christi is an hour ahead of us in time. Here's what we'll do," he responded. "Let's wait a couple of hours, then I'll call the King. If there is someone in Corpus Christi that he knows, I'll ask him to call that person."

Tame was not appeased. "His Highness will understand when you call and wake him up. His son is a Protector, too."

Decision made. She handed the phone to her husband who shook his head but made the call.

Chapter Seven

May 23, 2022
Corpus Christi Police Department

At the same time Moses Forsyth was calling the King of Exeter, his son was being escorted into an interview room at the Corpus Christi police station. Detective Sam Cessnas ambled in a few moments later, and sat down across a gray metal table from Forsyth.

"Mr. Forsyth, may I offer you some coffee?"

"Yes, black please," Cam Forsyth responded. "I also haven't had breakfast. Is there a donut shop around here, too?"

"I'll see what we can find. In the meantime, I'll be asking another detective to come in while we talk. Do you want us to wait until someone joins you?"

"As you said, I'm just being questioned because I found Catherine. If, however, I begin to feel you suspect me of murder, I'll stop talking until I have legal counsel. Until that time, you can ask me anything you want."

"Mr. Forsyth, no formal determination of homicide has been made in the death of Miss Austin. We're still just gathering information. This is simply part of that process."

Forsyth still knew better. *Regardless of what Cessnas says, Catherine was murdered, and I'm the logical suspect,* he thought.

A female police officer came in carrying two cups of coffee and a bagel. She put one cup of coffee and the bagel down in front of Forsyth and sat down with the second one. Cam now knew for certain his suspicions were correct and the conversation was being monitored. He took a sip of the strong coffee. "Since you've got someone listening in on our little chat, I have to assume you suspect me of something."

Cessnas smiled, "Mr. Forsyth, this is Detective Wendy Jo Vonderahe. She's been assigned to assist in our investigation. Now, what makes you think someone is listening to us?"

"What kind of cretins do you get in here, Cessnas? It doesn't take too much brain power to recognize I ask for black coffee and something to eat and this detective brings coffee and a bagel in almost immediately. Unless she's clairvoyant, I have to assume she heard me ask for it."

Cessnas looked at his partner. "Wendy Jo, take a note: No coffee in the future until I open the door and ask for it."

Wendy Jo Vonderahe nodded and pretended to write the comment down on the yellow pad in front of her. She offered her hand to the man across the table. "Mr. Forsyth, I've been checking your story out. From the information you gave my partner, I've been able to confirm your whereabouts for the past twelve hours."

"Really, and what exactly were you able to discover?"

Vonderahe read directly from her notes. "The crime scene report indicates the time of death was between one and two a.m. You checked your car with the hotel valet just prior to midnight last night. You retrieved it at approximately seven this morning. You ordered a sandwich from room service, which was delivered at one thirty this morning. You gave the room service delivery person a sizable tip. She remembers you clearly. A few minutes later, you made a long-distance phone call to a New York City number from your hotel room." She looked up at Forsyth. "Who uses a hotel phone to call long distance?"

"My cell phone battery was nearly dead. I had left the charger in my rental car and I didn't want to lose my connection halfway through the call."

Vonderahe just nodded at his revelation and continued. "At three this morning, you called the hotel operator and left a six thirty wake-up call." Wendy Jo Vonderahe looked up from her notes. "Mr. Forsyth, you keep weird hours, eat at odd times, and sleep very little, but I'm convinced you were nowhere near Miss Austin's apartment at the time of her death."

"I spent most of yesterday with Miss Austin. I was doing a magazine article on her. I finished the first draft and emailed it from my laptop to our New York office early this morning. Then I used my room phone to call New York to tell the night editor I was planning on adding someone to join me on my assignment to Cape Kennedy, Florida in a few days. That was the long distance call you noted. Those kinds of things are sometimes better handled by phone instead of by email. It makes it harder for the bean counters to say 'no' when I'm on the line.

"As far as your other observations, I work when I feel like it, eat when I'm hungry, sleep when I need it. And you're right, I was nowhere near Catherine's apartment from about eleven-thirty last night until I arrived back just before seven-thirty this morning."

"Did you touch anything in the apartment?" Cessnas asked quickly.

Forsyth thought for a moment before answering. "The front door knob, bathroom doorknob, and the water faucet in the shower. I also got a glass of water, but that wasn't until after you got there."

The detective's eyes narrowed as he leaned forward in his chair. "And why did you turn the shower water off? You told me yourself that you suspected this was a homicide. Why did you touch a possible crime scene?"

"I'm a water conservationist," Cam Forsyth answered sarcastically. "Listen, she was dead. I didn't think about it, I just turned the water off. There was nothing sinister." The memory of Catherine Austin lying there dead with water running over her naked body invaded Cam's mind.

Wendy Jo Vonderahe shook her head. "Mr. Forsyth, Detective Cessnas isn't accusing you of anything. He just has to account for any changes to a possible crime scene. That's why he's asking."

Cam Forsyth knew he was at the edge of losing his temper. "Look, I did spend a good bit of time in Catherine's apartment yesterday so you could expect to find my fingerprints in the kitchen, living room, and bedroom." He paused and then continued, "I've given you about as much time as I'm going to. Unless you have a very good reason to keep me here, I'm leaving."

Detectives Cessnas and Vonderahe looked quickly at each other.

Neither was finished asking questions.

A knock on the door interrupted them before either had time to respond. A rookie police officer stuck his head in the door. "Sir, I just got a call from the Mayor—not from the mayor's office—from His Honor Alphonse T. Ogg, personally. He told me to expect a call for Mr. Forsyth and to put it through immediately. Sure enough, right after I hung up from the mayor, someone called and asked for Mr. Forsyth. What do you want me to do?"

"Son," Cessnas said somewhat impatiently, "if the Mayor himself calls and asks you to stand naked in the middle of the Six Points intersection, I recommend you do so—at least until the end of your probation period. Give me the damn phone."

Police stations, like most places concerned with conversation security rarely have cordless phones. The rookie cop handed Cessnas a battered handset attached to a twenty-five-foot extension cord. "This is Detective Sam Cessnas. Can I help you?"

"Good morning, Detective. My name is Isha and I understand you have a friend of mine at your station. His name is Cam Forsyth."

"Well, Mr. Isha, it's against department policy to release information regarding citizens. I'm sorry I can't help you."

"Detective Cessnas, I understand your problem. You don't make policy. However, in about fifteen minutes, maybe less, your mayor will be calling back to see if Mr. Forsyth is still being questioned. If so, he'll want to know why and who made the decision. He'll also want to know why, in the absence of compelling justification, Mr. Forsyth has not been driven back to his car with the thanks of the Corpus Christi Police Department." The voice waited for a moment to see if there was a response. "I'm assuming you've already determined Mr. Forsyth had no personal involvement in your case."

"He found a body, Mr. Isha. That makes him a potential witness when the case comes to trial. No one, not even the mayor, will make me release this gentleman until I'm sure I have his testimony."

"I understand, Detective Cessnas. May I speak with Mr. Forsyth?"

Without saying a word, Cessnas handed the phone across the table. Cam Forsyth took it. He had heard the detective address the caller as Mr. Isha. He knew who was on the line. "Hello, sir. I'm a little surprised to hear from you."

"I'm actually here in Texas, Cam. My wife and I are in Temple, Texas. I've got an airplane here. We already have a flight plan filed for Corpus Christi. We should be there in a little less than two hours. We will land in time for lunch."

"Sir, I can't ask you to do all that."

"We belong to each other, remember?" *We belong to each other* was the motto of Exeter's Protectors.

"Yes, sir. I'll look forward to seeing you."

"When you're released, let someone at home know where you'll be. I'll be in touch, Cam."

The line went dead before Forsyth could answer. He slid the phone back across the table. Cessnas took it. He glared across at Forsyth, but said nothing.

Detective Sam Cessnas and Detective Wendy Jo Vonderahe got up from the table and stepped outside the interview room.

Vonderahe spoke first. "Listen, Sammy. The guy didn't do it. I personally checked out his story. He was in his hotel room from before the murder to well after it happened. That's confirmed. We have witnesses. The room service lady doesn't make too many deliveries at one-thirty in the morning. She remembers the tip. I have the phone log. I even checked to see if any cab company picked up a fare during that time frame anywhere within four blocks of the hotel. None did. This guy is not the doer. He was just unlucky enough to find the lady. They were probably going at it like rabbits, but he didn't kill her."

Sam Cessnas was an experienced investigator. He knew something wasn't right about Cam Forsyth. He also knew Vonderahe was right as well and there was nothing to justify keeping the man. "Okay, Wendy. Here's what I want you to do. We've played this good cop, bad cop scenario long enough. I want you to go back in and release this guy. Make sure he knows not to leave town. When His Honor the Mayor calls back—and for some reason I think he really will—tell him what we've done."

"Okay, Sam. By the way my mom wants to know if you're free for dinner this Friday night."

"Tell her I'll be there."

Wendy Jo Vonderahe and Sam Cessnas had been friends almost all of their lives. Some around the police force joked that they acted like a brother and sister or even husband and wife sometimes. They had joined the police force within a couple of months of each other and had risen through the ranks almost simultaneously. The two made an excellent detective team because each knew almost unconsciously what the other one was thinking. They had an uncanny gift for picking up tiny discrepancies in people's testimony. What one missed, the other was almost certain to catch.

Sam Cessnas and Wendy Jo Vonderahe were certain no one on the police force even suspected that they had been dating for two years and were getting married in four months. It was a source of great amusement to both of them that the detectives they worked with, who noticed the most minor details of a crime scene, were totally unaware of their off-duty relationship.

In reality, the detectives they worked with had already planned a huge surprise party in the next week for Sam and Wendy. They were tired of pretending they didn't know about the wedding plans.

Vonderahe was positive there was no discrepancy in Cam Forsyth's deposition. She was also concerned about Cessnas' adamant distrust of the man. Was she missing something?

For the time being, she dismissed her concerns and opened the door to the interview room.

Thirty minutes later an unmarked police car returned Cam Forsyth to Catherine Austin's apartment. Yellow Crime Scene ribbons were strung through all the palm trees he had admired only a few hours earlier. A few TV reporters were still mingling around in a feeble attempt to discover some spectacular or grisly detail that would spice up the evening local news. So far, the police had been tight-lipped saying only that a woman had been found dead in her shower. A friend of hers had made the discovery. Police were investigating. That was all anyone could get from detectives.

Just as Forsyth got in his car a distinguished looking man was escorted by police out of Catherine's apartment. Cam recognized him instantly as the president and CEO of Winter Triangle Physics.

Cam Forsyth got out of his car and walked to Schumer. The intense businessman was rapidly talking to someone Cam didn't recognize. The second man, Josh Tanner, had been appointed Schumer's new assistant only thirty minutes before. Cam surprised both men who did not see him coming up. Forsyth heard the last few words of Schumer's sentence. ".... who found her so damn fast." He quit talking abruptly when Forsyth stopped beside them. "If you're a reporter, I've no comment."

"My name is Cam Forsyth, Mr. Schumer. I'm the man who found Catherine this morning."

Nicholas Schumer studied the man before him. "What was your relationship to Catherine, Mr. Forsyth?" It was more of a command than a question.

Cam Forsyth decided immediately he did not like this man. "It was personal and none of your business." He turned and walked away without saying another word.

Schumer was unaccustomed to anyone being so abrupt with him. No one ever just walked away from Nicholas Schumer before being dismissed. Without removing his eyes from Forsyth's back, Schumer spoke to the man beside him, "Tanner, find out about that S-O-B. I never heard Catherine say anything about a Cam Forsyth. I want to know everything about him by the end of the day."

"Yessir, Mr. Schumer," Josh Tanner said as the two men got into the limousine.

As they drove back to Winter Triangle Physics, Tanner was on the speakerphone with Catherine Austin's secretary. He spoke, but both men listened. "Red, do you know anyone named Cam Forsyth?

He claimed to have some personal relationship with Ms. Austin."

Red, who had been sitting at her desk in shock since the early morning call informing her of Catherine Austin's death, took a second to place the name. "He was here yesterday to interview Catherine. He's some big-time reporter for Technical United magazine. Catherine left work early yesterday and spent the afternoon with him." Red checked her notes from the day before. She had, as was her custom, written Forsyth's cell phone number, hotel and room number down in case she needed to change his appointment with Catherine Austin. She read the information to Tanner.

"Okay, Red. I'll get back with you if Mr. Schumer needs anything else. In the meantime, don't let anyone into her office. No one—and that means even the police—is allowed in the office. Lock the office door right now. If anyone but Mr. Schumer or I want in, tell them you don't have the key. Do you understand?"

"I understand," Red answered weakly. "Has anyone tried to call Catherine's family to see about arrangements?"

There was no answer. Josh Tanner had hung up.

Chapter Eight

Corpus Christi International Airport was using runway 13 for landing. The weather was beautiful with only scattered altocumulus clouds but the pilot still tuned a navigation frequency for the instrument landing system (ILS). A cautious aviator, the man used ILS information to back up his visual approach to the runway.

"Corpus tower, November six eight two turning final for runway one three," the pilot transmitted.

"November six eight two, Corpus tower, you are cleared to land runway one three. Winds are calm, altimeter is three zero one zero," replied the almost bored control tower operator.

The pilot verified his altimeter setting and responded, "November six eight two is cleared to land runway one three."

Two minutes later, the pilot retarded the throttle and raised the nose of his plane just slightly to make a perfect touchdown on the runway centerline. He gently slowed the aircraft and made a left turn off the active runway. "Not a bad landing," commented the plane's only other occupant.

The pilot smiled, but said nothing. He simply pointed to the radio. "Oops, sorry. I forgot my assigned duties," the second person laughed. "I'm just always pleased when I can praise my dear husband." She quickly changed the knob on the radio to the ground control frequency.

"Corpus Ground, November six eight two is clear of the active. Please verify our flight plan is closed," the pilot transmitted.

"November six eight two is cleared to taxi to the ramp. Your flight plan was closed on arrival."

"Roger," was the terse professional reply.

The pilot was Isha, Prince of Exeter. He would, as the only heir of King Annu, someday rule the fifty-thousand citizens of Exeter. When Isha assumed the throne, he would also take control of a large international conglomeration of businesses.

King Annu owned companies in twelve countries. His assets were shrouded by several layers of consortiums and holding banks. Almost all of them were run by Presidents and CEOs who had impeccable credentials and resumes, but were in reality from Exeter. They handled the day-to-day operations, but their King was the ultimate authority for the businesses.

King Annu would, if he were living above, be worth over one point three billion dollars. Instead of accepting any personal wealth, he used his profits from the companies to send Protectors all over the world and to fund research. He chose instead to live a relatively simple life among his people.

Isha was, like his father, a true Renaissance man. His brown hair was straight and hung almost to his muscular shoulders. Chestnut brown eyes were set in a smooth tan face. He stood five foot ten inches tall, and was thirty-six years old, but could pass for his mid-twenties. Isha was a Protector, perhaps the best warrior Exeter had produced in several generations. He was a natural leader with a knack for recognizing the strengths of others. Most importantly, the Prince was remarkably popular with his subjects. He rarely exercised the privileges of his royal status.

The Prince and his wife stretched as they got out of their plane. Across the parking ramp, Prince Isha saw Cam Forsyth walking towards them.

"Cam, it's good to see you," Isha said while extending his hand.

"Your Highness, it's good to see you, too." Forsyth then looked to Deidre. "Lady Deidre, my name is Cam Forsyth. It's a pleasure to meet you."

"Cam, my husband has spoken highly of you. I'm very glad to meet you, too. Please just call me Deidre. I don't stand on ceremony, especially when Isha and I are away from Exeter."

"Thank you, Deidre."

As they walked from the aircraft Forsyth asked the question he had been considering since leaving the police station. "Sire, I was amazed to hear from you this morning. How did you get involved in this?"

"Easy. You called your father, who called my father, who called me. It's not a problem, Cam. I'm glad to be here."

"Also, who from Exeter called the mayor? That really got some attention at the police station."

"I honestly don't know, Cam. I suspect my father has business contacts in South Texas he felt comfortable calling. One of them probably made the decision to contact the mayor. Don't worry about it. The King was glad to help. I assume you have a car. While we're driving, why don't you tell us about what's happened to you in the past day or so."

Fifteen minutes later, while traveling on South Padre Island Drive, Forsyth was recounting his experiences. He left out the parts about his bedroom escapades with Catherine Austin. After all, they weren't pertinent, and the Prince's wife was present.

After hearing the story, Isha sat quietly for a full minute. Finally, he spoke, "Cam, basically you left the lady's apartment late last night and returned early this morning. During those few hours she died, and you're convinced she was murdered." Cam nodded, and Isha continued. "One thing bothers me. What was the motive? No one, except perhaps a psychopath, commits a homicide for no reason."

"You know, sir, that's troubled me, too. Catherine was an extremely driven person. At work, she was demanding of her staff. She seemed haughty, arrogant, and maybe even a little obnoxious. That was a front she put on. I found her to be a very warm person. I can't think of a reason why anyone would want to hurt her."

Isha and Deidre glanced at each other. Without a word spoken, both knew there was more to Forsyth's story. Isha spoke first. "Cam, the way you speak it seems like the lady was someone you might have wanted to bring home to meet the family someday."

"She was a terrific lady. I guess there was some kind of bond there. I only knew her a day, sir."

"Sometimes that's all that it takes," Deidre interjected. "The Prince and I only knew each other for a day, and I knew he was special."

Cam Forsyth, wanting to change the subject, asked quickly, "Really, tell me about it."

"I was living with my grandmother in Santa Fe, New Mexico. We were walking through the Palace of the Governors when some thug hit my grandmother and grabbed her purse. Isha was there, and stopped the guy from getting away. The mugger pulled out a knife and did his best to cut Isha. That was the first time I saw how a Protector can defend himself. A few seconds later, the man was unconscious and Isha was helping my grandmother up."

"My wife exaggerates more than a little, Cam. The only important thing about that event was I got an invitation from her grandmother for a home-cooked meal with her and Deidre."

"The only important thing?" Deidre asked, pretending to be hurt.

"Well, maybe there was more to the evening than just the meal," the Prince answered. "I also got to spend some—how shall I put this?—quality time with Deidre." The Prince and Lady Deidre had spent the last hour of that night making love beside a lake on the property.

Deidre continued, "It turns out my husband had been stalking us."

"Cam, the lady once again exaggerates. Her father was John O'Leary. Have you heard of him?"

"I know he was the King's friend from outside, but I don't really remember all of the story," Forsyth confessed.

The Prince reached over the back seat and took his wife's hand. "John O'Leary and my father met when both of them were thirteen. King Annu—he was then Prince Annu—was outside Exeter without permission from his mentor, Tomás. He was rock climbing when a ledge broke loose and he fell about twenty feet and was hurt pretty badly. John O'Leary was also in the mountains that day and heard my father's cries. Before passing out, my father told him about a cave nearby and the hidden passage that was there. Mr. O'Leary ran to the spot and began yelling. One of Exeter's sentries heard his shouts, and sent a mentor to investigate. They took my father to Exeter's medical chambers. The rescuers assumed John was also from home and allowed him to enter with them. After the mistake was discovered, my grandfather took John to our chambers and tried to explain how sacred our secret was. Right then Deidre's father promised to keep our secret, which he did for the rest of his life. John O'Leary was the first outsider to be adopted by Exeter. He was the best man at my parent's wedding, and gave the eulogy at my mother's funeral. When Deidre's parents died in an auto accident a few years ago, my father was devastated and Exeter had an official day of mourning. Anyway, the next time I was in Santa Fe, I decided to meet John O'Leary's mother. The mugger was just a lucky introduction for me."

Deidre spoke up to finish the story. "My poor grandmother still jokes that Isha was bad luck for her. The day after the purse snatcher incident, while Isha and I were on our first date, some men broke into her home to rob her. They beat her up and probably would have killed her. Anyway, we got home while all this was happening. Isha surprised the men and rescued my grandmother. He recognized how critical her condition was and made the decision to take her to Exeter."

"Well, it sounds like you didn't have a traditional courtship, Lady Deidre. How is your grandmother now?"

"Fully recovered. She still lives in her home in the mountains outside Santa Fe. King Annu had a passage tunneled to a point near her house. It only takes her about fifteen minutes to get from her back door to the King's chambers. Since the Prince and I married, she spends more time in Exeter than she does above."

Deidre continued her remembrances. "All of this happened just before that terrorist Azmud Salomi attempted to bring his stolen nuclear device into New York harbor. That's when Isha, his best friend, Kevin, and their team landed at night on the ship carrying the weapon. They destroyed the thing and saved the United States from the worst terrorist attack in history. That's also when we lost two Protectors. Ron Warren discovered the weapon in Germany and was killed. Then Skye died while on the ship. Ron's fiancé, Kristi, was the Protector who got to revenge his death by providing justice to the demon who started it all. Azmud Salomi's death was always described as from natural causes, but Kristi was really good at her martial arts."

Cam Forsyth knew well the story of the threatened terrorist attack and also had heard bits and pieces about the O'Leary family. Now the pieces fit together. "You probably don't remember this, but I was in the Protector honor guard for your wedding," he said.

The Prince nodded. "Sure. I remember. You were also with me on the honor guard when we buried Robert Grolier." Grolier, the oldest Elder in Exeter's history, had died from cancer shortly after the Protector's mission against the terrorist. His death came only a week shy of his one-hundredth birthday.

"Yes, sire. That was a sad day for all of us."

Cam Forsyth was aware that his mind was wandering to another funeral he would attend within a few days. "Prince Isha, something keeps gnawing at me. Whenever I tried to get Catherine to talk about her work for my article, she would clam up tight. I wasn't trying to get any kind of classified information, just background stuff to fill in the manuscript. I could tell she was uncomfortable with talking about the company or perhaps its research."

"Is it possible you're just trying to find answers to her murder and grasping at straws?" Deidre asked.

"Sure, I recognize that's a possibility. Security is always pushed at these high-tech companies. She didn't seem as concerned about security as she was about avoiding discussing her boss, Nicholas Schumer. He strikes me as a formidable man. I don't like him."

Isha looked across the front seat of the car to Forsyth. "You've met him, Cam?"

"Briefly, sir. I don't think he likes me either."

"Pity," was the only response from Isha. The Prince thought for a moment. "Is it possible she was working on something that may have led to her death?"

"Possibly. Like I said, she wouldn't talk about work too much." Forsyth made a decision. "You know, sir, I've been wondering if it might be possible to take a look at her files on the company server."

Deidre, who had a been a computer science major in college picked up on Forsyth's train of thought. "Are you thinking her files might give you an idea of who might want to kill her?"

"I don't know. It might be helpful to take a look. Do you think we can do it?"

Isha laughed out loud. "There are people in Exeter who love doing such things."

Cam made his decision at that moment. "Sire, I'm going to request a return to Exeter from the Elders. I want to be a part of whoever looks at her files." He was surprised at the powerful emotion he suddenly felt. "She was a nice lady."

"I'll make that call, Cam," Isha responded. "What about the police? Will they let you leave the area?"

"Oh yeah," Cam said. "Great question. They've made it pretty clear I'm not a suspect, but they did say I had to be available if they needed me. I'll call that detective and tell him I need to get back to work. He has my cell phone number obviously. All I can do is ask."

Chapter Nine

"Tanner, get your ass in here," Nicholas Schumer bellowed over the intercom system. It took mere seconds for the man to rush to his boss's office. There were no formalities. "What have you found out about this Forsyth fellow?"

"Sir, like Red told us, he's a reporter. It took a little doing, but I found out he was doing a series of articles on ladies in technology."

"Okay, that part checks out. What else did you find out?"

"There's one thing that is a little disturbing. His sister is Terry Lee. She's on the Sojourner crew."

An alarm sounded in Schumer's brain. "Catherine wanted to stop our work concerning Sojourner. I think we have to assume he knows about our plans for the shuttle." Nicholas Schumer looked up at Tanner. His dark eyes were locked on the man. "I want this reporter dead. Nothing can risk our project. Do you understand? I want him dead today!"

The soft tone of Schumer's voice sent chills through Josh Tanner.

Tanner was a researcher who was comfortable at a computer terminal, but not with engineering the death of another man. "Sir, I don't know anyone who can do something like that."

"Damn it, Tanner. I don't want to hear excuses." Schumer reached into the top drawer of his desk and threw a piece of paper at the assistant. "Here's a phone number! Go to our tech department and get a burner cell phone. We use them all the time for making calls we don't want linked back to us. Use that disposable phone to call this number then dump it somewhere it won't be found. The person who answers will handle the details. Get ten thousand dollars in cash from the safe. That's all it will take. Just don't use my name or the company name. Tell whoever answers that Starman told you to call. Just have Forsyth eliminated immediately—today!"

"Yessir. I'll take care of it."

Five minutes later, Tanner sat at his desk and nervously lit a cigarette. His hands were shaking as he began dialing the phone number Schumer had given him and waited. The call was answered on the first ring and was followed by a pager tone. He quickly punched in the numbers posted on the burner cell phone and hung up.

Tanner waited and stared at the phone. One minute passed, then two. Just as he was ready to really panic, the phone rang. Tanner quickly grabbed it. "Hello," he answered.

"You called me, man. What do you want?" the voice on the other end spoke.

"I have a job for you."

"I'm listening."

"There's a man who has been bothering my sister and I want him to stop."

"I don't handle family problems. Take care of your sister yourself, you wimp! Goodbye."

"WAIT!" Tanner yelled into the phone. "Okay, listen. The Starman told me to call you."

"You have my attention. Go ahead."

"We need someone eliminated. He said today."

A sinister laugh was the response. "You're new at this, aren't you? Nothing happens that quickly. If the Starman sent you, then you know my price."

"Ten thousand dollars."

There was a pause, then the laugh again. "That cheap bastard still wants me working at bottom dollar. The price is twenty-thousand cash. If he's interested in a quick job, it'll cost him extra."

Tanner thought quickly. Schumer had ordered that Forsyth be dead today. "All right. What's next?"

"Tell the Starman I want to meet you the same place I met him last time. Be there in one hour and remember to come alone. I get very nervous when I'm surprised by unexpected company, and I get very violent when I'm nervous. Do I make myself clear?"

"Yes, I understand. I'll be wearing a blue wind breaker. How will I recognize you?"

"Just come alone, bring the money, and don't be late." Suddenly, there was no sound on the phone and Tanner realized the call was ended.

Nicholas Schumer didn't flinch when Tanner told him of the extra expense in eliminating Cam Forsyth. "Cost of doing business" was all he said. He told Tanner exactly where to go and what to do.

Fifty-five minutes after making his original phone call, Josh Tanner was sitting down on the steps of the Corpus Christi Bay seawall. The exact spot was easy to identify because of its proximity to several key tourist spots in the vicinity. Within five minutes, a black sedan pulled to the curb. The back door opened and a voice Tanner had heard for the first time only an hour before spoke to him. "You still have that cell phone you called me on?" a deep voice called out.

"Yessir"

"Throw it as far as you can into the bay"

Tanner did as he was instructed then got into the car.

"What if someone saw me throw that phone, gets curious, and dives down to find it?" Tanner asked nervously.

"God! You are a cherry, aren't you!" came the tart reply. "If someone gave a shit about looking for it, they'd have a hell of time just finding it in the muck down there. And a phone like that sitting in 40 feet of salt water will be totally destroyed in just a few hours. Your ass is safe. I'm the only one you need to be afraid of now."

Tanner looked at the man sitting across from him. He couldn't help himself from staring into the face of death while being thoroughly frisked for weapons and any recording device. "So exactly what is it you and the Starman want done?"

Tanner spent the next several minutes outlining the expectations of his boss. The hotel Red had mentioned as to where Forsyth was staying was an upscale hotel on Ocean Drive. The room number for

Cam Forsyth had also been verified.

"I don't like capping someone in a hotel. There are too many possible witnesses and too few escape routes."

"Today. It has to be today. I don't care where you do it." Tanner tried to sound more forceful and confident than he felt.

"Listen, Tex, if you tell me one more time that it has to be today, I'll make sure you don't tell me anything else ever. Do I make myself clear?"

"Yes ... yes, sir," Tanner mumbled weakly. "My boss just asked me to make that clear. He said to tell you ..." Schumer's assistant caught himself just in time. "Well, you know."

The man pushed a button on his armrest. The driver immediately pulled to the curb. "Mister, your concerns will be handled today." He glanced into the manila envelope. "I assume the full payment is here."

"Twenty-thousand dollars. Yes, it's all there."

"Tell the Starman he'll read about this matter tomorrow in the paper."

When Josh Tanner got out of the limo, at first he had no idea where he was. The houses were run down and trash was strewn everywhere. "How am I supposed to get back?"

"Not my problem." The door slammed and the car moved quickly away.

"Bastard," Josh Tanner mumbled.

An old man sitting in a rickety rocking chair looked down from a porch that was in desperate need of paint. "You lost, sonny?" he called down to the stranger on his street.

"Yeah. I guess I am. I need to get back to Shoreline Drive. Don't suppose you might be interested in driving me there. I'll pay you."

The old man chuckled. "Sonny, I ain't had a car or a license for more than ten years. Guess I was scarin' folks with my driving. But, you can come in and call somebody to come get ya." He slowly stood up from his rocker and opened his front door.

Josh Tanner used the old man's phone to call for a taxi, gave him a twenty-dollar bill, and walked to the corner to wait for the cab.

Chapter Ten

It was well after dark when Cam Forsyth used the credit card style key and opened the door to his hotel room. The light over the door was on and Forsyth flipped the switch to turn on the rest of the lights in the room. He was annoyed immediately that his television was on and the volume was set a bit too loud. It was tuned to a music channel playing contemporary country. Since he rarely watched any television, and never listened to country music, Forsyth knew he had not left it that way.

He walked past the still darkened bathroom to his left and entered the brightly lit bedroom. Standing in front of the console holding the flat-screen monitor, he picked up the remote control and turned the TV off. Forsyth looked to the left and saw that the bed had been turned down for the night and a chocolate mint was on the pillow.

He decided the housekeeping service had turned on the television during their visit and had forgotten to turn it off as they left.

The second thing he noticed was that the thermostat was set too low and there was an uncomfortable coolness to the room. He adjusted the thermostat to 68 degrees. Forsyth walked past the room's garish tropical printed couch and arm chair with their brightly colored overstuffed pillows and lightweight blankets. He looked out the large sliding glass door to his tenth-floor balcony.

The events of the long day had taken their toll and Cam Forsyth opened the door and walked onto his balcony. The metal railing came a little above his waist. *Damn*, the thought. *This railing is really too low for my comfort.* His view of the night time Corpus Christi city lights reflecting on the bay was postcard picture perfect. To his left, he saw a large freighter leaving under the soon to be replaced harbor bridge.

Two days before, when he first arrived in Corpus, Cam Forsyth had walked along the Corpus Christi seawall and sat down alongside a couple of old-time locals. The two crusty codgers were looking at their iconic bridge while drinking something from a paper bag that they passed back and forth between them. Both men were bemoaning the bridge's impending destruction to make way for a much higher span.

"We don't need no bigger ships in our harbor," one man had grumbled. "If they can't fit under the bridge we've already got then screw 'em. Let them go somewhere else!" He slapped his leg to emphasize his feeling. The other old man just nodded his head in agreement without comment. The first guy had spoken for both and the bag made another pass between them. They graciously presented it to Cam, but he kindly rejected their offer to take a drink.

Back in the present, Cam watched the freighter and wondered where it was headed with its cargo seemingly balanced so precariously to the deck. He thought it seemed his conversation on the seawall had taken place weeks before instead of just two days ago. Nonetheless, Cam smiled at his mental picture of the two winos and then chuckled when he remembered their strongly worded conviction that the bridge should remain as is.

Because of his deep musings, Cam almost ignored the subtle perception that had warned him something was wrong. He slowly looked over his left shoulder. There, staring ominously back at him, was a man standing halfway to the hotel door.

The stranger was dressed as if headed to the board meeting of a Fortune 500 company. His suit was not off the shelf. It was made from fine pinstriped fabric and looked fitted with just a little extra room in the shoulders and front to allow for easy movement or perhaps a weapon. The man's shoes were highly polished and expensive as were the supple leather driving gloves he wore. He had cold eyes that sat deep in a tanned face. The man's dark eyes almost matched his jet-black hair which was combed straight back. He wasn't a handsome man, but he was an intimidating man... and he was carrying a wicked knife.

"Man," he said in a low, quiet, menacing voice. "I'm not sure how you pissed off the Starman, but I've been waiting in that shower of yours for more than two hours. I was getting bored."

"Well, at least that explains the country music," Cam answered. He was trying to calm his nerves at the shock of discovering this man, and that knife, in his room. "Since I don't know anyone called Starman, I don't suppose it's possible you've accidentally picked the wrong man's room."

"Clever, Mr. Forsyth. But, no. I have the correct room and the correct man. Worst yet is that you made me stand in that damn shower for so long and didn't even have the decency to take a dump when you first came in. I had practiced and practiced opening the curtain, seeing your shocked face and slicing your throat before you could scream. You ruined my plan, Mr. Forsyth. You ruined my fun. I don't like having my plans ruined."

Years of training and practice as a Protector had honed Cam Forsyth's fighting skills, and he recognized that this man was not a street thug who could easily be disarmed. He was a professional killer and as such was prepared for any kind of resistance. "Well, into every life a little rain must fall. I must assume this isn't your first experience in showers."

A faint smile crossed the man's tight lips. "For someone who obviously knows I'm here to kill, you are a very cool customer, Mr. Forsyth. Actually sir, you have the honor of being my 200th contract. That's quite a milestone, you have to admit."

"You have an impressive resumé, Mr..." Cam paused for the response he knew he wouldn't get. At the same time, he reached down and picked up a small, very lightweight blanket off the corner of the chair. Its designed purpose was for someone to cover just their legs while lounging.

Cam had a different use in mind. He slowly wrapped the cloth around his left forearm and, while never taking his eyes off the intruder, used his leg to slide the chair away. This opened the area. The assassin watched with mixed amusement and confusion. He had had people beg, cry, faint, try and negotiate, and even pray. He had never had someone so calmly prepare for the inevitable.

"Mr. Forsyth, you interest me. In case you plan on yelling for help, you're unfortunately kind of screwed. You have a corner room and the next room over is empty. I checked. The room directly below you is also empty. Now the room above is occupied, but we'll just have to assume they won't hear through the concrete flooring between you and them."

"With 199 contracts completed, I have to assume you're very good at what you do." Cam was slowly moving away from the sliding door and into the open area of the room. He now had some options for movement. The man noticed, but didn't really care that his intended victim wasn't going to die without at least attempting to get away.

"No, Mr. Forsyth. I'm not just very good. I'm the best." He slowly turned the knife so that the point of the blade was toward his elbow and the razor-sharp edge was away from his arm. Using this knife-fighting technique, he could quickly stab or slice his victim. There were many places a person could be cut or stabbed where death was almost instantaneous and, even more important, completely quiet.

A gunshot in a hotel gets a lot of attention and attention was the one thing this man didn't want. A quiet knife kill and a quick departure from the hotel was his plan. That afternoon, while entering the hotel, he had worn a very nice fedora that had matched his suit and completely hid his face from security cameras as he passed through the lobby. Overriding Forsyth's door lock had been child's play, and he had been waiting in the room for a couple of hours. With that much time in the hotel, he wouldn't look suspicious to security when he left. Plus, he would put the "Do Not Disturb" sign on the door as he left. That would keep housekeeping out an extra day, maybe two. After Forsyth's body was inevitably discovered, police would review the security camera videos to try and identify everyone who entered and exited around the assumed time of death. A man coming and going wearing an expensive suit would be disregarded by anyone reviewing the security videos. Murderers do not wear expensive suits.

Cam knew this man was not going to make a mistake on his own and decided he needed to force the man into action... any action. A moving man could be countered while a stationary one had all the advantages.

"So, I pissed off this guy you call the Starman. Did he happen to mention how?"

"I don't care how. All I care about is that you have to die today. I've already been paid and I don't give refunds or excuses."

"So, why the hell aren't you killing me? I don't seem to be leaking blood all over this nice carpet. I think you're full of shit. No professional plays with his victim the way you are. Only amateurs have to build themselves up first. Is this really your rookie job? From the looks of your cheap suit, you're really an undertaker, aren't you?"

The cheap suit comment was the breaker. "Cheap! You Mother fu..." In mid-sentence, the dark assassin came in for the kill. His right arm was up and across his chest. The knife blade was firmly and menacingly directed outward from his forearm. The man's left hand was clinched and ready to punch. He had the stance and attack of a professional for sure.

Cam Forsyth recognized the posture, and knew one way or another, this would be over fast. Nonetheless, he intended to walk out of this room, not to be carried from it.

As a Protector, Forsyth had begun his warrior training as a five-year-old. It continued until his graduation at twenty-one. He had kept his skills honed in the intervening years. Fortunately for him, Cam was the only one who knew the assassin was up against a professional, too.

With only two steps separating the men, the attack was almost instantaneous. The assassin crouched low and came in fast using the blade of his knife as a blocking shield. Instead of reacting in a defensive way and raising his arm as a block, Cam dropped to the floor on his left side and used his right leg to kick out into the attacker's knee cap. There was an audible crack as it was dislocated.

Forsyth was instantly on his feet again. He was amazed that the killer had not crashed to the floor in pain. Instead, he was still on his feet with ninety percent of his weight held by the undamaged leg. The knife was still being held in the most dangerous way and the man's fury was in control of the weapon.

"You son-of-a-bitch!" he screamed. "That will cost you. No fast death now. I'm going to make you bleed for a long time before you die."

"Come on, undertaker. Let me see you hobble over here and do your slow death thing."

The combination of excruciating pain, fury at being on the losing end of Forsyth's kick, and even a small amount of fear caused the man to react in a most non-professional way. Instead of cautiously picking his next attack, he blindly dove straight ahead with the plan to land on Forsyth and quickly stab his life out.

Using the most basic of all defenses, Forsyth rolled on to his back and met the killer in mid dive with his legs out. He then used his legs to keep the man's momentum going straight ahead. As the assassin landed hard on his back, Cam Forsyth quickly jumped back on his feet.

In almost slow motion, the killer stood and turned around. His curse of "You bastard" was stopped when Cam's flying kick landed squarely in his chest.

A split-second later the man was gone. Forsyth's kick was strong enough to propel him backwards across the balcony. His momentum sent him over the center section of the railing. The only sound was the word "Shit!" as the man fell ten stories to the large manicured lawn below.

Cam Forsyth changed his mind. He now thought the height of the railing was perfect.

The police were called within seconds of the man hitting the ground. As often happens in such cases, the 911 emergency dispatchers received six calls almost simultaneously. Two were from drivers on the side street next to the hotel; one was from the hotel valet at his station; two were from hotel workers who witnessed the fall from the lobby and one was from Cam Forsyth where he gave them his room number.

It took less than three minutes for five Corpus Christi police units to be at the hotel. It took less than three additional minutes for police to be in Cam Forsyth's room. They found him standing by the open door. "I didn't move anything," he said to the first officer.

"Are you armed, sir?"

"No."

"May I check, sir?"

Cam raised his hands well above his head and turned slowly to face the door, allowing the police officer to quickly and professionally confirm Forsyth's word.

Five minutes after that, Detectives Sam Cessnas and Wendy Jo Vonderahe walked into the hotel room.

"Mr. Forsyth," Cessnas began, "You are a most interesting man. In my career, I've been known to have a killer show up on multiple rap sheets in a single day. But, I've never had a material witness to two different deaths show up in a single day. Detective Vonderahe and I were getting ready to leave for the evening when your phone call was announced. We heard your name as the caller and we decided to hang around. We had dinner plans, which you have now screwed up."

"You're the second person in the past hour who has accused me of messing up his plans. I was happy to mess with the other guy, but I do apologize for messing up your plans with this lovely lady."

Detective Vonderahe smiled at the slightly angry look on Cessnas' face and quickly spoke before he could. "Mr. Forsyth, in our line of work we find coincidences like this either amusing or scary. You are one of the very scary kinds because you seem a little too prepared for the darker side of life. You found a dead girl this morning and fifteen hours later you are involved in the death of another person.... and not just any other person."

Her last comment caused Forsyth's eyebrows to go up. "You know who he is? This quickly?"

"That squashed lump," Sam Cessnas said, "if my somewhat hurried glance is right, was very known to us, the FBI and for all I know, any number of other law enforcement agencies. He wasn't pretty before his demise and is somewhat less so now, but I recognized him. That's J.P. Pearson. He's been a hit man for drug cartels, angry wives, and anyone else who could pay his fee for more than a decade. We've never had enough hard evidence to directly connect him to any murders and I suspect from what I saw downstairs that we'll likely never connect him to any future ones.

"He told me I was to be his 200th contract. Guess I got lucky and he lost his balance on the balcony before he could fulfill that contract."

Detective Wendy Jo Vonderahe looked at the disheveled chairs in the room. "So, you're saying there was no contact between you and Pearson? For some reason, I think you're being modest, Mr. Forsyth. If even half of what we know about Pearson is true, he was a very bad man. You weren't in the Navy Seals, were you?"

A slight smile came across Forsyth's face. "No ma'am. But, I did have an older brother who punched me a lot when we were kids. I learned to outrun him until our Mom saved me. Guess that experience paid off."

Cessnas called the police photographer over. "Have you taken pictures of everything?"

"Yessir."

Cam Forsyth commented, "Be sure to get some close-up pictures of the inside of the bathtub. And forensics may want to look, too. There may be residue from someone standing in there for a while."

The noticeably conflicted photographer looked at Cessnas for validation. All he got was a slight head nod and a few words. "Sounds like a good plan. Make sure they check the tub carefully."

"Yessir," was the only response. A moment later the photographer looked out of the bathroom and said, "There's a man's hat hanging from the shower head in here."

Cessnas walked to the bathroom, examined the fedora, and told the photographer to get pictures but not to touch it. The photographer almost reminded the detective that this was not his first day on the job, but decided not to.

Cessnas left the bathroom and returned to where Vonderahe and Forsyth were standing. "Would it be safe to assume you don't hang your hats in the bathroom?"

"I don't wear hats."

"You know, Mr. Forsyth, you have a knack for generating police paperwork. In particular, my paperwork. But, there is something about you I like. Tell me how you knew there was something in the bathtub."

"Pearson told me I pissed off someone he called the Starman. He mentioned in passing that he had been waiting for me to come back to this room and the bathtub was his spot. He said he liked to surprise people on the toilet—the pervert. Luckily, I didn't feel the call of nature and didn't go in there when I got to my room. Funny, I have felt the need to go several times in the past 30 minutes."

"You can tinkle at the station. You remember that place. It hasn't changed in the past few hours."

Detective Vonderahe was far more formal than her partner and continued her more professional questioning, "Why do I suspect we won't find Pearson's fingerprints on that sliding glass door lock? Did you open it?"

"I opened it, but for all I know so did Pearson before I got here."

"Did you push him off the balcony?" she asked quietly. "I saw the broken railing, but it would have taken a lot of force to make that happen. He didn't cause that just by leaning his fat ass against it."

"Fat ass?" Cessnas smiled at his partner. "I'm starting to rub off on you, aren't I?"

"I knew that term long before you," was the response.

Forsyth looked between the two detectives with amusement. He was certain there was far more than just a professional relationship here, but decided to keep that revelation to himself.

"Okay, here's what went down." Cam Forsyth told his story quickly but accurately. Both Cessnas and Vonderahe listened without comment. "By now, I suspect the officers on the ground will have found Pearson's knife under him or somewhere nearby. He had it when he left the room."

Vonderahe used her police radio to ask the officers photographing and gathering evidence from the body if they had found a knife. "No, ma'am," was the response. "But, we're about to roll him over. Standby." Several seconds later the voice came back, "There's a knife there alright. It has a composite handle and the blade looks about seven or eight inches long. We're about to search the pockets for ID and we'll put the knife in an evidence bag first if you need it."

"No. Thanks anyway. Just knowing you found it is enough." She thought aloud, "What are the odds they find any ID?"

"Zero," both Detective Cessnas and Cam Forsyth responded without hesitation.

"Mr. Forsyth, can I assume only Mr. Pearson's fingerprints are on that knife?" A yes nod was the response. "If that's the case and with Mr. Pearson's reputation, I suspect the DA will see a clear-cut case of self-defense and won't even bring this to the grand jury. But, obviously, the DA has to make that determination. In the meantime, let's take another ride to the station for you to make your formal statement. Can I expect another call from the Mayor?"

"Not this time. My discovery of Miss Austin was more suspicious. I understood that. It's pretty clear she and I had a romantic evening. That made me a person of interest. Not this time. I didn't invite this creature to my room. My only connection to him is that I was to be his 200th contract. Pearson's not my concern. The man who paid him to kill me is who I'm going to find."

"You called him 'Starman'?"

"Yes."

The two detectives looked at one another and both shrugged slightly indicating the name meant nothing to either. "If such a person exists, it's our job to find him," Detective Vonderahe said with finality.

Cam Forsyth did not respond has he grabbed his coat to leave the hotel room. Then he looked at Sam Cessnas. "My car or yours?"

"You can drive your car, sir. Detective Vonderahe and I will follow in ours. You will unfortunately have to get another room for tonight. I suspect this one will have crime scene tape in front of the door for a day or two."

"Can I take my laptop? I kinda need it."

"Is there anything on it pertinent to anything that's happened in this room in the past hour?" A head shake from Forsyth was the response. "If you happen to pick your laptop up on your way out, and I don't see you do it, how can I object? We will see you at the station."

Just a few minutes after 10 p.m., Cam Forsyth walked out of the interview room at the Corpus Christi police station. He was shocked to find his future King and Queen sitting in cheap plastic chairs in the outer room.

"Sir! Ma'am! What are you doing here?" he stammered.

A broad smile met his stunned look. "Well, it seems Lady Deidre and I cannot let you out of our sight for even a few hours without you getting involved in unwholesome activities."

"But how did you find out? I didn't call anyone this time."

"No, but we knew where you were staying and decided to get a room there, too. Your activities have produced no small amount of chatter around the hotel. Not too often someone leaves the hotel without using one of the ground floor doors. Trust me, it took no great detective skills to figure out your room was the one with police crime scene tape everywhere. Deidre and I figured you would want some company when you finished their questioning. Do we need an attorney? I can probably turn over a rock somewhere and get you one."

A smile cracked on Cam Forsyth's face. "No sir. The detectives made it pretty clear they believe this is a clear-cut case of self-defense. For some reason, the District Attorney moved really quickly, I guess because of who the guy was. She sent someone to the police station and got the details from the crime scene officers and from these two detectives. That guy then called the DA and filled her in with the information. With the facts she has now, the DA says she also feels it was self-defense and has no plans to present anything to the grand jury. That must be some sort of speed record for any DA action. I guess, this guy had a very bad reputation and they were not at all sad he is off their radar.

"So, nothing here is going to keep you away from coming back to Exeter tomorrow or to Cape Kennedy in three weeks?" Deidre asked.

"No, ma'am. At first, I was a person of interest in Catherine's death. I get the feeling, even though they haven't told me officially, that I'm off that list, too. When I told the detectives about the Sojourner launch and about Terry being my sister, they just asked me to keep them and the District Attorney's office updated as to my whereabouts. When they actually capture whoever killed her and it goes to trial, I'll be called back to testify about what I saw."

Isha and Deidre both decided to let that subject close.

The Prince then asked the question that had been confounding him all day. "Cam, who have you pissed off enough to want you dead? You've never struck me as the type to have a jealous husband on your trail." All three smiled.

"Sire, the only person I've even spoken to besides the hotel staff and police officials has been Catherine's boss. I put him dead-center in the Giant Prick column." His choice of words suddenly dawned upon Forsyth. "Forgive me, Lady Deidre. That just slipped out."

The future queen of Exeter laughed quietly and smiled warmly at the highly-embarrassed man before her. "Cam, I've heard the word before."

"Yeah, perhaps. However, I shouldn't have used it in front of Prince Isha. He's such a gentle soul and I shouldn't have risked offending his sensibilities."

Deidre's husband cut off her chance for a funny retort by interjecting, "Cam, we're away from home. Please call us Isha and Deidre."

"That will take some getting used to, but I will try. Thank you, sire."

All three laughed again and Isha just shook his head. "That's better. Come on. Let's find somewhere to grab a bite to eat. I'd wager there is some pretty good seafood around here somewhere."

May 23, 2022
Kennedy Space Center, Florida

At the same time Forsyth was leaving the police station with Isha and Deidre, his sister, Dr. Terry Lee, was sitting in her room within the crew quarters building and studying yet another procedural manual. She was reviewing procedures for an experiment she had first seen only four months before. It would involve an EVA (extra vehicular activity) which most newscasters called a spacewalk. Just the preparations for an EVA added six hours to an already densely packed schedule on the Shuttle. Added to the prep time was the actual time outside the airlock. Together it meant a ten-hour day for three people. That commitment of effort made no sense and Lee was angry.

Part of the time for this new experiment had come from the period allotted for her tests. *My work*, she thought as her anger grew, *was designed over three years. There were teams of Ph.D.'s who completed exhaustive peer reviews on my hypothesis and methodology. Then the boy-wonder shows up at the last minute and screws everything up. All because Maclemore has no balls to stand up to a corrupt and manipulative politician.*

Lee, whose drink of choice was sweet tea with lemon, instead poured herself a glass of merlot and decided on a ten-minute break. *I don't concentrate well when I'm angry*, she recognized.

Terry started to call her husband, an electrical contractor in Montana who very much liked to stay out of the spotlight. He rarely attended any of the obligatory press conferences, dinners, or junkets his wife was required to make. He chose instead to remain either in Exeter or on their Montana ranch. He chose to observe the cosmos from a hillside on a clear Big Sky night far from any city lights instead of from a space shuttle.

On a whim, Terry decided to call her folks. *It's only 9:15 at home*, she thought as she reached for her cell phone. From memory, she dialed a normal ten-digit phone number. After she heard a click, she added five more numbers. Deep within the caverns of Exeter the phone was answered by her sister, Melissa.

"Hi, Terry!"

"Hi, Sunshine," Lee replied. She instantly felt her spirits rise by just hearing Melissa's cheerful voice. "I was just feeling a little punk and decided to hear a happy voice."

"Well, then don't talk to Mom and Dad. If you want 'happy' you better stick with me."

Over the next few minutes, Melissa recounted the past two day's events in the life of their brother. She finished by saying, "Cam says he'll be here tomorrow. But, he's still going to be there with you for the launch." There was a pause. "Any chance I can come with him, too?"

"Absolutely! You won't be able to join us on the gantry, but I can get you into the VIP viewing area. You think Mom and Dad will want to come, too?"

"Not a chance. Mom says she can't bear to watch her baby girl launched into space without having a very strong drink in her hand and they won't allow that at the site." Both ladies chuckled. Their mother was not known for drinking much nor for being the nervous type. That said, she had adamantly refused to come.

"So, why are you feeling punk?"

"Me? I'm just angry at politicians and administrators right now. But, come to think of it, that's nothing new."

Melissa waited for her sister to add more to her comment. When it became evident that none was coming, she laughingly suggested, "Why not take a day or two off and come home?" Both women knew it was a comment meant to fill the quiet. There was no chance of Terry coming to Exeter before the launch and both women knew it.

Lee was quiet for a moment while considering an option. "I can probably slip away for a couple of hours tomorrow. Get Dad to schedule some time for me to visit. I'll sneak into Marlo Campbell's lab and use her equipment there."

Marlo Campbell was a NASA researcher who had worked two decades in developing holographic design projects. Her professional accomplishments were known world-wide in the physics community. However, surprisingly she had spent the first eighteen years of her life living in Exeter. As a child she had shown an unusual aptitude for scientific research. After studying with the best teachers of optics and physics in Exeter, it was decided to create an identity for her so she could continue her education above. Campbell had spent six years in Cambridge, Massachusetts where she earned bachelor and masters degrees in physics from the Harvard University. She had then moved across town. Four years later, she earned her doctorate in physics from the Massachusetts Institute of Technology (MIT).

Campbell would soon announce to the world a breakthrough in three-dimensional holograms which would have tactile capabilities. For years, holograms had been used around the world with increasingly dramatic clarity. What had always been missing was the ability to transmit holograms between two locations where each person would have the ability to feel the other person. Dr. Marlo Campbell had discovered a process where lightweight gloves worn by both parties would interface with each other. If two people were transmitting holograms of themselves while using Campbell's technology, they could reach out and shake hands and actually feel the other person's hand. There was the strong possibility that soon full body transmission would be reality. When that happened, two people on different sides of the world would be able to hug each other as if they were together. This would be just the latest technological gift that Exeter had allowed one of her scientists to release to the outer world.

"Great idea. What time do you want?" Melissa asked quickly.

"I'm unscheduled from 4:00 until 6:00 tomorrow afternoon which is two hours ahead of Exeter so factor that in."

Melissa was excited that she would get to see her sister the next day. "Thanks, Terry. I've missed you so much and you've been so busy. I know we'll all look forward to seeing you. Hugs!"

"Thanks, Sunshine. I feel so much better just having talked to you. See you tomorrow."

Chapter Eleven

May 24, 2022
Corpus Christi International Airport

Isha, Deidre, and Cam Forsyth were at the general aviation operations hangar by nine the next morning. Sitting on the ramp in front of them was a beautiful Bonanza G36. It looked almost brand new. Forsyth was initially confused. "Sire, this isn't the plane you flew in yesterday, is it? I don't know much about airplanes, but I can recognize most of the primary colors. The plane I saw you get out of was red and white. This one is bigger and is blue. Most non-aviators will assume they are different airplanes."

"Your powers of observation are commendable, Cam. The plane we came in seats four, but not at all comfortably. This Bonanza is a much nicer six-passenger plane. It'll easily reach Santa Fe without having to land and refuel. When I decided you needed to come to Exeter, I ditched the other plane and rented this one."

"You can just change planes like that?"

Deidre piped in, "Cam, we rented that other plane in Santa Fe and of course it had to be returned there. This place has a young instructor pilot who is already checked out in that other plane. He was thrilled to get the flying time returning it to Santa Fe for us. Then he'll just fly this plane back. That solved the little detail of two airplanes. As far as this plane goes, before a company will rent you a plane, they check your pilot's licenses, FAA medical, and logbook. Then they usually require the renter to pay for an hour or two for an instructor to fly along and observe the pilot's skills before letting them go solo. So, yesterday your Prince spent a couple of hours terrorizing some young man in the skies around Corpus Christi. That accomplished, we are now ready to head home together."

Forsyth did the math. Prince Isha had paid for two airplanes for the trip, plus the other pilot's charge for flying to Santa Fe and back, plus the money for getting checked out in the new plane. He had no idea how much airplanes rented for, but it was surely expensive. *His Highness spent a great deal of money and effort just so I could fly with them back to Exeter*, Cam thought. He knew the cost was not a burden to Isha, but it was an indication of how the Prince always thought of others instead of himself first.

Isha walked away from the flight planning table with his filed flight plan in hand. "Well, it's 740 miles to Santa Fe. If the weather guys aren't totally wrong, flying back at 10,000 feet we should have a nice tailwind. That means it should be just over four hours from takeoff to landing. I've had them load some nice inflight lunches on board, but everyone better tinkle before we take off." He winked at his wife who stuck out her tongue then walked to the ladies' restroom.

"Sire, I can't tell you how much I appreciate all this effort to get me home. The cost must have been ridiculous."

"Not really. I'm the one who is winning on this deal. I get to spend some time with my wife and my friend, and I get to fly a brand new and sweet airplane. Don't worry about the cost, Cam. It's not a big deal." He paused. "Now to avoid the inevitable abuse I would take from Deidre if we had to land somewhere for me to pee, I'm also going here."

Both men walked into the men's room.

Within thirty minutes Isha piloted the brand-new Bonanza into the air and Deidre dutifully raised the landing gear handle. The flight was uneventful with smooth air and, surprising Isha slightly, the forecasted tailwind was actually there which pushed the airplane even faster over the ground. True to his flight planning, four hours and ten minutes after takeoff, Isha was setting up to land on runway 20 at Santa Fe Municipal Airport. Even though the airport has what pilots consider high-altitude runways, the Bonanza easily met the challenge and handled perfectly. Runway 20 is 8,366 feet long, but Isha had the plane at taxi speed in about one thousand feet. He turned left onto Taxiway Golf which put the plane facing directly at the terminal and the only adobe-covered control tower he had ever seen.

Instead of going to the passenger terminal, Isha taxied to the general aviation hangar where he had rented the first plane. Sure enough, waiting there was the young pilot from Corpus ready to fly the Bonanza home. His uniform shirt had embroidered wings over the name Robert. "Come into the reception area with me, please," Isha said to the man.

Once there, Isha asked the young pilot what time he had gotten to work that morning. "Well, they called me at home last night and asked me if I wanted to fly to Santa Fe and back today. Of course, I said I would. I came in at five-thirty this morning to flight plan. I was told you wanted me here when you landed so I took off at six. That Bonanza flies about seventy-five knots faster than the one I flew here. Plus, I had to land in El Paso for fuel. So, I've only been here about thirty minutes. That was okay. It gave me some time to talk to that gorgeous young lady at the reception desk. I wish I had gotten here a couple of hours ago." He smiled more to himself than to Isha.

Isha did some mental math and responded, "We had a tailwind all the way over which means it'll be a headwind on your trip back. Also, you'll probably have to stop for fuel in the San Antonio area. That would get you back to Corpus after a very long day of flying. Okay, Robert, here's what we're going to do. I'll call your boss and tell him you're staying here for the night. I'll pay for another day on the Bonanza. It'll also mean you'll get a per diem. Finally, since you've really helped me I'll take care of your room and meal expenses for the night. That way you can fly back to Corpus fresh tomorrow. Do you have a wife you need to call?"

"No, sir. I'm single and fancy-free. But, sir, I can't let you do that. I can just sleep back there on a couch in the pilot's lounge. I've done that lots of times and this place is actually both clean and quiet," Robert protested.

Isha ignored him and walked to the receptionist. He had rented aircraft for many years from this company and everyone just assumed he was a local business man with deep pockets. "Please call the Hotel Magnificat and book a room for my friend, Robert. Tell them he is on my account and is not to be charged for anything, even gratuities. He'll need transportation over there and back here tomorrow. Okay?"

"Yes, sir." The perky receptionist with chestnut brown hair responded. "I'm about to finish my shift so I can drive him over there. I've always wanted to see the Hotel Magnificat. There aren't many five-star hotels around here."

Isha noticed the lack of a ring or even the hint that a ring was usually on the young lady's left-hand. He walked back over to the pilot who was gathering the overnight bag he always carried on cross country flights. Isha discretely gave the pilot far more money than he had contracted to pay. "Listen, Robert," he said, "that young lady has graciously offered to drive you to this hotel. The charges are all set up on an account I have there. If you feel duty bound to thank her for the ride by taking her to dinner at the hotel's restaurant, I would consider that part of our deal. Just sign for your meals and they'll charge it to the room. That's just my way of thanking you for your help today." He winked at the young pilot who was looking at the receptionist with new interest.

At that moment, a Mercedes limo drove to the door of the reception area. A silver-haired man gracefully got out of the driver's seat and opened the back door of the car. Deidre smiled warmly, "Sweetheart, when I first met Tomás years ago I thought he was old then, but he never ages. He still looks the same and is just as spry."

Tomás had been Isha's mentor during his training as a Protector. "Well, I think marrying your grandmother has a lot to do with that. Maria would keep any man young. They sure seem to be perfect for each other." Deidre's widowed grandmother and Tomás had married soon after Isha and Deidre did. They split their time living in Maria's home in the mountains outside Santa Fe and in Exeter where Tomás had his chambers.

"Let's go by way of my grandmother's home. I haven't seen her in a couple of weeks. Would that be okay?"

"Actually, that would be easier. Tomás keeps the car stored there anyway.

It took Tomás thirty-five minutes to drive Isha, Deidre, and Cam to the home he shared with his spry eighty-something year old bride, Maria. Maria insisted everyone stay for dinner—a request that was impossible to refuse.

Just before midnight, Isha was finally able to convince the old woman that they needed to leave. He borrowed a flashlight from Tomás for the short walk through the woods that brought the trio to the well-hidden entrance to a large cavern. The concealed room was what had been christened The O'Leary Station. It was part of a massive underground rail system that linked all of Exeter. They summoned two trams, one for Cam and one for Isha and Deidre.

At that late hour it only took them a few minutes to get to their respective homes.

Chapter Twelve

May 25, 2022
Exeter

The Forsyth family was together in a special circular room with equipment identical to that in Dr. Marlo Campbell's lab. It could comfortably accommodate twenty people, but plans were in works to enlarge it to handle fifty. Campbell had used the Exeter location to transmit holographic images without fear of them being intercepted and her technology stolen.

For decades, Exeter had possessed the capability to record events using holographic technology and to play those events back in near perfect 3-D images. Holographic transmissions were now being accomplished outside Exeter but the technology was primitive compared to Exeter's. Marlo Campbell's groundbreaking work would add a tactile component in real-time. There were rumors her work would be submitted for a Nobel Prize in Physics. If she were to win it, Marlo Campbell would be the thirty-second recipient of a Nobel Prize who was, in reality, from Exeter.

Moses, Tame, Melissa, and Cam were bathed in light projected from hundreds of low intensity laser lights from every area of the room. Suddenly, on a podium in the middle of the area, Terry Lee materialized from nothingness. Her image appeared completely solid from every angle. At her location in Florida, Lee saw her whole family with perfect clarity.

"Hi, guys!" Terry was genuinely thrilled to see her family. It had been months since her last visit to Exeter. "Glad to see you got my brother out of jail before he became some convict's surrogate consort."

"I wasn't in jail. I was just a guest of the police department." Cam smiled. "Twice in one day. But, I think my all-round superior personality won them over."

Terry made no attempt to hide her sarcasm. "Glad to hear that, Jailbird."

Melissa slid into the center stage and put on a pair of specialized gloves designed by Dr. Campbell. "They feel like surgical gloves. I don't feel any sensors in the glove," she said excitedly.

"There aren't any separate sensors. The entire glove is one sensor." Terry put on gloves exactly like the ones in Exeter. "Okay, Sunshine, hold my hand." With that comment, Dr. Terry Lee reached out her gloved hand to her sister. The two women could instantly feel the firm grip of the other. The tactile sensation was perfect. "Now Melissa, I want you to try to feel my pulse."

"Really?"

"It's an experiment. I don't know how sensitive these things really are."

Tentatively, Melissa touched the wrist of her sister. Even though almost 2,000 miles separated the two, Melissa could easily feel the steady beat of Terry's pulse.

"That's so cool!" Melissa exclaimed. "Try mine!"

Terry laughed at her sister's bubbly enthusiasm. "Sure, but I'm not sure I can count that fast." Despite her academic and professional demeanor, Dr. Terry Lee could barely contain the excitement she experienced feeling Melissa's pulse.

Every member of the family took turns trying on the tactile gloves and experiencing the new technology while at the same time carrying on a conversation with each other. Everyone felt as if they were sitting together instead in the same room and not several states apart.

Tame, ever the perceptive mother, stood directly in front of the holographic image of her daughter. "Okay, Kiddo, what's going on? I can see it in your eyes." She didn't move or prod any more.

After a moment, Lee answered, "They made a change to our crew a few months ago that has really affected everything I was going to try and accomplish. The new guy is working hard, but he isn't ready. That tiny detail doesn't matter. Because some politician threatened the entire program, we had to add this engineer and his experiments to the schedule." She paused. "I hate politicians."

Tame smiled wanly. "That seems to be a universal attitude." Again, the protective side of Tame emerged, "This won't affect safety on the mission will it?"

"No. Not at all, Mom. But, it's just crowding our schedule and all of us are having to give up some of the time allotted for our own experiments to accommodate his. We will make it work. That's what we do. Plus, we have Bubba Ledwell as our commander. He's got both the authority and the influence with NASA to keep us on track. He won't let the bureaucratic bozos put us in danger. I promise you that, Mom." Lee took a deep breath and smiled a genuine smile for the first time in days. The family time had been cathartic. "Oh, well. That's enough complaining."

"You're not complaining. You're just letting off steam," Cam said thoughtfully. "Who better to do that with than us? Besides, I'll be there next week." He felt a sharp jab into his ribs. "Damn, Melissa!" He smiled benignly. "Correction, Terry. I will be there next week and I will be bringing Melissa with me… reluctantly."

Melissa stuck her tongue out at her brother then quickly kissed him on the cheek.

Moses Forsyth had waited patiently and was the last to speak to his daughter. "Sweetheart, your mother and I are very proud of you. You've worked so hard all your life and we think you deserve the vacation you're about to take."

"Vacation? You call 12-to-14-hour work days a vacation?" She laughed knowing her father's sense of humor, then continued, "Yeah. I guess working in space for fifteen days will really seem like a vacation especially after all the work preparing for the mission. Thanks, Dad for putting it all in perspective."

Forsyth winked affectionately at the holographic image of Terry. "We do have one additional thing for you." He reached into his pocket and removed a box that looked like it could hold playing cards. "I know you'll be busy most of the time, but here is something from home for you to take into space."

"Dad, I can't get it from you. We're seven days from launch and we go into quarantine in a couple of days."

"Oh, but you can get it from us. Remember Cam will be the first journalist to ever ride with the crew to the shuttle. He's going to bring it with him and will slip it to you. Isn't there a pocket or someplace you can hide it? It weighs just a few ounces."

"Okay, Dad. Our suits do have an external pocket where we can carry personal items. There's room for something that small. What does it do?"

"Let's just say it's a gadget we're not ready to reveal to outsiders yet. When it's within six feet of you, it will lock on to your private communication channel and all the relay stations around the world. This little box will let us listen in to everything you say while in space without anyone knowing about it. It will have a hot microphone so that everything you say will be picked up."

"Can I hear you?"

Moses Forsyth smiled. "Don't you get to take a digital music library with you?" His daughter nodded. "Okay, when you plug your ear buds into this box, it will look like you're listening to your music player, but you'll be able hear us totally in secret. There has to be somewhere you can find a little privacy for a few minutes each day to talk to your mother. Right?"

Dr. Terry Lee smiled at her father knowing it was he who really wanted to talk with her every day.

"Sure, Dad. But NASA has a tight control over any communications from the shuttle. They won't like me having a private transmitter on board."

Tame Forsyth laughed. "Honey, don't worry about NASA. This system operates at a micro-frequency so precise that not even the NSA will know it's there. Exeter's research folks want to miniaturize it even more and give one to every Protector around the world. That way we could have instantaneous and secure communication with every one of them no matter where they are. Prince Isha made that a priority project after the communication problems he faced when that madman tried to destroy most of New York City. He's the one who asked Cam to slip it to you."

Cam stepped in, "Terry, I actually got the straight stuff from Prince Isha yesterday. He said when they were on that ship, he had to leave someone on the deck to relay messages home because the communications were too weak from inside the ship. He didn't want that to happen again in the future. The hope is that if it works through your hardened shuttle fuselage at orbital speeds, it will work from any Earthbound location."

"And you're sure neither NASA nor the NSA will realize it's happening?"

"They won't have a clue unless you get caught seemingly talking to yourself for no reason."

They all laughed.

Little did they suspect the small communication device Moses Forsyth was now holding might well soon be required to save the entire world from cataclysmic disaster.

Chapter Thirteen

May 26, 2022
Corpus Christi, Texas

Catherine Austin's funeral was a small gathering. Her mother and father had gratefully accepted Nicholas Schumer's generous offer to pay the expense for her funeral and burial. He had even sent a company jet to bring them to Corpus Christi. They knew their daughter had been valuable member of his staff and believed Schumer wanted to honor her years of service.

They would not have felt the same way if they had known Schumer had been the one who took Catherine's life.

No one from Winter Triangle Physics was there except Nicholas Schumer, Josh Tanner, and Red O'Callaghan. And only Red showed any emotion. Her flowing crimson hair accented the light freckles across her nose and the sadness in her bloodshot eyes. She was brokenhearted that something as tragic as Catherine's accidental death had been so quickly pushed into the irrelevant. Josh Tanner had already moved into Catherine's office. Her personal effects had been stuffed into a used cardboard box and relegated to an obscure corner of Red's office. Her instructions were to ship the box to Catherine's parents when she had the time.

Red knew she was not going to like working for the new guy. He required her to call him "Mr. Tanner". He even wanted her to schedule her bathroom breaks so she could have another assistant cover her desk while she was in the toilet. This, he said, would ensure he wouldn't miss any important phone calls. The idea that he might answer his own phone calls while she was away those few minutes had not even occurred to him. Red had already pegged Tanner as a jerk. Secretly she called him an ass-kissing jerk, but that term embarrassed her even if she never said it out loud.

Standing a discrete distance away and out of sight of the funeral party were two men. Cam Forsyth had returned to Corpus for the funeral. He had been flown there by Prince Isha. Going to the funeral had been Isha's idea. He believed his Protector needed the closure.

Cam had accepted the offer with one caveat. He wanted to avoid any contact with Nicholas Schumer. Their very brief encounter the morning of Catherine's death had been contentious. There was no reason to risk having another confrontation.

Even standing away from the actual funeral, Cam felt a bond with the woman in the silver casket just yards away. They had enjoyed each other's company and intimacy for only a short time. Yet rarely had he ever found any other person who had completely captivated his soul as Catherine had. He remembered her touch, her gentleness, and also the toughness of her spirit. Catherine was incredibly bright, unpredictable, commanding, and yet vulnerable. She would have always been a challenge to deal with in any long-term relationship, but it was a test he would have enjoyed taking. Cam really knew there could never have been any true romance. Catherine was married to her career and yet she had let him into her life in a way he knew was special. He didn't know what might have happened. Now he'd never have the chance to know.

Cam still believed Catherine had been murdered and he was going to find out who had done it. He was going to make that person pay dearly for taking her from him. He had even felt a bit of guilt about her death. Had he stayed the night in Catherine's bed as she had asked him to instead of returning to his hotel, she would still be alive. No one would have hurt her if he had been there.

Prince Isha was silent as Cam watched and secretly participated in the funeral. He wasn't there for the lady they were burying. He was there for his friend. The two men watched as the casket was slowly lowered into the grave. The mourners each tossed a handful of dirt in the hole and slowly walked away. From their hidden spot, Cam and Isha also silently left and found a nice seafood restaurant for a quiet lunch. Isha kept his Protector's mind off the funeral by asking questions regarding the maiden launch of the Sojourner, Terry's experiments, and his unprecedented chance to be with the crew.

Two hours later, Cam and Isha came back to the cemetery. Isha stayed with the rental car while his friend walked to the freshly-filled grave of Catherine Austin. As is so often the case in situations like this, Cam was having difficulty believing that just a few feet below him was the body of the vibrant, exciting, brilliant, but secretive woman he had held, caressed, and made love to just a few days before. He knew she had her demons, but she had put them to rest while they were together.

A current of rage was just beneath the surface of Cam's apparent calm exterior as he spoke to the small mound of dirt now completely covered with flowers. "Catherine," he said with conviction, "I will find out who put you here. They will pay. I promise you that."

The Protector of Exeter placed a single long stem rose on the top of the flowers and turned to walk away. Then he paused, turned to look one more time, and said, "Goodbye, Cathy."

May 26, 2022
Kennedy Space Center, Florida

At the same time as Catherine's funeral, Captain Thurman "Bubba" Ledwell was looking around the table at his team. In only six days, they would be on orbit. As time was getting short, he was becoming less and less patient with anyone he felt was not prepared.

"Scott, I was looking over your schedule requests. You're still asking for more time than was allocated initially. We don't have it. Pare down your requirements somehow." He waited for an answer from Elder but none came.

The tension became palpable as the seconds passed. When it became obvious Ledwell was not going to move on until Elder finally reacted. He moved uncomfortably in his seat. "I was told I could have whatever I felt I needed."

"You were told wrong. This is a team. We are not a team plus you."

"Dr. Maclemore said…," he started to respond.

Ledwell stopped him in mid-sentence. "Maclemore is not in command of this mission. I am. He got you on this mission but that doesn't mean you get carte blanche on orbit. Don't you dare try and intimidate me by invoking the Director's name. It won't work."

Ledwell stared directly into the eyes of Scott Elder. "Have I made myself clear, Dr. Elder?"

All the bluster Elder had attempted to project was deflated. Very quietly he almost whispered, "Yes sir."

"Good! Now that we've established the chain of command here, I'm telling you to come up with a new plan paring down your time requests to fit the time you already have allocated. It's your experiment so you know better than anyone what can be eliminated or shortened. I want it done by tomorrow."

"Yes sir," Elder repeated.

Bubba Ledwell shifted his attention to four more of his crew. "Jim, Patti, Janelle, and Terry, I want you guys to review our procedures for Tom's and Scott's EVA. We need to find another hour in the schedule for Day Three on orbit. The scheduling team will make their directives, but I want a backup plan from you. We all know those ground pounders are convinced we have thirty-hour days in space and they schedule accordingly. Work their plan and find ways to actually accomplish the mission objectives using a mere twenty-four hour day."

Tunes Dalton, the senior Mission Specialist, wordlessly reached into his worn attaché case and slid a bound package of papers to Ledwell. "Boss, we have been working on that for the past two weeks. Patti, Janelle, Tom and Terry have found several places where we can double up on responsibilities and run more than one experiment simultaneously and ideas on how to pare down some EVA work. If you can get the mission planners to approve these recommendations, we can make everything happen."

Captain Bubba Ledwell was not surprised that Dalton, Koch, McLain, Fredrick, and Lee had taken the initiative to improve on the official schedule. He leafed through the half-inch sheaf of paper quickly. "I'll look through this more carefully tonight but, if you guys are confident in your numbers, I'll tell the planners this is our new schedule."

Dr. Patti Koch caught Ledwell's attention and confidently stated, "It's good, Bubba. One small item I can't abide. Tunes and Terry decided we only get to have one toilet break every three days. I personally have problems with that, but it does save a lot of time in the schedule."

Everyone laughed except L. Scott Elder. He was in no mood for levity.

At noon, the crew broke for a two-hour lunch. Twenty minutes later, L. Scott Elder was on the phone with his boss, Nicholas Schumer. "Sir, I'm being ordered to eliminate some parts of my experiment. Captain Ledwell says there isn't enough time for everything."

Several seconds of silence followed as Schumer fought to control his temper. Finally, a slow and menacing response hissed into Elder's ear. "Don't you change one damn thing. I'll put that bastard in his place." He hung up without another word.

Dr. John Francis Maclemore, NASA's Director of Flight Operations, answered his private phone line. There was no formality in the greeting. The caller got right to the point. "Maclemore, this is Nicholas Schumer." Maclemore had only heard the voice on the other end a few times, but he knew instantly who it was. Senator Maxwell Bellow's wealthy "friend" had made an impression on Maclemore during their first meeting and it had not been a positive one.

"How can I help you, Mr. Schumer?" He knew he wasn't going to like what was coming.

"The experiment you personally approved for the shuttle launch is being tossed into the trash bin by Captain Ledwell. I need that to stop and for him to give my man the time he needs."

"I'll look into it, Mr. Schumer, and will get back to you."

"I don't want a call back. I want this problem handled now!" He then hung up.

"You son-of-a-bitch!" Maclemore said to the dead phone. Then he punched the intercom button to his secretary. "Find Thurman Ledwell. If he's in the building have him come see me please. If he's at home, ask him to call me immediately."

Ten minutes later, the Shuttle Commander walked into Maclemore's outer office. He was shown right into the conference room as the Director entered from the other door. "Please sit down, Bubba. This won't take long and I know you're busy."

"What's this about, John? I do have a full plate of things to finish today."

"Tell me why you cut Dr. Elder's experiments?"

"Really, John? That's why you called me in? That little prick hasn't had one second of his experiments eliminated. He wants us to give him another eight hours and we don't have it. That's what I've vetoed."

"Vetoed? Captain, who gave you the authority to veto anything? That responsibility rests on other shoulders, not yours."

"I'm the Mission Commander. I'm responsible for everything that happens on orbit. You shoved this jerk into my team and we've had to assimilate him into everything. There is no more open time in the schedule unless we cancel other experiments."

"Then cancel them."

"No."

"Captain, I'm the Director of Flight Operations and I say cancel them."

"Maclemore, I'm the Mission Commander and I say no." The two men stared at one another and neither one blinked. "I'll make this easy," Ledwell continued. "If you cancel one item on our schedule to give Elder another 30 seconds of time, I'll remove myself from the mission and have Russ step in and take Sojourner on her maiden flight."

Commander Russ Boda, the first United States Coast Guard pilot ever trained as an astronaut, was the backup Mission Commander.

"You wouldn't dare!"

"Goodbye, John. You call Russ and inform him he's got the flight." Ledwell got up and reached the door of the conference room before Maclemore called him back.

"Damn it, Bubba. Get your ass back in here! All right! Run your damn schedule. Just try and make Elder feel like he's being heard. I can't take the heat from that bastard in Corpus Christi calling his bought-off Senator."

Ledwell knew he had won. Inwardly he wondered if his resignation threat was real or a bluff. He was glad he didn't have to find out.

An hour later, the crew returned from lunch in the cafeteria and found their Mission Commander already in the study room. He smiled benignly at the seven faces around the table. "Dr. Lee, Dr. Koch, Dr. McLain, would you three please give us a few minutes? I'd like to speak to these gentlemen alone."

An uncomfortable quiet came over the room. Teamwork was Bubba Ledwell's mantra. He preached it, he practiced it, and he insisted upon it. Separating team members from a meeting was unlike him, but the three ladies slid their seats back, and quietly left the room closing the heavy door behind them

Captain Thurman Ledwell spoke quietly but slowly and distinctly. "Scott, what I'm about to say will never leave this room. Colonel Weaver, Colonel Fredrick, and Dr. Dalton will all swear what I'm about to say never happened." He paused to let that preface sink in. "I don't give a shit who you work for. If you ever go behind my back and call your Daddy again, two things are going to happen. First, these gentlemen and I will carefully but painfully make you aware of our disappointment in your actions. Second, the day before our launch, the flight surgeon will discover you have an inner ear infection and will ground you. You will not go into space."

Elder could not keep the look of shock and tinge of fear expressed on his face. "You couldn't do that!"

"You're the second person today to tell me I couldn't do something. I convinced the other individual. Please don't make me convince you. Yes, I could do it, I can do it, and am absolutely prepared to do it. Dr. Steve Ashy is our flight surgeon and has been my friend for twenty-five years. He trusts me. If I tell him you should not be on the mission, he will make sure you're not on it. He goes into quarantine with us tomorrow, so there will be no one to refute his diagnosis."

No one said anything for a moment, then Bill Weaver spoke in his characteristic clear-cut pilot vernacular, "Scott, I don't have a clue what you did to piss Bubba off, but I don't think I would do it again. Now to make this clear, I didn't hear a damn thing the Captain said after the ladies left the room."

Tom Fredrick, at almost six and a half feet tall, was an imposing figure even sitting down. "Scott, my buddy here just said what I also think. Please don't put yourself on the block by testing Bubba. You will not like the results."

Dr. Tunes Dalton did not have a military background. He was an engineer and biomedical scientist. However, he had been raised in a very tough neighborhood in Washington, D.C., then later in Erie, Pennsylvania. "Scotty," he knew Elder hated being called *Scotty*, "please don't do whatever it is the boss says to not to do. I doubt the flight surgeon would be required to diagnose any ear problems. Scientists don't usually heal quickly when they accidentally fall down stairs or slip in the shower. I suspect you wouldn't be physically able to launch. And, for the record, I didn't hear a damn thing either."

Elder knew he was not going to call Schumer anymore. He believed every word the four men before him were saying. If he was going to run his experiment on orbit, he had to make the launch. That required following Captain Ledwell's orders to the letter and he was certain that was in his best interest.

Bubba took a second to stare into Elder's eyes before speaking to Colonel Fredrick. "Tom, would you please ask the ladies to come back in."

"Yessir."

There was a look of confusion on the faces of all three ladies as they filed back into the study room. None of them asked any questions about their exile. The Sojourner crew spent the next three hours going over procedures and reviewing the new schedule.

Everything went smoothly.

Isha sat at the controls of his rented twin engine airplane as he and Cam Forsyth flew back to Santa Fe. The Prince could obviously tell Cam was deep in thought and kept his conversation to a minimum as they crossed the West Texas plains. Finally, in an attempt to distract his passenger, Isha mentioned, "You know, Cam, I once read that the person who doesn't fly misses half of God's creation."

Isha's comment interrupted Cam's reflections and brought his attention back to the West Texas scenery ten thousand feet below them. He gazed out the windows to the sprawling land dotted with green irrigation circles and numerous small towns. Cam wondered to himself who had decided to establish all those tiny communities in the middle of nowhere and far from any major city. From the air, even the checkerboard of county roads that outlined unnaturally shaped farms and ranches seemed disjointed. "Yes, sir. It really does give you a new perspective." Then Cam returned to his thoughts and Isha to his flying.

Cam was obsessing about the night Catherine died. There was something nagging at him, but not something he could put his finger on yet. He trusted his instincts when they alerted him and he was sure he would figure out the subtle incongruity that was there.

Two details bothered him in particular. *The cops said Catherine's time of death was about two hours after I left her apartment. Her bed was exactly the same as when we used it last. What had she been doing those two hours.* He remembered she didn't own a TV so that didn't occupy her. She had talked a lot about the pressure of her upcoming experiment. *Did she work on that? No! She left her laptop at Winter Triangle Physics when I picked her up. I wonder if she went there to get it?*

Then a lightbulb went off in Forsyth's memory. He recalled the police returning him to Catherine's apartment after their questioning that morning. He had walked up to Schumer and that other guy he had seen today standing by the grave, and he remembered overhearing the comment, "Who found her so *quickly*?"

That remark could only have one meaning.

Cam Forsyth focused his mind on the memory of Nicholas Schumer at the funeral that morning standing by the occupied grave. Schumer was picking up a handful of dirt and throwing it on to the casket.

A wave of undeniable consuming fury flowed through Forsyth's veins. "You bastard!" he exclaimed unexpectedly.

Isha smoothly looked over his right shoulder. He instinctively knew his Protector had solved whatever mental gymnastics that had been bothering him.

"Want to share your thoughts, my friend," he asked Cam.

"Sir, I need some help. I want to use your authority to have Exeter's computer section acquire some information from a company in Corpus. It's a high security organization so it will not be easy to bypass their corporate firewalls and encryptions."

"Is this for your job as a journalist?"

"No, sir. It's personal."

There was a perceptible pause before Isha answered. "Those guys love a challenge. Tell them I said to do whatever you want."

"Thanks, Isha."

The two men spent the next three hours of their flight talking about Cam's conviction that Nicholas Schumer had actually killed Catherine or at least ordered her killed. Isha mostly listened but occasionally played the devil's advocate to point out possible holes in Forsyth's logic. It was a good way to pass the flight. By the time they landed, Cam Forsyth had come up with a plan.

When the two men shut down the airplane in Santa Fe and walked into the flight operations hangar, they were surprised to see the young instructor pilot from Corpus Christi they had met just four days earlier. "Robert, you got another flight to Santa Fe so quickly?" Isha asked as they shook hands.

"Well, no sir. I found out they needed an instructor pilot on staff here and I decided I liked the area so I quit my job in Corpus as soon as I landed there from returning your plane. Then we packed my stuff up and spent a couple of days driving here."

"We?"

The young man smiled sheepishly. "Remember the young lady who drove me to the hotel? Her name is Constance. Well, Constance had several days of vacation time coming so she flew to Corpus with me and helped me pack and drive back here. She has an extra bedroom in her apartment so we decided I could rent it from her for a while."

Isha nodded and gave no indication he questioned the young man's version of the arrangement. He had actually noticed that the bill from the Hotel Magnificat had included one room, two dinner meals with a nice bottle of wine and two breakfast meals all charged to room service.

Chapter Fourteen

May 27, 2022
Corpus Christi, Texas

Nicholas Schumer was not a happy man. The local news was still reporting on the bizarre death at the bayside hotel. It was not the death he was wanting to hear about. Instead of reading Cam Forsyth was in the morgue, the news was saying an unidentified male had apparently fallen from a tenth-floor balcony. The insinuation was that the man had committed suicide.

"Tanner! Get in here."

Within seconds Schumer's assistant came scuttling into the office.

"Yessir?"

"What happened to Forsyth? He was supposed to be killed yesterday. You paid twenty-thousand dollars of my money to have him killed, didn't you? Why isn't he dead?"

"I don't know, sir. It appears from the news reports that he survived and killed the guy we hired. That doesn't seem to make sense. You said our guy was the best. Hard to believe a simple reporter could have survived our guy."

"Quit calling him 'our guy'. You're the one who set this up and paid the money. He was *your guy*. So, tell me how *your guy* is now dead and the person I wanted eliminated is still walking around?"

Tanner, was quite clearly unsure of the right response. He just looked dumb-faced at Nicholas Schumer with no idea how to answer.

"Next question. Since he's obviously still alive, where the hell is this Forsyth guy? I know he checked out of the hotel early the morning after your guy got himself thrown off the balcony, but where did he go?"

Tanner's face revealed the fear he was feeling. There was no way he could know where Forsyth was, but his boss didn't look at things logically. He demanded answers—immediate answers—to his questions. "Sir," he started haltingly, "I've been able to establish that he returned his rental car to the airport early the morning of the twenty-fourth. Our IT guys have searched all the flight manifests from the airline databases and told me he was originally scheduled to fly out on an American Airlines regional jet that morning, but he canceled that reservation right after he turned in his rental car. He did not rebook for another flight. Our IT department had no problems covertly breaking into those airline files. If Forsyth had been on a flight, they would have been able to see which flight and where he went."

Nicholas Schumer closed his eyes as if trying to shut out an annoyance in the room. "Tanner, there are only two ways out of the Corpus Christi airport. You drive or you fly. He didn't drive. You say he didn't fly commercially. Did it ever enter your pea-sized brain that perhaps he flew himself out? Check with the place we keep our jet. They are, I think, the only place at the airport that rents airplanes. They will know if anyone rented one."

Josh Tanner felt the color drain from his face. He knew Catherine Austin never wilted under the cold demands of Schumer, but she had felt his equal. Tanner was weak and knew he was weak. "Sir, I'll check that out right now."

"Get out of my office. I want to know something before noon today."

As it turned out, only one phone call was required. The general aviation manager of the fixed base operations where the Winter Triangle Physics' Gulfstream 150, 280, and 550 were hangared easily remembered that two men and a beautiful lady rented his Bonanza G36 on the day Tanner inquired about. "Yeah, they flew to Santa Fe and one of my guys flew the plane back the next day. That little punk pilot quit on me because of some little tart he met out there. Guess I can't blame him. She looked like a friggin' model or something."

"Who paid for the airplane rental?"

"Don't really remember. But I can look it up. Seems like it was some company from Santa Fe. I think the pilot was the owner of the company."

"Find out. I need to know." Tanner demanded.

"Okay. I do know that pilot could really fly. I checked him out myself in the Bonanza. Flew the plane like he was born in it."

"Glad to know that little bit of nonsensical bullshit. Now get me names!"

The flight operator raised his middle finger to the phone then hung up. The jerk on the other end represented a company that paid more than half of his operation's monthly profit margin with their hangar payment. He could not afford to really say what he was thinking.

An hour later, a receptionist from the flight school called Winter Triangle Physics and told Josh Tanner everything he wanted to know. The manager was unavailable to make the call himself.

May 27, 2022
Kennedy Space Center, Florida

With five days to go until launch, the crew of the space shuttle Sojourner were placed into quarantine. Ten days before the launch, the entire crew had been subjected to complete physical exams. They had had blood drawn and swab tests to search for any infections that might not yet be evident. The final isolation period was to minimize the chance the crew would be infected by any non-mission critical individuals. Last minute meetings with technicians and reporters and even family visits took place on opposite sides of glass walls.

Other than being isolated from the outside world, the life of the crew members did not change very much from the previous weeks and months. The focus of their study and simulator training sessions was now primarily dedicated to practicing launch procedures and malfunctions. Bubba Ledwell and Bill Weaver were rehearsing aborts and emergency returns to landing. Jim Dalton and Tom Fredrick, who would be strapped in right behind the commander and pilot, also practiced their emergency checklists and procedures. In the event of a pressurization system failure during the launch sequence, neither of the two astronauts actually flying the shuttle could reach their emergency oxygen activation switches. Therefore, Dalton would be responsible for activating Ledwell's system and Fredrick would activate Weaver's.

If a major malfunction occurred within the first two minutes after launch and Ledwell elected to blow the shuttle away from the solid rocket boosters and the massive external tank, he and Weaver would instantly have to control the unpowered craft to a landing at the Kennedy Shuttle Landing Facility and its 15,000-foot runway. In an emergency during those first critical seconds after launch, so much had to be accomplished perfectly that they practiced their actions over and over until every maneuver was second nature. Dalton and Fredrick were also practicing their support roles in accomplishing emergency checklists to ensure the shuttle was prepared for the immediate landing back at the Kennedy SLF. The four men spent hours practicing what would take less than thirty seconds should a catastrophe happen during launch.

In their simulator area, Janelle McLain, M.D., Patti Koch, Ph.D., Terry Lee, Ph.D., and L. Scott Elder, Ph.D. were practicing their procedures for setting up the initial experiments they would accomplish.

Elder's experiment was called the *Reflective Power Grid Generating System* or RePoGGS. The team had taken up pronouncing it "Repojis". Elder was having difficulty running his RePoGGS simulations. Unfortunately for Terry Lee, this was frustrating for her, too. Some procedures required two people to accomplish and she, as an electrical engineer, had been selected as the most logical second person. This meant she was having to take time away from her experiments to learn her role with Elder's evaluation. Lee was trying to help Elder resolve his problems, but even she could not decipher some of the strange parameters in the procedures. She attributed this difficulty to the fact that Elder was working on a corporate project that had several layers of secrecy. His company's security foolishly compartmentalized certain details even for those directly involved. Only Elder would know all the intricacies of the experiment, and that was a major problem for Lee. She was trying to help without being allowed to see the entire experiment. As the launch date got closer, Lee hated MacLemore even more for allowing, actually requiring, this travesty of experimental protocols to happen.

"Look Scott," Lee looked squarely into the eyes of the man beside her. "I really don't care about your company's security paranoia. No one on this crew, least of all me, is going to go out and sell your technology on the open market. All I care about is knowing enough to get your crap over with so I can do my own work."

"Dr. Lee," Elder never used first names, only titles, "I didn't write the paradigms for this experiment. My company designed it so automation would ensure success. All I have to do is make sure it is set up properly in space and all you have to do is monitor the instrument panel to ensure it remains within operation specifications. All you have to do is control of the electrical modulation system. When any surges or spikes in electrical signals happen, you will correct them. You don't need to know anything beyond that." There was a noticeable tone of superiority in Elder's answer.

It took all of Lee's self-control to keep her from telling him to screw himself and walking away. That, she was certain, would only cause more problems. Instead, she smiled sweetly at him, "Scotty,"—she also knew Elder hated being called *Scotty*—"if you ever use that condescending tone with me again, I'll put my foot where the sun doesn't shine. I have to work with you, but I don't have to put up with your crap. Now, from now on you will call me Terry. Only my university students call me doctor. You will treat me with the respect I deserve, and you will act like you are part of this team instead of some superior breed." She paused long enough to really enjoy the look of shock and surprise on Elder's face. "Okay, Scott?"

He nodded quietly.

Lee was not prone to using vulgar language, but she thought of Elder as a horse's ass who just needed to be reminded of his place in the universe. She had privately considered having the computer specialists in Exeter insert a discrete override to the Elder's security nonsense so she could have complete access. They could do it, but she knew that if an override was discovered it would cause a ruckus that she didn't need to explain. She had her own project to work on and it had critical importance to future military communications.

Secure mobile communication in wartime conditions have always been crucial for ground commanders in the field and for military pilots in flight. Since the early 1970s, the military has used a system called Have Quick. This encryption system uses radios programmed with several frequencies that are kept classified for each day. The radios are tied to each other by a tone sent from the leader's radio. Once the radios are synchronized by that tone, they would automatically sequence rapidly through the frequencies. To the operators, their transmissions sound perfectly normal, but the frequency swaps make interception virtually impossible.

As is always the case, advancing technologies eventually make older systems obsolete and new systems had to be developed. Lee was to experimenting with a new communication system that would allow coded communications between long distances. It involved a focused signal that would switch frequencies so incredibly fast that no one but the sender and receiver could speak or transfer data. Best of all, no secondary linking would be necessary. All the units were tied by the universal clock signal from the National Observatory in Washington, D.C. If it worked as predicted, secure military communications would take a major step forward.

Dr. Terry Lee's experiments were supposed to examine secure military communication equipment over a wide variety of locations. However, Senator Maxwell Bellow's under-the-table coercion of the NASA brass had proved political contributions to his office were more important to him than military security.

The corrupt politician's hubris would soon cause the entire world to be at risk.

Chapter Fifteen

May 28, 2022
Exeter

Isha was correct in assuming Exeter's computer section would enjoy the challenge of bypassing the firewalls, encryption, and passwords of Winter Triangle Physics' main database. They had no difficulty accessing the entry logs for around midnight of May 23, 2022.

J.R. Locklar, the chief of Exeter's computer section, visited Prince Isha as he was having breakfast with Deidre. J.R. was a tall woman whose face had gentle laugh lines and only the tiniest hint of gray at her temples. It would have been difficult to guess her age with any accuracy. Most of those who worked with J.R. described her as having a quick smile and an even quicker mind. No one seemed to know what J.R.'s initials stood for and she loved keeping that secret. The men and women in the computer section had all made it their supreme goal to discover the mystery of J.R. At first, they figured it would be easy. In the past, they had hacked into the most sensitive computers of governments and industries around the world. They had broken the encryptions protecting data in the most complex military databanks. They had once even obtained the personal phone number for the President of the United States. They could not, however, ferret out J.R.'s first and middle name. To the computer section breaking that code was considered to be the Holy Grail.

"Sire, we have the answer to your questions." Locklar was happy to have solved the Prince's request so quickly. "Winter Triangle Physics had the highest level of cyber security available to any company above." She continued, "They probably think no one could possibly retrieve data after their encryption, but we did it in less than thirty minutes." She glanced at her watch. "Twenty-six minutes to be exact."

"Was Miss Austin there during the time we discussed?" Isha asked quietly.

"Yessir." Locklar looked at the giant touchscreen monitor which took up a large part of the wall before him. There was a pause while she ran her fingers over the display to change the layout. "Sire, she signed in at twenty-seven minutes after midnight." Pause. "She signed back out twenty minutes later."

"How about the other subject?"

"Nicholas Schumer was signed out by the guard two minutes after Miss Austin."

"How do you know the guard signed him out?"

There was another pause. "Because in the computer log, there is a text in the notes section beside the time that says, 'The bastard is too important to sign himself out.' Guess the security guy was venting and figured no one would ever see the note"

"Wonder how long it took Miss Austin to get from the office to her apartment," Isha said more to himself than to the phone.

"Actually, I can tell you pretty closely." Once again, she deftly moved her fingers over the screen. "I've just accessed her driver's license records in Austin, Texas." Again, her fingers quickly tapped around the screen. "Assuming the address on her license is accurate, with the light traffic we can imagine at that time of the morning, it should have taken her twenty-two minutes to drive home."

"One more question, can you find the medical examiner's forms to see where he placed the time of death?"

Within a minute, Locklar had the answer. "Sire, the report says the TOD was between 1:00 a.m. and 3:30 a.m. He does mention that since she was in a shower with water running over the body, a more specific time was impossible."

When that information was related, the Prince of Exeter quickly did the mental gymnastics. "That means she probably died very soon after returning home."

"That's the way I see it, sir."

Isha thanked Locklar and walked her to the door to his chambers. He then called Cam Forsyth and relayed the information. After a few minutes, they had made a plan and reserved a plane to fly back to

Corpus.

By 9:30 they were taking off for their second flight to Corpus in two days.

May 28, 2022
Winter Triangle Physics, Corpus Christi, TX

Isha and Cam Forsyth drove their rental car to the headquarters of Nicholas Schumer's company. During their flight from Santa Fe to Corpus, the two men had hashed over everything they knew and suspected. At best, linking Schumer to Catherine's death was circumstantial, but Cam trusted his instincts completely and Isha trusted Cam.

Their plan was simple: Push Nicholas Schumer's buttons to see how he responded. His reputation as a hard-nosed, arrogant, narcissistic man was well documented. He would not be easy to catch off guard.

The majority of the Winter Triangle Physics' complex of buildings resembled a college campus. Each building had a facade of the same drab brown brick. Windows only revealed hallways. All the offices were located on internal walls. The spartan design ensured that security could not be compromised by someone looking in. Entry to each building required both an employee pass card and a five-digit security code. That code was changed monthly. Scientists working in the labs had all heard a rumor that retina scanners would soon installed to create an even higher security level. No one seemed to find that rumor too far-fetched for the hyper-security driven Nicholas Schumer.

Not even the most senior level scientist working in a Winter Triangle Physics' lab could carry their personal cell phone, laptop computer, or electronic tablet into the facility. Each time they entered a lab, they had to be rescanned for anything that might compromise sensitive data. More than one highly paid researcher had been fired on the spot for breaking the rules on personal electronics.

The main building entrance was different than all the rest. The front facade had three stories of glass which was tinted against the South Texas sun and hard tempered to withstand the straight-line winds from up to a Category three hurricane. If a more powerful storm was approaching, the building had been designed with quick connecting fasteners that would allow maintenance personnel to cover all the windows with high tensile strength alloy sheets. The building staff practiced covering the entire building twice a year. They could have the total area protected against a Category Five hurricane within three hours.

As the two men entered the beautiful headquarters building, they couldn't help but be impressed by the opulence. They walked on Tuscany marble floors that were immaculate, shiny, and obviously very expensive. There were three original paintings by Andy Warhol and several large bronze busts. Neither Cam nor Isha could identify most of the men immortalized in bronze, except for one of Albert Einstein and one of Stephen Hawking. Without speaking, both men quietly decided the rest of the figures were of other physicists both contemporary and historical.

A lovely blond receptionist with brilliant blue eyes looked up and smiled radiantly as the two guests approached her desk. "How can I help you today?" she asked cordially. Her name plate identified her as Linda Boldty.

"We're here to see Nicholas Schumer," Cam answered calmly.

"Do you have an appointment?" came the expected reply.

"No, Miss Boldty, but I suspect he'll want to see us," Isha answered for both men.

"Well, I'm sure you understand Mr. Schumer has a very busy schedule. Without an appointment I'm afraid there's no chance to get you in. May I take a message and have his assistant get back to you?" Her smile was just as beautiful as before but now looked a bit forced and uncomfortable.

"Tell you what," Cam said very calmly, "Let Schumer's secretary know that Cam Forsyth is here to see him." He smiled warmly. "We'll just sit over here and wait."

"Yes, Mr. Forsyth. Make yourselves comfortable. May I have coffee brought to you?"

"No, thanks. By the way, I was here just last week to interview Cathy Austin. I don't remember seeing you then."

"Catherine," the receptionist replied instantly. She looked solemnly at Forsyth and her smile evaporated. "Sir, I was off last week on vacation. I'm afraid I have to tell you that Miss Austin had a tragic accident and has passed away. It was very sad."

She reached for her phone to call Schumer's secretary.

"Yes, a tragedy," was Cam Forsyth's unemotional response. He sat down by Isha in comfortable leather chairs and for the first time really looked around the whole area. Suddenly, a large wall art caught his eye. He had been so impressed with the paintings and sculptures that the central design had escaped him.

Large shadowed brass letters spelling out Winter Triangle Physics were mounted on the wall. Directly below the name were three brass disks placed, not surprisingly, into an almost inverted triangular pattern. The pattern was slightly off balance because the right disk was higher than the left one and the bottom disk was skewed. Each disk had letters beside them, but the letters were too small to be read from the sitting area. Cam got up and walked to stand beneath the design. Isha was curious and joined him.

The circle on the top right was labeled Betelgeuse. The disk below was labeled Sirius and to the left was a disk labeled Procyon.

Cam suddenly realized what he was seeing. These were the stars that comprised the almost perfect equilateral triangle visible in the northern hemisphere from December until March. Cam studied the company logo and them mentioned almost conversationally to Isha, "That's the Winter Triangle. Sirius is the brightest star in this hemisphere. Betelgeuse is in the constellation, Orion. I don't remember anything about Procyon."

"Procyon is in the constellation Canis Minor," Linda Boldty interjected conversationally as she walked up. She had just answered a quiet buzz from her intercom and had spoken almost inaudibly into her headset. If the men had been looking her direction as she answered her call, they would certainly have noticed the surprise on her face. By the time she spoke to them, her professional demeanor had returned. "Gentlemen, I've been asked to escort you to Mr. Schumer's office."

"Thank you," Cam responded. "Do you happen to know how Schumer come up with the name of his company?"

The perfect smile returned. "As I understand it, Mr. Schumer has always been a student of astronomy. The orientation of those three stars in our logo are as seen here in Texas, but it's slightly different at other latitudes. Mr. Schumer even has an eight-inch refracting telescope on the roof of this building that he uses for his personal study. With his telescope in mind, he designed this particular building to block almost all of the surrounding light sources. Last Fall we had some NASA astronauts here on a visit and I was picked to take them up there to see the telescope. It was really cool to meet so many astronauts in person."

The final puzzle piece had fallen into place in Cam Forsyth's mind. Nicholas Schumer was going to pay for his crime of murdering Catherine Austin and for ordering his own killing by a hired assassin.

Josh Tanner was standing by his secretary's desk with his hands on his hips like some bad boss parody. He had just finished belittling Red for not getting his lunch order correct. He was looking at the food that had been delivered to her desk. He disgustedly muttered, "This will never do." To emphasize his dissatisfaction, he kept shaking his head back and forth.

Out of the corner of his eye, Tanner noticed two visitors walk by escorted by the front desk receptionist. He paid them no attention. Red, however, instantly recognized Forsyth. In her years working for Catherine Austin, there had never been another man to get Catherine to leave the office early. A slight gasp escaped the woman's lips and her look of shock caught the attention of Josh Tanner.

"Who the hell was that?" he demanded.

"The man on the left was the one Miss Austin left with the other afternoon." Red quickly glanced at her computer screen calendar for verification. "His name is Cam Forsyth. Catherine cancelled all of her afternoon appointments and left after their meeting. I think he was a reporter for some scientific journal. I don't know the other man."

Tanner could feel the blood leave his face. For a split second, he felt a wave of nausea and lightheadedness along with a flood of anxiety. Forsyth was the man who was supposed to have been killed by the assassin he had hired. He couldn't find Forsyth afterwards and Mr. Schumer was still angry about that. Now the man was actually being escorted toward Schumer's office.

"Oh shit!" Tanner mumbled out loud but only to himself. "I'd better get down there."

"Want me to reorder your lunch?" Red said to Tanner's back as he rushed out the door.

Linda Boldty was just leaving Nicholas Schumer's office after introducing the visitors to his secretary and leaving them in her care. She nodded curtly at Tanner as he rushed by. Her previous brilliant smile was not bestowed upon Tanner. His reputation among the support staff was already well known and she had no intention of being friendly to him. A distant and cordial acknowledgment was all he would get from her.

Isha and Cam knew they were being kept waiting on purpose. Nicholas Schumer was obviously a Machiavellian master at manipulating people and nothing says I'm more important than you than making someone wait. Since they knew what Schumer was doing, neither man was intimidated in the least.

Josh Tanner made no comment as he flew by everyone in Schumer's outer office and walked straight in and quickly closed the heavy mahogany door behind him. Nicholas Schumer looked up. He was annoyed by the interruption. "What the hell do you mean coming in here?" Schumer spoke quietly but with a menacing tone to his voice.

"Do you know who is sitting out there?" Tanner sputtered while pointing excitedly at the closed door. "Forsyth! Forsyth is sitting out there!"

Schumer closed his eyes and shook his head disgustedly. When he opened his eyes, they bore a look of arrogant disdain towards his assistant. "Of course I know he's here. Who do you think has him cooling his heels out there? Now get your ass out of my office while I meet this mystery man." Tanner turned to leave. "Not that door, you idiot! Go out through my conference room. I don't want him to see you again. You look terrified!"

"Yessir," came the meek reply.

Ten minutes later Nicholas Schumer buzzed his secretary and looked down at the papers on his desk with rapt attention. Moments later she brought the guests into Schumer's office where they stood waiting for him to acknowledge their presence. Instead of being ill at ease, the two men stood with their hands calmly crossed and looked around the room.

To their left were several large framed pictures of Schumer standing with movie stars, professional athletes, and politicians including Senator Maxwell Bellow. On another wall was a high definition screen displaying a massive digital star chart that changed minute-by-minute to show the actual location of all major constellations.

"That's the only one of those in existence," Schumer said unexpectedly. "I tapped into NASA's computers and use their data so I can see what's happening up there anytime I want to."

Isha didn't take his eyes off the screen. "'Tapped'? Is that the same thing as saying they don't know you've hacked their computer systems?"

"Well, some systems just begged to be hacked."

"How about the Winter Triangle Physics computers?"

"No one can hack into my computers," he said tersely. "Enough small talk. I'm a busy man, gentlemen. Tell me why seeing me was so important today."

Forsyth answered for both men. "You don't need to pretend not to know me. You know I'm the man who was with Catherine the day she was murdered."

"She slipped in the shower."

"She was murdered. I believe you know it and I am positive of it." Cam continued, "Second, there's a small matter of an uninvited guest in my hotel room."

"Why would I care about someone in your hotel room?"

"I think you sent her."

"Her?"

"Guess I misspoke. That was a nice catch. Anyway, he hit like a girl. Did you know he couldn't fly?"

"Get out of my office."

"Sure. But before we go I have one suggestion. Find a new nickname."

"What the hell are you talking about?"

Cam Forsyth leaned over Schumer's desk and very quietly said, "My friend and I are leaving, but you can count on meeting me again, Starman."

Chapter Sixteen

May 29, 2022
Kennedy Space Center

Because they were in quarantine, the Sojourner crew had virtually all outside distractions eliminated. There were no public appearances, speeches, and only a few interviews allowed. As a result, the crew could spend all their time fine-tuning procedures and practicing their responsibilities. Captain Ledwell and Lt. Colonel Weaver were still making the maximum use of the available simulator time. Their training remained focused on launch emergencies, but there was time carved out for integration with the other crew members. Today, they were practicing the maneuvers that would be required to facilitate L. Scott Elder's work on orbit.

Sojourner, like all the shuttles before her, actually had two levels where the astronauts, mission specialists, and payload specialists worked and lived. A simple ladder provided access between the spaces but most of the time on orbit, the ladder wasn't necessary because crew members simply floated from one deck to another. The top level served as the flight deck where the commander and pilot sat during launch and landing. Most people would recognize the front of the flight deck because it is what they had seen in countless movies. However, the back wall of the top level was less familiar. The entire rear wall held a complex communications and control panel with two large windows that looked down into the payload bay. During launch and landing, three additional seats were mounted behind the pilots in this area for crew members. The middle level of the crew compartment provided the sleeping and eating areas, bathing and toilet areas, storage, communication stations, and the entrance to the airlock which provided access to the payload bay. During launches and landings, all the additional crew members sat on this level in seats mated with the floor.

On future missions when the shuttle docked with the International Space Station, the actual connection would be through a vertical airlock located in the payload bay. To accomplish the docking, an astronaut pilot would look out the windows on the back panel of the upper level and maneuver the shuttle to the attachment. He or she would manipulate the massive shuttle precisely into position using a control grip mounted below one window. It was a very tricky procedure that required a fine touch and hundreds of simulations.

Since, on this mission there would be no visit to the ISS, no docking collar was installed. However, it was from the upper level aft bulkhead that Dr. Terry Lee would accomplish her role in Scott Elder's experiment. Once his array was deployed during the four-hour spacewalk, the shuttle pilots would move the spacecraft five hundred meters away from the package. The physics of focusing sunlight would potentially create a flash point that could endanger the shuttle if it was in close proximity to the experiment. Lee's responsibility was to use small thrusters attached to the package to precisely maneuver the experiment into the exact stabilized location.

Today, Lee and Elder were standing at that control station on the simulator's flight deck looking out windows into the projection of the payload bay. Behind them, sitting in their pilot's seats were Ledwell and Weaver. They had practiced their positioning maneuvers to move the shuttle into its holding spot away from Elder's experiment. It was now up to Lee to make her small thruster corrections to the array. Elder observed quietly but was privately furious that an outsider was required to control his experiment. Had Schumer allowed him to go on the next shuttle launch, he would have had time to learn the skills required. He felt he had been relegated to the support team but had decided he wasn't going to allow that to happen. Elder had devised an answer to this insult, but his plan would have to remain a secret until they were on orbit and he was on his EVA.

"Success!" Terry Lee exclaimed as the experiment package stopped exactly as planned. This was the twenty-first time she had done it perfectly. Ten of those attempts had been accomplished with no associated problems. For the past eleven attempts, the simulator operators had inserted malfunctions into the scenario. They had failed thrusters, frozen the array panels, and even caused the shuttle to shift locations. In each case, Terry had accomplished her checklist procedures quickly and saved the experiment. Everyone on the crew and in NASA Launch Control were completely confident in her ability to react to any foreseeable problem.

May 29, 2022
Exeter

Exeter was Cam Forsyth's true home. Every time he came back to the cavernous expanses, Cam considered leaving his life in New York City to return to the serenity of Exeter. It was only in the massive chambers that comprised the tribes of Exeter that Cam felt totally at peace. The advanced technologies that were commonplace here would be unimaginable to those living above.

Cam Forsyth was frustrated and angry. As he sat alone in his chamber, he sensed rather than heard his father enter. Moses sat down beside his son and held out a glass of a really fine Maker's Mark bourbon with a single ice cube. It matched the glass he held for himself. The two men clinked glasses together and then sat quietly for several seconds. Cam imported a case of Maker's whenever his family's stock in Exeter ran low. There were some things from outside his home he wasn't willing to forego. Exeter, for all its advanced technology, could not match this bourbon.

Finally, Moses Forsyth spoke to his son. "So, you want to tell me about the lady?"

Cam looked at his father in confusion. He had not mentioned Catherine Austin to anyone in his family. "How do you know? More important, what do you think you know?"

"Prince Isha shared the story with his father who has been kind enough to talk with me. Neither one wanted to get into your business, but both are concerned about you. That's what friends do, Cam."

"Dad, we only knew each other a single day."

"So?"

A mental picture of Catherine's lovely face grew unbidden into Cam's mind. "She was fascinating, Dad. She had a tough and unyielding personality. She was demanding to everyone around her. She was brash and bossy." A pause of several seconds passed before the son spoke again to the father. "Dad, this will sound wrong, but she was the first woman I had ever met who I thought was my equal. She didn't try and change one thing about herself to fit me. She didn't need to."

Moses Forsyth nodded his head quietly. He knew the comment his son had made would sound sexist to anyone who didn't know the man he had raised. The unspoken sentiment was that Catherine must have been totally self-sufficient and unshakable. It was meant as a compliment of the highest degree.

"Sounds like you two could have developed a nice long-term relationship."

"There wasn't time to find out. We did have a great time together. I don't think she would ever have been the kind of woman I'd have brought home."

Moses mentally filled in the blanks to his son's comments and recognized the physical attraction the two must have had. "Well, I'm sure you'll have wonderful memories of her."

"Dad, she was murdered. Before she can become a wonderful memory," he looked intently at his father, "I'm going to avenge her death."

In what Moses Forsyth later considered to be his greatest moment of sage wisdom, he said nothing.

The two men finished their bourbon in silence; each lost in his own thoughts.

"You want another drink son, or would you rather tell me your plans?"

"Let's do both," Cam said as he took his father's glass and went to refresh it. "We'll have to make this a quick one. Melissa and I are on the 8:00 flight from Santa Fe to the Dallas Fort Worth airport."

"Where do you go after DFW?" Moses asked as he took his drink from Cam and absentmindedly stirred the ice cube with his finger.

"We're going on to Orlando tomorrow. Tonight, we're having a little reunion with Kevin, Celia, Kristi, and Rob. I think the kids will be there, too."

Kevin was a Protector and Prince Isha's best friend. He had been with the group when they had stopped the terrorist attack on the United States more than a decade before. He and his wife, Celia, now lived in Texas where Kevin was the president of a multi-national company secretly owned by King Annu. Celia had become a successful graphic designer with a company who believed she was originally from a town in North Texas.

Kristi and her husband, Rob, until recently lived near and were very close to Kevin and Celia. Like Kevin, Kristi was also a Protector. During the threat to America, she had headed the communications team. Shortly afterwards, she had accompanied Prince Isha and Kevin and secretly entered the palace of Azmud Salomi, the demon whose plans had resulted in the death of two Protectors. The men had stood aside while Kristi served as the avenging angel and had permanently ended Azmud Salomi from ever masterminding another terrorist plot.

The two Protectors and their spouses often spent time together. Those visits had been curtailed recently as Kristi and Rob had two months before returned to live in Exeter when their daughter, Emmy, had begun her training to become a Protector. Their son, Aiden, would start his training in two more years, but he was already mimicking his sister as she practiced her elementary fighting skills.

Cam looked thoughtfully at the amber spirit in his glass. "Dad, are you and Mom worried about Terry? Exeter has had people in the space program for years, but always in the engineering and research areas. She'll be the first to ever go into orbit."

"Well, we're her parents so of course we're concerned. But she's confident in the program and we trust her judgment. I don't think anything is ever one hundred percent safe. You and Melissa are flying in an airplane tonight and we'll feel better when you land safely in Dallas. Parents never stop worrying about their children regardless of how old, independent, or successful those children become." Moses smiled. "Okay," he continued, "that's enough maudlin commentary. You have to get to the airport."

The two men clinked their glasses one last time and drained the remaining bourbon. "Melissa!" Cam yelled. "I'm leaving in twenty minutes with or without you."

Moses pretended not to hear his daughter's profane response.

May 29, 2022
Trophy Club, Texas

After landing in Texas, Cam and Melissa were picked up and were soon at Kevin and Celia's home. Kristi, Rob, Emmy and Aiden had already been there for a couple of days. The Forsyths felt completely at home with their friends from Exeter. The children, Emmy and Aiden, were allowed to stay up late, but by 10:00 they were asleep. The adults visited until well after 2:00 a.m.

Chapter Seventeen

May 30, 2022
Kennedy Space Center Crew Quarters

Cam Forsyth and his sister, Melissa, took the earliest flight from the Dallas Fort Worth airport to Orlando, Florida. Immediately after the airplane had taken off, they reclined their first-class seats and slept the entire flight to catch up on the rest they had missed the night before.

Melissa continued her napping while Cam drove the sixty miles from Orlando east to the Kennedy Space Center Visitor Building. There they were met by Dr. Marlo Campbell who escorted Cam and Melissa to the Crew Quarters building.

Before Cam would be allowed to enter the quarantine area, he was first subjected to swab and blood tests and a complete physical by the medical staff. Once the results of those examinations confirmed his health, Cam was finally allowed to enter the isolation area and shown to his room in the crew quarters. While all that was happening, Marlo took Melissa to a room where she could visit with her sister through a glass panel. Both sides of the glass were wired with microphones so the two sisters could talk naturally. Marlo Campbell left the room to allow them privacy.

"Hi, Terry!" Melissa could hardly control her enthusiasm. "Thanks for setting me up with Marlo. She's letting me stay with her and she pulled some strings so I'm getting to be in the Launch Control observation room when you launch. I'll be right there!"

Terry laughed out loud. "Well, you'll get a great show. Marlo is fixin' to demonstrate some of her research to the brass. I suspect she's going to practice doing her presentation on you. After all," Terry winked conspiratorially, "you've already seen most of it."

Both women laughed as Campbell closed her eyes and shook her head. She had not been happy to discover her research had been used for Terry to communicate with her family in Exeter. The danger of her research being compromised was always on her mind, but

Campbell begrudgingly acknowledged that a link to Exeter was as secure as could possibly be imagined.

"Listen, Melissa, I have to get to some training. I'll try and see you later tonight, kiddo."

"Terry, I'm proud of you." A touch of emotion touched Melissa's voice.

It was about at that moment that Cam Forsyth was escorted into the room with Terry. "Well," he said, "all the Forsyth kids together for once with only a sheet of glass separating us. Mom and Dad should be here to see this."

Terry hugged her brother and answered, "Never going to happen. Mom told me Dad had a television feed put into their chamber so they could watch the launch. He said she won't even turn it on. You can bet money there's no way she will come here to see it in person."

"I've talked with Exeter's communication section. They're going to hack my camera link and stream it live all over the chambers," Cam answered. "So Mom will have the best view possible and I'll bet Dad makes her watch."

Television had never been a big deal in Exeter. Most families did not even have it in their chambers. Instead books were the preferred pastime for both the adults and the youth of Exeter. However, a few homes and many businesses had televisions and the media was starting to gain more viewers.

Terry just shook her head. "Well, I have to get to work. We have our last pre-flight meeting in thirty minutes. That's where I'm supposed to introduce this pain-in-the-ass reporter to the crew. So far, I've been able to assure them that he was adopted and I have no real relation to him. Not sure I can pull that off much longer. We'll see how this goes." She blew a kiss. "Love you, kiddo. We'll talk later."

Marlo Campbell, who had quietly reentered the room, touched Melissa's shoulder and walked her out of the room and Terry escorted her brother towards the conference room.

Along the way, Cam stopped Terry and said, "This may be our last time to be alone before you launch." The Protector handed his sister the small, lightweight, gray case she had seen their father holding during the holograph conversation five days before. All she knew was that it contained a communication device of some kind, her brother filled in the blanks and reminded her of why the box was so important. "Terry, I know you remember when Azmud Salami tried to sneak a nuclear weapon into New York and only a team of Protectors were able to stop it. Prince Isha told me about the communication problems Exeter faced during that time. The Protector in Germany who found the bomb had to call Exeter by phone even though he was dying. He even had to use a code word because others were around. It took Exeter a while to figure out what he was trying to tell us. Later, when King Annu was talking to Colin Johnson, our Protector in London, he had to use secure telephones, and of course they weren't always available. The worst communication problems of all happened when Prince Isha and his team were on the ship in the middle of the Atlantic Ocean and needed to tell Exeter what was happening. It could have meant the failure of the mission."

Terry continued to look at the case as Cam continued. "Because of all those problems, the Prince made getting a communication system like this his highest priority. After Azmud Salami's threat was defeated, Isha asked Colin Johnson to return to Exeter from London to work with our engineers in developing a new way to communicate with our Protectors in the field. That team has made several prototypes and have solved problems as they came up. They think this one will be by far the best. Given the speed and complexity of your orbit, if it allows you to communicate as expected, it will work anywhere. The plan is to give one to every Protector around the world. We'll be able to have instant communication no matter where they are."

Cam took the case back and pointed to the uncomplicated controls on the side. "There is a simple on and off button and then this switch which has four positions. The first position will use a sensitive built-in microphone to pick up all the conversations within ten feet of you, regardless of who is speaking, and will transmit everything to Exeter. You will use this one when you are just talking to other crew members. We see it as most helpful during the launch phase. The second switch position is to be used when you are transmitting on your private frequency."

"I don't have a private frequency. None of us do."

"Terry, I think this is a matter of semantics. I was told each of the mission specialists have a discrete transmission channel they can use to communicate privately with support teams associated with their experiments. Is that right?"

Lee nodded her head. "Sure. That way I can discuss tests I'm running in space with the teams who actually designed them in Houston and Huntsville. We can't have those conversations cluttering the communications between Launch Control and Sojourner so we have separate channels. I guess I just never thought of it as a private line."

"Well, this box will automatically sync to that special frequency and to the Shuttle's main communication frequency. This is where I get a little fuzzy. The engineers tell me that any time your personal communication microphone is hot, this box is activated and we can listen in. It doesn't matter if you're just transmitting on that private frequency or talking to Launch Control. We will hear both sides of your conversation." He laughed conspiratorially. "Best of all, no one will know we're listening in."

Cam pointed to the switch and continued, "The third switch is used in conjunction with your earbuds. The engineers in Exeter say they have matched your voice pattern to this transmitter so they can tell if you are speaking into the mic or someone else is."

Terry examined the transmitter and found a small hole. "Is this where I plug in my earbuds?" Right then a thought popped into her mind. "Wait a minute. How did they get a digital sample of my voice to program this little wonder?"

"Really Terry? As many voice mails as you have left Mom and Dad over the years you have to ask that question?"

"Got it. Glad I watched my language when I called home." She laughed. "Okay, that mystery is solved. Let's get back to this little transmitter."

Cam pointed back to the switch. "As I was about to say, when you have your earbuds in and the switch is in the third position, you can hear us speak and the mic in the earbuds will pick up only your voice. Use it when you want to have a private talk with someone in Exeter. But, be careful when you're in the third setting because in that position, you can remove your earbuds and push this small button here." He pointed to a small spot on the top center of the box that would not be easy to activate accidentally. "This button will allow you to use the speaker function of the box. I doubt you'll use it on orbit since it'll be hard to conceal the conversation, but they designed the box for use in more group-like settings."

"So, this thing will let them hear me while I'm on orbit? Now that's pretty amazing."

"Yup. You can talk privately to the family. Annu had a receiver located in our chambers at home in Exeter. Just slide the switch to the third position with the earbuds plugged in." Cam looked around quickly. "Try it. Say something."

After verifying they were alone and the switch was in the correct position, Terry did as Cam instructed her. "Hi," she said tentatively.

"Hi, Baby!" Terry heard her mother's voice perfectly clear from her earbuds. "Dad and I can hear you just like you were in the room. This is amazing! I hope it works as well when you're on orbit."

"Me, too, Mom. This will be so cool. Let me try something." Terry whispered very quietly, "Can you hear this?"

This time, her father's voice came back to her. "Oh, yeah. They designed this for Protectors to use in secret. The mic automatically filters out extraneous noise and will only pick up your voice and automatically amplify it. That's why they programmed your voice into the transmitter. Even if you whisper when you talk to us, we'll hear you clearly. That will hopefully keep your team from wondering why you're talking to yourself."

"How about the battery life?"

"Not a problem. The entire case is a solar cell charger. If you can have it out for thirty minutes a day, it will keep a full charge. A full charge will last for a minimum of twenty-four hours of constant communication."

"Sounds like the engineering group thought of everything," Terry said quietly.

"Yeah," her brother said. "They did. For example, this really is a digital music player and Mom downloaded your entire playlist to it. That way, you can listen to music whenever you want. Just move that slide switch down to the fourth position and you can listen to your music. Speaking on behalf of our entire family I say please make sure the switch is all the way into the fourth position. That way the mic is turned off and we won't have to listen to your 1980's pop music collection."

Terry responded to her brother with a single finger…and a smile. She said goodbye to her parents and turned off the communications box.

The brother and sister team began walking again towards a conference room where last minute details were to be reviewed by the entire crew

Cam had never been one to miss the obvious. "I like your home here," he said looking down the long and totally monotonous hallway. "It looks like you're living inside a giant Milky Way candy bar." Every hallway, classroom, dining area, and even individual bedrooms were painted in the same caramel brown with a dark brown stripe at shoulder height. It was a long-standing joke in NASA that someone in Congress owned a paint factory that only produced brown paint.

The crew quarters building had existed since the earliest Mercury missions in the 1960's. In those days, with only a single astronaut and his backup in training, the facility had been significantly smaller. Over the years, it had been enlarged and modernized as the number of people comprising the flight crews and support personnel had grown. The building could now house and feed seventy-five individuals including almost half that number being completely segregated and in isolation for the five days before launch.

For most of their early training, the first-generation shuttle crews were in Houston where the primary simulator, classrooms, and facilities were operated. As training continued, the crews would spend several weeks at a time in Florida where tower egress training, water survival, and tests of the actual shuttle systems were added to the preflight drills. That travel back and forth between Florida and Texas, accomplished in T-38 Talon Air Force jets, was both time consuming and sometimes a disruptive factor in training schedules. Therefore, when the two new-generation space shuttles were under construction, it had been determined a second simulator and a payload bay mockup should be built in Florida which would eliminate the need for most of the flights between the different NASA training facilities. Construction had been completed at a substantial cost, but for once, Congress didn't even pretend to exercise tight of control over their fiscal responsibility.

Two months before launch, as training was reaching the greatest intensity, the crew began living in the now sprawling shuttle crew building. This gave them total flexibility in their scheduling and largely removed any outside distractions. The facility was little more than a very nice dormitory. The crew members and support personnel all had small private suites. Functionality was more important than decor and each room was furnished with what Dr. Jim Dalton called *spartan chic*. A bed, nightstand, and television were in the sleeping area. The adjoining sitting area had chairs for four, a study table and a compact refrigerator stocked with snacks, mostly healthy. Having wine or spirits in the rooms was strictly prohibited, so everyone on the crew kept their stock out of sight. On top of the refrigerator was a coffee maker and four mugs.

Dr. Patti Koch, who was not a coffee drinker, had asked for a hot water dispenser to brew tea. True to NASA form, one had been eventually approved for her suite after a lengthy requisition process had made it through channels. However, true to Dr. Koch's character, long before she had even filled out the requisition request, she had already persuaded a maintenance man to install the dispenser. Patti chuckled as she read the approval email. Sitting before her was a steaming cup of her favorite tea.

The closet in each suite was small because it only needed to hold a couple flight suits, underwear, and shoes. An adjoining bathroom, equally lacking in luxury, was the perfect size for a single occupant.

The food was as good as any institutional kitchen could produce with each meal offering two or three entrees with different side dishes. Everything was served cafeteria-style in a large room where tables were set for groups of four, six, or eight. There was even a tablecloth covering the faux-wood laminate.

One obvious decor component completely destroyed the college dormitory feeling. Instead of sports or broadcast television being shown on the multiple television monitors stationed around the hallways and dining area, live feeds from various locations around the pad and inside Launch Control were constantly displayed. A quick glance at key monitors by a trained eye would reveal any unexpected activity on the launch pad or in Launch Control. At the bottom of each screen was a ribbon with the current temperature and winds at the launch pad. In the corner of the display was a countdown digital clock showing the hours, minutes, and seconds until launch. It served as a constant reminder that time was precious and not to be squandered.

As Cam and Terry entered the conference room, the entire team stood to greet their visitor. A few minutes later, all the introductions had been made and a chair moved to allow Cam to sit beside his sister. Everyone was welcoming despite the intrusion Cam was certain he was to their routine.

May 30, 2022
Exeter

An alarm went off in the brain of J.R. Locklar, the head of Exeter's computer section. For all her intellectual skills, J.R. mostly loved the challenge of finding logic when someone's work didn't make sense. She rarely missed any subtle incongruity in data or mistaken logic of a subordinate's programming.

It was that sixth sense which alerted J.R. that something was wrong with the information in front of her. She hadn't yet figured out what it was, but she trusted her instincts. She had been looking at data from a search Prince Isha had requested on a company in Corpus Christi, Texas. For some reason, what she was examining was confusing. There was a large file of material instead of a few pinpoint items.

"Jim," she said to her assistant, "why are we still probing this company's computers? I thought the Prince only wanted to know when someone signed in and signed out from the headquarters."

"Yeah, but your guys got interested in their guys," he answered. "That company seems to be positive their firewalls and encryption make them completely secure. So, your team was just having fun looking at everything that seemed interesting."

"Okay. I'll bite," she responded while giving a "come-on" motion with her hands. "What are you telling me?"

"Why is a company that says it's focused on protecting communications and electrical systems from electromagnetic pulse working on ways to focus that same force to destroy communications and electrical systems?"

"Say that again."

"J.R., here's the deal. All we did initially was check some log times for the Prince. That was easy. We broke that info out in about twenty something minutes. But while doing the Prince's research, Christina Cantu realized the company had a layered paradigm. Basically, those guys use very strange software models to place some data into a much deeper level of security. That's what piqued her interest. Winter Triangle Physics has a sophisticated security system that is compartmentalized for this particular project."

"So?"

Jim knew he was on shaky ground. "Boss, why would a company that already has state-of-the-art cyber-security put another layer in for one program unless it was especially significant? That's what caught Christina's attention. So, naturally she was curious and kept looking." Jim wasn't sure he wanted to continue but decided he should. "That's when she discovered the discrepancy in projects and mentioned it to me."

"Let me see if I follow your somewhat convoluted logic. We have a company that does research in EMP protection but it's developing

EMP as a weapon. Right?"

"Yup. And to make it even more interesting, it seems they have found a way to potentially focus solar energy and then charge that focused beam with some sort of photon that usually only happens in a nuclear blast. This is over my head, but Christina got someone from the physics area to come here and look at the data." Jim paused and thought before speaking again. "Our physicist's best guess is that this focused beam could be aimed at any electronic or electrical center and instantly shut it down… actually destroy it. This program has bad mojo all over it?"

J.R. looked at Jim with renewed interest. "Mojo? Is that a technical term?"

"Yup," he responded and emphasized with a nonchalant nod of his head. "While EMP created by a nuclear detonation would only last a fraction of a second and would be more like the splash of a water bucket turned upside down and going in all directions, this would have pinpoint aiming capacity." Jim sighed and said, "It's really kind of spooky what this could do in the wrong hands."

"Alright. Keep this between as few people as we can for now. See if the physics section can figure this one out. If Prince Isha is interested in this company, and it's doing something that might have bad mojo all over it, he might want to know."

Chapter Eighteen

May 31, 2022
Kennedy Space Center - Launch Day

The shuttle launch was scheduled in six hours and preparation all around the Cape was a carefully orchestrated beehive of activity.

Hundreds of scientists, technicians, and support personnel were completing time sensitive tasks to ensure that nothing was done too soon nor too late.

Since both new-generation shuttles, Explorer and now Sojourner, were larger than the ones they had replaced, the solid rocket boosters and external fuel tank were more massive as well. Technicians were starting the process for filling the external fuel tank with almost six hundred thousand gallons of liquid hydrogen and oxygen. The solid rocket boosters would burn their propellent and jettison about two minutes after liftoff. Parachutes would then deploy to slow descent of the boosters into the Atlantic Ocean for retrieval. The much larger external tank would feed the three shuttle main engines for almost eight minutes before it, too, was jettisoned. The tank would then burn up on reentry into the atmosphere.

Five hours before launch, Commander Russ Boda, the backup shuttle pilot, Bob Paulus, and the other backup crew members entered Sojourner to set and verify switch positions, checklists, navigation and avionics systems. Their preparations ensured that when the primary crew strapped into their seats in about three hours, everything would be ready.

Boda was certain Bubba Ledwell would go over every switch position to verify for himself their correct position, but that made the backup pilot even more attentive to his procedures. If Bubba found a misplaced switch, he wouldn't say anything before the flight, but Boda knew it would be critiqued personally later. Bubba expected perfection and nothing less was acceptable.

The worst part for Boda was that Captain Ledwell was a hellofa great guy and his demand for perfection started with himself. Ledwell was, the backup pilot knew, a gifted leader and motivator for his crew. Boda wanted to emulate that quality on the next Shuttle launch when he was the prime pilot.

While the backup members were setting up the shuttle, the eight primary crew members were finishing a high protein breakfast. It would be several hours before any of them would have a chance to eat again and maintaining their metabolism was a priority. Steak, eggs, toast, hash browns, bacon and ham were all served in great quantity on platters. There were several carafes of coffee and, in deference to Patti Koch, one carafe of decaffeinated English Breakfast tea. There was one additional bowl in front of Captain Ledwell. It contained a steaming portion of grits with melted butter swimming on top. No one else on the crew appreciated the dish, but Ledwell was a Texan, and Texans needed grits to complete a full breakfast. Such traditions had to be indulged.

Cam Forsyth, who had slept soundly despite his excitement, planned on a far lighter breakfast. He was watching his weight and so a half grapefruit and oatmeal with skim milk were delivered to his seat as the choices he had selected. However, on impulse, he did take several pieces of bacon and placed them between two slices of sourdough toast to create a breakfast sandwich. After the first small bite, he added a large spoonful of scrambled eggs to the sandwich. The grapefruit and oatmeal were returned to the kitchen uneaten.

After breakfast, the team met in the main conference room. First on the agenda was a weather briefing. The Air Force meteorologist concentrated on the launch site and the immediate two-hundred-mile radius. At launch, the anticipated weather could not have been better…light winds from the northwest and a scattered canopy of clouds at 12,000 feet.

Ledwell leaned over to Weaver, "We'll plan on using Runway 33 as the initial emergency return runway." Weaver nodded and wrote that down on his notepad. Both pilots preferred runway 33 because the vast majority of the approach to landing took place over the Atlantic Ocean instead of Merritt Island and was less potentially dangerous to inhabited areas. Weaver would ensure the runway 33 approach chart was loaded in the cockpit navigation system.

The first adverse weather the shuttle might encounter on its climb to Earth orbit would be as it approached Lajes Field in the Azores off the western coast of Portugal. Therefore, that emergency landing airport had be switched to Zaragoza, Spain which was merely a formality. Shortly after passing the Azores, Sojourner would be on orbit and numerous landing facilities would then be available.

Forsyth was impressed with the massive amount of information the two pilots absorbed during the short briefing. Chart after chart covered with incomprehensible symbols and diagrams were flashed briefly before them with only the briefest of pauses. Neither man asked a single question. They gleaned what they needed, thanked the briefer, and walked together to be dressed for the launch.

At launch time minus four and one half hours, the two pilots and their guest journalist entered a large room crammed with eight specialized couches. Each couch sat between racks of test equipment with communication leads, oxygen and pressurization hoses. A team of three were at each station to assist the men and women in donning their multi-layer pressure suits.

Space travel does not allow for great modesty once on orbit but pre-flight conditions are different. Before any of the male crew members arrived, all three women had already dressed in their cooling garment and were in various stages of wearing the outer layers of their suits.

The men similarly went into a separate area to don their cooling suits. These garments actually resembled thermal underwear worn by winter hunters and fishermen. These, however, were made with dozens of small hoses where cold water was circulated to keep the astronaut cool inside their sealed outer pressure suit.

Beneath the cooling suit, each person wore what Tom Frederick called his man-diaper. They were only worn under the pressure suit for launch and landing. Frederick considered it a point of pride that during his first mission into space, his diaper had remained unspoiled. He never mentioned to anyone, however, his almost panicked rush to the lav immediately after removing his pressure suit.

The banter in the dressing area was lighthearted. All of the crew, even those facing their first flight into space, were confident and prepared...with the exception of L. Scott Elder. His heart rate was significantly higher than anyone else's and twice his technicians had to remind Elder to breathe slower. The three techs kept exchanging glances with each other that silently expressed their mixture of concern and amusement. Crew members were supposed to be calm and collected. In contrast, the techs could tell Elder was just this side of being distraught. They weren't sure what to do or who to tell. The three quietly conferred with each other and decided to simply make sure Elder's pressure suit was perfect. After that, it was up to someone else to ensure he was ready for flight.

Cam Forsyth was trying to stay out of the way while still taking notes on everything he saw. As much as he wanted to remain invisible to the people doing their tasks, he wanted to be near his sister as she donned her pressure suit. His journalistic objectivity was sorely being tested by his brotherly concern and the silent unexpressed fears he was feeling.

Terry Lee could sense his tension. "Cam, why don't you go over and talk with Tunes Dalton."

"Why him?"

"Because he's all the way across the room."

A discrete middle finger was passed from brother to sister. The three techs pretended not to see it, but they couldn't help but chuckle quietly. No further conversation could take place because everyone was now completely suited up and each crew member was about to undergo their final tests.

With their helmets on and sealed, a pressure check was completed using equipment at each couch. As the inflation and leak checks were accomplished, a communication test was simultaneously completed. Once both of those checks were done, the suits were deflated and helmets removed. The helmets would then be carried by life support personnel to the pad and placed in the clean room for the crew members.

While Bubba Ledwell and Tom Fredrick were getting their last-minute update on weather conditions, Howe Bucy, the mission Flight

Director, was polling all of his 16 mission controllers. Each person, responsible for a specific aspect of the launch, had to give their okay for the countdown to continue.

As Bucy was beginning his queries, Melissa Forsyth was escorted into a glass-enclosed observation area directly behind him. Comfortable chairs mounted on three tiers gave the twenty-one spectators an unrestricted view of Launch Control Center, which everyone called the LCC. The rows of complex consoles in Launch Control all had large labels on top. Dr. Marlo Campbell had prepared a cheat-sheet for Melissa with explanations of all the esoteric titles she was seeing. Melissa now knew that CAPCOM was short for "capsule communicator" and was the person who would make all the direct communications with the shuttle crew. FIDO and GUIDANCE would oversee the flight direction and trajectory. BOOSTER would monitor the solid fuel and external fuel rocket systems. There were others, but she was too excited to pay attention.

In all, fifteen primary controllers and more than two dozen specialists had to give their approval to proceed with the countdown at specified points. Bucy had handpicked the specialists he wanted on his team and had absolute confidence in their readiness. He began his check.

"CAPCOM, Flight."

The spacecraft communicator (CAPCOM), Mike Emmer, had already tested every shuttle communications channel with Russ Boda and his team. "Flight, CAPCOM is go."

"FIDO?"

"Go." Luther Robins responded in his characteristic taciturn manner. His West Texas accent made his single word last longer than most people's. Robins was a "good ole boy" in every sense of the word. A quiet gentleman with a Texas flavor. He never seemed to be a hurry, but he was never late for anything.

"Guidance?"

"Guidance is a go, Flight." The verification was spoken by Eric Corn, a tall engineer with a passion for rebuilding old cars. Corn had the distinction of being the guidance controller on the Explorer shuttle landing and had been instrumental in her safe return when the onboard computers had failed and Bubba Ledwell had flown the machine manually. Captain Ledwell had told the Flight Director he wanted Corn on the panel for launch for obvious reasons.

"Booster?"

Simmy Simcheck, a dark-haired man raised in Michigan, was known among all the controllers as quiet but intensely brilliant. He was monitoring the fueling of the external fuel tank. "Booster fueling is on schedule, Flight." His keen eye for detail ensured that the delicate loading of liquid oxygen and liquid hydrogen would go off without any hitch.

"DPS?"

The Data Processing Systems engineer, Jay Vandenburg, was responsible for the five onboard shuttle computers and other data collection systems. Vandenburg, a gregarious computer scientist who had an almost personal relationship with his computers could sense when a computer glitch was imminent. He had a reputation for recognizing potential problems and proactively making corrections before they became critical. Vandenburg instantly answered, "DPS is a go, Flight."

"GNC?"

"GNC is go!" responded David Parkerly after reviewing the guidance, navigation and control readouts on the multi-screen monitors before him. Parkerly was a mathematical genius with a Ph.D. in astrophysics and an intense love for the Green Bay Packers. He and his wife were known for their Sunday parties whenever the Packers were being televised. Parkerly was wearing a Packers ball cap, much to the Flight Director's annoyance.

"EECOM?" Bucy continued on.

The electrical, environmental and consumables systems engineer was a tall man with a full head of silver hair. Ken Cliner was known for his attention to detail. He could almost instantly detect the most minor deviation from the screen full of readouts before him. At the moment, Cliner was slightly concerned. "Flight, EECOM has one low fuel cell. I think it's probably an instrumentation problem, but I'll have it checked out and get back with you."

"Roger, EECOM," Bucy responded while jotting down the note into the log.

"MMACS?" Bucy pronounced the initials as "Max".

MMACS—maintenance, mechanical arm and crew systems—was monitored by Ken Quartoe. Years before, the other controllers had nicknamed Quartoe "Mr. Clean" because of his smoothly shaven head. He also had a small, almost invisible, hole in his left earlobe where he wore an earring off-duty. "Max is a go, Flight. I just got a call from Pad One saying they are ready for the crew," Pad One was Robert Emmidad, whose team atop the launch gantry would assist the crew in entering and strapping into the shuttle. They were also responsible for ensuring the crew was quickly evacuated in case of a major emergency while still on the ground.

"Roger, Max. Copy Pad One is ready," Bucy responded. "FAO?"

The Flight Activities Officer was responsible for the crew's activities, checklists, procedures, and schedules. Keeping the crew on schedule was not an easy task. This crucial position was being handled by Joe Bonoe, who had started his career with Grumman Aircraft on New York's Long Island during the Apollo mission days. His engineering background had been crucial in developing and writing most of the flight crew checklists.

"Instrumentation?"

Dr. Claus Dannenberg, had designed more than one of the myriad instruments both on the shuttle and in Launch Control. "Flight, instrumentation is a go… of course."

Bucy couldn't help but smile at the "of course" comment. It was very uncharacteristic of Claus and thus, especially humorous.

Bucy continued checking each of his controllers. Only one, Dr. Mike Sabos, the Flight Surgeon, was slow in answering. Since the crew had suited up for their launch, he had been monitoring medical sensors on each crew member. He was a little concerned about

Elder's heart rate and respirations. "Flight, let's go private," Sabos answered.

"Roger," came the Flight Director's response and he punched a button on his console. Now, he and Sabos were talking on a direct line between their stations. The words were still being recorded—everything said in Launch Control was recorded—but at least only the two men could hear each other, and the rest of Launch Control could not. "What's up, Mike?" Bucy asked.

"Howe, Elder is really hyped up."

"It's his first flight."

"Yeah, I know, but he showing borderline tachycardia. If his heart rate increases even a little more, I'm going to have to step in."

The Flight Director was well aware of the problems Elder had caused for the entire crew and in particular his friend, Bubba Ledwell. He wasn't too sympathetic toward Elder. "Want someone to evaluate what the hell that little turd is so wrapped up about?"

"Tell you what, Howe, The Flight Surgeon over there in quarantine is a buddy of mine. I'm going to ask him to make a quiet assessment. He can do it discreetly. That way Elder hopefully won't get even more tense. I don't want to stop the launch because of a medical problem. It doesn't look good in the press for one of our brave explorers to cancel a flight because they're about to pee in their pants or have a panic attack when the rockets light."

"Do it, Mike. Check out the guy, but try and stay under the radar."

"You got it, Howe."

Howe Bucy accidentally forgot to make an entry into his flight log about his conversation with the Flight Surgeon.

Chapter Nineteen

May 31, 2022
Kennedy Space Center - Launch Minus 4 hours 30 minutes

Cam Forsyth was in the prep room observing all the work of insuring the crew members were safely garbed in their pressure-suits. He had spoken to each of the members briefly and taken notes to use later. Even the serious and focused leader, Captain Ledwell, gave him a few minutes of his time. The rest of the crew, with the exception of Dr. Elder, had also spoken to Cam. Only Elder was uncommunicative. Cam sat down at a corner desk and kept up his observations.

As Bubba Ledwell and Bill Weaver were completing their preflight pressure suit checks, Dr. Steve Ashy sauntered into the crew prep room. Ashy and Ledwell had been friends for years. "Bubba! You're looking old and decrepit. Need a vitamin B-12 shot?"

"Ashy, you still treating chancre sores for a living?"

"Naw. I gave that up when you quit dating." Ashy looked around the room slowly and lowered his voice so that only Ledwell and Weaver could hear. "What's the deal with this chicken shit guy, Elder?"

"I'm assuming you've got a professional reason for asking," the mission commander asked.

"Yeah. He's freaking out Mike Sabos in the LCC. Guess his heart rate is near the top of the chart. I think there's concern he's going to go full-scale panic attack just when the boosters kick in? They want me to make some kind of magical prediction based upon a five-minute evaluation and they don't want him to know I'm doing it. Cute, huh?"

"Steve, let me be honest. In about four hours Bill and I are taking a shuttle into orbit. That shuttle with its loaded external fuel tank and solid boosters has a combined weight at launch just shy of five million pounds and engines that will produce almost eight million pounds of thrust. The weather at my primary recovery base is iffy and Bill and I will have to accomplish some serious mental gymnastics to safely return to land if any one of a couple hundred things go wrong. Worrying about that jackass is pretty low on my give-a-shit list right now."

Lt. Colonel Bill Weaver spoke in his quiet Texas drawl, "Elder has been a pain in our butts for the past three months, doctor. We've nursed him from day one and I for one am not thrilled with the prospect of babysitting him for the next two weeks while we're on orbit."

"If you want him gone, I can make that happen. He's already generated some high-level concern with Sabos and Bucy. Keeping his ass on the ground would not delay your launch at all. Bucy let me know, off the record, that Elder's experiment would simply remain on the shuttle all the way to landing so we wouldn't have to delay the flight to unload his stuff. Just say the word and I'll make it happen."

Ledwell responded, "Tell you what, Steve. You go make your assessment and while you're doing that Bill and I will give it some serious thought. You do need to know that he's got some pretty powerful mojo going for him. Whoever his boss is has Maclemore jumping through hoops. But, the call is yours and I'll back whatever decision you make."

"Thanks for the vote of confidence," Ashy said a little sarcastically. "But, I am glad you gave me that info before I made my totally professional and sound medical decision."

The doctor went to stand between Tom Fredrick's and Janelle McLain's couches. As a physician, McLain probably had a medical opinion on Elder, but Ashy knew she was too close to the group for an impartial assessment. He didn't mention his reason for being in the prep room and she didn't ask.

"So," Frederick started, "why haven't you ever volunteered to go into space, Dr. Ashy?"

"Afraid of heights."

"So am I, Steve," Janelle McLain retorted. "Do what I do. Don't look down."

The three laughed and Ashy moved to the next set of couches.

Patti Koch and Terry Lee were laughing about something when Dr. Ashy walked up. "Hey, Steve," Koch said.

"What's so funny?"

"Girl stuff, Doctor, and none of your business," Lee said in mock seriousness.

Ashy smiled and quietly responded, "I studied 'girl stuff' in medical school."

"Yeah, and what did they teach you?"

"They taught me all about girl stuff in my anatomy and physiology classes. They completely ignored the far more important training on how y'all think."

"It's a wise man who recognizes his limitations, Steve," Lee said with a big smile on her face. Then she continued conspiratorially, "We were discussing how much perkier we're going to be in microgravity on orbit." She slightly giggled, "It's been a while since I was perky."

Ashy, a man known for his great humor as well as his caring bedside manner, suddenly looked seriously at the two scientists before him. "I'm not sure how that could be empirically measured, but I would be curious in getting your feedback when you return. I might just write a medical paper on the subject."

"Go away, Steve," Patti Koch laughed.

Next, the flight surgeon walked to stand between Tunes Dalton and L. Scott Elder. Elder had been carefully watching Dr. Ashy since he walked into the room. He had felt a little better when it became obvious Ashy had stopped at each couch. He knew he was a little agitated, but that was certainly to be expected. *I'm sure everyone in this room is feeling exactly the same as I do,* he thought.

"Good morning, Tunes," Ashy said to Dr. Dalton. "Bringing your keyboard with you into orbit?"

"You know, Steve, I wanted to, but they gave us an eight pound limit for personal items. Even if I left my Pickleball equipment behind, I wouldn't be able to bring the keyboard."

Ashy was well familiar with the game of Pickleball and knew Tunes Dalton and Patti Koch had been playing it for years. "I heard you and Patti won some doubles tournament recently."

"Steve, my friend, you are talking to half of the gold medal winning team of the Southeastern US Pickleball tournament. Want to see my medal? I'll have them take my pressure suit off because it's hanging right next to my heart. Or, you can search us on social media. Our winning game was posted by one of our multitude of admirers."

"Tell you what, Tunes, when you get back I'll get you and Patti to take me out to a court and teach me some basics."

Jim "Tunes" Dalton laughed. "Dr. Ashy, my old friend, consider that a date. You can bring one of your bevy of bimbos and we'll make a day of it."

"Bimbos? I'll have you know that all of my girlfriends are MENSA candidates with advanced degrees."

"Steve, all of your girlfriends may be brilliant, but I believe their primary quality is that each is more than adequately blessed."

"Their bosoms do not keep them from being very smart and wonderful conversationalists."

Dalton just smiled.

Ashy turned to look at his last—and really only—patient. He tried to look nonchalant and friendly, but it did not require an M.D. degree to realize L. Scott Elder was scared... not nervous... scared. "Well, Scott, I'm sorry we haven't gotten to know each other. I'm Steve Ashy."

Elder raised his thickly gloved hand. "Pleased to meet you, Doctor. Are you checking us out?"

"Naw," Ashy lied. "I always walk through to see everyone before a flight to make sure all their inoculations are up to date."

Ashy's witticism was lost on Elder so the physician moved on. "Actually, Scott, this is just my tradition." A glance at the blipping monitor reflecting Elder's biomedical sensors told Steve Ashy all he really needed to know. "Scott, your heart rate and blood pressure seem to be a little high. How are you feeling?"

"Fine. I feel fine. Nothing's wrong. I feel fine." Elder spurted out the words with a bit too much irritation. "I'm just excited. This is my first time into space, you know. Anyone would be excited. I'm not scared. I'm just excited." The words flowed quickly, too quickly to be believed.

"Well, if you're not scared, you're the only member of this crew not a little scared." Ashy's carefully spoken words seemed to have the desired effect. A noticeable amount of tension left Elder's face. "Look. Just close your eyes and take a few deep breaths."

Elder followed the instructions and the monitor reflected a small, but nonetheless significant, drop in his heart rate. "That's better, Scott. Just do that every so often. Okay?"

"Sure. I guess I'm just excited."

"Probably. Just keep the slow, deep breathing going. You know this is the A team and everything is going to go perfectly." Ashy was continuing his friendly banter, but was still observing Elder and subtly glancing at the medical monitor. He was cautiously optimistic his five-minute tutorial in relaxation had worked.

"Thanks, Doctor. I guess I did need to relax a bit more. I'm not scared you understand... just excited. Maybe I was just too excited."

Dr. Steve Ashy smiled his best doctor smile. "No problem, Scott. Give me a call if you want to. I'll be around until y'all go out to the van." He offered his hand and L. Scott Elder took it. His grip wasn't exactly manly, but neither was it weak.

Ashy nodded and turned to walk out. He glanced around and noticed Elder's eyes were closed and he was doing the prescribed deep breathing exercises. As he left the room, at a spot where only Bubba Ledwell could see, he gave a thumbs-up signal. The commander made an almost imperceptible head nod.

Five minutes later, Dr. Steve Ashy and Dr. Mike Sabos were consulting one another over the phone. Sabos spoke first. "Steve, not exactly sure what you did, but Elder's heart rate, respirations, and BP have dropped a lot. They're still what I would consider high normal, but he meets mission parameters for launch. How did you do it?"

"Just my normal calming bedside manner. Plus, I slipped a couple Xanax into his orange juice."

Sabos knew his friend was kidding about the medication, but played along. "As long as nothing shows up in the post flight medical tests."

"He's just wound pretty tight and he's scared shitless. He's just too stupid to recognize that that is perfectly normal and he's making himself manic trying to hide his fear. He's not going to stroke out on us, but I'm glad he won't be at the controls if something goes wrong."

"Okay, Steve. Thanks for checking him out. I'll pass along your thoughts to the Flight Director. In the end it's his call, but he'll go with our recommendation and I'm a go."

"Me, too."

The two physicians were right in their conclusion of Elder's physiology. They just couldn't know that Elder was a master at hiding a mental condition that would prove disastrous within a few days.

Chapter Twenty

May 31, 2022
Kennedy Space Center - Launch Minus 2 hours 30 minutes

Just before the crew was set to leave the preparation room, Cam Forsyth was escorted out and directly to the crew transportation van. He was already belted into an observation chair when Captain Bubba Ledwell led his team out of the crew building. The van would take them the six miles to Pad 39 of the launch complex. The mandatory smiling and waving to the assembled photographers and television reporters was not Ledwell's idea of how to begin a mission. He knew most of them were wanting photos and video to show infinitum on news broadcasts if the shuttle blew up in a couple of hours. Bill Weaver, Tom Fredrick and Jim Dalton felt similarly. However, maintaining the intrepid space traveler image was important PR for NASA, so they smiled and waved, too

Doctors McLain, Koch, and Lee did wave, and they did mean it, not because they were females or unaware of the dangers, but because they were all far more naturally gregarious and friendly than the men in front of them. L. Scott Elder was the last out of the building. He was so obviously attempting to look calm and in control that it was clear he was neither. He looked like he was leaving home to take his ugly cousin to the senior prom… sullen and stiff. Even his tentative waves were stilted and awkward. Fortunately, the walk to the blue and white crew transport van was short and he was able to get in and sit down without too much drama. Elder was still trying to remember to breath slowly and deeply, but his tension was rising like an ocean tide in the evening. There was nothing that could stop it.

"Well, team," Bubba said to each of them. "Looks like a great day to go flying. I just got the last update from the Flight Director and he said everything is a go at this point. Pad One says the team is all set to meet us."

"Bubba," Terry Lee piped in. "I've got to pee."

"Told you before, Dr. Lee, you should have gone before we left home. Now you just have to wait until our next rest stop."

"Just kidding, boss. I'm good and I do have my diaper on in case of an emergency."

"I have a kid sister like you, Terry. We can't take her anywhere either."

As this short stress relieving conversation was taking place, Moses and Tame Forsyth were in Exeter sitting by themselves and listening in to every comment via the communications device Terry was carrying but had obviously forgotten about. Moses was laughing. Tame was shaking her head. Moses knew Terry's potty joke hadn't gone over well with her mother, but it could have been worse. A couple of hours earlier, he had been listening to his daughter's perky breasts comments. He had laughed then, too, but he was happy and relieved Tame had been out of the room and missed that conversation.

In the back row of the Launch Control observation room, Melissa Forsyth was paying rapt attention to Marlo Campbell's explanation of the beehive of operations before them. The two women had watched on closed circuit television as Cam was escorted unobtrusively into the van and moments later, the crew followed him in. Melissa couldn't help but feel the tension she knew Terry must be experiencing.

In Exeter, Tame and Moses Forsyth were holding hands and praying silently…as was much of the tribe.

During the ride to the launch pad, Dr. Janelle McLain had passed some of the time discussing the medical aspects of what they were facing. "I did a fellowship in neurobiology a few years ago. There was a classic study of the phenomenon that often happens during moments of intense stress, excitement, or danger. For some people, time often appears to slow down and they remember every detail and sensation with a clarity that is astonishing. I'm kinda hoping that happens for me today. I really want to relish every moment."

For seven of the eight crew members, especially the four on their first mission, this idea that time would seem to come to a crawl was something they looked forward to. L. Scott Elder worried it would only prolong what he called his excitement.

The crew reached the gantry elevator to the orbiter access arm

195 feet above the ground, which would give them access to the White Room and, from there, to Sojourner's entry hatch. Robert Emmidad, head of the White Room team, and known as Pad One, met them. "Good morning, campers! You've picked a beautiful day to go into space." He spoke to Ledwell, "Russ is still up here. I think he wanted to make sure you were feeling okay before he left."

Sure enough, Russ Boda came out of the orbiter, took off the clean booties he wore inside the craft and ambled over to the crew. Boda, who was very popular among everyone in the program because of his quick wit and infectious laugh, was also a gifted pilot and engineer. He was also known for his colorful expressions. "Bubba! You look a bit ill. Have you been exposed to malaria recently? If you're not 100%, I can just run down and throw on my suit and be right back up."

"Thanks, Russ, but I feel really good."

At this point, Boda spoke his most powerful phrase… one he used often to describe the most difficult situations. "You know," he began, "they almost had to belt-sand my nipples to get me out of your seat this morning." He smiled, "That said, everything is ready. There was a little concern about the number three fuel cell earlier, but they sent a team over and they replaced the flux capacitor or something and now it's reading fine."

"Thanks, Russ. I feel good knowing you've checked the bird out. You've been the perfect backup pilot, my friend. You go up in what…eight months?"

"Ten months. We're taking the Explorer for a docking with the ISS. That'll be the first for the new-generation shuttles."

"Yeah, I know how hard it's been being my backup and starting to build the crew for your mission at the same time. I want you to know I've appreciated it."

"Glad to help, Bubba. You've got a good one here. I've been tracking the R&D for the new avionics package. You know, during design and testing, this shuttle has had fewer faults and failures than any shuttle in the history of NASA. I think your little computer glitch on that last mission got some attention."

He laughed at his own cleverness. Boda was well aware how major computer failures had been on Ledwell's mission and how close to disaster his recovery of the crippled shuttle had come.

Russ Boda took one last look over his shoulder at the shuttle entry hatch. "Well, Bubba, if you are sure you don't have malaria, or anything like that, guess I'll head on down to the LCC."

"Thanks, buddy," Ledwell answered. "I meant it when I told you how much I've appreciated your friendship and the great backup you've been."

"See you, Bubba." As Boda walked away, despite his naturally positive attitude, he couldn't quite dispel an underlying feeling that this would be his last time to see Bubba Ledwell and his crew.

Dr. Terry Lee was uncharacteristically talkative as she stood on the orbiter access arm. She was chatting with Dr. Janelle McLain and Dr. Patti Koch about the view from the access arm. She mentioned the growing excitement she was feeling as the moment she would enter the orbiter and the pad crew would strap her into the seat between McLain and Koch. The banter, while not exactly out of place, wasn't really like Lee's usual conversations.

What the two lady scientists didn't realize was that Lee was actually giving secret color commentary to her parents 1,600 air-miles away. Sure enough, Moses and Tame Forsyth were listening in to every word their daughter was saying. On one level, Moses was happy to be hearing Terry's voice; on another level, as an Elder of Exeter, he was even more thrilled at the clarity and strength of her speech. It seemed to prove the new communication device was working perfectly. The real test, he knew, would come once she was talking to them from orbit.

Cam Forsyth was the odd man out. He wasn't part of the crew, nor part of the pad team. The permission for him to be here was totally unprecedented. The approvals had been sent to the launch team straight from Dr. John Francis Maclemore's office. As NASA's Director of Flight Operations, he was one of very few who had the authority to issue such an authorization. The fact Maclemore himself had given the authority meant the crew and pad team would accommodate Forsyth in his job of reporting behind the scenes activities of launch day…even though it was a distraction.

What the crew, pad personnel, and even the LCC Flight Director didn't know was that the request for Cam's participation had not really come from the public affairs office. Dr. John Francis Maclemore had never actually seen the falsified request. In fact, his office knew nothing about it. Maclemore's approval and signature on the document was just as counterfeit as was the original request. The Director of Flight Operations had never heard of Cam Forsyth.

Exeter's computer section had outdone themselves in creating the approval documents and inserting them in the NASA computer system. If Maclemore himself were to review the paperwork, he would have been forced to believe he had forgotten accepting and signing the approval. Like all high-level executives, he often signed documents he had not actually read, but were put before him by trusted subordinates. Exeter believed, and the results proved, Cam's fake permission documents would not be questioned. To the support personnel actually doing the work, having to deal with this reporter was just another example of how the top guys really didn't understand the problems they created in the name of public relations.

To Forsyth, the orderliness and precision of strapping the flight crew into their assigned seats was impressive. Each member of the pad crew had defined responsibilities and they carried those jobs out with a minimum of nonessential speaking. Cam had seen this kind of quiet efficiency only once before. While covering a breakthrough transplant surgical procedure, he had stood silently in an operating room for seven hours where the only sound was the surgeon's whispered orders and the tiny clink of instruments placed on metal trays. Like the operating room team, the pad crew demonstrated an intense focus because they knew any distraction from their procedures or any minor error of omission could spell disaster for their astronaut. Forsyth was trying very hard to be as invisible as possible.

This was the actual launch day—no longer a rehearsal—and tension blanketed each member of the pad crew. It was not a comfortable time…until Dr. Patti Koch shouted in exasperation. "Listen here, everyone." She waited for the inevitable silence—

inevitable because most of the people were taken totally by surprise with her uncharacteristic exclamation. "We've friggin' done this exercise two or three dozen times. We've never once done it like we were preparing for a funeral, so why are we doing that today?" She looked over to one of her pad assistants and continued, "Brad Killingsly! Usually by now you've made some bad joke about farting in our pressure suits. Get with it man!"

The tension was broken and everyone laughed. Koch's pronouncement had had the desired effect and the teams relaxed a bit as each person was led to the orbiter access.

A space shuttle crew compartment was actually comprised of three levels. The top level was the one most people were familiar with. It was the flight deck where the pilots flew the shuttle. The back bulkhead of this level was full of circuit breakers, switches, dials, instrumentation, and a control grip that would be used to operate the robot arm. The mid-deck was where crews entered the shuttle. It was also where the crews "lived". Sleeping, cooking, and sanitation areas were here as was the access hatch to the airlock. Finally, the lower deck contained the oxygen, water, and mechanical equipment that were crucial but that the crew didn't usually need to access on orbit.

To a novice like Cam Forsyth, the visual picture inside Sojourner was disorienting. The shuttle was attached vertically to the solid boosters and external fuel tank. Because of the launch configuration, the crew seats were attached to what, for the time being, was the left wall. Once each crew member climbed into their seats and were strapped in, they would actually be lying on their back.

Since the White Room is a small chamber and provides the last access point, it only held two astronauts and their pad assistants there at a time. From the White Room, the crew entry hatch gave access to the mid-deck. Once inside that level, the crew members who would be sitting in the top section went to the far end and turned to the right. Straight ahead now was a hatch that led into the upper flight deck area. Ledwell and Weaver led the way accompanied by their four pad assistants and Cam who was now wearing what he thought of as surgical scrubs and booties.

Temporarily installed on the flight deck level was a modified step ladder that allowed the commander and shuttle pilot to carefully climb onto their seats. Since these two front positions are more cramped and surrounded by flight controls, panels, and instruments, Ledwell and Weaver took as long to strap in as did the rest of the crew combined.

After the two pilots were set, the step ladder was removed. Next to enter were Dalton, Fredrick, and Koch. All three were stationed on the upper flight deck in seats positioned behind and centered between Ledwell and Weaver. While these seats were too far away from the nose of the compartment to see much out of the front glass panels, there were windows over their heads. As the last part of the insertion checklist, each crew member's helmet was carefully fastened to the metal ring on the neck of their pressure suit, but the visors were open. Finally, the rubberized seals and communication channels were checked between each other and the LCC. All five members on the upper flight deck gave their teams a final thumbs up signal.

At the same moment, Lee, McLain, and Elder were being strapped into their seats on the mid-deck. Cam Forsyth had been escorted from the upper area just in time to see his sister placed into her seat. Terry's brown eyes were bright with excitement, not fear. The next few minutes would be the culmination of years of schooling and training and the beginning of two weeks of absolute heaven for her research. She looked up from her seat to see Cam standing to her left and next to the entry hatch. She had carefully ensured the switch on her private communication device had remained on since she had left the crew quarters. There was little doubt in her mind that her family in Exeter were listening to her every word.

"Hey, cowboy," she jokingly addressed her brother. "You don't have to cry like that. I'll bring you something back from space." She knew her parents would get a laugh from her chiding. They did.

In an incredibly uncharacteristic show of sentiment, Cam gently touched the shoulder of Terry's pad assistant and moved over to look down on his sister. "Have a great flight, kiddo. I'm far more than just a little bit jealous. I'm proud of you." He leaned over and kissed her helmet. "See you in a couple of weeks."

Terry smiled but didn't speak. She didn't trust her voice.

With just two hours to go before launch, the hatch was sealed. Robert Emmidad and his pad crew were moved to a shelter not too far from the gantry in case they were needed quickly. If necessary, the gantry arm could be moved back in place within 15 seconds and the entire flight crew evacuated in 30 seconds.

Cam Forsyth was transported to the LCC where a seat was reserved for him in the observation room next to his sister, Melissa.

Howe Bucy, as Flight Director, was orchestrating his launch team with a calmness born of experience and demeanor. He had often said, and it was now accepted as fact in all of NASA, that the Flight Director's main job was to set the mood for the entire control center. He never raised his voice nor badgered a controller. He listened not only to the words but to the tone of every communication.

"CAPCOM," he started, "when was your last communications check?"

Mike Emmer glanced over his right shoulder to the next level in the tiered room. "Flight, it's been seventeen minutes since the last check. Not scheduled to run another for three more minutes. Want me to move it ahead?"

Bucy looked at the countdown clock centered above the three giant displays on the front wall. "We have a hold planned about then. It'll wait." The Flight Director didn't say, but no one needed reminding that as the launch got closer, time to correct minor problems was more and more limited. It had always been Bucy's policy to accomplish as many checks as possible early to free up time at the end.

Emmer needed no other hints. "Sojourner, CAPCOM."

The response was immediate.

"Go ahead."

"Thurman, let's go around the table for one last comm check."

"Well, obviously I'm good."

Weaver nodded. "Two's good."

Dalton, Fredrick, and Koch answered in turn. From the mid-deck,

Lee, McLain, and Elder also checked in. The voices were clear and had no static associated with the transmissions.

Emmer again looked over his right shoulder to see Bucy. "Flight, CAPCOM."

"Flight."

"Comm check is a go."

"Noted," came the expected reply. Bucy made the appropriate note on his log.

Inside the shuttle, for everyone except the two pilots it was a simple game of waiting. Unlike Bucy's flexible timeline, Ledwell and Weaver had checklist procedures that were very point-in-time specific in most cases. At launch minus one hour, they were right on schedule. They had a time to contemplate what was about to happen.

In the Corpus Christi complex of Winter Triangle Physics, Nicholas Schumer was sitting comfortably in the private study attached to his official office. Mounted on the walnut paneled wall before him were four screens upon which were broadcast different video feeds from Florida. He was watching the LCC, the MCC, the launch pad, and a video feed from the cockpit. Much like the celestial screen in his office, these feeds had been hijacked from NASA's closed-circuit lines. Schumer felt a quiet thrill in knowing the shuttle he was watching would soon be the vehicle for the greatest blackmail in the history of mankind…or the worst nightmare.

Chapter Twenty-One

May 31, 2022
Kennedy Space Center
Launch Minus 20 minutes

The NASA countdown had a built-in delay at twenty minutes before launch. This gave the controllers time to perform a last check on their consoles, engineers time to verify their readings, and a final safety check of the pad area. All those things were completed without any hiccups and Bucy resumed the countdown.

As the clock started the countdown again, Dr. Mike Sabos monitored a noticeable increase in the heartbeats of every crew member. Only L. Scott Elder's change was significant, but Sabos chose to not mention it to the Flight Director.

In the cockpit, several key events were taking place. All of the cabin vent valves were closed and pressurization was now from internal sources. The on-board computers were sequenced to their launch configurations and heating of the fuel cells was started.

The minutes passed quickly.

"Flight, Guidance," Eric Corn spoke while still looking at his console screen.

"Go."

"Flight, the primary and backup guidance computers are online and nominal."

"Roger, Guidance. Thanks."

On the flight deck, Weaver looked over to his commander. "Hey, Boss. Looks like we're taking this group on a trip." Behind him and on the mid-deck there were murmurs of approval and excitement from five other occupants in the shuttle. Only one person was completely silent.

The excitement was also growing in the viewing area behind the Flight Director. Cam and Melissa Forsyth were actually holding hands like they did as small children in the chambers of Exeter. Dr.

Marlo Campbell was as totally enraptured by the process as were her friends. In eighteen months, she hoped her holographic tests would be carried out on the fifth flight of the Explorer shuttle. Her work was still in development, but she was confident rapid refinements with her experimental gloves would allow Earth-bound researchers to actually touch and feel objects on orbit.

In Exeter, Moses and Tame Forsyth were sitting in a large observation room that the computer section had created. Four large screens were projecting the same hacked closed-circuit feeds as Nicholas Schumer was seeing in Corpus Christi. The Forsyth's had been joined by royalty. Sitting on Moses' left was King Annu and to Tame's right were Prince Isha and Deidre. Along the outer walls were representatives of every one of Exeter's many families and sub-colonies.

Television in Exeter was almost non-existent. It was considered a waste of time and hardly anyone had a set. Today's launch would be a first for Exeter. There had never been an astronaut from the tribe, and everyone was excited that that was about to change. Because of the historical significance, giant viewing screens had been erected throughout the caverns and were broadcasting the launch so everyone could watch.

Terry Lee's husband had returned to Exeter from his ranch in Montana, but, true to his quiet nature, had decided not to watch the launch.

Bubba Ledwell was focused on his last few checklist items. "Bill, bring the APUs online."

"Roger," Weaver responded. The activated auxiliary power units now pressurized all three hydraulic systems of the shuttle. At launch, the main engine nozzles were controlled by these systems.

In the cockpit and in the LCC, another significant light illuminated.

Dr. Claus Dannenberg flipped a switch on his console and spoke,

"Flight, Booster. APUs are online and pressurization is nominal." This was the last mandatory report to the Flight Director.

Bucy contacted all of his controllers once again to get a 'Go' for launch status from each one. Once again, Dr. Sabos chose not to notice L. Scott Elder's elevated heart rate, blood pressure, and respirations. They were within flight limits, but just barely. No previous crew member had ever been close.

As Bucy acknowledged the "Go for launch" calls, he made his normal status for this point. "Controllers, Flight. At the T-minus four minutes, go to silent mode." From that point until launch, a great number of significant operations and processes were automatically sequenced. Controllers could not report all of them. Instead, the Flight Director only wanted to know of any steps that failed to be accomplished.

In the shuttle, Bubba Ledwell spoke over the internal system to his crew mates. "Team, everything up here is absolutely textbook perfect. Bill and I are going into space in a couple of minutes and it's our plan right now to take all of you with us." He waited just a second more and continued, "Verify your helmet visors are down and locked."

Everyone reported in the affirmative.

For the past forty-five minutes, a highly sophisticated computer program, known as the Ground Launch Sequencer, had been monitoring hundreds of vehicle parameters. It had been controlling virtually all of the automated actions on and around the shuttle. Valves were closed, tanks were pressurized, pumps were started, and systems were activated all at the precise moment they were needed. Thirty seconds before launch, the onboard computers were sequenced to their terminal launch mode. At sixteen seconds to go, valves were opened releasing almost 400,000 gallons of water stored in a 290 foot tall tank. During launch, the main shuttle engines and the solid rocket boosters would create almost eight million pounds of thrust. This flood of water, aimed at the pad below the shuttle, would protect the vehicle from acoustic damage at liftoff.

McLain's comments about time seeming to slow down had

proven true for everyone except Bubba Ledwell and Bill Weaver. Their years of flying high performance jets and experience in space launches had made them immune. But for everyone else, in varying degrees, the last ten second countdown seemed to take forever. Their heightened senses were peaked and every moment passed at a snail's pace.

With 6.6 seconds to go, the three main engines started and began powering up to 90%. In the shuttle, a powerful rumbling vibration, an earthquake sensation, pummeled the crew.

As the launch timer reached zero, explosive bolts fired and released the hold-down points on the shuttle. The crew could not feel the release, but they could definitely feel it as the SRB rocket motors simultaneously ignited and added an additional 5.6 million pounds of thrust to that of the shuttle engines. The vibration became far more tremendous and every person on the shuttle felt a thrill of acceleration as the vehicle cleared the launch tower within seven seconds. Within 45 seconds, the five-million-pound vehicle was supersonic and accelerating rapidly.

The second the shuttle was above the launch tower, it was under control of the Mission Control Center outside Houston. Bud Stokesly, the MCC Flight Director calmly acknowledged the hand-off. He actually felt more at ease than he had for hours.

Stokesly was a deeply tanned muscular man who still had the same haircut he'd worn while in the military. He was a taciturn man who, when he did speak, had a slight Texas accent. The accent was not the result of living in Houston. When not working, Stokesly and his wife, Analyn, were often three hours west of Houston on their four-hundred-acre ranch riding horses, herding cattle or shearing sheep. The ranch was Stokely's way of escaping the pressure of NASA.

Before the launch, he and his team of controllers had all been at their stations, but had merely been observers while the LCC handled all the launch activities. Now that the shuttle was airborne and heading down range, the MCC controllers were busy with their jobs, and Stokesly was in charge. He was finally able to relax.

From her seat in the mid-level of the crew compartment, Dr. Terry Lee spoke for the first time since lift off. Since no one in the mid-level could see out, engineers had placed instruments in the area giving speed and altitude information and Lee was fascinated. "We're already accelerating through four times the speed of sound and we're almost one hundred and thirty thousand feet. I wish I could tell my mom and dad just how amazing this is."

Janelle McLain, sitting to Lee's left chuckled. "Well, you'll be able to do that in about six hours. Once we're on orbit, our ability to send emails will be up and running."

"Yeah, I'll never be able to write down this feeling to capture the moment. I'll just tell them that this is the most exciting moment of my life!"

McLain nodded her head inside her helmet. She had no idea that half a world away, Lee's mom and dad were in fact hearing their daughter's comments.

Chapter Twenty-Two

May 31, 2022
Winter Triangle Physics

"Tanner, get your ass in here," Nicholas Schumer bellowed over the intercom. Tanner was moving before Schumer took his hand off the button. It only took a few seconds for Josh Tanner to be standing in front of his boss.

"Yessir," he stammered.

"You know, Tanner, I've been thinking. The press was just reporting that that Forsyth troublemaker was the first reporter to be allowed into the White Room for the launch. That means he's in Florida. I want you to take one of the company jets and meet someone I've done business with there. This individual won't be like the rank amateur you hired to rid us of that meddlesome bastard."

Tanner wisely refrained from saying out loud that J.P. Pearson had been Schumer's choice. He just nodded his head. "Couldn't we just do it by phone?"

"You moron. Yes, use a burner phone for all your calls. You used one for this local botched job of yours, but I want you onsite to make sure it goes right. That pissant came into my very office and threatened me. He won't do that twice. Don't mess this one up."

Tanner could feel a knot in his stomach and a lightheaded feeling that took all his self-control to overcome. "Yessir, I'll be ready to go first thing in the morning."

"You can be ready first thing in the morning if you want, but you'll be somewhere else. I don't care how you do it, but be on the jet and airborne in less than one hour. The pilots have already been notified and the jet will be fueled and out of the hangar by the time you get there."

"But I don't have clothes or any personal items with me. I need to go home and pack," Tanner stammered weakly.

"Tanner, I don't care if your little beard grows out or not. I don't care if your odor can kill a skunk. I don't care if your underwear has to be burned later. Be on that plane! Questions?"

Josh Tanner meekly responded, "No sir. I understand."

He backed out of Schumer's office, stopped by the IT area and got an untraceable phone, and almost sprinted to his car. He told Red he was leaving for Florida and didn't know how long he'd be gone. She was to cancel all his appointments—there were very few—and to tell everyone he was on vacation.

As he sprinted out of the building, he failed to log out. That didn't matter. Linda Boltey, sitting at her desk, couldn't help but notice the quick departure nor the look of panic on Tanner's face. She dutifully logged him out.

In Exeter, J.R. Locklar noticed a small dialog box in the upper-left corner of her computer screen. Since Prince Isha's visit to the Winter Triangle Physics campus, and his less than cordial reception, she had maintained her hacked connection to that company's server. In particular, she had inserted a filter to notify her anytime Nicholas Schumer or Josh Tanner arrived or left their office complex. She didn't really have a good reason for having that information, but she had a hunch and that was good enough for her.

At the Corpus Christi International Airport, Josh Tanner arrived with fifteen minutes to spare before the scheduled departure of the company's Gulfstream 280. Winter Triangle Physics did not keep full-time pilots on staff. Instead, they used a company with contract pilots who flew on-demand trips. It was much cheaper since WTP didn't pay salaries and benefits nor for the very expensive periodic training all pilots are required to complete. Instead, those details were handled by the contract company. As a result, it was rare to get the same pilots every time a flight was necessary.

Standing beside the jet were two female pilots, both of whom were qualified to fly as pilot-in-command on either the Gulfstream 280 or 550 jet. Each pilot's uniform was adorned with four striped epaulets reflecting their hard-earned title of Captain. Between them they had almost 16,000 flying hours experience and were extremely proficient aviators. Nonetheless, both pilots recognized the look of concern or distain on the face of Josh Tanner when he saw two female pilots.

The captain with a name tag identifying her as Valerie Salfieri stepped forward as Tanner approached. "Mister Tanner, this is Captain Jennifer Davis. I'm Captain Salfieri. We have a flight plan filed across the Gulf of Mexico at 35,000 feet. There are scattered thunderstorms, but we will have the fuel necessary to divert if needed. There will be no problem reaching Orlando with plenty of fuel."

Tanner was not accustomed to having any woman be in charge of him. "Miss Salfieri and Miss Davis, I'm sure you are both very good at what you do, but don't we usually have other pilots on call?"

Captain Davis responded for both pilots. "Mister Tanner, if you're willing to accept pilots with less experience and qualifications just because they are men, then get them. Valerie and I get paid whether or not we fly you. For the record, it's not Miss. It's Captain. Now, you can either put your misogynistic crap in your bag and get your ass on the jet or you can wait and get two inferior pilots out here. We really don't care."

Both captains turned, walked up the stairs, and turned left into the cockpit. They were smiling.

Josh Tanner was to be the only passenger. He quietly sulked on board the airplane, turned right into the cabin and sat in the back seat. He paid no attention the pre-takeoff safety video played on the monitor at his seat. Instead, he stared out the window, thought about what he was supposed to do, and wondered if working for Nicholas Schumer was worth selling his soul.

As expected, warm water in the Gulf of Mexico had spawned several springtime thunderstorms. Knowing well the dangers caused by the intense weather, the pilots had plotted a path to give the billowing and towering cloud formations a wide berth. Most non-pilots lacked any concept of just how savage thunderstorms, even relatively small ones, could be. The familiar anvil shaped cloud gave

Captain Davis and Captain Salfieri distinct clues as how far they needed to be from the mass. Both knew that a cumulonimbus or thunderhead could throw damaging hail as far as twenty nautical miles. They stayed fifty miles from them.

A straight-line flight between Corpus Christi and Orlando was just under one thousand miles which would normally take two hours and fifteen minutes of flight time. Because of the necessary deviations around the bad weather they faced, it took the pilots an hour longer to land Josh Tanner at Orlando International Airport and taxi him to the civilian terminal.

Valerie Salfieri got out of her seat, wordlessly opened the cabin door and returned to the flight deck. Both pilots ignored their sole passenger as he left the jet.

They had been told the plane would be required for a flight back to Corpus in three days, perhaps two. They were to keep themselves available to fly Tanner back to Texas when his work—whatever that was—was completed. The main discussion between the two captains on the flight over the Gulf was deciding whether to take a car and drive an hour to a beach or to spend the day at one of the many amusement parks in the area.

May 31, 2022
Orlando International Airport, Florida

Josh Tanner used his throw-away phone to call the number Nicholas Schumer had given him. The call was answered after the first ring. The voice surprised him. It was low, sultry, and female.

"Hello, Mister Tanner. I've been expecting your call. Our mutual friend told me you were coming."

It took a long second for Tanner to find his voice. "Uh, then you know what I need?"

"Come on, Josh," the sexy voice responded mockingly. "Would I have answered your call otherwise?" There was a slight chuckle, "I was told the man who will be the recipient of my skills was somehow able to eliminate my old compatriot, J.P. Pearson. Now J.P. was not exactly a rookie. But, I have certain attributes that allow me to get a bit closer to my target."

Tanner had already figured out for himself. He was struggling to sound confident and unperturbed. "Well, Miss…"

"Come on, Josh. Do we have to play these games?"

"No."

He could tell she was mildly annoyed. "My name doesn't matter, Josh. All that matters is that your boss has already placed a sizable contribution to my retirement fund in a Cayman Islands bank account. Since the money is already there, I've already completed the first step in earning my fee. Your employer told me this man is a reporter for The Journal of International Tech Research and Development whatever the hell that is. I probably don't have to tell you it's a little embarrassing that most people of your gender will answer any question if it's asked with a sexy enough voice."

Tanner wisely chose not to respond.

"An hour ago, I called that august publication and asked for the managing editor's office. His secretary, a lady, answered and she could not have been less helpful. I told her I was from the NASA public affairs department and needed to speak to the editor. She reluctantly put me through. When he came on, I also told him I was from the NASA public affairs department. I just said we had neglected to find out where Cam Forsyth was staying in the local area and needed to contact him. It didn't take him thirty seconds to give me his cell phone number, his hotel and even his room information. He also thought he was reminding me that Mr. Forsyth is sitting in the observation room of the control center at that moment. I thanked him and he very nicely invited me to stop by the magazine the next time I'm in New York."

She laughed. "Guess when I eliminate his ace reporter, that invitation will be rescinded."

The mystery woman again laughed before continuing. "You know, Josh, the internet is a wonderful thing. I got on the magazine's website and found a picture of our guy. Now, here's the good news. I've been sitting in a parking lot where I can see every car going to his hotel." She gave him an address. "So, rent a car, drive to this address, and join me here. If I move, I'll let you know. Now, sweet thing, get moving."

"How will I know who you are?"

"Aren't you cute. Don't you think I know what you look like? Just come to the address I gave you. You won't be stood up. I promise."

She hung up.

The master schedule at Winter Triangle Physics showed Tanner's week had been cleared of all meetings and obligations, and Red had him logged as *Personal Time Off—Vacation.* Since one of the biggest perks of employment for executives was use of a corporate jet for a vacation each year, even that trip could be explained if necessary. As far as Winter Triangle Physics was concerned, Tanner was visiting Florida to enjoy the beach.

May 31, 2022
Titusville, Florida

Tanner had used his personal credit card instead of the company one to rent a car and was on the road in fifteen minutes. He had flown into Orlando instead of closer to the Space Center so he would have plausible deniability he was anywhere near Cam Forsyth when the hit took place. Pretending to be in Orlando made sense and it was easier to hide in a giant airport. The small airports closer to where Forsyth was would definitely remember a new corporate jet landing there—Orlando International Airport wouldn't.

It only took an hour to drive from the Orlando airport to Forsyth's hotel near the space center. He pulled into the hotel parking lot and found an empty slot on the back row. He looked left and right without knowing exactly who he was searching for. Suddenly a quiet tap on the passenger window startled him.

Looking at him was a gorgeous brunette with stunning blue eyes and immaculate makeup. Her red lipstick drew his eyes instantly and served to accent her perfect smile. The next thing he noticed were her deep-set dimples. Tanner couldn't help himself. He stared at the goddess before him.

"Josh," she said quietly, "do you mind unlocking the door so I can get in?"

"Sure," was all he could think to say. He pressed the button to release the lock.

The lady gracefully slid into the seat and placed her handbag on the floorboard. As she did, Tanner found himself torn between looking at her long tanned legs which were covered only by the shortest of skirts and the obviously unencumbered breasts beneath her blouse.

"First things first, Josh. My eyes are up here. Next put these on." She handed him a pair of latex gloves. "Now, let's go sit in my car. It's parked where we can see the driveway and yet it's blocked from the outside security camera."

As they walked to the second car, the woman put latex gloves on, too. "You're putting gloves on in your own car?" he asked astounded.

"What makes you think it's my car? I stole it this morning. It's a beauty though. Might actually buy myself one after this job."

About the same time Tanner was reaching the hotel parking lot, Cam and Melissa Forsyth were preparing to leave Kennedy Space Center. The observation room behind the LCC had rapidly cleared out as Sojourner was reaching its stabilized orbit. The craft had been in orbit for an hour when a second burn of the shuttle engines pushed her into final orbit. Since all of the monitoring and control was now in the hands of the MCC in Houston, activity in Florida was pretty much completed.

Meanwhile, life on the Sojourner was a flurry of activity. Seats for the non-flying crew were removed from their attach points and been stowed. This opened up all the work spaces on both levels of the shuttle. The critical action of opening the bay doors occurred soon afterwards.

Cam Forsyth had been riveted to his seat in the observation area with a laptop computer perched on his legs. Without looking at the screen, Forsyth had been typing almost nonstop since joining his sister, Melissa, and Dr. Marlo Campbell two hours before. He had already chronicled everything he had seen and felt starting from breakfast with the crew until he was escorted into the observation room prior to the launch. He knew he would revise and edit the document a dozen times before he submitted it to the magazine later tonight, but for now, he could savor the moment with his sister and their friend.

"Marlo, Mel and I are going to find the best steak house in town and celebrate. Come along and bring that guy you're dating. It's on my company expense account so we'll go big. Who's the lucky guy? You know your folks will ask me when we get back to Exeter tomorrow."

Marlo Campbell rarely dated anyone who wasn't from Exeter, but occasionally went out with what they called an 'outworlder'. "He's nice. The guy's an airline captain but I think he's on a trip."

"Well, since he's a pilot, he needs to meet Prince Isha. They could amuse themselves for hours talking all that pilot stuff. On second thought, I'm not sure I could stand that."

Campbell looked at the calendar on her smartphone. "You're off the hook, Cam. He's halfway across the Atlantic on his way to Madrid. Anyway, I'm going to pass, too. It's been a long day."

Cam made a mental note that Marlo was interested enough in this guy to keep his flying schedule on her calendar. He decided not to mention that detail to her parents.

"Cam," Melissa said as they walked to their rental car, "I got to sleep all the way here today while you drove. Then I got to nap in Marlo's office until we could go to the observation room. You were working. So, I'm far more rested. I'll drive."

Cam tossed her the keys in response.

Melissa drove the fifteen minutes to their hotel in almost total silence. The past several days had been intensely difficult for Cam and even for a man as powerful as he, the cumulative effects were taking their toll. He fell asleep before she had driven five miles, and he remained asleep until they pulled into the hotel parking lot. Melissa could have used the valet service, but saw an open parking spot and impulsively pulled in there. She parked carefully because the lot had just been repaved and there were no stripes to mark the spaces.

The car's engine had been the perfect white noise for Cam Forsyth as he slept. As Melissa turned the key and stopped the motor, he roused and felt strangely refreshed and alert. He glanced at his watch and saw that it was 4:00 p.m. He got out of the passenger seat and stretched his tight leg muscles.

Movement caught Cam's eye as he looked across the roof and over Melissa's shoulder. What he immediately noticed was an unbelievably gorgeous lady walking towards his rental car. The woman walked with the poise of a runway model and was carrying a designer bag that matched the color of her very short dress. He also noticed in passing that there was man walking slightly behind her. He seemed vaguely familiar, but for some reason, Cam didn't pay him much attention.

Before getting out of the driver's seat, Melissa had pushed a button on the console and remotely opened the trunk. She then walked around the back of the car to grab her small suitcase. She, too, noticed the lady, but her first thought was that the woman was probably a prostitute walking with her customer to his room in the hotel.

The Protector from Exeter came to the trunk to help his sister with their luggage. He was just reaching in when the woman spoke.

"Hello, Cam." Her voice was soft and seductive.

As her brother turned to respond, Melissa was the first to see the would-be temptress had reached into her bag and removed something besides a cell phone. She was holding a Glock 43 that had been matched with a silencer. When she pulled the trigger, the silencer wouldn't completely eliminate, but, would largely mute, the sound of the 9mm subsonic ammo she had chosen.

The assassin's planning and weapon meant no one in the hotel parking lot distinctly heard a sound as she pulled the trigger…twice.

In the split second before the shots were fired, Melissa recognized the pistol was not pointed at her, but was aimed directly at her brother's chest. Without thinking about it, she shoved Cam out of the way just as the first bullet was leaving the muzzle. She didn't initially feel the bullet enter her upper right arm. It went straight though without hitting any major blood vessels and was later recovered from a palm tree planted next to the parking lot. The second bullet, fired a split second later, wasn't as kind. It struck behind Melissa's injured right arm, entered her upper back, tore through her lung, and flung her violently to the ground.

It only took Cam Forsyth a split second to react after his sister had protected his body by sacrificing her own. The mysterious woman was already reacting too, and was shifting her aim to again fire at her intended target.

That split second was all it took.

As Cam was jumping from the pavement back to his feet, he grabbed a handful of gravel from the recent repaving job and hurled the rocks at the assassin's face with all his strength. Even a heartless killer has reflexes and this woman's reflexes were better than most. She couldn't stop her brain from involuntarily turning her face away from the rocks that were already pelting her. Blindly, as she reacted, she continued to pull the trigger three more times. None of the bullets went anywhere near Cam Forsyth. Unfortunately for Josh Tanner, one errant bullet struck him just above his right eye. He was dead before his body hit the ground.

Cam ignored the flurry of bullets as he tackled the lady. Her head hit the asphalt with a crunch, but still she tried to turn the gun on the man who was already supposed to be dead. Cam knew Melissa had been shot and he wanted this over quickly so he could help her.

He slammed his cupped hands over the ears of his would-be assassin. The intense pain of having her eardrums ruptured lasted just a second. The pain was ended as the Protector seized her head. With a strength born of fury, Cam violently twisted the woman's head far beyond its normal rotation. There was an audible crack and the woman instantly went limp. Her lips involuntarily moved silently and her beautiful blue eyes were wide open in shock. Within seconds, she joined the multitude whose lives she had cut short.

A glance at Josh Tanner told Cam the man was no longer a threat. All of his attention was directed to his sister. He rolled Melissa over on her left side to stem the blood flow from her chest and back. She was unconscious and had a weak pulse. But she had a pulse. Her arm wound was bleeding steadily but not pulsing with each heartbeat. Cam knew from this her brachial artery had not been hit. However, the frothy blood ebbing from the chest wounds told him her lung had been damaged. Calling on his years of Protector training, Cam quickly opened his suitcase and grabbed two thin plastic bags he used to transport his shoes. He emptied them and tightly held the plastic over both the entry and exit wounds.

Two men came running over. One had been waiting out front of the hotel for a taxi. The second man had been walking to his car. Both had seen the entire event.

Cam looked at the first one. "You! Call 911. Tell them we need the police and an ambulance. Tell them to prepare the hospital for a sucking chest wound." The man stood frozen in his place. Cam kicked out at him without letting go of his sister. "Do it!" he yelled. This time the man responded.

Cam told the second man to grab a t-shirt from the suitcase and use it as a bandage to put direct pressure on Melissa's arm wound. There was only a slight hesitation which Cam recognized. "Listen, mister, roll the shirt thick and wrap it around her arm. She's not bleeding bad enough for her blood to go through the cloth. You won't actually touch any of her blood." The man's eyelids blinked quickly as if he were making an instantaneous decision. He did as Cam had directed.

The man who was on the phone with 911 looked from Melissa to the other people laying on the ground, "Do we need an ambulance for these two?"

"No," was the simple reply.

Within one minute, a police car with siren blaring came screaming into the parking lot. It was followed three minutes later by an ambulance. Two paramedics from the Titusville Fire Department got their medical boxes from the ambulance and were by Melissa's side within seconds.

The senior paramedic, John Forrester, took charge of Melissa and told the second, Beja Clinton, to check the woman a few feet away. Forrester put an oxygen mask on his patient and started an IV with a sterile solution. He knew she had lost enough blood that fluid replacement was going to be crucial. The chest wound on his patient was by far the worst trauma. Nevertheless, he made a quick decision and first placed a sterile pressure bandage on Melissa's arm to replace the t-shirt being held there by an obviously shaken man. Forrester handled that wound first because he needed the civilian out of the way and the bandage only took a second to secure.

"You did a good job here," Forrester said to the man who was now seriously showing signs of shock.

"I only did what that guy told me to do," he responded nodding toward Cam. The man then sat down on the bumper of a parked truck and put his head down between his legs.

Forrester next directed Cam to remove his plastic bags and to move back. As Forsyth moved, the paramedic immediately secured an airtight bandage around Melissa's chest. Her breathing showed improvement right away. Forrester often saw civilians who were completely frozen by fear or shock when faced with an emergency medical situation. Very few people knew how to handle a chest wound. This man had cared for the patient's chest trauma while telling the other man how to handle the arm.

"Sir," he asked the man he'd replaced, "are you a paramedic, a nurse, or a doctor?"

"No," was the reply.

Forrester was too busy to follow up with any more questions.

Three feet away from Melissa, Clinton had already made her first assessment of the other two victims. One, the man, was quite obviously dead. A sizable portion of his frontal skull was in pieces and held only by skin and hair. His brain was largely missing. It didn't take a medical degree to determine this man was beyond care. Her second patient was a woman whose head wasn't quite in the right place. After failing to find a carotid pulse at the woman's neck, Clinton listened with a stethoscope to the patient's chest and heard nothing. Finally, she flashed a bright light into the woman's dilated eyes. Fixed pupils told the paramedic the woman did not need her attention any further either. Forrester looked at this partner, "Beja," he pronounced it Bay ha, "what's the word."

Baja Clinton shook her head at him, then at the policeman and moved to join Forrester with Melissa.

The policeman, whose name tag identified him as Mark Markham, had been the first on the scene. He had seen death many times before and the paramedic's pronouncement confirmed what he had already knew. Even though she was dead, the woman's lifeless hand was still holding a weapon. The cop had secured as best he could the crime scene and did not move the gun. Instead, he took a picture of the body. Evidence.

By this time, three more police cars had arrived and the two witnesses were being interviewed separately. Though neither had conferred with the other, their stories were basically the same.

It appeared that, as impossible as it seemed, the lovely lady and her accomplice had tried to rob the man and the wounded lady in broad daylight. They independently recounted how the woman had accidentally shot her own man while firing wildly. Finally, they told how the man who was about to be robbed had killed his attacker with his bare hands. They both admitted they had seen the whole thing but didn't approach until after the threat had been eliminated. The cops seemed to understand and didn't judge their discretion.

As the paramedics were loading Melissa into the ambulance, a detective named Jasper Priddy arrived on the scene. The detective didn't go to the parking lot. He saw the crime scene people doing their work there and wanted to let them finish uninterrupted. Instead, he carefully examined the exterior of the hotel then went in and found the manager. After showing his badge, Priddy asked the manager to see the security camera footage from the front of the building.

Cam was not allowed to travel with his sister to the hospital in the ambulance. Instead, Officer Markham drove him. It didn't take too much intelligence to know the police wanted to keep him under their control.

Ten minutes after the detective started reviewing the security camera video, he called Officer Markham who was now sitting with Forsyth in the emergency room waiting area. The phone call informed the cop he was no longer keeping Forsyth under surveillance. Instead he was now just sitting with a distraught brother.

About a half-hour later, Detective Jasper Priddy stopped by the hospital waiting room. After checking with the patient information desk, Priddy took Forsyth and Markham into a small conference room. He spent about fifteen minutes getting a statement from Forsyth which completely matched that given by the witnesses and the security camera. The incongruous part of the crime remained why a lady dressed to the nines and escorted by a businessman from Texas had attempted a robbery in broad daylight.

"Mr. Forsyth," Detective Priddy began, "you've told Officer Markham that you've never seen this woman before."

"That's correct." Cam was glad the detective had not asked about the man. Cam was certain he had seen the man before, but could not place him. Something in the back of his mind told Forsyth not to mention that detail.

Priddy just shook his head in confusion. After leaving his card with Cam and asking for a call if anything else came to mind, Detective Priddy left.

Back in the waiting room, Markham and Forsyth exchanged some small talk while waiting for word from anyone about Melissa's condition. The officer eventually asked the question he had been avoiding. "Is there someone you need to call?"

"Not yet. There's nothing to say until there's something to say. I'm not going to tell my parents about my sister until I know the whole story."

Markham nodded his understanding.

Almost three hours passed before a tall man with glasses, a kind face, and a balding head came out of the ER. His surgical scrubs were covered by a white lab coat with a stethoscope in the pocket. Embroidered on the coat were the words Tom Lemlock, M.D. and under the name in a smaller font were the words "Emergency Medicine". His calm demeanor and air of authority were the result of his years of experience and his keen intellect. As an ER physician, Lemlock had seen more trauma in a week than most doctors saw in their entire career. Instead of becoming calloused and numb to the never-ending flow of patients presenting with damage caused by auto accidents, gunshots, and critical medical issues he instead still found the challenges he faced each shift as an opportunity to serve and to heal.

The doctor walked directly to the man whose clothes were heavily stained with blood. "Sir, are you with the woman who was shot?"

Forsyth didn't trust his voice. He just nodded his head then quietly answered, "She's my sister."

"Sir, I'm Tom Lemlock. I was the doctor who saw you sister in the emergency room. I didn't do her surgery, but that doctor has been called back for another emergency operation so she asked me to come see you.

"Your sister is stable. She had two wounds. The first one went through her right bicep. It was clean and didn't hit any major blood vessels. She'll need physical therapy to regain strength in her arm, but it'll heal with no problems. The second wound was obviously far more serious. It appears the bullet entered under her right arm, broke the seventh rib, made quite a mess of her lung, then took out the inferior angle or bottom of her right scapula. When your sister arrived, she had what's called a tension pneumothorax. That's what happens when air can come into the chest, but not be expelled normally. The chest becomes almost like a balloon. When it's filled with air, it pushes the lung, heart, and central chest structures to the opposite side. Once we relieved that problem, your sister's condition improved immediately. Now, we've been able to get all her internal bleeding under control and I have every confidence she'll make a full recovery. Don't get me wrong, it's going to be a pretty long recovery, but she's going to be okay."

"Thank you, doctor. I'm very grateful."

"My pleasure, sir. I do have two observations. First, your sister is here and is going to live largely because of your emergency first aid. The paramedics told me how you sealed the chest wound. You probably saved your sister's life. Second, both of the other people from the scene went straight to the morgue.

"My first specialty was spinal orthopedics. I was asked to come down there to take a look at the body of a woman. The paramedic also told me she was the one who shot your sister and that you put her down. I've never ever seen such a clean break of the spine at the C2 vertebrae. Such a break is sometimes called a hangman's fracture for pretty obvious reasons. I'm not sure who taught you emergency medicine and self-defense, but you, sir, are a very formidable man."

The doctor looked over his shoulder to an ER aide. "Would you please get this gentleman a set of scrubs. I think his clothes are pretty much ruined and he doesn't need to be wearing these a minute longer."

He turned back to Cam. "Your sister will be in recovery for a while, then we'll move her to ICU. She'll stay there a day or two. You can see her when we get her to ICU in, say, four hours. In the meantime, try and get some rest."

He looked at the other man. "Officer, is this man your prisoner?"

"No, doctor. He's not. My supervisor said two eye witnesses have reported it was self-defense and the hotel security camera clearly showed Mr. Forsyth was defending himself and his sister. Actually, I got off duty an hour ago but I decided to hang around until we got your report."

Dr. Lemlock's kind face showed both compassion and concern. "Well, Mr. Forsyth, you can rest easy knowing your sister will be fine and it's because of you. Now, trust me, there's nothing you can do here for a few hours. Go get some rest."

Contrary to department regulations, the officer put Forsyth into his patrol car and drove him back to the hotel. The crime scene was still taped off, and therefore his suitcase inaccessible. That wasn't a major problem. The scrubs he was wearing were clean and the front desk had complimentary shaving cream, razor, and a small stick deodorant.

Chapter Twenty-Three

While in the hospital waiting room, Cam had decided not to call his parents to tell them about Melissa until he knew the outcome of her surgery. Now that he was finally in his hotel room and he knew she was stable, it was time to call home.

It was 8:30 p.m. in Florida which meant it was 6:30 in Exeter. Without really thinking about it, instead of calling his parent's number, he called Prince Isha. The phone was answered almost immediately by Isha's wife, Deidre, the Princess of Exeter.

"Cam, how nice to hear from you. We watched the launch with your parents today. It was so exciting!"

"Ma'am, may I speak to the Prince, please?"

There was something in his voice that chilled Deidre to the core. "Of course. Just a moment."

Within seconds, Isha was on the line. There was no exchange of niceties. "What's wrong, Cam?"

"Sire, there's a hard situation here and I need your help." The term "hard situation" was used among Protectors to describe a dangerous or challenging event. "Melissa and I were attacked this afternoon, and she's been shot."

"Cam…"

"The doctors said she's going to be okay, but I wanted to let you know. Since the King and my dad are friends, I was kind of hoping he could be there when I call."

"Stay on the line," was the terse response.

Forty-five seconds later a new voice came on the phone. It was that of Annu, King of Exeter.

"Cam, I'm sorry to hear about Melissa. She's very precious to me. My prayers are with her and all the medical people who are taking care of her." For Annu, this comment was not simply perfunctory. His faith was strong. "Tell me everything that happened."

Over the next several minutes, Forsyth recounted, with absolute clarity, the events of the day. He ended with, "The police are treating this as a daylight robbery gone awry. But it wasn't. The woman looked like she was headed to model in a fashion show which sure doesn't fit the crude robber image. Also, and I had forgotten this until just now, she said my name as she walked up. Obviously, I was a target and Melissa stopped her from killing me."

The deep fatigue and shock of the day was being overtaken by anger and the need for revenge. "Sire, there's only one person I know who wants me dead. This is the second attempt on my life in the past week."

Prince Isha, who was still on the line and listening in, interrupted, "Cam, I told my father all about your encounter in Corpus Christi. He also knows about our visit to Winter Triangle Physics."

At the mention of Winter Triangle Physics, the mystery of the man Cam couldn't identify in the parking lot was solved. "Shit. Sorry sir. I just connected a big piece of the puzzle. When everything was happening, I didn't have time to put it all together. Isha, do you remember that man who came into Schumer's office while we were waiting to see him? That's the guy who was with the woman who shot Mel. The woman's gun got away from her and she accidentally took him out. After that, I didn't pay him too much attention but now I'm sure it was him."

"Don't worry, Cam. You know he wasn't the actual one who ordered the attacks. You and I will make another visit to that place soon."

King Annu stopped that train of thought immediately by saying, "We'll look into that after Melissa is out of the hospital and Terry has landed from her mission. I give you my word this will be dealt with, but in its time."

"Of course, Sire."

The King continued, "Cam, this is completely your decision and I'll go along whatever you decide, but perhaps I should be the one to talk to your parents. Hearing news like this is sometimes easier in person instead of over a phone call. I'm sure they'll call you immediately but, by then, we'll have a good support system around them."

There was a pause as Forsyth considered the King's proposal. "Thank you, Sire. I believe you're right. I'm sure they'll take it better from you in person than they would from me over a phone call. Thank you, sir." The Protector continued, "While you go see them, I'm going to look into plane tickets for them. I'm sure they'll want to be here with Melissa."

Prince Isha responded, "Cam, while you were talking to my father and me, Deidre was on another phone line. There will be a corporate jet waiting at the Santa Fe airport in an hour and a half. The pilots will have already filed a flight plan and will be ready to fly to Florida. Also, someone here, I don't know who, has already located a private resort condo there in Titusville. They are taking care of renting it right now. Your parents don't need to be staying at the hotel where Melissa was shot. This will be much nicer than the hotel anyway. They said it comes with a chef and cleaning staff so that'll be one less thing to be concerned with. Do you still have a rental car?"

"Yes, sir. The police released the car a few minutes ago," Cam said immediately. "Sire, I don't know what to say. You're being too generous."

Isha ignored him.

Deidre handed Isha a piece of paper which he read quickly. "The couple that owns the resort are named Roy and Marie Colenart. It's 8:45 there. Right?"

"Yessir."

"We're texting you the address and contact information right now. The Colenarts are expecting your call. Let them know when to meet you at the condo to give you keys. Check out of the hotel and go on over there. Deidre told the Colenarts you wouldn't need the chef and staff until tomorrow, so grab a burger on your way over tonight."

"Sir, I can't afford all this and I don't want to take advantage of you and the King."

Isha ignored this comment, too, and continued on, "Deidre said we have the condo for three weeks. That'll cover the two weeks Terry is in space plus an extra week to relax after the shuttle lands so she can join us between debriefings. If we need it longer, we'll take care of that later. Deidre has just completed the rental details. We should be there in five or six hours. Can you think of anything else?"

"We?"

The Prince answered, "Cam, if you've proven anything to us, it's that you cannot be trusted to stay out of trouble when left alone. The resort has six bedrooms. Deidre and I will be with your parents in the plane. I'm planning on bringing a couple more Protectors with me. So far, the two attempts on your life have been unsuccessful. But, what if there's a next time and, instead of one person, there are two or three or four?"

Using a football analogy, Isha continued, "I'd feel better if there is a little depth to your backfield. From now until the King allows us to settle accounts with that smug bastard in Corpus, there will always be one or two Protectors with you at all times. Don't disagree with me, Cam. I'm your prince and this is not open to debate."

There was a subtle joke in that last comment, but Forsyth knew it was really not open to debate. The Prince had spoken.

"Yes sire. I understand. I have to admit, while sitting in the hospital this afternoon, I was thinking about the same scenario you mentioned. If Melissa, who is not a Protector, had not shoved me, I'd be lying on a slab in the basement cooler of the same hospital she's recovering in right now. Perhaps having a little adult supervision for me would be a good thing."

"There's no need to make this a high-profile operation. Let's keep it friendly. Your parents told us you visited a couple of ne'er-do-well Protectors before your trip. I'm going to see if they want to take a small vacation to Florida."

It had only been two days since Cam and Melissa had been with their friends, but it seemed weeks ago. "You know, sire, I've known Kevin and Kristi for years, and I like Celia and Rob a lot. Plus, those kids are wonderful. But I don't want them in any danger."

"Danger? What I'm proposing is three weeks of all of us soaking up a little sun, living in a nice condo, having a private chef to indulge our whims, and letting Melissa recover in a nice place.

"If you should need to leave the condo, your Dad, Kevin, Kristi, or I will just happen to need to go, too. There's no babysitting there."

Isha did a quick mental calculation and changed the subject. "With all of us from Exeter, plus Melissa when she gets released, and you, there will be ten folks staying there. If Melissa needs a hospital bed, we can have one delivered. Now let's get off the phone. I have some details to iron out."

"Thank you, sir."

There was no reason to argue with the Prince. Cam accepted the help as a fait accompli. He was amazed how quickly things could be arranged when you have money and people to make things happen. The plane and condo would have taken most people hours to arrange. The royal family of Exeter had it done in fifteen minutes.

Isha glanced at his watch. It was at 6:50 p.m. in Exeter, which meant it was 8:50 p.m. in Florida. It had already been a long and eventful day.

Prince Isha next called Kristi in her family chambers. He explained the situation and asked if they would go.

"What about Emmy?"

"I'll get Emmy a pass from her Protector training. You and Kevin can use the time to teach her some survival skills in the water and around the dunes. She won't miss too much anyway. Besides, Aiden will get some beach time in."

"Yes, sir. I'll start packing right now."

Isha had already thought about that. "Listen. Time is pretty short before we need to leave. We don't have time to pack enough for the whole three plus weeks, so just pack enough clothes for a few days. All of us will need more clothes and stuff once we're settled. We'll buy everything there. Time is more important than right now. We need to takeoff as soon as possible."

"I understand, Sire," was Kristi's response.

The details for getting to the airport were worked out.

Next Isha called his best friend, Kevin. That call was over in five minutes. Isha would call again from the airplane when they were an hour from landing at Meacham Field in Fort Worth. An hour would give Kevin and Celia time to leave home and to be at the airport when the jet landed.

Packing was easier for Kevin and Celia since they had several hours to prepare, but Isha made the same promise to take care of needs once in Florida. Everyone understood that the Prince did not want to delay the flight. He wanted the Forsyths with Melissa and Cam as soon as possible.

While Isha was setting up the trip with the other Protectors, King Annu visited the chambers where Moses and Tame Forsyth lived. They had one daughter who had been in space for just a few hours. Now their King was visiting, not as a sovereign but as a friend, to tell them their other daughter was in the hospital because of a gunshot wound. His assurances of the doctor's prognosis only mildly comforted them. As predicted, the first phone call after the King's arrival was to Cam.

Fortunately, their son had decided not to return to the hospital. A call to the ICU nurses station assured him that Melissa was asleep and stable and they discouraged visitation that late in the evening.

Forsyth called the condo owners and met them at 9:30. The facility had just been built and the owners had not expected it to be rented until a month later. Since the resort was ready early, the Colenarts were excited to have both condos unexpectedly leased for three weeks.

The resort had been designed for use by two different groups. Each condo had a master suite and two smaller bedrooms. The two resorts had common access between them so combining them into one large resort was easy.

Forsyth moved his suitcases into the smallest bedroom, and Melissa's into the one that was closest to the master suite their parents would occupy. In the other condo, he planned for Prince Isha and Lady Deidre to be in the master suite. The two other protectors and their spouses would each have their own bedrooms and the children would sleep on couches in the living area.

Fifteen minutes after Cam had everything planned, he was trying to fall asleep. It was not easy. Images of his sister's wounded body troubled his thoughts and plans of retribution towards the man behind her shooting flooded his mind. Schumer would soon experience a pain equal to the pain his sister would know in the coming weeks.

Forsyth intellectually agreed with the King that now was not the right time. But inwardly he vowed there would come a time when Protectors of Exeter would be free to bring punishment to the man who had tried twice to kill him and had almost killed his sister.

Cam finally fell asleep knowing his parents and his friends would be there in the morning.

May 31, 2022
Santa Fe, New Mexico Airport

The brand-new Gulfstream 650 was waiting outside the fixed base operations building when a stretch limo driven by a silver-haired man pulled up. Out of the back came six adults and two sleeping children. There were also several suitcases in the trunk.

The elderly driver had a lithely body that appeared to be incredibly fit and trim and he moved with the grace of a much younger man. Even though one would expect the driver of a limo to be responsible for unpacking the car, that was not the case this time.

The three men in the group made quick work of transferring the luggage to the plane where it was loaded and secured in the cargo area by an attendant. The driver of the car supervised. One of the men then addressed the driver.

"Tomás, I appreciate you driving us out here."

"My pleasure, sir. It got us a chance to get out of the house," came the reply.

At that moment, the front passenger door opened and out climbed Deidre's grandmother, Maria. She, like her husband, Tomás, was spry and seemed years younger than her actual age. She quickly hugged Isha and Deidre. She also gave loving hugs to Moses and Tame.

"I will be praying for all of your family until we are all back together in Exeter."

Finally, Maria looked to Kristi, Rob, and their sleeping children. "Keep those babies safe. Don't let them play too far from shore in the ocean." Once the perfunctory admonition had been made, the old woman hugged the adults and kissed the two sleeping children.

Isha quickly conferred with the two pilots to make sure all the details were in order and then made his pronouncement. "Wheels up in fifteen minutes. Let's all get on board."

Tomás and Maria drove away as the aircraft engines were starting. At that late time of the night, it took just a few minutes for the Gulfstream to taxi and takeoff.

Two hours later, during a thirty-minute stop in Meacham Field in Fort Worth, Kevin and Celia were added to the manifest. Shortly afterwards, the jet took off again.

It was 6:15 a.m. in Titusville, Florida at the Space Coast Regional Airport when the Gulfstream touched down on runway 18 made a left turn on taxiway A and taxied to the fixed base operator. Two vehicles, a Cadillac XTS and a Yukon XL Denali SUV were waiting. The SUV had been delivered with the correct child seats already installed for a six-year-old and a three-year-old. Isha, Deidre, and the Forsyths took the Cadillac while the families were assigned the van.

It took thirty minutes to reach the resort. Even though it was only 7:00 a.m., the chef was already there and had prepared a full breakfast. Everyone had been able to grab several hours sleep on the plane and the smell of frying bacon and eggs acted as an alarm clock. The whole group was instantly wide awake and ready to eat.

Chapter Twenty-Four

June 1, 2022
Titusville, Florida

While the group was devouring their breakfast, Cam was bringing everyone up-to-speed on the events the previous day. The chef, a genial fellow named Raul, had made smiley-faced pancakes for the children and they were eating on the veranda overlooking the beach and the Atlantic Ocean. Emmy was reading Aiden some favorite books that had been brought for their entertainment.

They were out of earshot as Isha described the attack in great detail.

Moses wanted to make sure of one point. "Son, are you convinced this attempt was somehow tied your experiences last week?"

"Dad, I am," came the simple reply. "The woman called my name as she was raising her weapon. I chose not to mention that detail to the police and so they're still treating it as a bizarre daylight robbery, but it wasn't."

"Why didn't you tell the police she knew who you were?"

"If I had, they would still be investigating me to see if I'm involved in any sinister activities that would warrant my elimination by parties unknown. I'd probably still be in some room at the police station answering probing questions instead of being here."

Moses Forsyth looked at Prince Isha. Both men silently nodded their heads at each other in silent agreement to Cam's judgement. "Sounds like good logic, son. The police aren't looking at any charges against you?"

"Not a chance. The two witnesses and the hotel security cameral all confirm it was self-defense. I've given the police my cell phone number and this address so they can find me if necessary, but that's all they asked for."

Isha addressed the one fact that had escaped everyone except Cam, "Let's just hope they don't do a search for your name in a national crime database. If they discover there was an assassination attempt on your life a week ago, they might decide you are a lightning rod for bad people." The prince laughed, "Heck, I'm not sure you *aren't* a lightning rod for bad people."

Deidre just shook her head at her husband.

The subject was quickly changed. "Dad, should we tell NASA about Melissa so they can pass the information along to Terry officially or should we tell her using our private device?"

Moses Forsyth had already considered that question. "We're not going to tell her privately using our communication device because it would inevitably reveal its existence."

That settled that question. Then, as was his habit when making a difficult decision, Moses verbalized a few questions to himself and then answered them as well. It was his way of looking at a problem from different perspectives.

"Is there anything she can do from up there? No. If we tell her, will her inevitable worry affect her work on orbit? Probably, yes. Will not telling her affect anything that happens down here? No." The Elder had already made his decision. "We're not going to tell NASA and we're going to keep Terry in the dark until she lands. She's going to be pissed then, but I'll jump off that bridge when we get to it."

Once everyone had completed breakfast, the three Forsyths left to see Melissa in the hospital ICU. Prince Isha decided to tag along.

Melissa was awake but groggy when her family entered the glassed walled enclosure of ICU. Isha decided to stand in the hallway that led to the area. Earlier that morning, nurses had removed Melissa's ventilating tube and begun the process of bringing her out of the induced sleep she had been in since surgery the day before. Now she was aware of her surroundings, but was surprised to see her family there. Time had stopped for her the previous afternoon and Melissa had no idea how long she had been in the hospital.

Not surprisingly, drugs had fogged Melissa's memory, but after a while her eyes seemed to clear up and she looked intently at her brother. "Cam, that lady was going to shoot you, wasn't she? She didn't, did she?"

"Nope, Sunshine, she didn't shoot me. You saved my life." Cam leaned in close to his sister's ear. "Thank you," he whispered.

Melissa smiled wanly and immediately fell asleep. The ICU charge nurse stuck her head in and gave the family an update. She assured them her patient was doing well and would sleep most of the day. She suggested they come back in the evening.

June 1, 2022
Winter Triangle Physics

In Corpus Christi, Linda Boltey had just put her purse in a desk drawer and was reaching for her first cappuccino of the day in preparation for whatever might come. After work the previous evening, she and Red O'Callaghan had decided to take advantage of happy hour at their favorite bar. Linda's drink of choice had been a nice chilled chardonnay while Red had ordered a vodka and grapefruit.

With Josh Tanner out of town, Red was ready to celebrate. Two beautiful single ladies in a bar drew a lot of attention and never ending offers for free drinks. Despite the drinks and several charming opening lines from different well-tanned and muscular patrons, neither lady found a reason to stay late in the bar. They both had work in the morning

Like most large corporations today, WTP had an automated phone system where a synthetic voice prompted callers to press different numbers to navigate eventually to a real person. However, WTP also had an unlisted direct number that would bypass the synthetic voice and go straight to a receptionist. Linda Boltey was sipping her cappuccino when the direct phone line rang. She answered with the slight Texas accent that made callers glad they had reached her.

"Winter Triangle Physics. This is Linda. How may I direct your call?"

"Ma'am, this is Detective Priddy of the Titusville, Florida police department. I need to speak to someone who can answer some questions about a Mister Joshua Tanner."

Boltey responded quickly. "Just a moment please. I'll connect you with his assistant." She put the caller on hold and quickly pressed in a three-digit number. It was answered immediately. "Red, I've got some police officer on hold. He says he needs some information about Tanner. Want me to put him through?"

Red responded with a slight hesitation. Inwardly she was thinking *What has that bastard gotten himself into.* But she instead said aloud, "Sure, Linda. Put him through." A moment later the click in her headset let her know the call had been transferred. "Good morning. This is Anastasia O'Callaghan. I'm Mr. Tanner's assistant. How can I help you?"

"Ms. O'Callaghan, I'm Detective Jasper Priddy of the Titusville, Florida police department. We got this phone number from a business card in Mr. Tanner's wallet. I'm very sorry to tell you he was killed late yesterday afternoon here in Titusville." Priddy waited a moment to let his words sink in before continuing. "We have his Texas driver's license with a picture of him, so the department feels confident in the identification of the victim. Can you verify that Mr. Tanner was indeed in Florida yesterday?"

The shock of the pronouncement had not fully hit Red, but she nonetheless responded. "Mister Tanner's on vacation there. He got to Florida yesterday morning."

The police had found a key in Tanner's pocket and used it to search out his rental car. The vacation story and chronology jived with the rental papers they found in the glove compartment.

"Can you tell me if he knew a Miss Samantha Holder?"

Red efficiently opened her boss' contacts file. "I don't see anyone by that name in his listings. But these are just business contacts. I can't say if he knew her outside of the office."

The police were still trying to figure out Tanner's part in the shooting the previous afternoon. The two witnesses and the video tape both confirmed he was walking with the female shooter, but nothing else made sense. He was not armed and he was carrying identification that indicated he was some sort of business executive. To further confuse the matter, he was on the receiving end of a 9mm bullet fired by the woman he was apparently escorting.

It had taken a few hours to identify the shooter as Samantha Holder. She had been on the FBI's radar for several years, and, if their dossier on her was even partly correct, was a highly effective assassin. They had never been able to gather enough evidence to arrest, much less convict, her. Making prosecution even more difficult, there were never any witnesses alive to pick her out of a lineup. Her beauty made her stand out in a crowd of fifty. A line up of ten would have been a snap.

"Do you have any next of kin information?"

Next of kin? Hell no. No one would have stayed around long enough marry him much less have a child by him.

Red mentally chastised herself for having such thoughts about a dead man. "I know his parents are dead and he was an only child. He was never married or had any children I know about." Red thought about it for a moment and made a decision. "Detective Priddy, would you hold for a moment? I need to get someone else."

"Certainly."

Red put her line on hold and dialed the extension for Nicholas Schumer's assistant. "Is he in?" was all she asked.

"Sure, but he's busy."

"He'll want to take the call on line three. Mr. Tanner has been killed in Florida."

Within fifteen seconds the blinking light on line three went solid indicating it had been answered by Schumer.

Priddy, who had gotten used to hearing the sultry southern accented voices of Linda Boltey and Red O'Callaghan, was momentarily taken back by the next voice he heard.

"Who is this and what the hell happened?"

"Sir, I'm Detective Priddy of the Titusville, Florida police department. Who am I speaking to?"

"My name is Schumer. I'm the president of Winter Triangle Physics and Josh Tanner's boss. Now, tell me what the hell happened."

Priddy knew instantly he didn't like the man on the other side of this conversation. "Mr. Schumer, I'm not at liberty to discuss the details because it's still under investigation. I can tell you that Mr. Tanner was killed yesterday by a gunshot during what we think was a robbery."

"Don't give me that 'under investigation' bullshit, detective. Who shot Tanner and is that person in custody?"

It took considerable effort on Priddy's part not to hang up. His professionalism won out. "Sir, I've given you all the information I'm at liberty to share. You may call the police chief if you wish. Perhaps he has more releasable information."

"I'll do that!" The line went dead.

Priddy walked down the hall until he reached the open office door of Police Chief Mario Salfonsi. The chief had his foot on the open bottom drawer of his desk and was leaning back in his chair while reading a report of the previous day's shooting.

Priddy walked in and announced in his most cheerful voice, "Boss, unless I'm completely wrong—and I don't think I am—you're about to get a call from a," he referred to his notes, "Nicholas Schumer. He's the head of that company our male victim worked for. I gave him all the info I'm allowed and he threw a hissy-fit."

About that instant, the voice of the switchboard operator came over the chief's intercom announcing she had just dealt with a most obnoxious man who had demanded the chief's personal office phone number.

The chief looked at the phone as if looking for verification of what he had just heard. "My private number?" he asked incredulously.

"Yep. I told him I'm not allowed to release that. He gave me his phone number, ordered me to get your number and to call him back. Then he hung up. Just like that…he hung up on me," she said incredulously.

The chief looked at Priddy, quietly laughed, and just shook his head. "Detective, close my door and sit down. Let's enjoy this together." He got the man's number from the switchboard operator and thanked her for not being bullied into giving out his information.

The chief called the number he had been given and put his receiver on speaker phone. The call was answered before the second ring. Without preamble, the voice demanded, "Okay, what's your chief's number?"

Even with Priddy's warning, the man's arrogance was a surprise. "This is Chief Salfonsi from the Titusville PD. I understand you are interested in some additional information about your deceased employee."

"What the hell kind of name is Salfonsi?"

"Sir, my ancestry is Italian and not germane to this conversation. What information do you want that my detective was unable to give you?"

"All I know is my chief of staff was shot and killed yesterday. Did you catch the person who shot him?

"We have her," was the terse reply.

"Her?" Schumer felt a momentary thrill of concern as he considered the possibility his plan had been discovered. "Who was she? Did she say why she shot him?"

"No sir, she didn't speak to anyone after she shot him."

"What kind of amateur police force do you have there? Why haven't you gotten a statement from the bitch?"

Chief Salfonsi's mouth momentarily got the best of him. "Because her mouth and brain are no longer connected, Mr. Schumer. The woman who killed your employee had another intended victim who took umbrage to her attack and broke her neck with his bare hands. She died almost instantly."

Silence was all that the chief heard for several seconds. Then, "So, somehow Tanner got in the way of this alleged attack and got himself shot."

"Mr. Schumer, we have two eye witnesses who independently told us almost an identical recounting of the event. We also are in possession of sixteen minutes of security camera video that began when the intended victim arrived in the parking lot and ended when the crime scene personnel arrived. I don't know why your employee was killed. That's one of the things we're trying to determine."

"My attorneys will be contacting you. They will be my point of contact. I'm sure you'll make it a priority to keep them informed of the progress." Schumer hung up.

Chief Salfonsi sat in total silence for several seconds before speaking. "You know Jasper. I spent thirty years in law enforcement before deciding to retire in Florida. After being here about a year, someone on the city council heard about my time in uniform and visited me. Shortly afterward, this chief position was offered to me and was described as an easy and quiet job. In short, they lured me out of retirement. I messed up. I believed them. Instead of lounging on my boat and occasionally catching a fish or two, I'm here and listening to that SOB questioning my ancestry and denigrating my police force." The chief paused to carefully light the single cigar he allowed himself each day. As he inspected the burn, Chief Salfonsi continued, "I have come to the conclusion that Schumer guy is not a nice person." The chief took a contemplative puff on his cigar and chuckled. "He's the only man I've ever come close to suggesting he go perform an anatomically impossible feat on himself." He took a long and satisfying draw then slowly blew out the smoke. His anger and tension left him with the exhale. He raised the report he had been reading. "Okay, this preliminary report looks good. Please make sure I'm thoroughly briefed as the investigation continues. I have a feeling I'll be hearing from this man's representatives soon."

"Yes sir."

Chapter Twenty-Five

June 2, 2022
Shuttle Sojourner
Day 3 On Orbit

Day three of Sojourner's fifteen-day mission had passed with everything on schedule. The crew had settled into their work and sleep schedules. There had been the usual bouts of nausea and resulting vomit from a few crew members on day one. No one said anything about it because the situation was so common in microgravity. The symptoms almost always subsided within a day or two.

In the case of Sojourner's crew, everyone was back to normal except for Dr. L. Scott Elder. While everyone was enjoying the thrill of floating around the crew compartment and trying little games of floating tag, Elder was instead using handholds and equipment racks to pull himself around. No one had seen him even him attempt a single passage anywhere by floating there.

Earlier in the day, Ledwell and Weaver had made minor corrections to shuttle's orbit, and she was now exactly where programmed to be. The absolute perfect apogee and perigee were required for Elder's experiment to be run the next day. Time had been built into the tight schedule to ensure perfection in this positioning. Ledwell and Weaver had locked it in perfectly on their first use of the maneuvering jets. They pretended not to be surprised, but secretly, both were.

Several of the crew members were already busy with their individual and corporate projects. Jim Dalton, in his usual methodical and reasoned way, was calibrating the biomedical equipment he had designed. Patti Koch was interested in Jim Dalton's experiment. She had grown up in an area of Pennsylvania where people got severe frostbite every winter. When infection set in, many lost fingers, toes, noses and ears and Patti knew his work would have an application that would save those people.

"Tunes," she started off, "I know you're working on a synthetic skin of some kind. But, don't we already have that?"

"Yeah, we've had artificial skin for grafting burns since the 70's and, starting in the mid 80's, it was being used to help build ears and noses using cartilage as the foundation. Then stem cell research started expanding into creating actual replacement parts for the human body."

"Okay then, if we can do it on Earth, why do it in space?"

"Simple, cells expand in microgravity. If I can create a culture of super cells in microgravity that can then be replicated on Earth, we'll be able to giant step forward in a new-generation of skin grafts."

Koch, an astrophysicist, nodded her head in understanding...but in reality, had none. There weren't too many men in NASA who could match her intellect, but Tunes Dalton was one who did. They already had a successful off-the-clock relationship as Pickleball partners and it was her sincere goal to expand that athletic partnership into a more personal one. She was being patient and would wait until after the mission to begin her plan to charm Dalton.

Dr. Janelle McLain's experiments had also started producing significant results. NASA had long known that bone and cellular degeneration would be a factor on long-term space voyages in the decades ahead. Astronauts who had spent long periods aboard the International Space Station had suffered, to varying degrees, deterioration in both cellular structure and bone density. Before astronauts could be safely in space for a year or more on the planned missions to Mars, the cumulative effects on the body needed to be determined and nullified. In a sealed case, McLain was carrying numerous tissue and bone samples. Each sample had been subjected to a different potential therapy. Even on a fifteen-day mission, McLain believed there would be measurable variations in the samples that would provide insight into which therapies were showing promise.

Dr. Terry Lee's studies were scheduled for the second week on orbit. In the meantime, she and Lt. Colonel Tom Fredrick were busy helping Scott Elder prepare for the launch and positioning of the RePoGGS. The precision placement of his antenna array was the most critical factor in the initial success of the experiment.

Tomorrow, Fredrick and Elder would enter the payload bay and remove the experiment package from its lockdown mechanism. From her position in the upper level of the crew compartment, Lee would be looking down into the payload bay to monitor the process. After the men were clear of the bay and were moving their container into position, she would look through a sighting scope to direct them to the exact location they were to place it. Later, small maneuvering rockets attached to the experiment would fire to maintain the package in a geosynchronous orbit at precisely that spot.

The shuttle had been in its high orbit for nearly three days. With the first-generation shuttles, orbits were usually anywhere from 170 to 350 nautical miles from the Earth's surface. Sojourner was established at 406 nautical miles because Scott Elder's experiment required a very high Earth orbit.

Around 6:00 p.m. in Florida, Terry Lee was in what could best be described as a sleeping bag attached to the left bulkhead of the mid-level. Her schedule allowed for a one-hour nap and she was making full use of it. With her earbuds in, anyone who glanced at her would assume she was listening to music to drown-out the sounds around the shuttle. They would have been correct if Lee had not moved the switch of her music device to the third position. She was quietly carrying on a very quiet conversation with her mother. Both sides of the conversation were crystal clear.

"This is amazing, Mom. Right now, we're approaching Italy's coast. There's quite a bit of cloud cover down there, but a few minutes ago I was up on the flight deck I could easily see the whole United Kingdom and Ireland to the left and out front I could see Lisbon, Madrid, and Barcelona—all at the same time. That's when I came down here. Right now, we're doing an orbit about every ninety minutes so every forty-five minutes we have a sunrise or sunset!"

Tame Forsyth, fresh and relaxed after her earlier hospital visit with Melissa was sitting on the back veranda of the condo and watching the ocean waves breaking on the beach a hundred yards away. "Well, Baby, I know how you love your sunsets. How many times have you sent me a picture of some beautiful Montana sunset you were looking at from your ranch?"

"Yeah, but the sunsets in Montana are even more beautiful than up here… at least, they last longer," came her reply.

"Remind me again when you became a Montana lover?" Tame asked innocently.

"Took about a whole day after we moved there," Terry laughed. "Just can't beat the best."

"I'm sure your father—Remember him…He's an Elder of Exeter—will be pleased to know you've changed your team colors."

"Mom, I'll always be first and foremost from Exeter," was the exasperated reply. "But, you guys are the ones who recommended we expand our views and the Big Sky pretty much did that for us. I've even gotten used to the winters. Just before launch, I got an email from Mark and Karla Smolender. Remember them, Mom? You met them the last time you visited us in Bigfork. They're the folks who are our closest neighbors at the ranch. Mark told me the runoff from the snow melt has the Swan River flowing like mad. Karla has taken some pictures and videos to show me the next time we're up there in Bigfork."

"Yeah, I do remember meeting the Smolenders. They were a really nice couple," Tame responded a little too absentmindedly.

Her daughter immediately picked up on it. "What's the matter, Mom?"

The answer was quick, "Nothing. I'm a little tired is all. We had a long night." Tame decided a little bit of truth would be appropriate. "Believe it or not, I'm just a few miles from the Kennedy Space Center. Your Dad decided if I wouldn't come for your launch, I had to be here for your landing. King Annu and Prince Isha actually had us flown out here last night and they found us a beautiful place to stay right on the beach. So, your chicken Mom will be here when you land."

"Wow! That's wonderful—and really generous of them. I'm sorry Cam couldn't stay, too. I know he had to be back in New York the day after he went with us to the White Room."

"Oh, Cam will be here, too. He got permission to stay here in Florida. Maybe he's writing more about the Sojourner's maiden flight into space." Tame felt a little uneasy with her stretching of the truth but knew it was best.

"Is Melissa staying with y'all, too?"

"She's not with us right now, but she'll be here when you land. I promise."

"Great. Listen Mom, one of the other folks is coming down to take a nap, too. They'll be right next to me and carrying on a conversation with myself won't go over well. I'll talk to you later. Love you. Give my love to Dad, Cam and Melissa, too…and tell the royal family I really appreciate them getting you to Florida." There was one of Terry's characteristic giggles and the line went quiet.

The connection was broken as Terry moved the switch on her device to the fourth slot. She was immediately enjoying her playlist of Adele, Ed Sheeran, and Andrea Bocelli favorites. That playlist was a little eclectic she knew, but that's what she liked.

In Corpus Christi, Nicholas Schumer was deep in thought. With the RePoGGS on the Sojourner and ready to be deployed tomorrow, he should have been relaxing. However, the fact that Cam Forsyth had survived two attempts on his life by the best assassins money could buy troubled him somewhat, but he knew there was no proof that could tie him or WTP to those attacks. Schumer believed in a philosophy that when it came to the law, money could not buy protection, but money could buy politicians and bought politicians would provide protection. Schumer had bought and paid for a lot of politicians.

Starting tomorrow, he wouldn't need his Senators and Congressmen. Tomorrow, governments from all over the world would want to arrest him. The US would have to get in line with other panicked rulers in futile attempts to stop his crushing threat to their countries.

Melissa's recovery was nothing short of miraculous. When the Forsyths and Cam came to the ICU. Tom Lemlock there, too. Dr. Lemlock had been Melissa's ER physician and had kept up on Melissa's case, as he often did on trauma cases he had stabilized in the ER. The physician was studying Melissa's medical chart at the nurse's station and noticed Cam entering his sister's glass enclosed area. Lemlock assumed the other two people were his parents. The doctor replaced the record, thanked the nurse on duty, and walked to the small room.

Cam introduced Lemlock to his parents as the doctor who had saved their daughter's life. Without actually thinking about it, Tame Forsyth hugged the imposing man in the white lab coat. She left a telltale remnant of makeup and lipstick on his shoulder for which she apologized profusely. "Don't worry, Mrs. Forsyth. My wife, Cynthia, is a very trusting lady. She's seen similar things before on my coats." He smiled kindly at Tame. "Your daughter is showing remarkable progress. We'll keep her at least three or four more days to make sure there are no complications, but I feel confident she's in no longer in any danger."

His words were exactly what the Forsyths wanted to hear and Tame spontaneously gave him another hug.

Chapter Twenty-Six

June 3, 2022
Shuttle Sojourner -
Day 4 On Orbit

Tom Fredrick and L. Scott Elder were sitting in the suit-up area on the mid-deck level of the shuttle preparing for their spacewalk. Getting ready for the extravehicular activity had actually started nearly an hour before when the two men had started breathing one hundred percent oxygen through masks.

Scuba divers would understand the reason for this precaution. They all knew the danger of rapidly changing the pressure exerted on their bodies. For divers, rising too quickly from deeper water could result in nitrogen gas bubbles expanding in the diver's bloodstream. Those gas bubbles could cause severe reactions, even death. The exact same thing could happen to the astronauts if they went from the pressurized environment of the shuttle to the much lower pressure maintained in their space suits. Breathing one hundred percent oxygen would purge the body of nitrogen and prevent the threat.

Because of his experience on previous EVAs, Fredrick only took about fifteen minutes to suit-up. Elder required three quarters of an hour. On space shuttles, different modular units were designed to latch together. The lower body and upper body units were selected to fit astronauts of different heights. The arm units, gloves and helmets were also slightly different sizes to accommodate various sized astronauts. Underneath the actual space suit, each man was wearing what was essentially an adult diaper and a cooling suit that circulated cold water around their bodies. Their life support and communication equipment were carried in a large backpack. Once the parts were all connected, they formed a well-fitting space suit and backpack that would protect its wearer from the airless void and temperature extremes of plus 250 degrees in sunlight to minus 250 degrees in the shade of the shuttle.

Preparation for this moment had begun right after Elder had been added to the crew four months before. While in training, Fredrick and

Elder had spent much of their time in Houston at the Johnson Space Center's Neutral Buoyancy Laboratory. The world's largest indoor pool containing more than six million gallons of water was where astronauts practiced extravehicular activities or spacewalks. A full-scale model of the shuttle payload bay sat at the bottom of the forty-foot pool depth. It was there the two men rehearsed what would be their work once on orbit.

In training, Fredrick and Elder had worn modified space suits that were weighted to make them neutrally buoyant. This meant they could maintain their depth without rising towards the surface nor sinking and was as close to the feeling of weightlessness as could be duplicated on Earth.

Each man had spent more than two hundred hours in the pool practicing their spacewalk. Fredrick had the hardest task to master in the pool. During the space EVA, he would be wearing the Manned Maneuvering Unit to allow him unattached operations. Elder would be tethered to the shuttle with a 150-foot-long umbilical that would provide him with oxygen, electrical power and far greater security. He only had a small handheld maneuvering unit for small movements around the payload bay. For any greater distances, he would be tethered to Fredrick for towing by the MMU.

Anytime Fredrick and Elder were in the pool, a team of divers were always close at hand. Each diver wore scuba gear with full-face masks that contained microphones and earpieces to allow constant communication between the surface, the lead diver, and the astronauts. The team always stayed a discrete distance away to avoid inadvertently interfering with the training. Only the lead safety diver, Nic Oldman, remained close by the astronauts to handle immediate emergencies.

Oldman, whose ancestors had come to the United States from Sweden, had been a member of the Ohio State University swim team and that background had prepared him for his work at NASA. After only two years on the emergency dive group, Oldman's had earned a well-deserved reputation for having a cool head. He was hand-selected for the crucial position as NASA's head safety diver. In the water, he was the final authority regarding safe operations. Oldman personally checked the astronauts' suits before each training session in the pool. During the training cycle, Nic Oldman had twice stopped the session and returned the astronauts to the surface when the flight surgeon had been concerned with the information she was reading from Elder's biomedical sensors. Nic trusted the Flight Surgeon's judgement. After all, they had been married twenty-five years. Dr. Kim Oldman had grown up in Texas and met her husband at Ohio State. After medical school and her residency, the diminutive physician with the quick smile and even quicker mind recognized she would never be happy in a practice where she saw the same types of cases every day. She and Nic had realized NASA would be perfect for both of them.

The Oldman marriage was not unusual in NASA. There were actually several husband and wife teams working in different groups. It wasn't surprising given the long hours and commitment the organization required.

Fredrick didn't particularly like Elder, but decided small talk would at least make the time pass quicker. "So, Scott, did you know that during the Mercury, Gemini, and even Apollo missions, the space suits were customized for each astronaut. In fact, each astronaut had three suits—one for training, one for the mission, and a backup spare." Elder at least appeared to be listening. "Of course, once the space shuttle began flying with regularity, there was neither time enough nor the budget to continue using customized suits and things were changed to what you and I are wearing."

Elder would never admit to his pure ignorance about this bit of space history. He didn't like admitting ignorance about anything. He was the outsider and knew his truncated training had prepared him for only the most basic tasks during his spacewalk. In fact, Lt. Colonel Tom Fredrick was actually tasked with doing most of the actual work. Elder resented deeply being merely an onlooker to his own project.

Why the hell did Schumer force them to get me on this shuttle? he often thought to himself. *There is another launch in six months. I could have run this focused energy project by myself instead of having this military cretin do it for me.*

Fredrick decided to at least try to keep some conversation going. "Scott, obviously I know the mechanics of your work. I completely understand what procedurally we're going to accomplish out there. I still haven't really had the time for me to grasp the underlying theory. We're going to set up and deploy an array of focusing antennae and then calibrate their localizing sights. Somehow then they will then generate a beam of energy capable of being converted into electrical power back on Earth. Is that essentially it?"

When Elder didn't respond after several seconds, Fredrick silently decided he had had enough small talk with the arrogant little ass.

Finally, reluctantly, Elder responded, "Colonel, nuclear power plants have been seen as the long-term answer to the world's power gluttony. But, the problems with disposing radioactive waste make that a poor option for our ecological survival. So, right now when it comes to totally renewable energy we have two options. In some places, mostly in the desert southwest, there are fields of solar panels that charge batteries for use by associated communities. There are a couple of problems with these. First, they aren't effective at higher latitudes because the length of daylight hours is so short in winter. Secondly, during extended periods of heavy rain or thick cloud cover, there is enough disruption of sunlight to negatively affect solar array efficiency."

Elder's tone made it plain he felt like he was talking to someone total incapable of understanding, but he continued. "We also have giant wind farms where dozens of huge wind-powered turbines spin powering generators that create electricity. Again, these have some inherent problems. First, there is what is called visual pollution. People resent seeing a great amount of their surrounding landscape blocked by these mammoth windmills. Secondly, when the wind is calm, there is no generation. That makes both solar and wind power a little unreliable and makes communities have to be attached to traditional electrical grids, too."

Fredrick, who had grown up in Nebraska, knew well about the short winter days and about long periods without seeing the sun. He had also driven through areas of west Texas and seen hundreds of the massive wind driven generators—he agreed they ruined the beautiful landscape. He understood Elder's argument and was beginning to grasp why he had spent two months practicing setting up the array antennas in the water pool at the Houston Space Center.

"So, Scott. I get the problems of the current systems. What exactly will the arrays we put up out there do to solve those problems?"

Elder spoke as if to a college freshman instead of to a career military officer. "Okay, right now there are twenty-four satellites in geosynchronous orbit, plus some spares. Those satellites have very precise clocks and locations and kind of talk to each other and to ground stations. All of them are constantly updating their precise location. Each satellite also sends out signals that pinpoint their location." He stopped and looked carefully at Fredrick. "Got me so far?"

Fredrick, who had been using GPS receivers in supersonic jets, his car, his boat's fish-finder, and his hand-held hunting device for almost thirty-five years, nodded his head silently. "Keep going," he said patiently.

Elder continued on. "Receivers gather bearing and distance info from several satellites simultaneously. When the receiver takes that data from several satellites and then triangulates the positions from each, the receiver's location can be determined with a few inches of accuracy." Elder waited for the expected nod indicating Fredrick was paying attention.

"I'm still with you," Fredrick said while still trying to sound interested. He finally had Elder talking and didn't want to shut him down by pointing out that GPS fundamentals were common knowledge.

"Now, instead of sending location signals, picture satellites in high Earth orbit that will have access to solar energy every second of every day. That solar power in space can be intensified exponentially by means of internal transformers to create an electromagnetic generator capable of sending a power signal directly to Earth. Receivers on Earth will be able to translate that space-based power signal just like solar panels do today, but at hundreds of times greater efficiency. No more massive fields of solar panels and none of the inefficiencies I mentioned before. RePoGGS will be the first such focusing satellite.

"We're going to provide proof of concept focusing power from outside Earth's atmosphere. Her arrays will direct this concentrated power to receivers on the ground. If all goes as planned, by this time tomorrow, a corner of Nevada will be the first to be on an electrical grid powered from outer space.

"Well, that seems possible during the day," Fredrick responded, "but what about during night hours?"

"When our array works like we expect it to, there will be thirty-four additional satellites placed in geosynchronous orbit. Twenty-six of them will be placed in high Earth orbit and eight others in a far lower orbit. When the twenty-six high-Earth satellites are in place, at least half of them will always be facing the sun. These satellites will focus their energy towards the lower satellites which will then refocus and reflect that energy to the Earth stations. Despite the curvature of the Earth, there will never be a time when the low orbit satellites cannot receive direct energy from the high ones that are in sunlight. It's actually pretty simple physics, but it's a really important experiment."

"Okay, with RePoGGS we're taking care of the high-Earth orbit satellite. Where's the low-Earth satellite coming from?"

"For today's experiment we are going to use a dead satellite that's already in low orbit. It was a weather satellite, but has a reflective surface that was designed so its cameras could have a much broader range-of-view by focusing off the mirrors. There are actually nine other satellites that have ceased working but haven't been pulled back into the atmosphere to burn up. Any one of them would work and all of them are in the satellite's targeting database, but our expectations are that the one we've chosen will reflect well enough to prove our concept." Elder paused then unloaded his frustration. "I just wish everyone would give me a break for being here. I didn't choose the flight!"

Tom Fredrick nodded his understanding. "You know, Scott, when an experiment goes through the normal vetting process, everyone becomes totally involved in the whole project. Your abbreviated program bypassed all the normal protocols and nobody got to become familiar with your work. It's been difficult for everyone to accommodate something they didn't get to work on. I talked to some of the support engineers and even they are in the dark. It seems your company claimed proprietary control whatever the hell that is. It's not really you they resent. It's your boss, whoever he or she is. People don't respond well to politics invading their professional realms."

Silence was the response. Fredrick knew he had pissed off Elder, but he really didn't care. After their long EVA, all of Elder's experiments would be completed and he wouldn't have to talk to the jerk again until they landed…maybe not even then.

Their pre-breathing of 100% oxygen complete, Dr. Janelle McLain made the final check of the men's equipment before they moved into the pressure lock. As a physician, she was the logical crew member to monitor the biomedical readouts of Fredrick and Elder while they were beyond the relative safety of the shuttle.

McLain checked her instruments from the biomedical sensors attached to each man's body. Everything looked okay with Fredrick. He had completed three EVAs on his last shuttle mission and was one of the most experienced space walkers in all of NASA.

Elder was a rookie and therefore expected to be a bit more agitated. He was. However, just as before launch, the flight surgeons in Houston were closely evaluating the signals they were receiving from his biomedical sensors. Unofficially the flight surgeons in Houston all knew that Doctors Sabos and Ashy had almost pulled him before launch. Dr. Janelle McLain did not know that. She of course recognized Elder was slightly hyperventilating and his heart rate was significantly faster than Fredricks. She did see him close his eyes and take slow deep breaths like Steve Ashy had taught him. That seemed to help and the flight surgeon in Houston gave his okay for the EVA.

While McLain was monitoring the health of the men from inside the airlock, Ledwell and Weaver were inverting the shuttle so that the tail was going first. After the satellite was set in position, the orbital maneuvering system engine would be fired for twenty-two seconds to slow the shuttle enough to drop to a lower altitude of one hundred thirty nautical miles where she would stay the remaining days of her mission.

Terry Lee was standing in the upper fuselage area gazing down into the payload bay through thick glass ports. Her job was to keep an eye on the health of Elder's RePoGGS experiment. Looking through thick clear windows, she could peer directly down into the open payload bay to see the mammoth antenna area. Once Fredrick and Elder manually deployed the solar power array, she would have immediate feedback on the response of the equipment. She would use her instrumentation to verify and document the resulting electrical grid and to give instructions for the two men help them make minute adjustments to maximize the array performance.

Next to Lee, Tunes Dalton was standing by for his part of the teamwork. This would be the first time the newest variation of the shuttle robotic arm was to be used in space. Explorer, the other shuttle, had a robotic arm that was of the old style, which would be replaced with this new version soon if no major flaws were uncovered.

To stay easily in place, Lee and Dalton were wearing what looked like ballet shoes. The soles of the slippers were half of a fabric hook and loop fastener. Mounted on the floor of the work area was the other half of the fabric. As the two stood at their work stations, the bottoms of their shoes held them in place. The natural tendency to float in microgravity was eliminated by this elementary procedure. It was one of those things that made science fun for Lee. It always fascinated her that sometimes the solution to a difficult problem was something very simple.

On the mid-deck, the hatch from the crew compartment into the airlock was opened. Tom Frederick went in first. He was the senior astronaut on the mission and as such would be the one to operate the airlock controls. Fredrick looked back into the crew compartment. He was not surprised to find Elder hesitating.

"Okay, there Scott. It's show time. Come on in." The tall Nebraska native tried to sound confident and yet soothing.

Janelle McLain actually gave Elder a slight but unmistakable push and he floated into the airlock. Relying solely on the ritual he had practiced countless times in the neutral buoyancy pool, Elder got into the correct position. Behind him, McLain closed and sealed the hatch. While the airlock was not spacious, neither was it tiny. Nonetheless, once the area was sealed shut, the walls seemed to close in as well.

Dr. Janelle McLain verified the seal and spoke to the two men in the airlock. "Okay, guys. We're good on this side. You are cleared for depressurization."

The only person who could actually initiate the venting of pressurization into space was Lt. Colonel Tom Frederick. He was the last cog in the safety system designed to ensure protection for the shuttle from a pressurization crisis. "Beginning to vent," was his simple reply.

Elder immediately tried to put out of his mind the vacuum that now was only microns away outside his suit. There was some slight stiffening of material as the pressure that kept him alive pressed against the airless void he would be working in.

The first order of business was to attach the 150-foot umbilical cord to L. Scott Elder's suit. He would now use a small handheld maneuvering device and handholds to move about the payload bay for the initial part of the mission.

Tom Fredrick moved himself to the manned maneuvering unit attached to the forward payload bulkhead. There had only been three first-generation MMUs built and they were only used on a few missions. Even those short operational experiences were enough to convince NASA the remote arm and tethered EVAs would accomplish the same tasks in a much safer way. The new shuttles and more challenging spacewalks would require updated MMUs that would allow astronauts to accomplish more complex missions.

Planned shuttle missions for next year included repairing satellites in orbit. This had been done as early as 1992 when the shuttle Endeavor had captured a damaged satellite in an incorrect orbit. Astronauts had repaired it and the shuttle then moved to the correct orbit and released the now operational unit. Pulling a satellite into the payload bay was difficult and dangerous.

The new-generation MMU would allow astronauts to leave the confines of the shuttle to repair satellites in open space. The MMU Tom Fredrick would be wearing was next-generation equipment and far superior to its predecessor. Both used 34 nozzles powered by compressed nitrogen. In the past, an astronaut had to constantly fire maneuvering jets of nitrogen to stay in a specific spot. That constant fine tuning required a great deal of attention which distracted from the mission and of fuel which shortened the time for accomplishing the tasks.

The new-generation MMU had addressed that issue. Once an astronaut was in the position he or she wanted, the pack would lock on to the spot and would, using something akin to an autopilot, use extremely fine adjustments of the jets to stay there. Since the unit could make tiny adjustments instead of larger ones the astronaut would use, consumption of fuel was expected to be reduced almost 40%.

Another huge safety consideration for the new MMU was the addition of an automatic homing command. A fear in the past had been that a wearer might become incapacitated well away from the payload bay and would be incapable of returning from their untethered spacewalk. The new MMU could be commanded from the flight deck of the shuttle to return to its docking point. From there, a tethered astronaut could recover the injured crew member. This return home feature had addressed the greatest unspoken fear astronauts faced during untethered space walks. No one wanted to become a footnote in history books as the unfortunate astronaut spending decades as a lifeless satellite and doomed to eventually burn up when gravity finally won. At least with this feature, they would return home with the rest of the crew.

Dr. Jim Dalton was in his element. He and Terry Lee were standing side-by-side in the upper flight deck and looking down into the payload bay. Lee had verified RePoGGS was healthy and all the required powered instrumentation was operating perfectly. Dalton's responsibility was to use the robotic arm to move the twelve thousand pound, compact sedan-sized package out of the payload bay and to a spot where Elder and Fredrick could activate it and manually adjust the sighting lens. The first crucial step was to be initiated by the two space walkers as they visually checked the release links that held the six-ton experiment in the payload bay. Once the locks were confirmed open, Dalton attached the robotic arm to the RePoGGS and slowly raised it out of the holding blocks and straight up into free space.

A tethered Elder held on to the satellite as it moved beyond the extended open doors of the shuttle. His participation was essentially that of Assistant in Charge of Tool Management. Lt. Colonel Tom Fredrick was completely in charge and Elder relegated to a backseat role which he was convinced was a slap to his face by the mission commander, Thurman Ledwell. For his part, Fredrick used his total untethered freedom of movement to transport himself around every point of the RePoGGS. He knew exactly how everything should look and his examination went precisely as he had practiced it over fifty times.

"Hey, Tunes," Fredrick spoke, "give me another minute and you can plan on releasing this thing."

"Roger," Dalton responded.

"Scott, I can't see you from here. Are you clear of the arm for release?" Fredrick knew Houston was listening to every communication. He didn't want them to suspect he was concerned about the man on the opposite side of the satellite.

"Uh…yeah, I am clear. Is it really okay to let it go?"

Well, so much for sounding confident…

"Scott, this is what you and I have been practicing for the past three or four months. Take a deep breath and relax. Let's do it just like in the tank. The only difference is we don't have those pesky scuba divers in our way. In about four hours, this baby will be doing its thing and we can have a nip of bourbon to celebrate."

In Houston, the Flight Director, Bud Stokesly, closed his eyes, slowly shook his head side to side and allowed a small smile to escape the corners of his mouth. "CAPCOM…don't respond to that last comment. I'm certain Colonel Fredrick would never consider bringing any spirits aboard the shuttle in direct disobedience to NASA directives about such things. I'm positive he's joking with his partner out there." In reality, there was little doubt in Stokesly's mind that there was indeed a flask of good bourbon in Fredrick's personal items.

Floating over the top of the experiment package and looking down on Elder's helmet, Fredrick said, "Hey Scott. Look up and say 'cheese'!"

There was no movement at all. Elder appeared locked on to the hardware in front of his visor.

"Never mind, Scott. I'm coming down." Within fifteen seconds the two men were side by side. "Okay, buddy. Give me the release spanner from your left front pouch."

As if in a dream, L. Scott Elder retrieved the specialized wrench from its holder and passed it wordlessly to Fredrick. After verifying the wrench was the correct size, the tall Nebraskan worked it into a locking grid and then stepped onto a plate welded to the bottom panel. The plate was just big enough for the front half of the man's boots to rest there. Because of the foothold, Fredrick was able to exert his full strength to pull up on the wrench. His significant strength had been necessary for this procedure while practicing it in the neutral buoyancy pool. But here in space, the wrench moved with ease and Fredrick felt a satisfying snap as his action released the solar panels which had been latched alongside the blocks. The jet-black panels glistened as they reflected ambient light during the seconds it took to fold out on both sides of the package. Fredrick pointed his finger at one panel and Elder reluctantly nodded his head. He gingerly moved hand over hand along the solar panel until he reached the hinged mechanism at the end. Elder was already breathing heavily from this small exertion but nonetheless, he did his assigned task. Tentatively he slid the single locking pin aft and the entire remaining portions of the solar panel unfolded and deployed. Fredrick had already accomplished the same action on the other side and had moved away into free space to observe the entire experiment. The RePoGGS now looked like a tall cylinder with almost twelve feet of flat-black panels attached midway up each side. She was ungainly and yet beautiful floating against the pitch-black sky.

Ninety feet away, Terry Lee was both observing the process through her viewing port and simultaneously watching as the electrical systems of the newly hatched RePoGGS showed the solar panels were performing perfectly and actually generating more potential energy than was expected.

The team of space walkers had done their job in less time than either had expected. It had only been three hours and thirty-five minutes since they had left the airlock. It was just before 1:00 p.m. and Fredrick was satisfied with the accomplishment of the procedure. He had not expected to be finished for another forty-five minutes. Even Elder had done well.

"Terry, before we leave, how do things look over there?"

"Tom, you guys have Repojis dead center," she responded using the phonetical pronunciation of the RePoGGS package. "She's showing green lights across the board. Looks like she's locked on to the target low-orbit satellite. Come on in and we'll move away so she can operate like the good girl I'm sure she is."

"Roger," Tom Fredrick responded.

The plan now was for Elder to use a three-foot long linkage to attach himself to Fredrick for a tow back to the payload bay. Tom positioned himself for the return to Sojourner.

This was the moment L. Scott Elder had been waiting for.

Instead of attaching on to Fredrick, Elder rotated to face the control panel at the top of the RePoGGS. Weeks before, Schumer had decided that since Elder was the Head of Development for Winter Triangle Physics, he was going to initiate the first operation of his satellite. He grasped the handle that locked the controls and pressed two large red buttons simultaneously.

Terry Lee and Jim Dalton were both looking towards the RePoGGS at that moment and were instantly blinded by a bright discharge that was close to the intensity of looking at the sun from the ground.

At the same instant, all communications between the two men performing the EVA and the shuttle were completely disrupted.

On the flight deck, Captain Thurman Ledwell and Lt. Colonel Weaver had seen the bright flash that had come through the windows behind them and heard the muffled sounds from Dalton and Lee as they tried futility to see through the blindness they were both experiencing. The two pilots would normally, by reflex alone, have looked over their shoulders to see what was happening behind them, but instead were both staring transfixed at something they had never seen during any of their training simulators.

Every screen on the panels before them was blank. Ledwell instantly pressed his microphone button and tried to sound as calm as possible as he spoke, "Houston, Sojourner." No response. He tried a second and a third time before looking at Weaver. "Bill, try your transmitter."

Weaver moved a wafer switch to go to his backup radio and frequency. "Houston, Sojourner on secondary." No response. Weaver continued using every secondary and tertiary communication system in a fruitless attempt to speak to Houston.

Patti Koch, who had been in the mid-deck eating, and Janelle McLain, who was preparing to receive the EVA astronauts into the airlock, both heard the commotion on the deck above and quickly pushed off to glide over to the access port for the upper deck.

Once on the flight deck, McLain went immediately to her friends, both of whom had their palms covering their eyes. Koch, as an astrophysicist, decided her place was with the pilots.

Ledwell saw her and commanded, "Patti, pull out the systems checklists for communication and avionics failures." Even as he spoke, Bubba Ledwell was certain there was nothing written there that would address the emergency they were facing.

Patti went to a closed and rarely used locker on the left bulkhead behind Ledwell's seat. The locker had been designed with protection of the contents in mind. The walls were layered with composite and thin lead skins to provide shielding from any anticipated threat in flight. That foresight had never considered the current situation

Sojourner's crew found itself in, but it had nonetheless worked.

From it, she pulled out a four-inch notebook. Bound inside were holders for six computer tablets. The tablets were loaded with every manual and checklist a crew could possibly expect to need in space. If the material had been printed out into books, they would cover an entire wall. Instead that same information in electronic format fit in this small binder.

The electronic checklists were a redundant reference because in the event of an inflight emergency, the CAPCOM in Houston, who was a fully rated astronaut, would have the checklist in front of him and would lead the crew step-by-step through whatever procedure was called for. That procedure for handling emergencies had been practiced countless times in the simulator, however, this was not the simulator. Sojourner had a communication system designed for reliability and redundancy. With six totally independent radios and receivers aboard, no one ever really considered the possibility that a total radio failure could happen.

After fifteen minutes of futile searching for any pertinent checklist, Ledwell directed Koch to return the useless tablets to the storage locker.

Despite everything that was happening all at once, Captain Ledwell was still mindful of all his responsibilities. "Patti, look out the port and see if you can find Tom and Scott."

Koch could see both men. Scott Elder was unmoving and floating limp in space. Tom Fredrick was moving and appeared to be going towards his teammate. No one on the Sojourner yet knew Fredrick had been turned with his back toward the satellite and so was protected from the blast of light that had come from it. He had, however felt like someone had hit him in the back with a baseball bat.

It had taken several seconds for Fredrick to regain his senses and realize something very bad had just happened. It was also then he realized he couldn't move his left hand. The metal control joystick mounted on the MMU left arm was missing. As impossible as it seemed to him, Fredrick realized the force of the blast had driven his arm against the control with sufficient power to break it off. Fredrick was sure his left arm was broken above the wrist. There wasn't a great deal of pain, but that would come soon enough.

Trying to control the MMU using just the right controller would be impossible. For the moment, Tom was deciding how to reach Elder who was motionless. Fortunately, a small length of the umbilical cord would be within reach if he could just move a few feet.

Very carefully, he used the right control stick and made a short burst of the jets. Without a counteraction from the jets controlled by his left hand, Fredrick just slowly rotated like a space ballerina, but each revolution brought him closer to the umbilical. On the third revolution, he grabbed the hose and gave it a sharp tug. In the vacuum of space, Scott Elder's inert form was yanked into range of Fredrick's good arm and the Nebraskan captured the second man immediately.

During the entire EVA crisis, Tom Fredrick had been trying unsuccessfully to communicate with Sojourner or Houston. He wasn't hearing static, just dead silence. Total silence was more frightening than static. Fredrick was certain his left arm was broken and knew he could not control the MMU. The seasoned mission specialist was forcing himself to remain as calm as possible while holding on to an unconscious or dead Scott Elder and feverishly searching his mind for any procedure that could save them.

Back on the Sojourner, Ledwell and Weaver were trying to restore their communications with Houston while also attempting to reboot the computers that generated their flight screens. For a pilot—any pilot—not having the avionics screens was one of worst possible scenarios. For a shuttle pilot, it was significantly worse because it would be impossible to fly an arrival like Ledwell did on his last mission when the autopilot failed.

McLain had gotten patches from the first aid kit and covered Lee's and Dalton's eyes. She doubted there was any permanent damage, but the patches would help them rest their eyes.

Patti Koch was still watching Fredrick manhandle Elder. She couldn't tell what the problem was, but Fredrick was obviously having trouble. She unilaterally made a decision and looked over her shoulder to the mission commander.

"Bubba, I can't tell why, but Tom's having trouble getting the MMU to work. I think we're going to have to control it for him."

Ledwell's decision was immediate. "Do it."

Patty Koch looked down at her bandaged friend. "Terry, how do you activate the return to base function on the MMU?"

With her eyes covered, Lee had to visualize from memory the very complex control panels that were so packed with instruments, controls, switches, and circuit breakers. She started giving instructions, describing where each switch was and how to activate it. Lee could have completed the task in fifteen seconds, but it took almost a minute to describe it to Koch. There was no small satisfaction to both women when Koch said she could see the two men steadily moving under automatic control towards the payload bay, indicating the procedure had worked.

Dr. Janelle McLain could do no more for her patient's retina flash burns. But she could definitely knew the two men doing the EVA would need her care. She floated the medical kit before her and exited the flight deck moving through the floor hatch to the mid-deck. Patti Koch followed her.

Every astronaut for years had received advanced emergency medicine training as part of their mission preparation. They could all start an IV and administer injections. The fear of a crew member becoming seriously ill or injured in space was a daunting one. With that concern in mind, the shuttle first aid kit was more like a crash cart in a major emergency room and was stocked with a wide range of drugs and support equipment that could be used if approved by the flight surgeon in Mission Control.

In the entire history of the space program, the first aid kit had been required, but never used for anything except very minor injuries. On this mission, it had to be opened to hopefully save the life of L. Scott Elder. Fortunately, especially since a doctor was not available by radio, a physician was aboard. McLain and Koch were standing by the airlock hatch. They could not see what was happening in the payload bay since the MMU docking area was to the side of the airlock.

Fredrick had difficulty disconnecting from the MMU once it had reattached itself to the bulkhead locker point, mostly because his left forearm was now throbbing with every heartbeat. Elder still hadn't moved and there was no way to tell if he was alive or not. The good news for all was that once free of the backpack, he was able to make his way to the airlock while still holding on to Elder. Activating the airlock using his right hand, Fredrick pushed Elder in the compartment first, gingerly moved in himself next, and painfully closed the airlock hatch.

After the re-pressurization was complete, Dr. Janelle McLain opened the shuttle side hatch and removed Elder. Fredrick was able to maneuver himself out. It only took five minutes for McLain and Patti Koch to remove L. Scott Elder's pressure suit. He was alive, but barely.

Janelle McLain had become a medical doctor not because she wanted to treat patients, but because she wanted to cure diseases. She has spent her entire career doing medical research. Long gone were the days where she saw patients, but to her it was like riding a bike. It only took the doctor a moment to determine Elder probably had internal bleeding, but where and how bad it was would be impossible to tell under these circumstances. McLain felt her chances of saving him were a long shot, but there were some options.

She first started an IV and opened the flow to full open. Getting fluid into his veins would be a first step. While that was happening, Patti Koch helped Tom Fredrick out of his suit. It didn't take an x-ray to diagnose the swollen and misshaped area right above the left wrist as broken. All that could be done for him was to put his arm in an air splint that would immobilize him from his fingertips up to his elbow. McLain offered pain medications, but Fredrick, recognizing the shuttle's dire circumstances, decided not to risk fogging his mind.

In the Houston Mission Control Center, it took all of Flight Director, Bud Stokesly's leadership skill to restore order. On every console, where data from the shuttle was expected to be displayed there were blank screens. No telemetry or voice communication had been received since the instant the RePoGGS had been activated.

Long range scanners had been able to confirm the shuttle was in one piece and in its assigned orbit, but nothing more definitive could be determined. The fact that the shuttle was in the highest orbit ever established for a mission made everything more difficult.

With everyone talking at once and protocol being ignored, the Flight Director acted decisively. He grabbed a bull horn from an aide and turned the volume to its highest setting, "Everyone…shut the hell up!" No one could ever remember hearing a single vulgar word come out of Stokesly's mouth. Hearing this one, even as mild as it was, shocked most of the people in Mission Control into silence. The few who were so self-absorbed that they missed Stokesly's announcement were immediately brought back to attention when their name was called loudly over the bullhorn followed by a colorful admonition to be quiet. Within seconds, the bullhorn was no longer necessary. The room was as quiet as a tomb.

"Now," Stokesly continued, "everyone take your seats. Pick up the phones to your support staffs wherever they are and let's find out what the fu…what the heck has happened. Keep all the other chatter down."

Stokesly then picked up a red telephone on his desk which instantly connected him to Dr. John Francis Maclemore, NASA's Director of Flight Operations. "John, we have a serious situation here. I think you should come over."

"Bud, you don't know the half of it. Las Vegas has just lost its entire electrical grid. The damn thing just fried for no reason. They're already predicting it may take weeks to get the entire system back operational. Stokesly, did your shuttle experiment cause this?"

"You rotten SOB," was Stokesly's only comment as he slammed the phone back into its cradle.

Chapter Twenty-Seven

June 3, 2022
Las Vegas, Nevada

Pandemonium was the best description for the entire city of Las Vegas. Every home in a fifty-mile radius was completely without commercial electrical power. The mega-hotels all had backup generators, but they only powered essential areas. On emergency power, most of the hotel elevators were inoperative which meant thousands of guests were trying to exit using the stairs, lighted only by emergency lights, while carrying or pulling their suitcases. The resulting logjam of people was a powder-keg. In some cases, the emergency lights failed to come on and in the resulting darkness panicked people fell and were trampled or froze in fear and were shoved down flights of stairs.

No traffic lights were operating and terrified drivers weren't using common sense in trying to leave the city. Accidents were everywhere and police were powerless to address the problem. Cell phones would turn on but could not get service. After all, cell towers needed electric power to operate and without it were useless.

Television and most radio stations had backup generators but with almost all homes without power, their audience was counted in the hundreds—not millions. The governor of Nevada, a career politician with a huge practiced smile and zero managerial skills, was clearly unsure of what to do. His only action was to mobilize the National Guard to provide manpower for essential protection in the blacked-out areas. He wanted patrols on the strip to prevent looters. This was a ridiculous action since the casinos all had more armed guards than there were soldiers on the street.

June 3, 2022
Corpus Christi, Texas

Using an encrypted network, Nicholas Schumer sent messages to every major newspaper and television station news desk in the country taking credit for the blackout in Las Vegas. He identified himself as "The Starman" and promised to hit a second city shortly to prove his ability to strike at will. He knew that despite the sophistication of his encryptions, it would not take the government long to figure out who he was. What they would not be able to do is figure out where he was.

Schumer decided to prove his claim quickly. After consulting the star chart attached to his wall—the one with hacked data from NASA—he made his decision.

"What an irony that I'm using their own technology to hold the world hostage." He mused.

A small command on his computer produced a very slight position shift in the angle of the free-floating RePoGGS satellite and he activated the system. The instruction was transmitted straight to the control system of the satellite and was sent over a network that would take even the NSA several hours to break. By then, Schumer knew he could create a new routing. This hopscotch of technology would only work a day or two, but by then Nicholas Schumer would be rich beyond even his avaricious dreams.

As the command from Schumer's computer was sent, a flash of light, just as bright as earlier in the day, erupted from the RePoGGS. This time, fortunately, the shuttle was well away from the satellite and the blast caused no injury nor damage.

June 3, 2022
Cambridge, England

Within two seconds of the flash outside of Sojourner, almost three quarters of million people in a forty-mile radius of Cambridge lost their electricity. The entire electrical grid had been fried. Every major substation had suffered severe damage. The devastation was so widespread that it would require at least six weeks to bring everything back online.

The panic seen in Las Vegas a couple of hours before was much less dramatic in the rural areas of England especially at this evening hour, but the economic havoc would be every bit as extreme. As the center of high-tech development companies for all of England and much of Europe, Cambridge was often seen in the same category as the Silicon Valley in the United States. It had the largest research and development complex in Europe and was also a banking center. The blackout would result in millions of pounds being lost every hour to the UK economy.

Scientists and government researchers had very little trouble deciding on the cause of the power system destruction. There were few things that could create such catastrophic damage.

Based upon very initial findings, they were certain the power grids around Las Vegas and Cambridge had both been destroyed by a highly focused electromagnetic pulse, but they were at a loss to know how that could happen. Scientists had known about EMP for decades but had studied it mostly because the phenomenon was only produced after a nuclear detonation. Researchers now knew that in the microseconds after a blast, charged particles traveling out at incredible speed would destroy electrical and electronic devices. Decades ago, during the high-altitude detonation test of a nuclear device, electrical devices almost 1,000 miles away were inadvertently damaged. Focusing EMP was the problem.

Every year, thousands of people around the world lost electronic devices such as computers, television sets, and sound systems as the result of a lightning striking their house or business. The same damage caused by a lightning strike to a single place would be far worse if wide areas were affected simultaneously. Protecting systems against such events was a high priority for Winter Triangle Physics.

In early 2018, a research team working on improving Schumer's early disputed patent had stumbled on a way to direct the energy flow using a highly-charged electrical beam. Essentially, they could create a lightning bolt that could be aimed with absolute precision. The WTP team's goal had been to discover a new way to protect critical components from damage like that caused by a lightning strike but on a grander scale.

Nicholas Schumer had followed his team's progress with interest knowing they would be completed by the end of 2018. He would implement their experimental protection system as soon as it was operational. However, it wasn't the protection system he was the most attracted to.

He was fascinated by the device his team had built to create the test energy. Schumer had wondered if it could be modified and be made exponentially more powerful. The more he considered options for the mechanism, the more it morphed from a ground unit to something that could be deployed in orbit. Schumer's design and development group had taken eighteen months of intensive work, but by May of 2021 it was ready for production.

The satellite had been designed to be built in modules, and each component was built by a different subcontractor. The module concept provided two distinct advantages. With each subcontractor working independently, a huge amount of time was saved as compared to one company building everything. Secondly, and most importantly, no one company had the whole picture. They only knew about their one component. Taken as individual units, there was nothing of a weaponizing nature. It was just the combination of all the parts together that produced a dangerous synergy.

Once the final assembly was completed at Winter Triangle Physics, the device had the power to direct a highly charged electrical beam through the vacuum of space with the capability to destroy entire electrical grids on Earth. The research teams were under the false impression they were working on a top-secret military project and had no idea of Schumer's actual plan for the satellite. He knew the technology could be sold to the Pentagon for use as a tactical attack system to cripple an enemy's infrastructure. That sale would bring WTP billions in revenue.

Schumer also recognized it could be used to blackmail governments and organizations around the world. The second option seemed the more lucrative venture to Nicholas Schumer personally.

While his scientists, designers, and engineers were busy in creation, Schumer had been very busy buying off politicians like Senator Maxwell Bellow, Chairman of the Senate Appropriations Committee. Political influence had been critical to the success of his plan.

The work had gone slowly but steadily ahead. The satellite had been built and shipped to Florida after the top brass at NASA had somehow been convinced to place it, and WTP's head of development, L. Scott Elder, on the first flight of the shuttle Sojourner. Everyone was a little nervous. It had been tested only once and only three people had even known that. Two of those three, Catherine Austin and Josh Tanner, were now dead.

To be validated, the theory needed to be tested against a highly sophisticated target, so a month before in Nevada, a miniaturized focused energy blast had been used to cause the crash of a highly secret supersonic jet during a low altitude run. To keep his test as secret as possible, it had been conducted by Nicholas Schumer himself. There was absolutely no question the technology worked at least on a small scale.

June 3, 2022
Corpus Christi, Texas

Schumer gave the world thirty minutes to come to grip with the magnitude of what was happening. For decades, individual countries in every corner of the world had suffered from terrorist attacks. This time, Schumer wanted all countries to feel threatened at the same time. The massive attacks had been directed not at an individual country, but at two major locations half a world apart. This time, panic griped the entire world.

Schumer decided it was time to close the noose.

As the world was beginning to react to the attack on Cambridge, a second email was sent to the same newspapers, television stations, radio stations, and social media centers around the world. This time the email threatened to destroy power grids in every major city in every country.

Those transmissions to news organizations had had the desired effect. It didn't matter how much elected national leaders from every country tried to reassure their people, broadcasts of the populations in Las Vegas and Cambridge totally without any power and no hope of having any for an indeterminate time was enough to raise the fear factor.

Schumer was no fool. He knew governments would never capitulate to threats. He didn't care because he had no intention of negotiating with any politician regardless of their title. Schumer had a different target audience.

Around the world there were hundreds of men and women who had wealth measured in the billions. These people had their fortunes vested in businesses with headquarters in major cities on almost every continent. The loss of electrical power to those nerve centers would cost them millions of dollars or euros or yen or yuan each and every hour that passed. Preventing that power loss would be of critical importance to those individuals.

Schumer's plan had its foundations in the racketeering days of big cities like New York. Businesses often paid protection money to local gangs or crime bosses who would then prevent undesirable things from happening. If the money wasn't paid, the business might be robbed or burnt to the ground.

Schumer's plan was along those very lines. He now controlled the satellite that could annihilate huge areas of any company's production, distribution, or management by simply destroying their power grids. His destruction would be so complete, and over such a wide area, that recovery would be measured not in hours or days but in weeks or months.

Communicating with these corporate leaders, as individuals, would not really be that difficult. In 2004, the founders of the three biggest technology conglomerates in the world at the time decided that email was much too slow and congested when it came to maintaining contact with each other. They didn't have time to peruse a thousand emails a day and didn't always trust subordinates to do so.

Men and women with the rarified title of billionaire wanted a way to communicate without layers of assistants and sub-executives getting involved. Sometimes they had items to discuss that they would not want government watchdogs to discover later. The solution came as the three worked together and developed a new and highly encrypted network. Encryption was virtually unheard of at the time.

Over the years other billionaires had been added to the classified network. Owners of highly competitive companies often wanted to let each other know their strategy concerning private projects.

Even though, to the public and to the government, these companies were in direct competition, the network was used to provide each other with insider information which was highly illegal but extremely profitable to both.

Those men and women each paid ten million dollars to be a part of the group. That pittance was an insurance policy. Should someone get a conscience and decide to reveal the network, they would not be able to claim innocence about the group's activity since they had paid to be a part. The insurance policy was never needed. There was too much money to be made from the network.

In the early days, each member had to sign into the system in order to communicate with the group. In later years, each member had been given a single dongle that would fit into the USB port of any computer. When a message was sent to an individual, the dongle would vibrate wherever it was. The individual had two minutes to insert the dongle into a computer to receive the message. After that amount of time, the communication would auto-erase. That feature was an incentive to encourage prompt attention to messages.

After a few years, owners of the dongles decided they wanted the ability to present potential business opportunities to the other members anonymously. That way, if the deal was rejected, no one's reputation was hurt. To make secret communication possible, the system was modified to provide a way for a member to send private notes. Recipients could then respond to an anonymous proposal in equal confidentiality so that only the sender knew who was interested.

Since 2004, the number of members in this elite group had grown to 265. The secrecy and exclusivity of the network had only been broken once and only two people knew about it—the owner of the dongle and Nicholas Schumer. The owner was an extremely wealthy United States senator who had used his money to buy his seat. Six months into the man's first term, he was blackmailed by a lobbyist for a major Chinese company. She was demanding millions of dollars in exchange for forgetting about their carefully photographed sexual trysts. Money was not a problem for the Senator, but anything that could come back and hurt his chances for eventually reaching the White House was. The senator turned for help to a man he knew had contacts in the woman's Chinese business and in governmental circles—Nicholas Schumer. There was agreement made between the two men. For making the lobbyist go away—which he did—Schumer wanted access to the Senator's business contacts. The dongle had swapped hands and no one in the network ever knew.

Schumer had researched all 265 in the private network and selected specified individuals who had direct control of their business instead of those who were figurehead leaders. All had controlling stock and therefore were in total control of their Board of Directors. Schumer wanted people who would personally be financially wiped out if their business centers were left without power for an extended period of time. That criteria brought the number of billionaires who used the private network and were susceptible to blackmail down to 56. Schumer's anonymous note to the 56 was a simple offer of protection to the operations and centers owned by them.

Dear Friend,

As a business man myself, I know how difficult times can be when catastrophes happen to a company's infrastructure. Floods, hurricanes, tornados, fires, and earthquakes can disrupt our manufacturing and distribution for days and what a financial hit that can be.

Imagine your company headquarters or manufacturing and distribution centers were to lose all electrical power for several months. In all candor, I can make that nightmare happen as I've proven today in Las Vegas and Cambridge. I have both the technology and the ability to hit anywhere on the globe I desire.

To avoid that unfortunate event from happening to your company, I offer you a proposition.

At the bottom of this note is information regarding a

numbered bank account in a location that will afford me a level of protection I find appealing. You have 24 hours to transmit one billion dollars in US currency into that account. This will be a one-time payment. I will not be needing to do this type of transaction ever again, so don't fret about me contacting you with future proposals of a similar nature. However, at the end of 24 hours, anyone who has not decided to participate in my offer will discover their entire company is powerless...literally.

I'm sure you will agree that this one-time payment is a trivial amount of money compared to the effects on your personal bottom-line should an unfortunate power interruption become reality...and it will happen in 25 hours if you don't participate.

Because Schumer's note had been sent using the anonymous feature, the recipients would not be able to tell who had originated it. They only had two minutes to access and read the note. As the sender, Schumer received an electronic acknowledgement as soon as a receiver opened the note. Sure enough, all 56 received and opened the note within the allotted two minutes. Schumer laughed out loud thinking about the looks on the faces of those billionaires as they realized they could easily be bankrupted within a few days.

These were not people accustomed to being threatened nor likely to be intimidated. They had not become billionaires by backing down from a fight in the boardroom nor in the marketplace. However, they were, for the most part, pragmatists who knew when to fold their cards.

Every one of the 56 recipients made phone calls immediately after reading the correspondence. Most called their corporate security heads, information technology (IT) departments, or attorneys. The most ineffective calls of all were to their senators or congressmen. With the world reeling from the Las Vegas and Cambridge attacks, everyone was understandably concerned about their vulnerability and ability to protect themselves against a similar attack.

Within two hours, investigators for governmental agencies around the world already knew the source of the Las Vegas and Cambridge attacks. There was no doubt the satellite just placed into orbit by the Shuttle Sojourner had discharged some kind of massive and highly focused electrically charged beam. NASA was already widely being denounced for not ordering Sojourner's crew to immediately destroy the satellite.

The problem was that Sojourner was not responding to any radio calls. It appeared the shuttle had been a victim of the satellite, too.

Chapter Twenty-Eight

June 3, 2022
Shuttle Sojourner

Physics was now in charge of the Sojourner's orbit. Without instrumentation or communication, Ledwell and Weaver didn't dare attempt any changes to their path. It was obvious to everyone on the crew that their predicament had been caused by Elder's satellite, but they had no idea how to alleviate the severity of their situation. The second flash had done no further damage, but that brought no comfort to anyone. They had been trained to handle emergencies on orbit, but nothing like what confronted them now had ever been envisioned. They were totally unable to re-establish communication with Houston and the flight information displays in the cockpit were as black as the sky outside.

Thankfully, both Lee and Dalton were slowly regaining their sight. The bright image that had seemed burned into their retinas was now almost gone. Tom Fredrick's wrist was still throbbing, but he continued to reject Dr. McLain's offer for pain medications. The only crew member still in danger was the unconscious L. Scott Elder, but at least his blood pressure and heart rate had finally stabilized.

In Houston, Flight Director Bud Stokesly had Mission Control working efficiently. The initial shock and bedlam of losing all contact with the shuttle had been overcome and the controllers were now in contact with teams of engineers from every company who had any component on Sojourner. Since no one knew exactly what had happened on the shuttle, a great deal of time was being spent brainstorming and investigating possible causes for the blackout.

The only thing that was known without a doubt now was that the power crisis in Las Vegas and Cambridge had been caused by the satellite the shuttle Sojourner had put into orbit. No one knew how nor why that could be possible, but the facts were clear that no city was now immune to a total power failure. The Mission Director was not a man prone to rash actions, but he decided to be proactive about one important item. He stepped away from his desk in Mission Control and called the only name on his cell phone speed dial.

"Analyn," Stokesly said when his wife answered her phone. "I want you to go to the ranch and stay there." He paused a moment. "Before you leave, call our supplier and tell him to come out today to make sure the propane tank is full." Another thought came to him. "Also, have him fill both the gasoline and diesel storage tanks. I think they each hold a thousand gallons and I'd like them full."

"You afraid we're going to lose power, too?" Analyn Stokesly asked quietly.

"Sweetheart, I get paid to plan for worst-case scenarios," he said. "Okay, here's my thinking. The ranch is pretty much already off the main grid. We're six miles from the nearest town and have our own well water. We've got herds of game and a large garden. The only thing we really get from off the ranch is electricity. So, with full tanks, if something happens, we'll have propane to cook, gas to drive our cars, and diesel to run the backup generator which will give us electricity for the well pump and for the house. If nothing happens, we've got plenty of fuel to last us for a year or more. I'll meet you at the ranch as soon as I can get there. Don't wait up."

"Okay."

June 3, 2022
Shuttle Sojourner

"Mom, Dad…can you hear me?" This was the first time since the shuttle had be crippled Terry Lee had been able to slip away and try her communication box. For all she knew it, too, had been disabled by whatever had damaged Sojourner.

Inside the resort house on the Florida coast, Tame Forsyth cried for the first time all day. "We can hear you, Terry. Your voice sounds so good. We were afraid…"

"I know, Mom. I'm fine for the moment, but everything up here is pretty messed up. We don't have any radios that work and our flight instruments are out. I'm really glad to know this contraption you sent me still works. When I get home, I'll have a big hug for whoever designed it." Terry had caught herself a split-second before saying If I get home.

Tame and Moses had been listening to radio and television news since the incident in space and were well aware of the danger their daughter was in. They had been fighting the urge to attempt to contact her. The Forsyths had found themselves in a very peculiar situation. Every day, they had been leaving the resort condo and driving four miles to visit Melissa in the ICU. This afternoon, they had not told Melissa about the danger Terry was in. Now, talking to Terry, they were keeping Melissa's wounds and hospitalization a secret, too.

Their situation would only continue a few more hours. Keeping Melissa in the dark had been an easy thing since her ICU room had no television set. However, in the morning, she would be moved to a regular hospital room. Since every television channel was covering the terror attacks on Las Vegas and Cambridge and the shuttle's communication failure almost exclusively, the Forsyths would have to talk with their daughter before her transfer. That would wait. Right now, they were savoring each word from their daughter in space.

"Honey," Moses Forsyth started, "what happened? All they're saying down here is that there was some malfunction with the satellite you launched and it knocked out your radios." He didn't mention the electrical problems in Nevada and England. There was no reason to add that to Terry's concerns and there was no way she could explain knowing about it were she to slip up and say something to anyone on orbit.

"Dad, that's pretty close to it. We're not sure exactly what it did, but not only are the radios out, but so are the flight instruments. We're pretty much blind up here. Even Bubba is at a loss to figure it out."

"Terry, I want you to keep your transmitter on the first position. That way we'll be able to hear everyone around you and that may help our people in Exeter to figure something out. Don't let on about the box yet. We may be using it later, but for now keep it a secret."

"Yes sir. Do you really think our people will be able to come up with something?"

"If anyone can, it'll be them," Moses responded. "I'm going to call King Annu in a few minutes and ask for his help getting people started. Let's give Exeter a chance."

"Yes sir," Terry repeated. "I'll keep my device on the first position." There was a slight pause, then Terry continued half-jokingly, "Listen Mom and Dad, it's a bit tense up here. If an unladylike utterance should come out, I'd appreciate a little understanding."

Tame answered, "Honey, if the Pope was up there, he might slip some, too. Don't worry. All is forgiven in advance."

"Get some rest, Terry. We'll be standing by and available anytime you can have a personal chat. In the meantime, keep your spirits up and try to encourage your teammates. We'll figure out some way to get you home. I promise," Moses said to his daughter.

"Thanks, Dad. Good night, you guys. Kissy noise."

"Kissy noise to you, honey," her mom responded.

June 3, 2022
Winter Triangle Physics, Corpus Christi, Texas

Nicholas Schumer expected at any time to have federal agents come arrest him. By now, every law enforcement agency imaginable knew his satellite had caused the blackouts on two continents. He wasn't too concerned. As founder, president, and CEO of Winter Triangle Physics, he was the responsible party for any proven acts of terrorism committed by his company. However, Schumer had carefully documented the research into power generation that RePoGGS was designed to accomplish. To prove his company's innocence, he had over 200 four-inch binders with reams of investigation studies, meticulous reports on hundreds of experiments, and an army or researchers all of whom would swear their satellite was designed to create electricity, not destroy it. The official story would be he could not fathom what had happened during the deployment of the satellite that had led to the tragedies.

Schumer had made a few preparations in case his story did not hold up. Three hundred fifty miles off the west coast of Africa were the ten islands of Cape Verde. Schumer had, in the past year, built an immense and luxurious estate on Santiago, the largest of the ten islands. At his current worth and with the money he had hidden over the years in off-shore accounts, he could live here in absolute comfort. With the billions of dollars he was soon expecting to have in those same accounts, he would live like a king in his new home.

Cape Verde had been carefully chosen because it had no extradition agreement with the United States. When the inevitable island fever struck, Santiago had the Nelson Mandela International Airport which would easily handle the Boeing 757 he was planning to customize for himself and keep there. Considering the number of nations in Africa, Europe, and the Middle East which also had no extradition treaties with the US, he would be free to travel extensively.

Returning to the United States or Great Britain would never again happen, but he could live with that.

June 3, 2022
Exeter

"Sire, I know it's late there, but have you been following the shuttle mission?" Moses Forsyth was talking to his king, not his friend.

"Yes," was the reply. "How can we help?"

"We're still in communication with Terry. Obviously, no one knows about her device, but if they can't re-establish radio contact with Houston, would using the device be an option? Also, is there a way our people can supplement the NASA engineers to help get the shuttle and crew back safely?"

Annu thought several seconds before answering. "I'll get our engineers to access everything NASA has. Perhaps we can find something that will help."

He was still considering the ramifications to letting anyone from above know about the communications device Terry was carrying. For one thing, Exeter did not want the technology revealed for another ten years or so. For another, how would Terry explain how she came in possession of it? Her identity would forever be compromised and she would have to return to Exeter and abandon the work she was doing above.

"Moses, let's have Terry keep her ability to communicate a secret for now. If we can figure out a way for NASA to re-establish radio contact with the shuttle, there won't be any need to share our technology. Let's give our guys a day to work on it first. Does that sound okay?"

"Yessir. I'll tell Terry that's the decision so she will be careful not to reveal too much."

"Now then," the king continued, "how are things in Florida? When will Melissa get to join you?"

"I'm sorry I haven't kept you informed on Melissa. She's being moved to a regular room tomorrow. There's a possibility she'll be released in a few days. It's wonderful being young, isn't it?" There was a slight chuckle of relief at the end of the sentence.

"Yes, it is my old friend. I don't know if he's told you, but my son has arranged for a nurse to stay at your Florida home during the nighttime hours. That way you and Tame can get some rest instead of being up and down with Melissa all night."

"Sir, that's too expensive! We can take turns getting up with her when she needs us during the night. The cost of a nurse all night on top of the expense of this condo and the flight out here must be astronomical. I don't want to know how much this all costs."

"Good…because I have no idea how much it costs and don't really care. You and Tame have served the people of Exeter your whole lives. Now, you need Exeter and we will be there. Do not let the subject of money cross your minds again. It is not a burden nor a charity. It is a repayment for your services rendered."

There was no reply. Annu could not see his friend, but he knew the powerful leader and virtually invincible warrior was momentarily choked up.

"We will talk again tomorrow, Moses. Get some sleep."

"Yes, sire."

The phone line went dead. Annu placed a new call and it was answered almost instantly by J.R. Locklar, head of Exeter's computer section. She assured the king she would wake up whoever was needed to start working on the shuttle problem.

Annu felt better. If anyone could get the shuttle safely back to Earth, it was his team, not NASA's. Locklar was a genius with computer technology, and she had created a team with members who possessed a wide variety of skill sets.

Her cybernetics group would be able to figure out a solution of some sort, or so J.R. Locklar prayed.

Chapter Twenty-Nine

June 4, 2022
Concord, North Carolina

President Thomas Rogers was enjoying his second cup of coffee of the morning while sitting on the veranda of his home in North Carolina. This had become his morning ritual since leaving Washington D.C. and politics. Completing two terms as President and turning over the reins of government to President Roberson had felt like getting released from prison. His decision to stay completely out of the limelight had been a good one. He never made public comments about President Robertson's administration and he had steadfastly refused to be a guest on any political talk show.

Rogers had a reason for his denials. He had had to deal with the President he replaced. That man had left the presidency and immediately commenced a worldwide tour of public speaking appearances where criticism of Rogers' administration was his favorite topic. That kind of vanity was not in Tom Rogers' DNA.

As a former President, there was secret service detail still assigned to him and his wife, Ruth. For that group of agents, life was pretty dull. Since Rogers didn't do public appearances and rarely travelled far beyond Charlotte to the south or Greenville to the north they mostly patrolled the parameters of the fourteen acres around the boss's house. Another advantage of this posting was the way President and Mrs. Rogers treated them. Unlike some individuals from previous administrations who saw their agents as glorified servants, the Tom and Ruth Rogers treated their secret service detail like good friends who just happened to be carrying weapons.

The lead agent had been given the unfortunate name of John by his parents, Franklin and Sarah Smith. John Smith was a tall and imposing man with salt and pepper hair, emerald green eyes, and an intelligent face. He had been protecting his boss during the White House days and decided to follow him to North Carolina after the second term ended. After another four of five years, he planned on retiring, too.

There was a running joke in the Rogers home that when John Smith retired, he was going to start renting a room from the former President. That wasn't true, but the agent had fallen in love with the forested hills of North Carolina and had quietly bought a one-acre tract of land only a couple of miles away with plans for a modest home in the woods.

Smith came to his boss with an encrypted cell phone. Even former presidents did not want their conversations to be susceptible to being hacked. "Sir, there's a Mister Annu on the phone for you." He immediately saw the look of confusion, perhaps concern, on Rogers' face. "Sir, he had this number so I assumed he was on your okay list."

"John, I'll take the call, but just so you know, if you changed this number right now, Annu would have the new number in five minutes if he wanted it." He took the phone from his baffled agent.

The last time he had spoken to Annu had been from the Oval Office. Annu had somehow acquired the private phone numbers for Rogers' Chief of Staff at home, the Presidential residence and the Oval Office. He had had the audacity to tell them the United States was the target for a terror plot to detonate a dirty nuclear weapon in New York harbor.

The President had rejected Annu's claim outright and hung up. Later, when a freighter named the Pelegroso plowed into Liberty Island and was found to have in fact a disarmed weapon in the hold, the ship's crew told everyone who would listen that a crack military unit had somehow boarded the ship in the Atlantic and killed the terrorists who were behind the attack. They didn't know any more because they had been under guard the whole time.

The crew publicly praised President Rogers for the way he had sent the secret unit to save all of them and the city. President Rogers knew who was really responsible…the mysterious Annu. Now he might finally get to thank the man.

"Hello, Annu. It's been quite some time since we last talked. I hope this time it's not for the same reason as before."

"No, Mr. President. This call is to ask your help with a somewhat tricky situation."

"If it is in my power, the help is yours. I owe you a debt I cannot repay…that our country cannot repay. What can I do for you?

"I need President Robertson's influence on NASA to let us help return the shuttle crew safely home. I don't have time to convince him of my position or my ability to get difficult problems solved. I had some difficulty doing that last time." Annu actually chuckled, but Rogers remembered how he had labeled the king a madman with access to some tightly held phone numbers.

He had rejected Annu's offer and, while understandable, that decision could have cost millions of lives.

"You want me to call the President and tell him about you?"

"Yes, Mr. President. I have a way to open a door of communication with the shuttle, but it's along the same lines as the team who boarded the Pelegroso and then left it without revealing themselves. I need a certain degree of autonomy that NASA might not want to give us."

Rogers considered the request and how he would have responded to a call like the one he was certain he would make. "I will make the call right away. Unfortunately, the President is not always able to drop what he's doing to answer my call. Once I am able to talk with him, how can we reach you afterwards?"

"Actually, Mr. President, my people learned something from the last time you and I worked together to stop Azmud Salomi's terror attack. I could call you, but there was no way for you to contact me. Since then, my people have set up a system that provides me with a phone number that will ring where I am. As before, I'm afraid even your NSA won't be able to use that number to find me. My computer section was pretty proud of that detail." Again, there was a slight chuckle. Annu passed the number along to Rogers.

Ten minutes later, President Larry Robertson looked up from the work spread out on his desk when his private secretary, Donna Morr, walked in. The President of the United States had already been in the office for three and a half hours, as the crisis in Las Vegas and the almost certain shuttle disaster was occupying almost all of his time.

"Mr. President, President Rogers is on line one." Donna announced.

"Really?" Robertson asked a little surprised. Rogers had only called him once or twice in the past two years. Donna Morr nodded her head yes as her boss reached for the phone on his desk.

"Mr. President, how the heck are you?" President Larry Robertson asked. Then suddenly concerned the call might be personal continued, "Tom, are you and Ruth doing okay?"

"Mr. President, we are both well. Thank you for asking." There was a very slight pause before Rogers jumped right in. "Larry, obviously you remember the aborted nuclear attack on New York City a decade or so ago. Well, there's more to the story and I need to let you know some behind the scenes information about it."

Over the next several minutes, President Thomas Rogers revealed details of how King Annu had intervened to save the country despite Rogers' failure to act. He then encouraged Robertson to take seriously, no matter how farfetched, whatever he was going to hear shortly.

Robertson listened without interrupting. Since becoming President, he had been briefed on military and international secrets that to the normal civilian would seem impossible. He knew Tom Rogers was a man of honor and integrity and not prone to exaggeration. Robertson decided he would be open to whatever this Annu fellow proposed.

The two Presidents ended their phone call with an invitation for Tom and Ruth Rogers to attend a state dinner next week honoring the British Prime Minister. It would be the Rogers' first visit to the White House in quite a while.

Roberson pushed the far-left button on his console and said, "Di, come in here for a moment, please." Twenty seconds later, Di Dennington, White House Chief of Staff, came in from the side door that was almost concealed in the paneling of the Oval Office.

"Yessir?"

"Di, I'm about to make a phone call that I want you to listen to, but I do not want you to say anything. The call will be just between me and one other individual. You will have a lot of questions if the conversation goes the way I think it will, but hold them."

"Yessir," Di Dennington repeated. The next thing she heard did surprise her.

President Robertson pressed the far-right button on his console. "Donna, turn off all the recording devices in here and on my phone line." He didn't offer a reason and Morr didn't need one.

"You got it," a moment later Donna Morr continued, "Everything's off, Mr. President."

"That means you, too, Donna," Robertson laughed.

The only sound that came out of the intercom was a raspberry.

President Larry Robertson dialed the number Tom Rogers had given him. He could not remember the last time he had actually placed a call himself. It was answered almost instantly.

"Good morning, Mr. President. I see this call was placed from the Oval Office which tells me you have spoken with your predecessor. Thank you for calling."

Robertson wasn't sure what to expect but was ready to listen. "Do I call you King Annu or…?"

"Mr. President, please call me Annu. How much did President Rogers share with you?"

"Enough that I'm completely impressed and completely bewildered by your ability to remain hidden. I don't think I'd be betraying a confidence if I told you President Rogers spent a considerable amount of time and resources trying to locate you and your people after the New York incident. He really wanted to give you credit for saving the city and the country."

"Which is exactly why he was not able to find us. With due respect, nor will you. My people value our privacy above all."

"So, tell me how my administration can help you."

"One of my subjects is on the shuttle."

"That is impossible. No one could get near the shuttle, much less on the crew, without the most thorough background investigation. Every member of that crew has years of experience in their fields of study and have extensive vita."

"Mr. President, I'm not going to debate my every assertion. You can believe me or not, that is your prerogative, but your disbelief will not change the fact that a citizen of my realm is on that shuttle. That individual is carrying a miniature communication device that has been secretly allowing us to communicate back and forth since before takeoff."

"You don't, I assume, want to reveal which crew member has this device."

"That would have been our preference, but we recognize that will not be possible. We have decided saving the shuttle and her crew will be worth the very small risk to our privacy. Once there is communication between the crew and your mission control, we can start solving the problems associated with getting them home. My people are standing by to help NASA in any way to that end. We have accessed all the engineering data of every electronic instrument and communication system on the shuttle and are looking at finding options. The key, they tell me, is discovering exactly what could have been affected the shuttle in the same way as the power stations in Las Vegas. There are some theories that I suspect are the same as the ones NASA has developed."

Robertson found himself powerfully inclined to point out NASA had the finest minds in the country working on the problem, but was able to control that impulse. "Annu, we will gratefully accept any help you can provide. Establishing communication using the device you have described will be an amazing gift."

"It's not a gift, Mr. President. We will want our communication equipment back after this is over. I will tell you the device has been built to melt its own electronics if someone tries to open it in an attempt to accomplish reverse engineering. We are not yet ready to release it anyone outside our tribe." Annu let that sink in for a moment before continuing.

"We will deliver a single transmitter/receiver to NASA's mission control. My engineers have modified it to be compatible with the system you already use for communicating with the shuttle. Your CAPCOM will transmit just as always but the communication will be carried by our system, not NASA's. What we need from your office is an order to the top of NASA directing them to give us the access we need. You can couch it any way you wish. Tell them we are a top-secret section of any governmental agency you wish. I don't care, but we don't have time to go through their bureaucratic hoops. We just need to set this up without answering a lot of questions."

"I'll call NASA's Director of Flight Operations, John Maclemore, immediately. He will be directed to give you anything you need without question."

"Thank you, Mr. President. Our engineers will be there within three hours. Let's make it easy. They will have identification credentials saying they are with the Defense Intelligence Agency. Trust me, the credentials will be authentic which will make it easier for your misdirect."

"Authentic? Do your people really work for the DIA?"

Annu chuckled. "I have access to the DIA if I need it, but no, these people do not work for them. It's just an effective ruse for your convenience."

"There will be people at the main entrance to Mission Control who will be ready when your people get there, Annu. You have my word on it."

"Thank you, Mr. President. You can call me using this number any time you wish."

"If you need me, I'll tell the White House switchboard to put you through immediately."

"Thank you, but if I need you, I'll call a direct phone line wherever you are. There is no reason to trouble your switchboard. Goodbye, Larry. Thank you for making this easier."

Robertson didn't even seem to care that Annu had used his first name. That seemed a trivial infraction of protocol for anyone capable of the things this Annu guy was able to do.

June 4, 2022
Tortola, British Virgin Islands

Nicholas Schumer was having his first brunch in Tortola. His overnight flight in the company jet had left just before midnight and landed in this tropical spot in the British Virgin Islands six hours later. The flight plan had been to Puerto Rico, but an hour out from that destination, the pilots had followed Schumer's instructions to cancel their flight plan and then flown at a much lower altitude to Tortola. Schumer didn't believe this would hide his location long, but he would only be here a few hours.

He had a Gulfstream 650 standing by at the Terrance B. Lettsome International Airport for an overnight flight across the Atlantic to Cape Verde. He was confident he would shortly have billions of dollars streaming into his account. He was equally confident many of the industrialists he was blackmailing would doubt his resolve and soon dozens of locations around the world would suffer from the loss of their power supplies. Cape Verde would give Schumer the protection and the lifestyle of a king. It didn't bother him in the least that he would probably never again be in Corpus Christi nor even in the United States.

So far, none of the recipients of his message had responded with their payments. Schumer had decided to make a symbolic hit on a random member of the 56 as an encouragement to the others. For no reason in particular, he decided on the number 42. He checked his list and number 42 was Roald Ibsen, a shipping magnate from Stavanger, Norway.

Starting in 1972 with a single ship, the seventy-five-year-old Norwegian now had a fleet of sixty ships delivering oil and shipping containers to destinations around the world. His headquarters were located on the outskirts of the city and would make it especially easy to hit since only one grid powered the entire complex. The fact that the rest city would be almost completely spared meant nothing to Schumer. That was just their luck.

The miracle of cyberspace thought the Machiavellian entrepreneur as he referred to a list of coordinates in his database. He typed in the correct numbers and activated the satellite weapon. Since the satellite was in a geosynchronous orbit and the shuttle was orbiting at seventeen thousand five hundred miles per hour, Sojourner was fortunately on the opposite side of Earth this time.

In an instant, Ibsen Shipping found itself powerless. This time, the power station struck from space was very near the headquarters and that proximity also caused every computer and server in the building to be destroyed. The company had ships in thirty-one ports around the world and sixteen on the open ocean. There was now no way for the company to be in contact with the ships.

Worse yet, while company procedure was for files to be backed up to an off-station server every evening, that had not been accomplished in two weeks. The business was instantly crippled and Roald Ibsen knew why. He had already decided to ignore the messaged threat and not pay the protection money, but there were still eight hours left before the deadline. Why had his business been attacked early? Reluctantly, Ibsen realized a quick payoff of one billion dollars would have been infinitely cheaper than what he was facing.

Ibsen's personal laptop computer was not on his company system and so was saved from the total destruction of his company network. He was furious, but he was on the message channel within an hour telling all of the members that the lunatic could and would do as he threatened. Ibsen admitted his company was in ruins and would take quite some time to get everything going again.

Within three hours, everyone was responding. Most were asking for more time. Even people with wealth counted in the multi-billions had some difficulty getting one billion dollars in cash within 24 hours. Schumer had actually expected this and sent a note giving everyone a generous 36 hours. Nonetheless, before the end of the first eighteen hours, six billion dollars had been deposited into his accounts and almost everyone else on the list had promised to meet the demand. Schumer was pleased his little extra show of force had been so successful.

Tomorrow he would be in Cape Verde and his new life would be beginning.

Chapter Thirty

June 4, 2022
White House

President Larry Robertson's phone call to Dr. John Maclemore had not gone exactly as he expected. NASA's Director of Operations was not keen to have outsiders on his turf.

"Mr. President," he began, "just have these people drop off this magical device and we'll set it up."

"John, they will be there in about an hour. You will make sure someone is there to meet them, escort them to Mission Control, and give them all the assistance they need."

"Mr. President, I resent this intrusion into our process. NASA is perfectly capable of handling this."

"Dr. Maclemore, after this is all over and Sojourner is safely back on Earth, we can discuss your resentment." He waited a moment to consider his next comment, then went ahead. "If I hear you have not given this team your full and unwavering support, your assistant will have the opportunity to do so when I relieve you. Is that clear enough?"

Maclemore wasn't really sure the President had the authority to remove him as Director, but did not want to risk the possibility. "Yes, Mr. President."

As soon as the one-sided phone call was over, John Maclemore told his assistant, Dr. Angela Robinson, to personally see to the team when they arrived at the main gate. They were to get whatever they wanted. An hour and ten minutes later, two men with DIA identification were at the controlled entry portal as expected. Dr. Robinson was there and waiting with NASA badges encoded to allow the person wearing it entry into every area of flight operations. The men were carrying a slightly oversized brown leather satchel not unlike one a salesman might have samples in.

Robinson escorted the men into mission control and to the desk where the flight director on duty, Stephanie Blissett, was overseeing the increasingly frustrated team of controllers. In the thirty hours since they had lost contact with Sojourner, these controllers had been trying in vain to discover a way to communicate with the stricken crew. Long range scanners continued to show the shuttle was intact but could not give any indication of the crew's condition. The complete loss of all data from the shuttle led them to believe Sojourner's flight and navigation systems were probably inoperative, too. That meant their friends on orbit would most likely die there and these professionals found that demoralizing because they could not alter that outcome.

Three Flight Directors alternated eight-hour shifts the entire time a shuttle was on orbit. Each one always arrived at least an hour early to get up to speed on the current situation. Blissett was briefing Bud Stokesly and made no attempt to hide her irritation when the Assistant Director of Flight Operations walked up with two strangers.

"Excuse me," Robinson began, "can we step into the conference room for a moment?" She led the group fifteen feet to the glassed enclosed room that overlooked the bustle of activity going on in Mission Control.

The conference area allowed the five people to speak without being overheard. Blissett was not pleased with the interruption of her briefing and allowed her impatience to control her tongue, "Lady, I don't give a crap what your title is, but in Mission Control right now, I am in charge. You will have to wait until I am finished here!"

While Angela Robinson was taken back by the woman's outburst, the two men she was escorting were not. The one carrying the attaché simply asked, "Would you like to talk to Dr. Terry Lee?"

"Shit, you bastard, that's what we've been trying to do for almost thirty hours. Now if you and your little party will leave Mission Control, we'll get back to it."

Bud Stokesly interrupted Blissett by asking, "Are you suggesting you can talk to Terry right now?"

The man didn't answer. Instead he opened the attaché and removed a small device no larger than two packs of cards. He moved a switch on and said, "Terry, this is David Marcus. How do you read me?"

To the utter shock of everyone except the two outsiders, Terry Lee answered, "David! I never expected to hear your voice. Are you with my parents?"

"No, Colin Johnson and I are in Houston at Mission Control. King Annu made it possible for me to talk to you." There was no response. Terry was too surprised at hearing Annu's name to answer. "Terry, his highness spoke this morning to President Robertson and together they have decided to allow NASA to use your communication device to bring you all home."

"Thank God! No one has actually said it up here, but I'm pretty sure no one really expects to be on solid ground again. It'll be nice to dispel that feeling."

"You will be back and probably sooner than you expect. Our people have designed a patch that will give NASA fairly normal communication to the Sojourner. King Annu himself has given you permission to reveal your device to Captain Ledwell and the rest of the crew. You are released from your promise to keep it secret."

The relief in Terry's voice was obvious. "Thank you. I've wanted to so bad, but decided someone from home would contact me whenever there was a plan. So, you have that plan?"

"Sure," David Marcus lied. "Now that we're talking, stuff will start coming together."

Of the five people in the conference room, three were so dumbfounded by what was happening that they were at a loss for words. They were hearing something about a king nobody had ever heard of talking to the President and getting permission to somehow talk to the shuttle using a box no one had ever seen. Even these seasoned veterans of the space program were having difficulty processing what they were hearing.

On the flight deck of the Sojourner, Dr. Terry Lee asked her mission commander for a moment of his time. "Bubba, I have a small confession to give you."

"Terry, I'm not a real priest, but I'll hear your confession," Ledwell said in an overly pious tone.

"Yeah… not that kind confession." She handed Ledwell the box. The switch was in the third position and the small button on top activated. "Here."

He looked at it carefully. "Okay, I give up. What is it?

"Bubba, this is Bud Stokesly here in the MCC. How do you read me?"

The look of astonishment on Ledwell's face was instantaneous. "Bud? What the… ." Words escaped him.

"Bubba, when you get home, you and I and a very few others will sit down with a nice bottle of bourbon and try to get our stories straight about the little device you're holding and a long list of other surprises we've learned about in the past hour. But, for now, we're going to start by you detailing exactly what put you in this position and what you're looking at from a systems standpoint. Everybody on the engineering and design teams will want to know where to start looking for solutions. We've been shooting in the dark trying to figure what happened, but we have a pretty good idea it started with that satellite you guys launched."

"Yeah, it did. Terry and Tunes saw Elder activate the switches during the EVA. That wasn't in the plan. There was a very bright light and there must have been some sort of force generated because Elder was knocked unconscious and Tom broke his wrist. The wrist has been splinted, but Elder is still out. Janelle really can't do much for him up here other than keep an IV going." Ledwell made no mention of Terry and Tunes' flash blindness since they were totally recovered.

"Okay, Bubba. Listen. We are getting zero telemetry from you guys, so we can't really give much support right now."

"I'm not surprised. We're looking at black screens up here, too. Whatever the hell happened out there, it must have generated some sort of electromagnetic pulse because we instantly lost everything."

The man who had identified himself as Colin Johnson spoke to the flight directors next. "Ms. Blissett, Mr. Stokesly, we brought equipment and tools to patch this box into your sound system in Mission Control. Everything that is transmitted from the shuttle will be heard by everyone in the room. However, only one person will be able to speak to them."

"Only one person ever speaks to the crew anyway. I'll ask one of you to brief our CAPCOM on the use of your magic device here."

"Again, we will patch our box to your normal channels. Your CAPCOM will use his or her normal system. That will make the process more familiar."

Ledwell, who had been listening in to the hot-mic conversation, chimed in. "Whenever you get us on the loudspeaker, Bill and I can give the teams a synopsis on what we have going on up here."

Bud Stokesly took over as flight director but Stephanie Blissett hung around, too. It only took twenty minutes for the box to be installed and become operational. David Marcus and Colin Johnson seemed to know exactly where every connection needed to be made.

Once everyone could hear, for almost an hour, Captain Thurman Ledwell and Lt. Colonel Weaver described every switch position and circuit breaker on the entire flight deck to the engineers and scientific teams at NASA. Without knowing it, they were also describing everything for the engineers and scientific teams in Exeter.

Dr. Janelle McLain also used the system to give the flight surgeon in Mission Control her best assessment on L. Scott Elder's condition. Without telemetry, the consulting doctor could not really give much advice. McLain did tell him she was beginning to have hope that Elder would survive his injuries. His vital signs had stabilized and he was showing indications his coma was lighter. McLain could not be sure, but she thought being in microgravity might have saved his life. Without the pull of gravity on his torso, the internal bleeding seemed to be actually stopping. Elder was making sounds for the first time. There was nothing coherent, but it appeared he was wanting to talk. There were only four more bags of saline IV fluid in the medical supplies and after that was gone, McLain knew she would have to get Elder to a major medical center if he was to live.

Melissa was in her hospital room and was slightly disappointed that the television set was not working. After Moses mentioned to her doctor that Melissa's sister was on the shuttle Sojourner, the two men decided jointly to have the television unplugged. The physician did not want his patient worrying about her sister while still so weak.

Moses and Tame had purchased a tablet reader and loaded it with several books they knew Melissa liked. She would have had difficulty holding a hard copy of the books and turning pages, but she could easily handle electronic editions on a lightweight tablet.

When the Forsyths also informed the doctor their condominium was being furnished with a hospital bed and that there would be a registered nurse in the room from eight p.m. until eight a.m. every night, he decided Melissa could be discharged sooner than she normally would have been. He decided he would release Melissa from the hospital to their temporary home in twenty-four to forty-eight hours. That would be soon enough to learn about Terry.

As the Forsyths entered their condo, Cam was waiting with the communication device in hand. Tame's deep brown eyes widened and her face paled. "What's happened, son?" she asked fearfully.

"Nothing bad, but a lot of good," came the reply. The events of the past few hours were shared with Terry's relieved parents. "I don't think we should talk to Terry anymore. The channel is full of back-and-forth between the crew and Houston."

Everyone agreed and the mood among the entire group was elevated as a near celebration broke out. Kevin and Rob announced they were driving to the store to get the largest steaks they could find to grill. Kristi and Celia took the kids across the sand dunes to the beach and the refreshing Atlantic Ocean. Emmy and Aiden, growing up in the subterranean world of Exeter, had known only the numerous lakes of limestone filtered water that were in almost every community in the tribe. The crystal-clear water in those deep pools was always cold, but children from all over Exeter swam in them year-round anyway. Standing on the beach and looking out at endless blue salt water was exciting and yet a little intimidating for the children. They would not, however, allow the boundless expanse of sea to frighten them into staying on shore. Both were in the water, splashing and laughing with every wave that knocked them down.

After an hour in the ocean, Celia took Aiden back to the condos while Kristi took her daughter into the medium-sized dunes for some training on how to find fresh water at a seashore. Protector training was designed to prepare the warriors to survive in any weather condition and on any type of terrain, so why not take advantage of this golden opportunity.

Chapter Thirty-One

June 5, 2022
Santiago, Cape Verde

Nicholas Schumer was in his new home and settling in. His seven-hour flight from Tortola had been smooth and comfortable. As the sole occupant of a fourteen-passenger business jet, he had eaten a gourmet meal with a world-class wine, then slept for his usual six hours in absolute comfort. The flight attendant assigned the task of making his trip as close to opulent as possible had been largely ignored after dinner. She had spent most of the remaining time either in the cockpit chatting with the pilots or napping in her seat.

Since his plans were being achieved with far fewer complications than he had expected, Schumer was able to enjoy a relaxing late lunch with no demands requiring his attention. After the Norwegian shipping magnate had been removed from the original 56 recipients of his message, that left 55 billionaires to contribute to his retirement fund. In the past twenty-five hours, his bank account had grown to an astounding thirty-four billion dollars and the messages coming in told him nineteen of the remaining twenty-one individuals were raising funds to make their payments.

With thirteen hours left until his deadline, Schumer was feeling no pressure. The time limit was set in concrete, and he had already identified the two remaining holdouts and had their locations programmed into his database. One minute after the cutoff point, those two enterprises, one in India and one in Canada, would be shut down. Unfortunately, the company in India was located right in the center of a major city. Annihilating that company would also leave almost one million people without power, but that problem resided with India, not Schumer.

There were still a few details regarding the new compound in Cape Verde left to be completed. The ten thousand square foot house with five bedrooms, eight bathrooms, and various entertaining areas was finished, but the thirty-seat movie theater, swimming pool, putting green and exercise room still had two weeks of work ahead.

The first thing completed had been a twelve-foot solid concrete fence with imbedded spikes around the entire three-acre estate. Sensors attached to the wall would alert the security staff if anyone attempted to climb over the enclosure. Those same sensors would automatically focus high-definition and infrared cameras to the exact spot on the fence where an alert originated. Schumer had a multi-million dollar contract with the same company that provided protection for almost every elected leader and dictator in Africa. A team of fourteen guards were on duty twenty-four hours a day and armed with an impressive array of weapons. These men didn't care one bit about who they were protecting nor how they earned their money. All they cared about was making sure their contract continued which meant killing anyone they even thought might be a threat.

June 5, 2022
Kennedy Space Center

Commander Russ Boda had been in the Kennedy Launch Control Center when NASA lost all contact with Sojourner. He had felt powerless listening to Houston's unsuccessful and increasingly frantic radio calls on every possible frequency and radio. As the hours passed, Boda became even more frustrated. He was certain the shuttle simulator in Houston, not the one in Florida, would play a key role in trying to save his friends, and because he served as Ledwell's backup pilot, no one knew the flight deck procedures better than he did. He called Bob Paulus at home. Boda got right to the point. "Bob, wanna take a trip to Houston? I'd rather belt sand my nipples than stay around here." Paulus, who had been the backup pilot for Bill Weaver, had been considering the same thing as his buddy. After Boda's usual colorful expression, the rest of the conversation lasted only two minutes.

Believing in the adage that it is better to beg forgiveness than ask permission, neither man told anyone they were flying to Houston. The personnel in charge of maintaining NASA's T-38s assumed when Boda and Paulus showed up and filed a flight plan to Houston that they had all the necessary approvals. They didn't.

Nonetheless, within an hour, they were wheels up for a planned trip across the Gulf of Mexico to Ellington Air Force Base in Houston.

Each pilot had more than a thousand hours flying the incredible two seat T-38 which NASA used as its preferred transportation jet for astronauts. They were fast, sleek, and relatively economical to operate. Plus, the pilots loved to fly the highly maneuverable jet.

Since both pilots in this case felt time was of the essence, they flight planned to cruise at the T-38's highest allowable altitude, 45,000 feet or flight level 450. This would put them above all commercial airliners and would allow them to go straight to Ellington instead of having to follow established routes used at lower altitudes. Being at that extremely high altitude presented a major problem with the T-38. Because of the very thin atmosphere, the airplane would stall at a much higher airspeed than at a lower altitude. However, staying above the stall speed put the aircraft close going supersonic. Going faster than the speed of sound created a huge shockwave that caused drag on the jet to increase four times. With that additional drag on the jet, they would not have enough fuel to reach Houston in one hop. That meant staying above the stall speed and yet less than supersonic; a very small speed envelope. Being at FL450 required smooth control and careful operation of the throttles.

Both pilots felt comfortable with their skill in flying the jet in that extreme situation. Boda requested and received a clearance for an unrestricted afterburner climb to FL450 immediately after takeoff. Unrestricted climb let them fly straight to that altitude without stopping at any intermediate altitudes. Incredibly, even with the Florida temperature, they would reach the jet's maximum altitude in less than two minutes after liftoff. Once there, they would cruise at nine tenths the speed of sound.

The weather Gods were in their favor and even the high-altitude jet stream was cooperating. There was virtually no headwind and their time from the Space Center in Florida across the entire Gulf of Mexico to Ellington Air Force Base in Texas would only take an hour and fifteen minutes. Twenty minutes before landing at Ellington, Russ left Houston Center's Air Traffic Control frequency long enough to call Ellington tower. The tower supervisor was happy to call Mission Control's command center to inform the MCC the two pilots would be available if needed in the simulator.

Kel Trotter, the astronaut serving as CAPCOM, was sorting through a stack of diagrams and checklists covering his desk. To him, it seemed every engineer in NASA had a personal theory about the best way to reestablish Sojourner's flight instrumentation.

Trotter was an Air Force Academy graduate who had flown two tours after pilot training and then been accepted into the astronaut corps. He had an aristocratic, Nordic appearance with a tall, slender build and short blond, almost white, hair. In private conversation, Trotter spoke with a quietness that drew listeners in to him, but when in his role as capsule communicator, he spoke with a calm clear voice that demanded attention. Trotter had been Ledwell's shuttle pilot on the near disastrous Explorer mission two years before and was scheduled to be the mission commander on a shuttle mission in twenty-four months. He was the perfect man for the CAPCOM job in the current situation.

Trotter had been told Russ Boda and Bob Paulus were en route and keyed his mic to address the Flight Director. "Boss, any chance we can send those two straight to the simulator when they land? Having them in the box would sure make it better when we get to running checklists that were written by engineers, not pilots. I'd appreciate their experience."

"Done," was the response.

One phone call from the flight director's desk was all it took to ensure there would be a staff car waiting at Ellington to transport the men. With Boda in the simulator left seat and Paulus in the right seat, the work would be significantly more streamlined.

The supervisor of flight simulation was Deb Trotter, a blond beauty with radiant blue eyes that could melt an ice cube. She had met her husband, Kel, while he was going through his Explorer shuttle training and the attraction between the two was instantaneous and powerful. Six months later, they were added to the list of NASA married couples.

Not surprisingly, the NASA shuttle simulator operations group was extremely proficient. Trotter's team had, based upon Bubba Ledwell's description, reconfigured the simulator to duplicate Sojourner's situation. As Kel evaluated different procedures, he would read them off to Boda and Paulus in the simulator just like he was hoping to do over the radio to the shuttle. Any ambiguity in the phrasing would show up doing it this way.

In Exeter, engineers and scientists lacked the simulator to try out options, but they did have something else…a brilliance of minds known nowhere else on Earth. They had decided on an entirely different course of action than NASA was considering. Instead of trying to restore instrumentation though resetting switches and circuit breakers, Exeter wanted the crew to physically rebuild the system on orbit. They considered that since the mission commander's left seat flight instruments came from an entirely separate computer than the shuttle pilot's instruments in the right seat, they could possibly build one good system from the two broken ones. Exeter had hacked into all the technical drawings from the shuttle's designers and found a way to access the modules they would need.

Within three hours, they were in contact with David Marcus and Colin Johnson in Mission Control with recommendations and preliminary procedures.

With their carte blanche freedom in Mission Control, the two men from Exeter went straight to the Flight Director's desk which was something no controller would dare do. Marcus asked quietly, "Can you afford a few minutes with us? We have a recommendation for a procedure that we want to present you and any technician you choose."

"Sure," Stokesly replied. "We'll make the time."

Bud Stokesly would go off duty in an hour and his replacement, Bill Techman, had just walked into the Mission Control Center. "Bill, would you ask the guys in the bullpen to send someone over who is current with what they're working on?"

"Absolutely. I don't think they've settled on much of a plan, but I'll bring the team chief."

Ten minutes later, a composite group of NASA engineers had joined the two flight directors to listen to Marcus and Johnson. The NASA scientists were under the impression the unknown guests were from a contractor think tank. They were not pleased to have been pulled from their problem solving to listen to someone else's nonsensical proposal.

Johnson put a dozen pages of schematic drawings on the conference table. "Gentlemen, we've been treating this problem the same way we would treat an electrical or communication failure on a modern commercial aircraft. That's understandable since we tend to think of the shuttle as highly specialized flying craft. In a modern jet, a power distribution failure can often be reestablished by opening and closing a series of circuit breakers and switches in a specific sequence. Those procedures are designed to force relays to reset in a distinct order. The problem, as we see it, is that this is not a power disconnect that can be reestablished using sequencing. Instead, we think entire computer boards are burned out. As all of you know, that's usually the kiss of death for a computer system, but this time it's possible we've found a solution."

David Marcus picked up the briefing. He placed several diagrams side-by-side on the desk. When combined, they were a schematic of the flight computer system.

"Ladies and gentlemen, our engineers picked up on an interesting design quirk. For some reason, probably cost, one company developed the computer interface to the mission commander's flight instruments in front of the left seat. An entirely different company developed the computer interface to the shuttle pilot's right seat flight instruments. We think this may actually be the most providential cost saving decision in the history of the space program. The power input and display output for each flight computer actually follow similar yet unique pathways. That difference may be our saving grace. For a moment, think of a circuit breaker in a home. If there is an electrical surge into a house, the circuit breaker trips and the danger stops there. The electrical system is designed for the circuit breaker to be thrown offline before a surge can damage the entire house wiring system.

"Computers like the ones we're dealing with do not have circuit breakers. Reviewing the computer design schematics, our people noticed both companies, as a cost saving measure, used material in the board that will actually melt when subjected to a high electrical load. The composition of these particular components may hold our solution."

Marcus waited until he was sure everyone was nodding in agreement or at least paying attention.

"Alright, here's our theory. When Sojourner's computer system was struck by that power surge, the first mother board would have melted almost instantly. Once that component was fried, it's possible, we hope probable, that the destroyed mother board worked like a circuit breaker to the components downstream. This is where having two computer contractors is in our favor. The design means different motherboards in the computers would be melted first."

Marcus looked momentarily around the room. "Our suggestion is to make one operable computer out of two inoperative ones. We believe we can instruct a crew member how to cannibalize parts from the right seat computer to replace components in the flight commander's computer. That single operating computer could then drive Ledwell's flight instrumentation for re-entry and landing."

It didn't take much skill to read the skepticism on the faces of almost everyone. Marcus decided to continue before they could start shooting down his idea.

"There is a mountain of problems to climb for this to work. Assuming the surviving components are the ones we need, and assuming someone, probably Dr. Dalton, can fabricate an operable computer.

Kel Trotter spoke before the flight director did. "It still won't be a complete system. Captain Ledwell will have flight instrumentation, but autopilots require two operable computers to handle the flight. Bubba will have to hand fly the re-entry and landing. Without his computer, Bill Weaver will also have to manually control the engine burn to decelerate the shuttle and start the descent. Ledwell's maneuvering will have to be on a paper-thin arrival corridor without the aid of an autopilot. I know first-hand he's done that before, but the

Explorer shuttle was already on the descent profile and was stabilized when we had our problem.

"This time, if we're able to make this composite computer happen, the two pilots will be required to fly the shuttle with the same precision as the autopilot. If Bubba's even a little too shallow, the shuttle's descent path will be high and no one can guess where they would crash but probably somewhere in the Atlantic Ocean. The weight of Sojourner and the sink rate at touchdown means a water landing like that brilliant flight crew did a few years ago in the Hudson River is totally impossible. The shuttle would disintegrate the second it hit the ocean. If on the other hand, Ledwell is just a tiny bit too steep, the shuttle will burn up in the atmosphere."

Everyone in the room already knew those two outcomes. Trotter ended the discussion stating the fact no one really wanted to mention.

"Of course, if nothing is done, the guys in the back room estimate the shuttle orbit will decay in approximately thirty-seven years and…"

"What about the International Space Station?" one of the NASA engineers jumped in. "We've got long range detection on the shuttle and we can talk with them now. Give them vectors to the general vicinity of the ISS. Within a hundred miles or so, they would be able to visually maneuver the rest of the way. After they rendezvous with the ISS, we can move them over and keep them there until we can come up with a rescue plan. The ISS would be very crowded, but she was just refurbished with food and supplies so the group would be sustainable."

Bill Techman, a man with a brilliant mind for logistics and complex planning, had already considered that option. "I thought about the ISS, too, but had to discard it. There isn't a shuttle docking port installed in Sojourner's payload bay, so a direct entry is impossible. That leaves transfer by EVA. Only Tom Fredrick is qualified using the Manned Maneuvering Unit and every transfer would have to be made using the MMU to drag the second member between the two craft. We know Tom has a broken wrist which makes controlling the unit with precision a near impossibility and from what we've been told, the MMU control stick may be broken. Secondly, there are only two suits on the shuttle which means it would take seven round trips to transfer everyone. That won't be possible. During Tom and Scott's EVE, we lost telemetry from the backpack at the same time as the shuttle. We know the fuel remaining in the MMU at that moment and can estimate the amount used to return the men to Sojourner. Gentlemen, there is only enough fuel in the MMU right now for four, perhaps five round trips at best. That number would be valid only if Tom is able to go straight between the two ships which is somewhat unlikely. When he no longer had fuel for a round-trip EVA, Tom would be forced to stay on the ISS and leave whoever was still on the shuttle.

"I've known Tom Fredrick many years, and I'd put a sizable bet he wouldn't do that. He would use the remaining fuel to return to Sojourner and spend his remaining time with his friends there. He would choose that ending over surviving while they died."

With the International Space Station off the table as a rescue site, the computer rebuild concept started gaining status.

Stokesly, as the senior mission director and de facto leader, looked over at Bill Techman who gave him an almost imperceptible nod.

"Okay," Stokesly began. "We have another week's supplies on the shuttle plus a day or two of reserves. I want a plan, procedures, and a list of contingency considerations in twenty-four hours. Tell the simulator people we're going to try whatever procedures you come up with on one of the ground-based cockpits before we try it on the full motion one." He looked at his watch. "Change my times. I want all that data in twenty-two hours."

People started to move out of the room but Stokesly stopped Techman, Johnson, and Marcus. "Bill, do you mind coming in a couple of hours early tomorrow? I want you here when everyone presents their ideas. I'll ask Stephanie Blissett to come in, too. The three of us should get the plan at the same time. I have a feeling these two gentlemen already know something they haven't shared yet." He smiled benignly at the two from Exeter. "Am I right?"

David Marcus looked thoughtfully at the ceiling, then at Johnson, then at Stokesly and Techman. "Well, you already know we smuggled a very small, but extremely powerful communication device on the shuttle. What you don't know is that it is a prototype for devices of this kind. We wanted to monitor how it was working on orbit, so we incorporated a sensor to evaluate the signal strength."

"Why am I not surprised? Listen, I don't imagine you're going to tell us who the hell you are or where you come from. I'm not buying for one friggin' second that you're from the DIA," Techman said. "We've put too many satellites into orbit for the NSA, or DIA, or CIA, or any other set of letters not to recognize their handiwork. Not to put too fine a point on it, but your stuff is way ahead of anything I've ever seen…and I've seen a lot in my time."

"When questions like that come up, my boss just likes to say, 'we're friends.'" Marcus replied. "I'm afraid that will have to do for now."

"Is your boss the guy you called 'King Annu' when you spoke to Terry?" Both men nodded but added no more explanation.

Techman and Stokesly quietly nodded their heads in acceptance. They both knew they would learn nothing more from either of these two men. They also had, for some inexplicable reason, complete confidence in their highly illogical proposal.

Chapter Thirty-Two

June 6, 2022
Santiago, Cape Verde

Nicholas Schumer was a very rich man. Attached to his accounts in four off-shore banks were fifty-five billion dollars. Even for organizations accustomed to large balance sheets, this was an extraordinary amount of money.

At the last moment, there had been no need to disrupt power associated with the two reluctant businessmen after all. With three hours left until his hard deadline, Schumer had sent private messages to the men. All he mentioned was the time remaining and the exact latitude and longitude precise to the half-second of their key facility and the phone number for Roald Ibsen in Stavanger, Norway.

Neither man called Ibsen. Instead, they each transferred a billion dollars to the bank listed on their first message.

June 6, 2022
Titusville, Florida

Melissa Forsyth was brought to the condominiums early in the morning and was settled in her rented hospital bed.

"Well," she said jokingly, "this isn't as luxurious as my hospital room, but I suppose it'll have to do." She looked to Cam. "What happened to the lady who shot me?" The look in her brother's eyes revealed the answer. "Quickly?" He nodded a barely noticeable yes. "Okay," was her only response.

Tame Forsyth told everyone to leave the room. Her tone was such that no one, not even Moses or Cam, even thought of staying. Over the next thirty minutes, Tame's gentleness tempered with strength was put to the test as she told Melissa all about her sister's situation. Tame kept the information upbeat and positive yet honest. When everything was out and in the open, both women hugged and cried together for a few minutes. It was the first time since the shuttle crisis had started Tame had allowed herself that outlet.

After the tears passed, it was as if a massive load was lifted off Tame and washed into the nearby Atlantic Ocean. Melissa also made the decision everyone else in the residence had made…no television set was turned on. There was no reason to listen to the doom and gloom reporting.

They kept up with the progress first-hand. Since the Forsyths had a communication device with them, everyone had been listening to the transmissions between the shuttle and Houston. Before David Marcus had made his first contact with Terry from mission control, King Annu had called Isha to give him advanced warning. The king did not want the Forsyths talking to Terry any more. All communications would be focused on saving the crew; personal conversations would have to wait.

June 6, 2022
Johnson Space Center Simulator Building

In Houston, a team of engineers were dissecting two working computers installed in one of the simulators. Kel Trotter was reading the detailed checklist instructions he had been given for the procedure and were following them to the letter.

The biggest obstacle they had to overcome was the requirement to only use tools and materials aboard the Sojourner. Even on a ship as large as this new-generation shuttle, space was at a premium.

To reach the computers, the shuttle pilot's seat had to be removed which was difficult because the unit was extremely heavy, but microgravity would negate that problem for the shuttle crew.

It took an hour to access the motherboards and another three hours to swap out the components. Finally, the moment of truth arrived. One circuit breaker at a time was pushed back in. After each push, fifteen seconds were given to see if it would trip. None did. When the sixteenth circuit breaker went in, there was an immediate flicker on the four screens mounted in front of the mission commander's left seat.

A cheer went up from everyone around. There had been very few missteps in the process and just a few places where the directions were not perfectly clear. Those were addressed and corrected.

On orbit, Dr. Jim "Tunes" Dalton was ready to start what he had taken to calling his computer surgery. Ledwell and Weaver had removed the right seat and lashed it safely to the aft bulkhead. Dalton had enlisted Patti Koch to help him with the assembly procedure. All the tools they had been told to have ready had been placed in a canvas bag which would give Koch easy access.

Mission Control was quiet as controllers, sitting in front of their blank screens, stopped all their small talk and listened in to the communication going on between the CAPCOM and the crippled shuttle which was still in the highest Earth orbit any shuttle had ever attained. Sojourner's altitude of 407 nautical miles had not changed since the first day of orbit, but no one knew for sure that was accurate. Her precise position was also a guess since long range sensors could only give rough location readouts. Interestingly, the astronauts actually had a better idea of their location. They had passed almost directly over the Hawaiian island of Kauai three minutes before, which meant it was 850 nautical miles behind them. In less than nine minutes they would be over the west coast of California. The skies over the Pacific Ocean were crystal clear with only a few high cumulus clouds as contrast against the azure blue water to disrupt visibly from space. The mission commander and shuttle pilot were so familiar with the geography before them, they could pinpoint their position purely by sight alone.

Ledwell and Weaver were both a little uncomfortable trying to stay out of the way of Dalton by standing behind the flight deck. Their domain looked naked with one seat missing and lower panel covers removed and exposing the guts of their flight computers. Tunes Dalton was well aware his work in the next couple of hours would probably determine if the shuttle and her crew would ever stand a chance of being safely back on Earth.

"Tunes," Patti whispered quietly, "get this right and I'll make sure you get that Steinway grand piano you've been lusting over for years."

"The ebony one?"

"Is there any other kind?"

"You do know, Patricia," Dalton answered. "I needed that extra incentive because just saving our butts wasn't enough pressure. Now you've added my second biggest lust object on the pile. Thanks for that extra motivation."

"Second? What's first?"

Tunes Dalton smiled shyly. "Not really a 'what'. It's a 'who'."

"Are you at liberty to name this mystery person?"

"No. It wouldn't be appropriate. She's married," he shook his head in mock sadness. "I will just tell you she's a goddess who plays jazz piano like no one else can and has a sultry singing voice that is the soundtrack of my dreams."

Koch slowly shook her head resignedly. "Can't help you there, Romeo, but I'll make you a deal. Get these screens working and I'll make sure you get the Steinway a week after we land. It'll take me that long to cash in my 401K and take up a collection from the crew and everyone in Mission Control to make up the difference."

Suddenly, impulsively, Dalton kissed his friend. Both of them were surprised.

"Are you two finished?" the voice of Bud Stokesly came from the speaker of the communication device held in place by cords. They had forgotten they were hot mic. Stokesly continued, "Because if you are, we have a checklist for you." There was a pause then he whispered as if only Koch could hear, "Patti, put me down for one hundred dollars to the Dalton piano fund."

Dr. Jim "Tunes" Dalton took a deep breath and said, "Okay, guys let's go."

In Houston, the CAPCOM, Kel Trotter, began reading the step-by-step process that had been practiced four times in the simulator. He silently prayed they had rooted out and revised all the confusing or misleading directions. There would be no chance to fix any errors this time.

"Tunes," he began, "if you have even the slightest doubt about what I'm telling you to do, stop and ask me to clarify the step. We're going to take this nice and slow. I'm on overtime now and feel absolutely no pressure to speed through."

"Gotcha, Kel. I'm ready."

In the simulator, the fourth attempt to replicate the procedure had taken a little less than three hours. The timer in Mission Control was reading four hours sixteen minutes elapsed when the CAPCOM said, "Okay, Tunes, that's it. We have sixteen circuit breakers to reset. I'll call out the position and I want you to repeat it before pushing the button back in. Once it's in, we'll wait fifteen seconds before continuing. Okay?"

"Roger. I've got both Bubba and Bill here with me and listening in. We'll all follow you."

There were eight electrical panels on the flight deck and circuit breakers on each had been pulled to un-power specific components. Each circuit breaker was identified first by the panel name then with a letter designating which row, then a number designating which circuit breaker position on that row.

"Aft electrical panel three…circuit breaker C-16."

"Aft three, C-16." In the shuttle, all three men nodded. "In."

"Right overhead panel…circuit breaker B-3."

"Right overhead, B-3." Again, the nods before the button was pressed in.

Finally, there was only one remaining circuit breaker. "Tunes, left overhead panel…circuit breaker A-6."

Dr. Jim "Tunes" Dalton crossed himself unconsciously and repeated, "Left overhead, A-6."

Everyone on the crew, except for L. Scott Elder, had come up to the flight deck level. Elder was still unconscious and secured to a reclined seat on the lower level. All seven held their breath as Jim Dalton confirmed the position with Ledwell and Weaver, then pressed the last circuit breaker in.

Nothing happened for five seconds. Ten seconds passed with blank screens in the cockpit. Just as everyone in the shuttle was about to give up hope, a voice came from the black box lashed to the floor. It was muffled which meant the person was not right by the CAPCOM seat.

"Flight! I've got data!"

Another voice chimed in, "Flight! I've got data, too."

Five seconds later, the four screens mounted in front of the Mission Commander's seat flickered on. The colors had never looked so beautiful to any of the crew.

In a condominium on the Florida coast, eight adults had been listening in to the broadcast in total silence. The two children had been kept busy playing in the sand that covered the courtyard. Suddenly the children heard everyone inside yelling. They ran in and found all the adults laughing and hugging each other. The two children had no idea why everyone was so happy, but they were enjoying the celebration.

Within fifteen minutes, every major news network had broken in on their regular broadcasts with news communication had been restored with Sojourner and Mission Control was now receiving data. No mention was made as to how it had all happened.

In Washington, D.C. and in rural North Carolina, two Presidents privately celebrated some guy named Annu and his people…whoever and wherever they were.

Chapter Thirty-Three

June 6, 2022
Houston

Moses and Tame Forsyth were invited, as were family members of every crew member, to a briefing at NASA. There, Flight Director Stephanie Blissett brought everyone up-to-date on the ongoing efforts to return their loved ones home. She was known as someone who believed in giving all the facts without glossing the truth or using platitudes to build false hopes.

Blissett started by giving a synopsis of what had transpired the day before. She gleaned over how communication had been reestablished with Sojourner so all of the listeners, except two, assumed NASA had been responsible for the radio contact.

"Having communications and flight instrumentation on the mission commander's side are only the first two challenges in a long list of complications that have to be overcome or solved in order to safely land the shuttle. Our next concern has to do with the orbital maneuvering system engines located on the tail of the shuttle. Those engines, which are tiny compared to the main shuttle engines, will have to fire in order to slow the orbiter enough to enter the atmosphere. We won't know if the blast from the satellite has damaged these smaller engines until it comes time to operate them in the morning."

"Why are you waiting so long to bring them down?" the anxious mother of L. Scott Elder asked. "You can talk to them and have the instruments you said you needed. Why are you waiting? I want my son on the ground right now! He's been hurt up there in your shuttle." Several others in the audience nodded their heads in support of the question.

Stephanie Blissett was able, just barely, to control her immediate impulse to remind the lady it was her son's experiment that had put them in this situation.

Instead She instead answered calmly, "First of all, we are not sure exactly what happened to your son. He is getting the best care possible considering the location. Regarding the timing, there are actually two reasons for waiting until in the morning. First, we need the shuttle to be in the correct spot for decelerating. Because of the Earth's rotation, relative to the shuttle's orbit, we have to wait until the correct place on Earth coincides with the shuttle's location. That will happen at 0630 tomorrow. Second, we have to practice all the new flying procedures in the simulator to make sure our computations are correct for Captain Ledwell's maneuvering. I'm sure you understand now why we have to wait until in the morning."

Stephanie Blissett smiled, but there was no smile in her eyes. She continued, "Okay, if the OMS fires and begins the deceleration, the next unknown will come immediately. The shuttle has what is called fly-by-wire flight controls. Essentially that means when Captain Ledwell moves the control stick, he doesn't actually directly move any control surfaces. Instead, his movement sends a message to a computer and that computer commands changes in the directional controls. In space, the shuttle uses twenty small thrusters at the front and rear of the fuselage to move around. We won't know for sure if the fly-by-wire computers work until he actually tries a maneuver after the deceleration engine burn. We believe they will because, unlike the flight instrumentation computers that are on the more vulnerable flight deck, the flight control computers are located deep in the belly of Sojourner. That area is surrounded by the thick heat resistant tiles used to protect the shuttle during landing and by heavy metal sheeting. Our analysis, based largely on guesswork I'm afraid, says the flight control computers will work."

Stephanie Blissett looked at the blank stares from most of the people in front of her. She was attracted to one couple, Terry Lee's parents she recalled, who seemed almost at ease. *Obviously, they don't get the danger their daughter is in. That's okay. Let them bask in ignorance for now.* "The final major hurdle to jump before the shuttle can safely land will come after the deceleration burn and use of the initial flight controls to set up for re-entry. Can Captain Ledwell, or any pilot, manually fly the shuttle all the way from space until landing? On a normal flight, the autopilot flies the entire re-entry from orbital altitude until approximately eight thousand feet above the ground. This time, Captain Ledwell will be responsible for flying all the initial, very precise, maneuvers without the aid of autopilot. Now I'm going to be very honest with you. This will be the most dangerous and unforgiving part of getting everyone home. The shuttle data readout in Mission Control is only half of what we usually have, so we won't be able to provide much advice to the commander as he flies the arrival corridor, but I'm convinced Captain Ledwell and Lt. Colonel Weaver are up to the challenge."

After the briefing, many of the family members went on a guided tour of the Space Center. Moses and Tame returned to their condo to tell everyone else what they had learned. Isha found a media video that showed a graphic illustration of what would be going on tomorrow as the Sojourner began her descent to landing. For first-generation shuttles, the time from when the orbital maneuver engines fired until touchdown was only slightly more an hour. However, because of Sojourner's much higher orbit, it would take an hour forty-three minutes which would seem like an eternity.

On the mid-deck of the Sojourner, L. Scott Elder awoke suddenly and seemed to be fully conscious. Dr. Janelle McLain and Dr. Terry Lee were the only two near him at that moment.

"Where am I?" he cried out. "What happened?" Then the cloud in his head lifted and Elder blinked his eyes several times and seemed for a moment to calm down. He looked at McLain, but didn't really speak to her. Instead he was talking to himself as if no one else were around. "That bastard knew. He knew and he didn't tell me. That son of a bitch!"

Terry called up the hatch for one of the men to come down. She was afraid Elder would become violent and she didn't want to be here with only McLain against him. Almost immediately Thurman Ledwell, Bill Weaver, Tom Fredrick and Jim Dalton floated quickly to the mid-deck leaving Patti Koch to mind the flight deck. The mid-deck was crowded, but no one really seemed to notice.

Elder's eyes were wide with a combination of fear and anger. His skin was as pale as the clouds below them, but his expression was impossible to decipher. "Schumer did this. He meant for me to die. That bastard!"

Ledwell, usually one hundred percent business and no nonsense, spoke instead in a quiet, almost fatherly tone. "Scott, we've got the shuttle fixed well enough to land her. You're going to be in a nice hospital soon. Just relax. Everything is okay."

"No! I'm not going to relax until I see Schumer behind bars for murder, racketeering, and trying to kill me."

"What are you talking about, Scott?"

"He told me there would be no blowback from the satellite. He said it would hit the power station and no one would know how it happened." Elder paused letting his mind clear a bit more. "He told me that he wanted me to fire the first attack during the EVA in case his ground control unit didn't work. He said I was in no danger doing that, but he lied. He wanted me to die in space so I couldn't expose his work after the mission."

Ledwell still believed Elder was confused and probably suffering from either a head injury or the effects of Janelle's drugs, and still tried to calm the man down. Elder would not rest until he said what he needed to say.

"Josh Tanner, was my best friend…probably the only friend I ever had in life. He was working for the same man I am, Nicholas Schumer. Josh told me that Schumer had killed some military pilot and then Catherine Austin. Catherine's death almost put Josh over the edge. I think he loved her, but she wouldn't give him the time of day. Josh told me Schumer ordered him to have some reporter named Forsyth killed. Josh was afraid of Schumer, but said he wouldn't have to work for him long. Schumer had some plan to use the RePoGGS to somehow make a bunch of billionaires pay him for protection money. Josh discovered, but wasn't supposed to know, Schumer was going to take all that money and live somewhere the US government couldn't reach him. Josh didn't care where he went as long as he'd soon be free of that murderous son of a bitch."

In Mission Control, everyone listened in to the confession uncomprehendingly. Sitting at a table in their temporary home, Cam

Forsyth and Prince Isha were listening in also, and the confession meant everything to them. The obvious calmness in Forsyth's face worried Isha. The Prince recognized the look because it was the same one he would get when he became very angry, which didn't happen often. Isha would become extremely quiet and soft spoken instead of being his usual far more gregarious self. He was aware the same thing was happening to his friend.

"Cam, you don't have any foolish plans in that brain of yours, do you?"

"Sire, I was thinking two things. One is that Elder was already in space and doesn't know his friend Josh Tanner was killed during a second attempt on my life ordered by Schumer. Second, Schumer must have activated his plan after the satellite crippled the Sojourner. That means he initiated his protection money extortion plot after our visit. He must have thought Catherine Austin had betrayed his plan and he killed her for it. Then he tried twice to have me killed believing I knew something."

Forsyth spoke his next words very carefully. "Sir, if what Elder said is true, Nicholas Schumer has probably received some very large payoffs somewhere. I don't know how much, but since Elder identified his targets as billionaires, we can assume it's a lot of money. Do you think we can find out where the money went?"

Isha didn't answer immediately. Instead, he grabbed his phone and dialed a ten-digit number then he added three additional numbers. The phone was answered after the second ring.

"How can I help you, Sire?" The sweet voice of J.R. Locklar came through clearly.

"J.R., how did you know it was me calling? I'm not even at home."

"Sir," she responded with a saccharine voice. "Where do I work? I know everyone who calls here. I also know you're not here. At this second you are, let me see,"—she paused to refer to her computer—"Right now you are in Titusville, Florida." She gave the exact address where everyone was staying.

"I want you to use your powers for good now, J.R. Remember that guy you were checking out for me named Nicholas Schumer? He has come into a sizable amount of money in the past two or three days. Can you find out where it is and who gave it to him?"

"If it's a lot of money, he didn't use any American or Canadian bank. They have strict rules. However, there are some banks in the Caribbean that have a more relaxed standard of rule keeping. Can I call you back in a few minutes?"

"I'll be waiting. Thanks, J.R."

The two men discussed possible ways to cause Nicholas Schumer's life to be difficult and unpleasant.

Within twenty minutes, Isha's phone rang, "Hi, J.R. What did you find?" he asked.

"Well, I don't know exactly what this guy is investing in, but I want some of that stock. He's received fifty-five billion dollars into four off-shore accounts in the past thirty-nine hours."

"Okay, J.R. here's where you get to have some fun. Back trace all those deposits and return every penny to whoever made each one. If you can empty those four bank accounts in less than an hour, you'll have that new computer system you've been nagging my office for."

"Nagging? I don't nag, Sire. I express my desires clearly and sometimes frequently, but I never nag."

"Sorry. Allow me to rephrase my statement. If you can empty those four bank accounts in less than an hour, you'll have that new computer system you've been clearly and sometimes frequently requesting from my office.

"Sire, I'll get out my catalog and have everything I want for Christmas circled for your people to see."

"Christmas is six months away. If you do what I'm asking, I will personally make sure you get your new computer system long before then. Deal?"

"Deal, your highness." J.R. chuckled.

It wouldn't require an hour to empty those bank accounts.

Transferring funds back to the depositor would be easy. She didn't realize how easy it was. Seventeen minutes after she had hung up from her conversation, J.R. was back on the phone with her Prince.

"All four accounts are empty, sir. While I was poking around in Mr. Schumer's banking activity, I found his personal accounts. This boy has been taking in quite a bit of personal wealth lately. He's worth a tad more than one hundred and fifty-three million dollars. Here's the funny part. I'm looking at his encrypted files in the Winter Triangle Physics mainframe. I love that he really believes no one can break his encryption."

She laughed then continued, "He's got a couple million in cash, but that's about all. Looks like for the past year he's been converting his wealth into diamonds. He's been using brokers in Toronto, New York, Sydney, London and Johannesburg to buy caches of certified flawless D color diamonds of two to three carats. Wow! Here's a single transaction where he bought just twenty-six diamonds and the price was just over almost three million dollars. Guess there aren't too many diamonds at that quality."

Cam answered her, "Diamonds that are certified means an international gem agency has graded the stone. 'D' is the most perfect color and 'flawless' means exactly what it sounds like. A flawless D color diamond would be absolutely the highest possible quality. Then when you consider the larger carats, you've got the most expensive stones in the world. I hate to admit it, but you could keep millions of dollars of diamonds of that quality in a single safety deposit box."

J.R. Locklar had been quiet during Cam's explanation, but she'd been going through more of Schumer's accounts.

"Wow!" She exclaimed. "I love this guy. He's so arrogant that no one could break his encryption that he made no attempt to hide anything in the files. Here's a list of certified diamonds that totals…" —she searched the screen—"sixty-three million dollars and change. At the top of that page is a bank name in Denver. Beside the bank's name it says…wow!" she repeated, "Here's another page with a different bank name and number. The list on this one totals forty-six million dollars and change." Locklar was quiet for almost fifteen seconds. "Sire, there's a lot of stuff here. Give me a few minutes to compile all this together. Okay?"

Within half an hour, J.R. Locklar was back on the phone. "I've found six banks in different cities that have safety deposit boxes that combined hold a total of nearly one hundred forty-nine million dollars in diamonds, rubies, and sapphires. The balance of his negotiable wealth is stuck in banks in Corpus Christi and San Antonio. He's got a bunch of accounts he has scattered around. Each account is at the maximum FDIC secured balance. Together, there is a cumulative balance of three point three million dollars. Best I can tell, that's all his liquid assets. Now, there is his business, but it looks like he's mortgaged it to the hilt to build this satellite deal. It's almost like he wouldn't care if the place went under. As it is, he won't be able to get a farthing from it."

"You might be on to something, J.R. It's very possible he never intended to return to that business again."

Changing the conversation's direction Isha said, "You know, Cam and I have been thinking of how to make Schumer unhappy. We've come up with an idea. I want you to create a new 401c3 philanthropic charitable organization based anywhere you want it. Transfer all of his bank balances into one account in that organization's name. I know making such an organization is easier said than done, but set it up where it can't be traced back to Exeter or any of our people. I trust you to do it right.

"Also, ask someone in your section to research charities around the world that have a history of actually using donations to help people instead of just the administrators. Come up with one hundred and fifty of such charities if you can. I believe our little philanthropic endeavor might help people around the world with Mr. Schumer's money. Of course, he's much too humble to take credit for that kind of work, so we'll let our organization do it anonymously. When your group comes up with the list of charities they trust, we'll split the nice man's money evenly among them." Isha became serious again for a moment. "I'm sure you see why I want to make sure it's a charity that really does use donations to help others and not just enrich the administrators."

"I understand, sire. We'll find a good list of reputable charities.

With that kind of endowment, the more the better. I feel confident we can do all you ask, sir. Creating a paper philanthropic organization like you describe will take a few hours. The hardest part is putting all the right security and exchange and IRS data into the correct computers to ensure it'll pass the scrutiny it's bound to get. I'll make it look like the organization has been around a decade or so. That'll give it some credibility. Now, researching the spending and effectiveness of that many charities will be easier, but will probably take several hours, too."

A spark of mischief flared inside the mind of J.R. Locklar and she quietly chuckled and asked as an aside, "Any chance I can set up the J.R. Locklar Benevolent Fund as a charity?"

"No. But that was a nice try. Has anyone ever told you that you have a wily and somewhat devious streak just under that sweet and calm facade you present?"

"No sir, but thank you. I'm going to add that to the strengths column of my resumé." She laughed. A thought popped into Locklar's mind. "You know, that Schumer guy might take his money and run, so while we're setting up that organization here, how about I lock his accounts so he cannot access any money? As soon as everything is set, I'll make the transfer."

"I do like the way you think," the Prince replied. He started thinking out loud, "Now we need to find a way to get to those safety deposit boxes."

"Oh sire, when will you ever cease being amazed at my skills? I've already done some research on Mr. Schumer's choice of banks. Seems they all have cipher locks on their safety deposit boxes. I'm guessing he doesn't like carrying a bunch of keys. Anyway," she paused and took a deep breath, "from what I can see, each bank's procedure is very similar. First a bank officer verifies the identity of whoever wants into the vault. They both go in the vault and the officer uses the bank key to open half of the box's locking system. Now, all that's left is for the banker to plug in a cable into a slot in the door. That cable is attached to a digital fingerprint scanner. Once the owner sticks his or her thumb on the scanner—voila! —an opened door. Of course, at this point the bank officer takes the scanner from the door and leaves."

"Let me guess, you have the capability to change the owner's fingerprint and identification so we can have someone go shopping for precious stones."

"Yessir, that's about the extent of it. May I suggest we pick some Protectors and dispatch them now. I suggest we reach all the banks at the same time. That way, if any one of them gets suspicious and contacts Schumer he won't have time to contact all the other banks."

"J.R., that's another brilliant idea. Don't let it go to your head."

Isha really liked this terrific lady. She wasn't the least bit intimidated by his royal status. That, plus the fact she really was a computer genius who could access any database in the world, elevated her significantly in his opinion. "I'll call my father and make that happen…or would you rather call him?"

"Let me do it. We haven't talked in a while."

With that, J.R. Locklar hung up on her Prince.

An hour later, every billionaire who had paid a protection fee found the money back in their account. Several of them, believing it to be an error, immediately tried to re-deposit the money only to find the off-shore account had been closed. A flurry of messages using the secret message system confirmed every one of them had received their money back. There was nothing they could do except wait for whatever was coming.

Chapter Thirty-Four

June 7, 2022
Johnson Space Center

All three Flight Directors were in Mission Control. One way or another, within a few hours there would be no need for a Flight Director to sit on the top tier of the massive room and oversee the beehive of activities happening in front of him.

Bud Stokesly, with no small amount of self-control calmly addressed all the controllers.

"Ladies and gentlemen, the next couple of hours will be very intense for all of us. Take a moment now to mentally prepare yourself. Keep your small talk to a minimum."

He paused for a second then made a decision. No matter how things went today, starting next month, he and Analyn would be living at their ranch and enjoying the retirement they had dreamed of, so he didn't care if he offended anyone.

"I'm about to quietly pray up here. Feel free to take a minute to pray, however you wish, for God's blessings on the events we face. I know you all have done everything possible to bring our friends and the Sojourner safely home. The results now are out of our hands and so it's appropriate to ask for divine intervention."

Mission Control, usually a very serious and unemotional place, was now a setting where people of Protestant, Catholic, Non-Denominational, Jewish, Muslim, and Hindu faiths found a common thread to approach their deities. There were no atheists among the group, but even the few controllers who considered themselves agnostic found themselves silently praying in case their skepticism was unfounded.

After a ten second break, Stokesly brought the room to order with a simple call. "CAPCOM, Flight."

"Flight, CAPCOM is ready. The mission commander reports the crew are all strapped in and they are prepared for OMS burn."

"Roger." Everyone in the room knew the orbital maneuvering engines would have to burn for precisely three minutes and sixteen seconds. Lt. Colonel Bill Weaver would be responsible for this critical action.

"GNC?"

"GNC is go!" responded the guidance, navigation and control controller.

"Instrumentation?"

"Flight, instrumentation is a go," responded the controller.

The list of other controllers Stokesly wanted to query was much longer, but they still had blank screens in front of their position. They would just have to assume their areas of responsibility were a go, too.

"CAPCOM, inform Sojourner she is go for OMS burn."

"Roger."

There was now a short wait for the shuttle to reach the exact spot on their orbit to begin the deceleration. The guidance controller and the instrumentation controller had been moved next to the CAPCOM station so the three would consult instantly.

"Sojourner, you are go for OMS burn in thirty seconds."

"Roger," was Ledwell's only response. He glanced over at his buddy, "Ready, Bill?"

"Sure, what's the problem? I turn it on and I turn it off." Weaver was ready.

"Sojourner, OMS burn in five, four, three, two, one."

There was a collective sigh of relief when the orbiter maneuvering engine did start and everyone in their shuttle seats could feel a slight, but definite push, against their backs. At the three minute six second point, Ledwell started a ten second countdown. Precisely three minutes and sixteen seconds after he started the engines, Weaver stopped them. The Sojourner had only slowed a few hundred miles an hour, but that was enough for gravity to start its pull and the shuttle to begin descending.

Sojourner was at this moment traveling with the tail first and upside down in relation to the Earth. On orbit and in microgravity, neither of those conditions meant a thing. Now as they slowed and began to once again enter the atmosphere, this position would become problematic. Within a half hour of slowing from orbital speed, if nothing was done to turn the shuttle around, the tail would disintegrate from the heat of reentry and they would all die almost, but not quite, instantly.

The OMS burn had gone according plan, now the second unknown was about to be faced. Ledwell put his hands on the control stick in front of him and very gently pulled back on it. There did not appear to be any response at first, then the nose of the shuttle started down. The maneuver required Ledwell to fly the back half of a loop. Once the shuttle was now heading nose first, Ledwell continued his control inputs until the shuttle was pointed forty degrees above the horizon, and almost thirty thousand silica tiles were facing into the oncoming atmosphere.

"CAPCOM, be advised Sojourner flies like a dream. She's stable and responsive. Tell the boys and girls in engineering that placing the flight control computers in the belly of this beast surrounded by all those layers seems to have protected them perfectly."

"We'll pass the word, Bubba. I wish we had put the flight instrument computers down there, too."

"Kel, make a note to bring that detail up in our engineering debrief," Ledwell responded.

For some reason, everyone in Mission Control felt better knowing Bubba Ledwell believed there would be a debrief.

In Cape Verde, Nicholas Schumer was furious. He had just received several emails from his various banks confirming his special accounts had all been cleared out. The emails did not inform him who had emptied them, but nonetheless all that remained were a few thousand dollars from interest that had been paid on the billions that had been there for just a couple of days. Schumer believed only the United States government could have made this happen. He didn't know how they had reached his accounts, but the facts spoke for themselves.

There was just one thing to do…make them pay. He would destroy the shuttle and all her crew in the most public way possible. They would not be exploded miles in the air and the destruction captured only in some fuzzy pictures. He would do it seconds before the landing. Cameras operated by international news organizations would capture it in vivid crystal-clear color. His plan had gone perfectly but they had ruined everything and taken his money and they were going to pay.

Now that his decision was made, Schumer started to get his fury under control and sat down with a nice glass of Italian Amarone wine. Vengeance for what they had done to him required a high price in return. He had always had a doomsday plan, but had decided early-on he would not need to execute it. That decision was going to be reversed.

His thoughts revealed the vitriol he was feeling. *Now, that the government has taken away my money, I'm going to do the same thing to her.* In an hour, the shuttle would be blown out of the sky. That was just the icing to his retaliation cake.

Immediately after the shuttle event, the doomsday plan would start. He would destroy power supplies to crucial sections of ten US cities. This time he didn't pick targets like Vegas or Cambridge. First, he was going to annihilate power to all of Washington D.C. and Manhattan. Then the downtown areas of Boston, Chicago, Los Angeles and Houston would go. Finally, the seaports of Miami, New Orleans, San Diego, and Seattle would be in the dark. Destruction this devastating would take several months to repair. The loss of those critical locations for that long would be enough to crash the stock market and cause a worldwide financial meltdown.

Of course, since the vast bulk of his money was in easily marketable high-grade precious stones which would still hold their value even when money was diminished, the crash of the world economies would not affect him at all. He would continue to live like a king the rest of his life.

Schumer didn't care about the United States. After all, they had taken the billions of dollars he had worked so hard to get. Now, in return, he would remove the United States from being the world's primary financial force. By this time tomorrow, the US would be finished as a world power.

As Schumer was finalizing his plans, Sojourner was still more than 5,000 miles from landing and traveling at sixteen times the speed of sound. The air was becoming more dense by the second, and this aerodynamic fact meant Bubba Ledwell had to constantly fight to keep the nose of Sojourner precisely forty degrees above the horizon.

This pitch was critical for generating friction from the atmosphere to slow his orbiter, but transitioning from airless space to the atmosphere meant the feel of the orbiter changed constantly and required all of Ledwell's skill to control. Already the orbiter's silica heat shielding tiles were beginning to heat up.

This was where it was going to get tricky. The flight guidance computer required two operable computers to operate. Since there was only one, Ledwell had no descent path information and no symbology in the heads-up display to guide him. Houston had devised a plan to give Bubba his best shot. The controllers were getting data from Sojourner including her altitude. They had designed side-by-side comparison screens which were being shown on the massive screens at the front of mission control. The left screen showed a dot where the shuttle was as she crossed the ground and gave a readout of the orbiter's actual altitude. The right screen gave the same information and the altitude the shuttle should be passing. Every minute, CAPCOM transmitted if the shuttle was above, below, or on the desired descent path.

Captain Thurman Ledwell was concentrating intently on every altitude correction he was receiving from Houston. He used bank angles to increase or decrease his descent speed to stay at the precise altitude. He needed to keep the Sojourner's nose high so the atmosphere would continue to slow the craft, so using pitch to control altitude was impossible. The solution was to use bank angle to control descent. Just like on a conventional aircraft, when the wings were in a turn, they produced less lift and the descent rate increased. When Sojourner was too high, Ledwell rolled the shuttle into a bank to descend faster until the shuttle was back on the correct path. If he were slightly low, he rolled out of the bank to where the stubby, inefficient wings created more lift and the descent decreased. It was this constant left and right banking to different degrees that required precision few people in the world were capable of.

The greatest control challenge was coming soon. The heat generated by entering the atmosphere would soon reach almost 3,000 degrees, and shortly after that, the super-heated compressed air under the shuttle would cause a layer of ionized particles which would block all radio transmissions. Exeter and NASA had no reason to believe that would not happen with their special communications device just as it did on normal radios. Ledwell wanted to be exactly at the correct descent point when the communications blackout began. He'd maintain the same rate of descent until communications were restored. Hopefully, that would minimize any corrections needed then.

"Sojourner, we expect you to go com-out within a minute. You look right on profile. We're in uncharted territory with you hand-flying, but expect it to last approximately sixteen minutes."

"Roger," Weaver responded.

No one heard him. They had entered the period of communications blackout much earlier than expected. Hopefully they would be out earlier, too.

Virtually every major news feed in the world was live streaming the crippled shuttle's descent and providing their viewers with color commentary by anyone they could find who was even remotely involved in the shuttle program and thus described as *experts*. Fox News had the only two actually experts available. Both Russ Boda and Bob Paulus were on-screen describing in minute detail exactly what was happening in the orbiter. Nicholas Schumer was watching them from his villa on Cape Verde. He had checked and knew the winds at Kennedy Space Center were from the north which meant they would be using runway 33 for landing. Computing an exact spot two miles from the end of the runway was a snap and Schumer programmed that location into his satellite so it would be ready for instant use. If just being near the satellite had done so much damage to her computers, he reasoned, a direct hit of a full beam would completely devastate every electronic component onboard. He relaxed knowing Sojourner would be in full view of everyone when, two miles from landing, she went uncontrollable and crashed.

In the Titusville condominium where Melissa's hospital bed was installed, pizza boxes were open and spread out on the large kitchen island. Hardly a single piece had been touched. Everyone was watching television reports while simultaneously listening intently to the silence coming from their communication device. They were trying hard to stay positive. After all, everything that could have gone wrong so far had not. If that streak continued for just another few minutes, Terry would be safely on a runway less than fifteen miles away.

No one spoke. Even the two children could feel the tension in the room and were playing quietly in the corner. There were half eaten slices of pizza on paper plates on the floor next to them.

Every fifteen seconds the group heard the exact same transmission from the CAPCOM. "Sojourner, Houston. How do you read?" Every fifteen seconds silence was the only response.

Isha and Cam left the group and walked out on the veranda overlooking the beach and the vast Atlantic Ocean. There was an uneasiness they felt that no one else in the group knew about. Cam spoke first, "By now, Schumer must know his extorted money has been returned. He can't be taking that well. To be honest, I've been waiting for him to hit another city…probably a big one."

"Yeah. The same feeling has been bothering me. Wish we could get in that cesspool of a brain of his and think like him for a minute."

"That thought alone makes me want to take a shower. But—"

An explosion of cheering interrupted the conversation. Both men ran back into the living room.

Moses Forsyth glanced over at his son and his prince. "They just checked in and said everything appears to still be working. Houston told them the shuttle was low and said to roll wings level until they re-intercepted the descent path."

Cam whispered a silent prayer of thanks and then started hugging everyone in the room.

Isha, suddenly stopped smiling and instead took on the look of a man who had just seen a tragic accident. Kevin noticed it first. Isha had been his best friend since they were young boys. He had seen the same look on Isha's face once before. It had happened deep in the bowels of an ocean-going freighter carrying a nuclear weapon bound for New York harbor. The young protector named Skye had just died and Isha felt the responsibility for his death and a sense of powerlessness in the face of his almost certain failure to protect millions of lives.

"Isha, what is it?" Kevin asked so quietly that only the prince heard him.

"Get Cam and come outside." With that short command Isha left the room while pulling out his phone.

It only took ten seconds for Kevin to get Cam's attention and point outside. They closed the door to the veranda just in time to hear Prince Isha speak rapidly. "J.R., we have just a few minutes. As hard as this is to believe, we have to assume Schumer has some kind of control over that satellite. When it was first used, we now know it was targeted at Las Vegas. After a short time, he hit Cambridge. That means he can control the aiming from down here. We need to know how to disrupt that control."

"Sir, I have noticed his company Wifi system has an amazing bandwidth. I'm a little jealous. Anyway, it's so much more than that whole company should be using. If he's got signal boosters, I wouldn't be too surprised if it could reach up there."

"Shut down all communication to the satellite. Better yet, you take control of the damn thing and aim it into space."

J.R. Locklar recognized this was not the time for levity. "Sir, I don't understand."

Cam and Kevin felt a sudden chill as Isha said, "Schumer has been too quiet and I know why. He's planning a massive attack. Knowing that SOB, I think he'll want to start with a big kickoff. Look, he tried to have Cam assassinated just because he might know something. He doesn't take failure lightly. Using Cam as an example, we know Schumer tried to kill his operative on the shuttle to prevent him from spilling his guts about everything he knows. As soon as the media started reporting Elder was conscious, Schumer realized he was about to lose control of that situation. In his mind, he's got to kill that guy to protect himself, and the best way to eliminate Elder is by destroying the shuttle. We only have a couple of minutes before they land, and he could attack at any moment. J.R., we've got to stop him somehow. Find a way to either override his control of the satellite or destroy it."

"Sire, I don't know how…" Locklar's voice trailed off as she felt an unfamiliar moment of defeat. "If only I knew how he coded messages to the satellite…and he's no longer at his business. I've tracked him to an island off Africa so he's using his laptop now. He's…Wait! I've got it!"

"You've got what?"

"Leave me alone. I need to concentrate!" No one was offended by her curt response. "Listen, he was at WTP when the satellite hit Las Vegas and Cambridge. I'll bet he was using his encrypted company computer to send those commands. We broke the firewalls and encryption for the company's server when you needed to know about that lady's arrival and departure times last month."

Cam felt a strong sense of sadness. He hadn't thought of Catherine in several days. He let out a deep breath which he thought was silent. He was slightly startled when he felt Prince Isha's hand on his shoulder as a gesture of comfort. No words were spoken.

The three men could actually hear the sound of J.R.'s fingers flying over the keyboard in front of her. After an eternity that was actually twenty-five seconds, she let out a shriek. "I've found it, sire.

I've found it!"

Celia stuck her head out the door. "Guys they're less than three minutes from landing. They've already got television cameras on the shuttle. Get in here." She was confused when the men didn't immediately start towards the door. Celia just shook her head and decided she wasn't going to miss it and went back inside.

Nicholas Schumer was watching the exact same broadcast half a world away as everyone was watching in Florida. His finger was poised over the transmit key of his computer. In forty-five seconds, the shuttle would be gone and three minutes later, all the cities he'd already designated would be wastelands of dead houses, businesses, schools, and infrastructures. Nothing could stop him now.

She didn't know it, but J.R. Locklar only had fourteen seconds before her efforts would be in vain. The clock was moving faster than she had ever seen it move. The shuttle was only twenty seconds from landing when she found exactly what to do. She hit her send button three seconds before Nicholas Schumer hit his.

From four hundred six nautical miles in space, a burst of destructive energy was fired from the RePoGGS satellite. Four seconds later, the shuttle landed on the centerline of runway 33 at the Kennedy Space Center and the burst of energy from the satellite hit Earth somewhere six miles off the coast of Florida in the vast Atlantic Ocean. Locklar's command had only shifted the satellite slightly before Schumer's fire command reached it, but that tiny move had been enough.

J.R. Locklar knew she would have all the computer equipment her heart desired for a long time. Immediately after disrupting Schumer's plan to destroy the Sojourner, she had sent a new override access code into the maneuvering computer of the satellite. From now on, no one except her could ever control that disgusting creation ever again.

The cheering in Mission Control was surpassed only the cheering in the condominium. In the shuttle, right after coming to a full stop on the runway, Navy Captain Thurman Ledwell allowed himself a few seconds to release the tension that had been building in every muscle of his neck and shoulder. He looked over to Lt. Colonel Bill Weaver who had released his seat restraining straps. He rolled left and held out his right hand. Bubba Ledwell shook it.

Neither man said a word to each other until Weaver spoke, "After landing and shutdown checklist…"

It took twenty minutes to complete the entire procedure which also gave the Florida winds time to blow away any residual gases from the area which allowed support teams to finally enter the shuttle.

"Welcome home, team," was Ledwell's only comment to the group. He didn't trust his voice for more than that.

Ten minutes after the Sojourner landed, Marcus and Johnson had all of their communication devices from Mission Control in their attaché case and were gone from NASA. Before Terry Lee walked off the shuttle, she put the communication device that had been crucial to saving them all into a pocket of her suit.

Chapter Thirty-Five

June 9, 2022
Cape Verde

In the two days since Sojourner had landed safely in Florida, several things had come to Nicholas Schumer's attention which did not make him happy. It had not taken him long to realize his dream of living surrounded by the trappings of wealth had been dashed. That realization had started as he called every bank where he had a safety deposit box containing his precious stones. Each and every one had confirmed that the box had been visited by the alternate authorized individual on the account. That was impossible. The only alternate had been Catherine Austin until she betrayed him. He was going to have Josh Tanner placed as the alternate but that man had proven incapable of doing the simplest tasks.

As a fatalist, Schumer accepted the cards fate had dealt him. But, for now, he would have to live as best he could. In his attaché case was about a million dollars in precious stones and one of his large suitcases contained one hundred thousand dollars cash. That would be enough to see him through until he figured out his next move.

In Florida, Kevin, Celia, Kristi, Rob, Emmy, and Aiden remained in the condominiums and enjoyed Raul's cooking for the two weeks remaining on the agreement. Isha had convinced them this was the best use of the place since it had already been paid for and there were no refunds. They couldn't argue with his logic.

Moses, Tame, and Melissa Forsyth returned by private jet with Lady Deidre to Santa Fe. Isha had decided on the private transportation since he wanted Melissa to avoid the inevitable jostling that he knew takes place on commercial airliners.

The returning Sojourner crew, minus L. Scott Elder, were being heralded as heroes by virtually every media in the free world. Everyone on the crew had been given a couple of days off before debriefing began. Terry spent the time with her friends in the private condominiums. There wasn't time to fly to Montana and her husband wouldn't want to fly to Florida. That didn't matter. She had already told him she was leaving NASA and coming home to Montana. She could find a teaching job somewhere, or she could just sit on their ranch and enjoy the sunsets.

From his hospital bed and under heavy police guard, L. Scott Elder was telling everyone who would listen how Nicholas Schumer of Winter Triangle Physics had bought off Senator Maxwell Bellow, the senior senator from California. Senator Bellow had used the threat of withholding funding for NASA to get his friend's satellite on Sojourner without proper vetting. Elder's colorful assertions had been met with widespread acceptance. He freely admitted his complicity in everything that happened. Senator Bellow had already started making the rounds of every major news talk show vehemently denying the allegations. Dr. John Francis Maclemore's only response had been "No comment."

An hour after the shuttle's landing, Bud Stokesly submitted his retirement papers to NASA. He and Analyn had their ranch as ready as it ever would be for his retirement. His tractor was brand new, the deer feeders were set up, and the four-acre lake had been stocked with bass.

Prince Isha and Cam Forsyth were nowhere to be found. Both men had just told their families they'd be in touch shortly. Everyone knew better than to ask for more information. No more was going to be said.

On Cape Verde, things were settling down after Sojourner's landing two days before. As the sun was just setting over the crystal-clear waters surrounding Cape Verde, the head of Nicholas Schumer's security team entered the reading room. Schumer was enjoying a nice snifter of brandy and his evening cigar. He felt perfectly safe in his villa. As long as the guards were getting paid well, Schumer knew no one could touch him. It wasn't unusual for the security chief to visit. He often stopped by to ask about Schumer's comfort and to see if he needed anything special to be flown in. This time however, he had a slightly different look. He was a security man and Schumer believed it was part of the job description to occasionally look concerned. That made the protected individual, who was paying the bills after all, feel like he was getting his money's worth.

"Mr. Schumer, our office on the mainland just contacted me. They have been informed by their sources in the United States that a secret military team is about to be put ashore on Cape Verde. They will be inserted using a submarine off the coast with the intention of kidnapping you back to the United States. The home office says the reliability of their informant is very high. If this team is who they suspect it is, your safety will be difficult to ensure. The office has sent a jet to fly you to Algiers, the capital city of Algeria. Our people there will keep you safe until such time as you can return here."

"Isn't there any place closer?"

"No sir. It's a four to five-hour flight, but you will again not be listed on the manifest which means your anonymity will be protected. They have picked Algiers because our presence there is strong. It's a beautiful city and you will find it has great food, fine wine, and temporary companionship should you wish that. Sir, time is of the essence. I've asked your butler to pack your bag for a week-long trip, but let's hope it'll be considerably shorter. I have a car waiting outside and the jet is at the airport. I've been informed the flight plan is filed and you'll be able to leave as soon as you get there."

"Okay," Schumer sighed, "I pay your company a significant amount of money to keep me safe. It would be foolish to ignore your recommendations." He left the room and walked immediately to the car where the door was being held open by a guard.

Twenty minutes later, the car was waved through the security fence at Praia International Airport. As promised, a Gulfstream 550 jet was on the tarmac. Beside the entry door were two stewardesses, or flight attendants as he remembered they liked to be called. The sun had dropped to below the horizon and the airport lights were just coming on. As the car approached the jet, Schumer noticed the epaulettes on each woman's shoulders. On each were the four stripes of a captain. Obviously, Schumer thought, those are part of the company's flight attendant uniform.

The car stopped just outside the wingtip of the Gulfstream 550 and a porter came up. The limo driver pushed a button and a noticeable click inside told the occupants the trunk had been opened.

As the porter transferred Schumer's luggage to the jet, he walked up to the two women and extended his hand.

"Nicholas Schumer."

"Good evening, Mr. Schumer, I'm Captain Valerie Salfieri and this is Captain Jennifer Davis. We'll be taking you to Algiers, Algeria. The weather en route at 35,000 feet will be smooth with only occasional light chop. I'm afraid you won't be able to see many lights on the ground. There will be overcast skies all the way. I'm sure you'll choose to sleep anyway. Now, because of the speed this trip was put together, we didn't have time to get a flight attendant, but they did load several different meals for you to choose from."

"Thank you, Captain."

Captain Jennifer Davis spoke next, "We've already filed our flight plan and are ready to go. If you wish, there is time for you to use the facilities in the building, or of course, we do have a lavatory on board."

"I'm fine. Let's get in the air." Within ten minutes, the engines were running, the plane had been taxied to the end of the runway, and the power added for takeoff. Three minutes after that, the plane was out over the ocean, climbing right up to 35,000 feet, and Nicholas Schumer was asleep in the plush leather reclining seats.

Five hours later, Schumer was awakened when the constant drone of the engines changed pitch. He recognized the pilots must have reduced power to start their descent in Algeria. He got out of his seat and went to the lavatory. He washed the sleep out of his eyes and combed his hair. He then went forward to where the galley was located. Sure enough, there was a fresh pot of coffee and a china mug. He poured a cup and then opened the door to the flight deck.

"Good morning, sir," said one of the pilots, he couldn't remember her name. "We'll be landing in about ten minutes. There are a lot of snacks in the cabinet to your right. Help yourself. I'll be turning on the seatbelt sign in a moment. But feel free to take an extra cup of coffee back with you to the seat. There are holders that fit those cups in the arm rest or on the corners of the desks."

Even though it was still dark outside, looking through the front windscreen he could just make out where the water ended and land began. He could see the lights of the city. It looked just as he expected Algiers to look like. That was the Mediterranean Sea, there was the city and that looked like a runway.

"Where are we? Never mind. I can see the city. Either of you want a cup of coffee before I go back?" Schumer figured he could be nice. After all, both of these ladies were beautiful. Maybe one of them might be interested in visiting the sights of the city.

"No, thank you, sir," the other pilot said. He couldn't remember her name either.

"Then I'll go back. See you on the ground."

Schumer closed the door to the flight deck and went back to his seat. Within a minute or two the descent of the jet increased and he felt the rumble caused when the spoilers came up on the wing. Then came the familiar whirling sound as the flaps and slats were deployed from the leading and trailing edges of the wing. That was followed by the noticeable bump of the landing gear being extended. There wasn't much to see of the still dark landscape, but now the lights of the city were far more evident. It was only moments later the engines were obviously at idle power and then the wheels touched down very smoothly.

Schumer believed in tipping pilots one hundred dollars each for a trip like this. *Whoever did that landing just earned an extra hundred-dollar tip*, he thought. Another thing he liked was that the pilot didn't use full reverse thrust power. Instead, she just left the reversers in idle power and the braking was very smooth. It must be a long runway, he figured.

"Mr. Schumer, please remain in your seat with your seat belt fastened." The soft but very professional sounding voice said over the intercom. "Ground control just told us we may have to taxi a little farther. These aren't the smoothest taxiways and ramps and we don't want you knocked around."

After a few minutes, he could see out the side windows the bright lights of a parking ramp.

Once again, the voice of one of the pilots spoke, "Mr. Schumer, we're here on the ramp, but it looks like they have to move some baggage carts so we can get to our spot. I apologize for this, but it's better you stay in your seat so we can move quickly if we need to."

Thirty seconds later, without having moved another foot, the engines were both shut down. As Schumer stood to his feet and stretched, one of the pilots came out of the flight deck and closed the door behind her. She smiled quickly then lowered the stairs from the cabin level to the ground and quickly walked down them.

When Schumer reached the door to the fuselage, he didn't see, as he expected to, the pilot standing at the bottom of the stairs to make sure he stepped down safely.

He held the handrail and carefully stepped down the stairs. As soon as his feet touched the ground, a voice surprised him. "Nicholas Schumer, you are under arrest under an international warrant issued in the United States and received in the United Kingdom. Raise your hands and turn around."

"You can't touch me," Schumer responded. "This country has no extradition treaty with the United States."

He turned, but did not raise his hands. Immediately, several heavily armed men came from under the aircraft. One of them roughly grabbed the Schumer's left arm and with a practiced action twisted it to put Schumer on the ground. Another man had his right arm now and he felt the cold metal of handcuffs tightening around his wrist. Looking up from his position on the ground, it became obvious the pilots had stopped the jet in such a way that these foolish policemen could approach from the nose where he could not see them from his seat.

"I keep telling you Algeria has no extradition to the United States. That Interpol warrant has no power here."

The man who had forced Schumer to the ground and then frisked him for weapons smiled. "Well, lad, you're half right. Algeria has no extradition, but you have just landed at the Exeter International Airport outside Exeter, England. I guess your pilots must have gotten confused." He pointed and said, "Algiers is about 1,600 kilometers that direction or for you Yanks it's about 1,100 miles. You have unfortunately landed on Her Majesty's soil."

Realization came to Nicholas Schumer like a wave. He had been tricked. *This wasn't right. This wasn't fair!* As the policemen lifted him to his feet, Schumer found himself staring into the coldest eyes he had ever seen. The man walked up to Schumer and wordlessly stared him down until the prisoner could no longer bear the gaze and looked away.

At that moment, the man spoke quietly but with a deathly menace in his voice. "You killed Catherine Austin. Then you sent two people to try and kill me. The first one died quickly. The second one missed me, but shot my sister. I might have forgiven her for shooting me, but not my innocent sister. I broke her neck and watched her die." Cam looked around at the armed men on the ramp. "Schumer, I told these men we could save time and money if they would just give me fifteen seconds with you, but my friend here convinced me it would be better watching you spend the rest of your miserable life in prison without any creature comforts. You are a fortunate man it went down like this."

The police hustled Schumer away. His extradition was expedited after the President of the United States placed a personal call to the Prime Minister.

Prince Isha called the pilot from behind the baggage cart where she had been hidden after coming down the stairs. "Captain Davis, please ask Captain Salfieri to join us. I've booked four rooms at the best B&B in all Exeter. After a good night's sleep and a great breakfast or lunch, we'll fly back to the States."

Salfieri asked, "Why do you smile that way every time you mention, Exeter. It's one of the oldest towns in all England. Is it some kind of private joke we don't know about?"

Isha responded with a slight laugh, "Yes, ma'am. It is.

Postscript

Immediately after the near disastrous shuttle flight, President Larry Robertson ordered the creation of a blue-ribbon panel to investigate the entire event including the attack on Las Vegas.

Six months later, investigators released their comprehensive report. They found NASA's Director of Flight Operations, Dr. John Francis Maclemore, guilty of bypassing protocols in placing the RePoGGS on the shuttle without proper testing and evaluations. While no evidence was presented of criminal intent or conduct, Maclemore's cavalier action was found to be a direct causal factor in the tragedy. He was retired in disgrace.

The inquiry found Senator Maxwell Bellow guilty of accepting bribes, extortion, and misuse of his office. He was publicly censured by the Senate and retired rather than face expulsion from the body. A month later, charges were presented to a federal grand jury which indicted the discredited politician on three counts of bribery. Three days later, Bellow took his own life. He left no suicide note.

The panel's report specifically recognized each individual crew member, with the exception of L. Scott Elder, for special commendations. Ledwell retired from NASA, as he had always planned to do. Every other member returned to either military commands, academic professorships, or to industry jobs with impressive titles and large paychecks. None of them ever flew in space again.

L. Scott Elder was found guilty in federal court of conspiracy for his part in the satellite attack on Las Vegas. He was sentenced to prison for a period of not less than twenty years. He was placed in the Federal Correctional Institutional in Marianna, Florida. A British High Court also found him guilty in absentia for the attack on Cambridge and ordered him to Newport Prison on the Isle of Wight for a period of not less than twenty years. The High Court deferred its sentence until such time as Elder completed his prison term in the

United States. In an accord between the US Department of Justice and the British Home Secretary, a binding agreement was made guaranteeing extradition of Elder to the United Kingdom immediately on completion of his US sentence.

Both Las Vegas and Cambridge had their power restored in a matter of days instead of months. For Vegas, a brand-new power generating system, one tenth the size of the destroyed one was trucked to Hoover Dam and installed far faster than anyone would have imagined. The team of engineers who came with the generator knew every detail. The new generator, though a fraction of the size produced forty percent more electrical power than all the generators in Hoover Dam combined. This single generator would suffice until other conventional generators could be built and installed. No one in Las Vegas could know an identical unit, beneath a massive underground waterfall, had been supplying power in a subterranean community named Exeter for almost sixty years. Tourism was not affected by the temporary power disruption.

Cambridge faced a different problem. Her electrical power was generated miles away. It was the complete destruction of twenty-three relay stations that had crippled her. President Robertson called the Prime Minister to tell her he had been made aware of a previously secret power transformer and switching unit capable of handling ten times the energy as had previous units. The day after the President's call, three of these units were on an Air Force C-17 Globemaster transport jet en route to the Royal Air Force Base, Mildenhall, England with all the specialists required to install them. With linemen from all over the UK working around the clock, all twenty-three stations had cables installed connecting them together into three groups, and the three new units were positioned in the combined locations. All were operating and power restored twelve hours later. The specialists performing the work just smiled when asked what company they worked for. They were back on the transport jet and airborne for Dover AFB, Delaware eighteen hours after first arriving in the UK.

After six months of working with precious gems brokers in several countries, a cache of previously unavailable stones was offered by auction houses around the world. Collectors, investors, and jewelers had numerous places to buy these highest quality stones. At the conclusion of the sales, almost one hundred eighty million dollars had been received. Then, within a month after the sales, an anonymous donor presented almost two hundred charities around the world with a gift of nearly a million dollars each. The charities represented a vast array of causes and were from every part of the world.

In perhaps the most unique state visit ever made to the White House, President and Mrs. Larry Robertson and former President and Mrs. Thomas Rogers welcomed three guests for a private dinner in the upstairs residence. King Annu along with his son and daughter-in-law, Prince Isha, and Lady Deidre, were welcomed by both Presidents as if old and dear friends. The seven people laughed when remembering all the subterfuge King Annu had been forced to use twice to convince these skeptical Presidents they needed his help.

President Robertson momentarily considered having his intelligence agencies track the three to learn where they lived. He decided against it knowing the organizations would inevitably be embarrassed by their failure.

Nicholas Schumer died in prison at the hands of a convict serving two life sentences. All the man said in his defense was that he used to live in Las Vegas.

ABOUT KEN ARTHUR

Ken Arthur is a native Texan whose career has been a wild ride.

Flying jets has been the core of his life, first as an Air Force fighter pilot flying both in the US and Europe, and then as a captain for a major US airline. Still later, he became a captain, instructor pilot, and certification evaluator on a new generation corporate jet.

Arthur is now retired and enjoying the simple life of a pickleball player and writer.

Made in the USA
San Bernardino, CA
05 April 2019